"I'm worn out," Rio grumbled. "Can we just get the rest of my clothes on so I can go to sleep?"

Binney tucked the single crutch under his bare arm and slipped her arm around his damp waist. "I'll be quick."

It took them a while to make it across to the bed, where Rio sank back with a groan.

Binney was totally unprepared to experience a punch in her gut from merely looking at him sprawled on his bed In nothing but briefs. Averting her eyes, she started at his feet and worked up his legs, and felt his suspicious gaze track her every move.

Privately she chanted, *You're a nurse. He's a patient. You're a nurse. He's a patient.*

One fine-looking patient who showed by his grin that he'd begun to enjoy the whole process way too much as she smoothed lotion over his chest and the nicely rippled muscles along his lower abs.

TEXAS BABY SURPRISE

Roz Denny Fox

&

USA TODAY BESTSELLING AUTHOR

Marie Ferrarella

2 Heartfelt Stories

A Baby on His Doorstep
and *The Rancher and the Baby*

Recycling programs
for this product may
not exist in your area.

ISBN-13: 978-1-335-44884-2

Texas Baby Surprise

Copyright © 2022 by Harlequin Enterprises ULC

A Baby on His Doorstep
First published in 2017. This edition published in 2022.
Copyright © 2017 by Rosaline Fox

The Rancher and the Baby
First published in 2016. This edition published in 2022.
Copyright © 2016 by Marie Rydzynski-Ferrarella

This edition published by arrangement with Harlequin Books S.A.

For questions and comments about the quality of this book,
please contact us at CustomerService@Harlequin.com.

Harlequin Enterprises ULC
22 Adelaide St. West, 41st Floor
Toronto, Ontario M5H 4E3, Canada
www.Harlequin.com

Printed in U.S.A.

CONTENTS

Roz Denny Fox's first book was published by Harlequin in 1990. She writes for several Harlequin lines, and her books are published worldwide in a number of languages. Roz's warm home-and-family-focused love stories have been nominated for various industry awards, including the Romance Writers of America's RITA® Award, the HOLT Medallion, the Golden Quill and others. Roz has been a member of the Romance Writers of America since 1987 and is currently a member of Tucson's Saguaro Romance Writers, where she has received the Barbara Award for outstanding chapter service. In 2013 Roz received her fifty-book pin from Harlequin. Readers can email her through Facebook or at rdfox@cox.net, or visit her website at korynna.com/RozFox/.

Books by Roz Denny Fox

Harlequin Western Romance

Snowy Owl Ranchers

His Ranch or Hers
A Maverick's Heart
A Montana Christmas Reunion

Harlequin Heartwarming

Annie's Neighborhood
An Unlikely Rancher
Molly's Garden

Visit the Author Profile page at Harlequin.com for more titles.

nd raised there. Not that Ryder cared, although
e someday he'd change his mind. Championships
t far more to him than they ever had to Rio.

aving traveled across the States since junior rodeos,
d be glad to get off the road. Several years ago his
rents had sold all of their cattle to happily retire at a
nior living complex in San Antonio. At the moment
hey were on their dream vacation in Australia.

Bronc riding had been good to him, though. A win
today would be a fine way to go out, plus give him more
than enough funds to buy a palomino mare he'd had his
eye on for a while.

All at once he heard a commotion in the chute. The
bronc he'd drawn to ride today, Diablo Colorado, Span-
ish for Red Devil, was new to the circuit. Rio had given
him a cursory inspection earlier and noted the horse was
a big, powerful sorrel gelding. Rio guessed the animal
was living up to his name based on the difficulty handlers were having getting him into the chute.

"Don't envy you this one," Colton Brooks called
down to Rio.

He smiled and acknowledged the warning, although
feisty horses weren't anything new to him. Over the
years he'd suffered his share of hard knocks, bruises
and even a few broken bones. Probably another reason
at thirty-two to hang up his spurs and leave serious
competition to the young dudes. Unlike his brother, a
hypercompetitive bull rider who reveled in piling up
points in his sport to be acclaimed in the professional
standings, Rio had been content to seek out smaller
venues with fair winnings. Rather than sticking with
the PRCA, he figured after today to keep his hand in
by joining the RHAA. The Ranch Horse Association

A BABY ON HIS DOORSTEP

Roz Denny Fox

I'd like to dedicate this story to
my daughters and their families.
You make me so proud, and
you complete my life.

Chapter 1

Rio McNabb vaguely registered the sights, sounds and
blended odors of hay, animals and concession stands
at the regional rodeo in Abilene, Texas. Really he'd
honed in more on the bronc rider who preceded him
who'd failed to make the required time to be in money
contention.

Striding toward his chute, he smiled at the handlers
preparing the mount that would be his last ride with the
PRCA. He'd earned enough over his years on the Professional Rodeo Cowboys Association circuit to buy
the Lonesome Road Ranch from his folks. Like most
ranchers they'd been land rich and cash-strapped. But
after today he could cut back rodeos and concentrate on
building his horse-breeding business. The ranch, situated well off any beaten path, was a secluded spot where
he and his twin brother were third-generation McNabbs

on will be back to check your breathing around sup-
time. This is Nurse Murphy. Do what she says. Say,
rph, Mr. McNabb wants his phone. Is it among his
rsonal effects you've put somewhere?"

She went to a cabinet and took out a sack with a list
apled to the front. "Yes, we have his cell. I'll let him
make a call while I record his vitals. This pain med you
ordered will send him nighty-night."

Shrugging at each other the doctors left the room.

Rio took his phone and with some difficulty called JJ
Montoya. "JJ, it's Rio. I'm stuck in City Hospital. Will
you ask Rhonda to take you to pick up my truck and
camper from the rodeo grounds? I left Tag while I rode."

"I'm ahead of you, Rio. Rhonda already drove me
over there, and I brought your rig home."

"You did? Is Tagalong okay?" Rio had been worried
about the ginger-colored stray dog that had found him a
couple of years ago in the Mesquite Rodeo parking lot.
His vet had called the stray an Australian Labradoodle.
To Rio the big mutt was simply a great companion on
lonely treks between rodeos.

"Tag's fine. How are you?"

"Docs say I'm pretty stove-up, JJ." He listed the injuries Layton had named. "Say, will you check on the
bronc that dumped me into the fence? His name's Diablo Colorado. He's from Weldon Walker's rodeo string."

"I ran into Colton Brooks. He said a vet checked the
horse. He may have fared better than you. Only had a
few scrapes."

"I'm thankful he didn't break a leg and have to be
put down. Not that I envy the next rider who draws
him," Rio mumbled. "But this was his first rodeo. You
know, JJ, I'd decided that ride would be my last in the

of America showcased skills of true cowboys. His twin
scoffed at those events, and at the notion of ever returning to the homeplace Ryder called Hicksville Ranch.
Thinking about that had Rio grimacing. He loved the
Lonesome Road and would be happy to live there until
he couldn't climb aboard a horse anymore.

Tightening his gloves, he resettled his dove-gray
Stetson before climbing up to join the handlers who'd
finally gotten Diablo into the chute.

Rio sank onto the saddle, then vaulted out again as
the horse bucked inside the enclosure and wildly tossed
his head. Rio considered asking for a tie line to run from
the bit to the cinch. A head-tosser could easily break a
rider's nose, or blacken his eyes. But hearing the crowd
cheer and chant his name, and because he alone knew
this was his goodbye ride, he decided to ride this devil
and give the fans their money's worth.

Gingerly taking his seat again, Rio wrapped the reins
tight, slid his boots into the stirrups, raised his right arm
and let out a rebel yell.

The gate slammed open. The sorrel bucked stiff-
legged right in the opening. And instead of bolting
or bucking into the larger arena, Diablo rose on his
hind legs and without warning crashed over backward,
crushing Rio between seven hundred fifty pounds of
muscled horse and a well-built, steel-reinforced wooden
fence that he felt crack around him.

Even as he tried to haul in a deep breath, Rio heard
a collective "oh" roar from the crowd. There was a
momentary cacophony of curses amid fast-shuffling
booted feet, seconds before everything in his world
went black.

The strident sound of sirens awakened Rio to the urgent shout of old Doc Kane, a much-appreciated rodeo doctor. Rio tried to ask a question, but pain battering him from all sides seemed to clamp a fist around his voice box.

Doc called for morphine, and before Rio could object he felt the sharp sting of a needle entering his thigh and he was lost in oblivion again.

Rio opened his eyes, but didn't recognize anything around him. He felt weighted down in a sea of white. Odd beeps came from somewhere overhead. Two men, both blurs of ocean blue, bent over him. He tried to move to see around them, but couldn't seem to do that. He felt his heart begin to pound as panic set in.

"Dr. Layton, he's awake." The figure at Rio's left shined a bright penlight in each of his eyes.

Blinking, Rio attempted to sit up. A heavy hand pressed him down. Excruciating pain followed. Enough to have him gritting his teeth.

"Settle down, son. I'm Arthur Layton, chief of general surgery at City Hospital. This is Dr. Mason, our surgical resident. A horse fell on you at the rodeo. You're not long out of surgery and still in pretty bad shape."

"Is the horse okay?" Rio croaked. He began to remember bits and pieces, like seeing the chute open, feeling Diablo rear right before something went terribly wrong.

"You're worried about the horse?" The surgery chief snorted. "Worry about yourself, Mr. McNabb. I'm afraid your rodeo days are over. You broke your clavicle, cracked two thoracic vertebrae we may still later need to stabilize. You have a fractured left wrist

and badly sprained right ankle. [...] pneumothorax we hope stays fix[...]

Surfacing through the pain, R[...] pneumo what? What is that?"

"Collapsed lung," the resident su[...]

The older doctor unwound his ste[...] to Rio's chest, then typed on his compu[...] a chest tube to reinflate your left lun[...] good. We'll keep a close eye on it, thoug[...] pain meds as needed. With luck, by nex[...] move you from ICU into a ward."

"I can't stay here," Rio said. "I've got[...] ranch." For one thing, he was seeing dollar [...] this surgery stuff.

Dr. Layton's voice gentled. "According t[...] our nurses you're famous. I know performi[...] rodeos makes you tough, but I can't release y[...] you're able to get up and around. You don't have [...] tured skull, but you shook your brain."

"Famous? Not me. They must mean my twin[...] bull-riding champion." Rio tried again to scoot u[...] bed, but yelped when pain gripped him.

Scrolling through Rio's computer chart, Layto[...] frowned. "I figured you'd have someone at your ranch to cook and clean. But I see the last time you were seen here for a concussion you signed yourself out against staff's advice. This states you're single. If that's still the case, who'll care for you at home?"

"I'll take care of myself," Rio growled. "Health insurance companies don't like guys in my line of work. Paying my bills depends on me getting home to help my only ranch hand ready our colts and fillies to sell."

The doctor shook his head. "Sorry," he said, clos-

PRCA. The surgeon says it'll likely be my last bronc ride anywhere."

"What do doctors know about cowboy grit? You've been banged up before and have healed fine."

"I hope you're right and he's wrong." He glanced up at the nurse who had finished recording his temperature and pulse. "Listen, there's a nurse here with pain medication, and I'm starting to think I should take it. I'm, uh, not going to be able to help wean and train our young stock the rest of this year. We can talk about hiring you part-time help once I'm home." The two men signed off and Rio let the phone fall to his side. That was when he realized he'd forgotten to ask if JJ knew a Binney Taylor.

"I'll set the phone on your tray table," Nurse Murphy said. After doing so she took the cap off a syringe, swabbed Rio's upper arm and administered the drug.

"Don't they have pain pills? I hate sh-shlots," he muttered. But clearly his ability to speak was already compromised.

At two o'clock, after donning a sterile gown, booties and gloves, Binney Taylor entered the ICU room where Rio McNabb lay trussed up like a Christmas goose. She could hear the soft whiffle of a snore indicating her arrival hadn't wakened him. And that was good. It gave her time to collect her thoughts at seeing him in person again.

In high school the popular and handsome McNabb twins were crushed on by every girl in school, including her. As someone who didn't travel in their sphere, she'd been particularly drawn to Ryder McNabb and had loved him from afar. Then in her junior year, Ryder had asked her to the spring dance. Beyond thrilled she'd borrowed a nice dress and then spent money she didn't have to spare on having her hair done. And she'd arranged for a night off from her after-school job. Ryder never showed up to collect her at the group home. Nor had he called. Later it'd been cruelly pointed out by mean girls at school that he'd taken Samantha Walker to the dance. He had never bothered to apologize, and the rejection lingered until she got to nursing school, where in time she'd learned to value her self-worth.

She hadn't run into either twin since they graduated from high school the year before her. She knew they were both following the rodeo. As she gazed at Rio, she was transported back to a time when the very thought of administering care to either of the hot, popular twins would've left her feeling awkward. Now Rio McNabb was just another unlucky cowboy in need of nursing.

Binney opened his computer chart with her access card. Reading over the many injuries diagnosed in ER, her empathy for him grew. His recovery was going to be arduous. It was easy to see why Dr. Layton thought she might hesitate being stuck on such a remote ranch, forced to ride herd on someone the surgeon had indicated could be cantankerous. But she was well trained and good nurses handled all types of grumpy patients.

She closed out of his record, and glanced up to find the patient in question studying her with serious gray eyes.

"If you're here to deliver another shot for pain, forget it. I don't like how they knock me out. I can't recover if all I do is sleep my life away. And tell that hospital advocate who came by to say I need to book an ambulance to take me home next Saturday, and rent a hospital bed for a month or so, that the wrangler who works for me will collect me in his pickup. No one's gonna turn me into an invalid."

"Actually, I'm not on your nursing team. Dr. Layton said he told you I'd drop by around two today so we could talk about your home care. I'm Binney Taylor, a private duty nurse. I see you don't remember me. We attended the same high school. You and your brother graduated a year prior to me."

"You're a home nurse? You look so young," he blurted. "Layton said we went to the same high school, but I assumed he meant you went there years before me."

"I believe age is just a number. But if you have questions as to whether or not I'm competent," she said testily, "I can provide you with references."

"Sorry. I suppose you're capable. High school was a long time ago for both of us. To be truthful, I don't remember you." He closed his eyes. "The shots they give me mess with my head. I wake up fuzzy. I don't like it, not thinking clearly, I mean."

Frankly it irritated her to hear so bluntly that she was totally forgettable, although it shouldn't surprise her. Back then all kids who lived in the group home were made fun of by cliques of their popular peers. That didn't mean she had to endure his slights now.

Taking out her cell phone, she phoned Lola Vickers, the former private duty nurse. "Hi, Lola, it's Binney. Dr. Layton has a patient at City who's going to need home care in a week or so. Can you take this job?"

"No. Arthur called me. I'm retired. My husband and I plan to travel. Why can't they get that through their heads?"

"Oh, I didn't know Dr. Layton had contacted you.

Sorry." She chewed the corner of her lower lip and eyed the man in the bed. "I know you turned the area over to me, Lola. I am free to take this assignment. It's more that this patient wants a nurse with more experience. But I understand. Enjoy your trip. I'll talk to you later. Bye."

Rio glared. "Did I question your experience? I just don't want anybody caring for me at my ranch." He rubbed the furrows that'd formed between his eyebrows. "Can you cut me some slack? I feel like I'm navigating through fog."

Binney reopened his record. "I see you are on a heavy-duty opioid. Are you aware that you sustained serious injuries? While you're here you should let them do whatever they can to keep you pain-free. Really, though, I am happy to hear you'd rather not take painkillers. Once you get home and settled we can certainly start cutting back." Jerking upright, she keyed out and guiltily met his searing gaze. "Uh, that's providing you elect to hire me. I didn't mean to be pushy. Dr. Layton called Lola Vickers, but she's not available."

"Do I need to decide right now? I've been tossed off horses before, and even been kicked in the head. After those docs patched me up I recuperated on my own at the ranch. Anyway, the Lonesome Road, my ranch, is well named. It's two hundred acres in the middle of nowhere." He gestured with his hand and once again the IV lines rattled. "Someone like you would get bored there before a day passed."

She began backing toward the door. Seeing the shape he was in she probably shouldn't take personally his reluctance to hire her. After she'd taken over from Lola as the only private duty nurse in the ranch community around Abilene, her jobs were mostly caring for ranchers or their wives following simple surgeries. There was Tom Parker, who'd been gored by a bull and gangrene had set in. Besides nursing she'd done their cooking so Tom's wife could get their cattle to market. She could handle McNabb's job.

To be honest she felt rattled over the possibility of working for the fancied McNabb brother. Someone who had matured and had definitely gotten more muscular. Even amid all his casts and bandages, and with the scruff of a five o'clock shadow, Rio McNabb was still handsome as sin. Had he become better looking than Ryder? The deeper question—was he nicer?

Quickly contemplating what it'd be like to share his home if it was as remote as he indicated, all while handling his most intimate needs, left her thinking this was probably a bad idea.

She was almost out the door when Rio called, "Hey. In high school, did you date my brother?"

The pain caused by that query even so many years later sent Binney spiraling in anger. But, loath to admit that his brother had stood her up, she stepped fully into the room again. "Are you kidding? I never garnered Ryder's attention, although it wasn't for the lack of my hoping to."

Rio might have responded, but Nurse Murphy came into the room and stopped to greet Binney. "Hey, hello. How's Raenell Foster? I heard you were taking care of her after her heart attack. What a shock. She's my age, you know. And she was never an ounce overweight. Nothing like me," the woman said, patting her ample girth.

"I completed my stint at the Fosters'." Binney glanced at her watch. "In fact I'm filling a few shifts in ER until another outside job comes up. I'm working three to eleven tonight. Guess I'd better go grab the elevator to keep from clocking in late." She dredged up a smile for Rio then peeled off the sterile gloves and gown she'd donned to enter ICU.

Gertrude Murphy shot a furtive glance between her patient and Binney. "Oh, so you two are friends." She broke into a wide smile. "Or more than friends? I forget you younger nurses have lives outside of the hospital. If you two are dating, feel free to stop back anytime."

Binney choked. "We're not friends. Dr. Layton thought Mr. McNabb might have need of home nursing once he's dismissed from here." She wadded up her used gown. "He doesn't think he'll require home care."

"Of course he will." Gertrude made a face. "Wait'll the morphine wears off and we try to get him up to see if he can manage crutches. The tougher these cowboys are, the harder they go down. You'd better keep in touch."

"I'm not deaf," Rio exclaimed, gray eyes thunderous. "And I don't think I said for sure I wouldn't need help, only that I didn't want it. Dr. Layton or the resident said they'd be back to check me this evening. Earlier I wasn't thinking straight. Now I have some definite questions for the doctor as to my prognosis. So, Binney…er, Nurse Taylor, keep in touch, okay?"

She felt a childish urge to stick her tongue out at him. Instead she inclined her head, and murmured to Gertrude, "The hospital has my phone number and ER schedule." With that, she spun away, dumping everything in the trash receptacle situated right outside his room.

"It doesn't sound as if you made a very good impression," Gertrude chided, marching to Rio's bedside.

He scowled all the way through her taking and logging in his vital signs. He practically growled when she pulled a syringe from the deep pocket of her uniform. "No more shots for pain."

"Dr. Layton ordered a shot every three hours through tomorrow. Then he'll reevaluate."

"The stuff you give me knocks me out cold."

She grinned. "That's the point. Sleep facilitates healing. Come on. Don't make me call in an orderly to hold you down."

Rio noticed pain had begun to seep back. "Is there a reason I need to sleep sitting up?"

"You had a collapsed lung. You don't want it deflating. I expect if all sounds good later, your surgeon will give us leeway to adjust the head of your bed. Between a tightly taped clavicle, a neck brace and recovering from a pneumothorax, sleeping reclined for the time being is preferable. Has anyone suggested you order a hospital bed to use at home?"

"Yes." His scowl deepened.

"So is that what you and Binney were fussing at each other about?"

"Were we fussing?" Rio didn't care to tell a friend of Nurse Taylor's that his irritation at the younger nurse centered on the fact she'd all but admitted to lusting after Ryder. Not that he wasn't used to women flocking around his more flamboyant twin, like bees buzzing over a flowerpot. He wondered when it had started bothering him so much. Possibly when he heard admiration for his twin falling from the kissable lips of the attractive blonde nurse with the striking green eyes. Those eyes were memorable, and yet he couldn't place her. Damn!

Since his head had cleared a little, he searched his memory bank back to high school. It annoyed Rio that he continued to draw a blank when it came to Binney Taylor. He could phone Ryder on the PBR circuit and run her name by him. Given their last falling out, he quashed that thought. JJ was a bit older, but he might remember Binney Taylor. Or his fiancée, Rhonda, who'd also attended their high school.

Why did any of this matter? Why waste time worrying about the past when he didn't even want to hire a private duty nurse?

In spite of telling himself that, Rio was beset by a longing to see her again. As he tried to sort through why that was, Nurse Murphy popped him with the needle she brandished, and in seconds Rio slipped out of the real world again.

Chapter 2

A bright light blinding Rio in one eye ejected him from a dark stupor. He tried to move his head to get away from the light, but was hamstrung by an immovable plastic collar he vaguely remembered someone clamping around his neck. His opposite wrist and ankle hurt like the devil when he moved either one, so he lay still until he could get his bearings.

"You are still alive," Dr. Layton said, shutting off the penlight as he continued to loom above Rio.

Devoid of words, Rio simply blinked. Ever so slowly his thoughts coalesced with his body. "Barely alive," he finally got out.

"Did you insult one of our nurses?" Layton pulled up a stool and sat next to Rio's upper torso. He unhooked his stethoscope and plugged in one ear tip, all the while checking Rio's pulse.

"If I did it's probably because you're doping me up like some street junkie," Rio managed to feebly say. "I don't recall insulting Nurse Murphy. But I didn't mince words objecting to that last pain shot. I can't remember what happens after one of those."

"So I've heard from a few staff members. Including from one who claimed she couldn't wake you to eat the soup I ordered for your supper." The doctor clamped in his other ear tip and slid the metal chest piece over Rio's lungs and diaphragm. After he finished listening, he sat back and slung it around his neck. "Both lungs are getting good air. Any chest pain now will be from the vertebrae and clavicle. You're lucky you have strong ribs. A broken rib on top of everything else would've added months to your recovery."

"Lucky. Yeah, that's me." Rio wrinkled his nose and tried to scoot up in bed, but couldn't get any traction between his hand being in a cast and his opposite ankle in an inflatable one that extended below his heel.

"We need to try and get you up. I'll have our orthopedic man on staff drop by and see if the swelling in your ankle is down enough to exchange the temporary cast for an Ace wrap. That should give you some better mobility. How's the rest of your pain?"

"Manageable, I think. I guess I don't really know since I'm zoned out more than I'm awake. Out of curiosity, who did I insult? If I swore at one of the nurses, I'm sorry."

"Nothing that bad. You apparently have issues with Nurse Taylor. Whatever transpired between you two gave her second thoughts about working for you. Since Lola Vickers opted out, you'd best get used to the idea of spending a few weeks at Baxter Rehab." After typing on Rio's chart, the doctor then clicked off the system and rose.

Rio's main issue with Binney Taylor was that she looked like a model, and in her own words once, and maybe still, harbored a desire for his brother. But were either of those things reasons for him to dismiss her services? Hell's sake, he didn't want to spend weeks away from his ranch.

"To tell you the truth, Doc, my conversation with Nurse Taylor isn't totally clear. Could you apologize for me and ask her to come back to talk again?"

"I can do that." Layton glanced at his watch. "In fact, she's due to clock out of ER in a few minutes. I want someone to get you up to see if you can stand with crutches, and with help walk a few steps. The night duty nurse will check your vital signs, but if Binney's available, let's see if she can assist you out of bed. We'll be more inclined to release you to go home if the two of you manage walking. Provided she'll take you on as a private patient."

The doctor talked so fast Rio had difficulty processing everything. Enough registered for him to know he needed to be on his best behavior with Nurse Taylor. Really he just needed to satisfy Dr. Layton. Once he got home what would hold him to keeping a private duty nurse? Couldn't he tell her he no longer required her help? What was most important was for him to go home, where, even if he was housebound, he'd be there to confer with JJ and do the ranch bookkeeping and such.

A nurse Rio didn't remember meeting bustled in to remove the inflatable cast and rebandage his ankle. Her badge said her name was Janet Valenzuela. In the course of their short conversation she revealed that she knew JJ and Rhonda. "I watched you ride in last year's Abilene rodeo," she said as she attached the clips to hold Rio's Ace bandage in place. "My son and a friend do team roping."

"Would that be Carlos? If so, I know him. He and his partner are moving up in PRCA standings. Even before the accident this was going to be my last circuit ride. I did think I'd sometimes enter ranch rodeos." He tried to move his newly taped ankle. Pain shot up his leg and made him catch his breath. "Plainly that won't be for a while," he said through compressed lips.

About that time Dr. Layton walked back into the room accompanied by Binney Taylor. They both heard his last exchange.

"Working here the last fifteen years I've met a lot of you stubborn rancher and rodeo types," the doctor said. "I've seen a few who don't take my professional medical advice end up in the obit column of the local paper. You can be one of them, Rio, or you can follow my orders and be content raising and selling horses. Barring being caught in a tornado, you could live happily into old age."

Rio caught Binney and Janet both wincing at the doctor's blunt statement. Because his previously addled brain was beginning to connect to the truth of his situation, Rio thought he could accept Dr. Layton's advice. "Some rodeo jocks don't have options. I'm lucky to have the ranch as a fallback." Rio mustered a smile. "Earlier I may have sounded like a blockhead. I understand my life has drastically changed. Truly I'm not like some guys who see rodeo as their whole life. I have a twin like that," he added, his gaze boring into Binney as he spoke.

"You act as if that's significant to me," she replied. "Until today I hadn't seen you or Ryder since the night of your high school graduation, when, as a junior, I helped set out snacks. You both went on the all-night party. I worked two jobs all through high school. That's how I paid for nursing school. Which reminds me," she said, handing him a manila folder, "as I'm the only private duty nurse currently in the area, here's a copy of my nursing diploma and recommendations from nursing professors. The hospital HR had them on file. If you'd like I can get references from my private duty jobs over the past two years."

"We're wasting time," Dr. Layton said. "I'm vouching for you, Binney. This guy has two choices, go to Baxter Rehab or hire you. Without further ado, can you ladies help our patient out of bed? Janet, I ordered crutches for him. Will you see if they were delivered to the nursing station?"

Acknowledging the doctor with a nod, the older nurse hurried from the room.

Resolving to make this work for Rio's sake, Binney slid her arm behind his back to give him support so he could ease his injured torso off the pillows. When her hand accidentally burrowed between his loosely tied hospital gown and the naked flesh of his muscular back, she and Rio both sucked in shocked breaths.

"Sorry about my cold hand," she hastily mumbled. "My bad. But someone needs to tie your gown tighter. It's only loosely done up at the top."

Having quickly jerked back fingers that still tingled from touching him, Binney made sure to have cotton fabric between her hand and Rio's smooth, warm back during the next attempt to sit him up. *Her reaction made no sense.* She was, after all, trained to see bodies as machines. In all her seven years as a registered nurse caring for young, old and in-between men and women of all shapes and sizes, she didn't remember ever having experienced such an immediate visceral reaction to simply touching anyone's skin.

A nursing aide entered the room carrying a set of adjustable crutches. "Janet got called to a patient having problems in another room. She said she may be a while."

The surgeon huffed out an irritated sigh. "I could help you, Binney. But the object is to see if you can get him out of bed."

"I'll manage. Are the crutches set for someone Rio's height?"

Dr. Layton took them from the aide, who quickly retreated. "I'm six-one and he's about the same. These would work for me. Just see if you can help him stand, Binney. I'll save ordering him trying to walk until tomorrow."

Not in the habit of arguing with attending physicians, nevertheless Binney knew it would be a disappointment for Rio to have walking put off. He'd made plain earlier how he resented feeling like an invalid.

Lowering her voice, but speaking directly to him, she said, "This will be awkward considering you have injuries to both sides of your body. Might I suggest you try using one crutch? The one opposite your usable foot. Let me act as the stabilizer for your right side. I can keep you upright and guide the portable infusion hanger, while you sort of hop along on your good leg."

"That's risky," the doctor said. "He must outweigh you by fifty pounds, and could bowl you right over."

"I'm five-eight and stronger than I look." Binney smiled encouragingly at Rio.

"All right. I'll be here this time to catch any slip." Dr. Layton walked over and passed Rio one crutch.

"Dang. The cast makes it hard to grip the handhold," Rio muttered. "Are you sure you want to try bearing my weight?" he asked Binney, who'd settled his right arm over her shoulder, and this time had her arm firmly around his waist as she slid him to the edge of the bed.

"Trust me," she murmured near his ear.

Totally caught off guard by the force of tremors running from his toes to his head as he experienced her touch and warm breath at his ear, Rio tested his uninjured foot on the floor and stood. Determined he could do this, he nevertheless needed a moment to get used to the feel of Binney's soft breast and other womanly curves pressed tight into his side and hip.

"I've got you," she said in a sure voice from somewhere in the vicinity of his chin. "I know you want to use the bathroom. It's about twenty steps to get you there. Are you game to try?"

Rio felt cool air from the room's A/C blow across his exposed backside. His hankering to use the facilities warred with an ingrained manly pride that said it was wrong to show off his naked butt. He certainly didn't pretend to be holier than the Pope, but neither was he in the habit of displaying his man parts to a woman he didn't know.

"Is this enough for today?" Binney queried quietly. "I'll help you back into bed and you can try again tomorrow."

"No," he grated. "When I get to the bathroom you don't have to stay with me, do you?"

"I do until you can navigate better on your own and not require help getting up off the commode, Rio. Earlier you mentioned at least one older injury. Did all modesty not go out the window then?"

"Even when I had the concussion I walked on my own. So, no, I handled everything I needed to do in privacy." Sucking in a deep breath, he took a tentative step forward.

"I'm glad to hear that solid breath," Dr. Layton said from behind Rio. "That tells me your lungs are performing well. Tomorrow, Dr. Darnell, the orthopedic doctor I've asked to see you, wants an MRI on your neck. He'll decide if you need cervical vertebrae four and five fused or not."

Rio straightened swiftly, a movement that caused him to swear. "Uh, sorry. I don't like the sounds of fusion. Will that mean I can't turn my head?" His question came out in fits and spurts, because Binney gripped him tighter and they were inching toward the open bathroom door.

"That's something you'll have to ask Dr. Darnell." Layton spoke over the sound of his pager going off. "Blast it all, I'm on call and ER is sending an auto accident victim to surgery. Binney, you seem to be holding up okay. Would you rather I help get Rio back to bed? I've already written orders to get him up in the morning."

"It's up to Rio. I'm good so far."

Rio was close to choosing to return to bed rather than be left alone with Binney for such an intimate excursion, when Janet Valenzuela rushed back into the room.

"Land sakes! That looks painfully slow. Here, let me get on his other side. Ditch that crutch for now. I'll support you so you can hop a little faster."

"I'll leave you in their capable hands," Layton said, striding toward the door. "I will check you again on morning rounds. It'll be after I consult with Dr. Darnell."

Watching the surgeon dash out, Rio had no idea why he'd feel relieved to have a totally strange woman witnessing his humiliation. Possibly it had something to do with Janet being more the age of his mother. In fact he knew she had sons in their twenties. Maybe he could find a way to dismiss Binney without sounding ungrateful. Especially if, as it appeared, he was going to need to hire her for a while in order to leave the hospital. His fervent hope was that by then he could work the crutches enough on his own to not need help getting to the bathroom.

Between them, the nurses maneuvered their patient into the small bathroom. It so happened that Janet entered first. With her short but plump body and Rio's six-foot-two-inch rangy frame filling the space, Binney was left unable to fit inside.

She disengaged her hold on Rio's waist and slid her hand the length of his right arm so he could maintain balance as the older nurse helped him be seated.

"Here, I'll close the pocket door to give you some privacy," Binney murmured, backing fully out. "Holler when you're ready for a return trek to bed. By the way, Janet, we noticed his gown needs tying farther down the back." Her words were cut off as she shut the pair into the small space.

Rather than hover outside, Binney hurried back to straighten the rumpled bedsheets and fluff up Rio's pillow. She'd unhinged the right bedrail to get him up. Now she checked the left one to make sure it was secured. The last thing he'd need would be to fall out of bed in the middle of the night. As it was she couldn't help but think how tall and broad-shouldered he'd grown since she'd last seen him that evening in his cap and gown. She had thought about the McNabb twins over the ensuing years. Texas was big on rodeos and their accomplishments were often in the Abilene news. Rio and Ryder were homegrown boys who made names for themselves on the professional rodeo circuit. She assumed their rodeo accomplishments were a big part of who they were.

She gave the pillow a last thump, feeling sympathy for Rio, who in all likelihood was going to lose a career that had helped make him more popular. However, he'd been brought up having the fallback of a ranch, and he hadn't sounded disgruntled.

As she responded to Janet's call that they were ready for her again, Binney made a mental note to take a run out to said ranch tomorrow. What had Rio called it? Lonesome Road. The name didn't denote a place rolling out a welcome mat.

"Thanks for your help," Janet told Binney after they returned Rio to his bed.

"Yes, thank you," he rushed to add. "Listen, the doctors gave me your business card, Binney. Now that I know I can navigate to and from the bathroom with a little support, I'll probably check out of here next week. Depending on how I'm doing, if I need your services I'll give you a jingle. Okay?"

The two nurses exchanged slight frowns. It was Janet who said, "The doctors may move you from ICU to a room next week. But did Dr. Layton or Dr. Mason not tell you that you won't qualify for release home until you can get around with crutches all on your own?"

"They did. But we'll see. I'll recover faster at home," he ended with a plainly dismissive note.

"A lot will depend on whether or not you need those vertebrae fused, Rio," Binney reminded him.

He closed his eyes and didn't respond.

Binney sighed. "Right! Okay, bye, guys. It's late." Shrugging, Binney left. She'd been here two hours past her ER shift. She had noticed they'd scheduled her the next day for the 11:00 p.m. to 3:00 a.m. slot again. While she appreciated having the ability to earn money between private duty nursing jobs, she sometimes wondered if it'd be better to go back to hospital duty altogether, where her hours would be more consistent.

Thinking himself alone again at last, Rio yawned. He opened his eyelids a crack when he felt fingers wrap around his right wrist.

It was Janet taking his pulse. "I can see you're wiped out from the exertion of hobbling to the bathroom. I want to be sure we didn't put a strain on your heart or lungs." Dropping his wrist, she donned her stethoscope and had him breathe in and out normally.

"All sounds good." She patted his hand and engaged the bed's side rail. "Murph told me you hate the pain shots, but I have to give one. Doctor's orders. He also wants you to eat some yogurt." She brought a carton over and removed the lid. Arranging double pillows behind him, she handed him the container and a plastic spoon.

"I'd rather have a hamburger." After saying this, Rio dug into the yogurt and ate it all in about four spoonfuls.

"You'll be on soft foods awhile. At least until after they see if you need vertebrae surgery." She whisked away the empty carton. "Okay, Rio. Sorry, but it's shot time."

"Tired as I am right now, just give it to me. I hope I'll feel a whole lot better after a full night's sleep."

The nurse disposed of the container, logged on and wrote on his chart then went to a tray an aide had brought in. She picked up a preloaded syringe and checked that it was the right medication.

"Before you hit me with that, can you tell me a little bit about Binney?"

Janet eyed him quizzically. "What do you want to know? She's an A-1 nurse. Everyone who has ever worked with her says so. Far as I know there's not a person on staff who she doesn't get along with. And she does more than what's required. If you're wanting gossip, I've never heard any." She rubbed an alcohol wipe over his upper arm.

"She claims we went to the same high school. It bugs me that I can't remember her."

"I can't help you there. About the time you two were in high school I was through nursing school and was probably long married. This will sting," she warned, jabbing the short needle through his skin. "If you want my advice, you'd be smarter to hire Binney rather than spend a couple of weeks out at the rehab. There you'll be one sheep in a flock, if you get my meaning. At home with one-on-one care—well, think about it, you'll be the recipient of all the attention."

Rio closed his eyes. He had been thinking about all that individual attention from the pretty nurse with the smooth hands and sparkling green eyes.

After finally leaving the hospital around 2:00 a.m. Binney only managed to sleep until ten o'clock in the morning. There were no calls or text messages on her cell phone. But had she really thought Rio McNabb would get in touch so soon asking to hire her?

Maybe she didn't want to work for him, she thought in the middle of scrambling eggs for breakfast. The hospital would keep her busy until some other private duty job came up.

At the very least, supposing he did offer her a position, she ought to inspect his ranch first and judge for herself if it was more isolated than she cared to be cooped up on with a young, too-handsome cowboy.

Thank heavens for GPS, she thought an hour later when finally she turned her motorcycle onto a graveled ranch road that led to the Lonesome Road horse ranch. Binney wondered how her predecessor ever found her way around this rural community without one.

She slowed considerably as a flock of wild turkeys flapped across the road in front of her. The road wound through high desert brush, shaded along the way by gorgeous old live oak trees. A moment before the road opened up to a clearing, Binney spotted a white-tailed deer bounding through a thicket of mesquite and juniper.

As she stopped completely to take the measure of a stone ranch house that had a wide porch running clear across the front of the structure, a fuzzy-faced barking dog ran up to her. She bent to let him sniff her hand and then gave him a rub when he rolled over. She supposed someone was on the property caring for the animal. From reading his chart Binney knew Rio McNabb wasn't married. But she hadn't thought ahead to wonder if he had a live-in. A lot of cowboys did. And surely a man as handsome as Rio could have his pick of any number of rodeo followers. She refused to refer to them as buckle bunnies because that was so demeaning.

Continuing to pet the friendly dog, she eyed a wind-mill that told her the ranch was on a well. Two barns in the distance boasted new paint, as did split-rail fences that enclosed grassy pens where several beautiful golden horses grazed in late summer sunlight.

As she rose from where she had crouched to pet the dog, thinking to stroll over for a closer look at the horses, a man seated atop a long-legged horse appeared out of nowhere, bearing down on her.

He pulled the snorting horse to a standstill even as Binney scrambled out of its path. The dog barked louder, and ran circles around the dancing horse.

"Are you lost?" the rider asked. He removed his hat and she met the dark, curious gaze of a handsome man, probably a few years older than Rio.

"No. I came in search of the Lonesome Road Ranch. I'm Binney Taylor, the area's visiting nurse. It's not definite the ranch owner will request my nursing ser-vices when he's released from the hospital. But since his surgeon recommended me and Mr. McNabb and I spoke about the possibility, I came out to get the lay of the land. I apologize if I interrupted your work."

The man swung out of the saddle. "I'm JJ Montoya. I train horses for Rio, and look after the ranch when-ever he's away. I only spoke briefly to him yesterday. He was more concerned about the horse that injured him than he was about much else except making sure I collected his pickup, camper and Tagalong, here," he added, indicating the dog that had gone to lie across Binney's feet. "Tag doesn't generally trust strangers. He seems to like you."

Bending, Binney scratched the animal behind his floppy ears. "I'd love to have a dog or cat, but since my work out in the community often takes me away from my apartment for weeks at a time, I can't have one."

"How is Rio, really?" the man still holding the reins of the golden horse asked suddenly. "He didn't sound his old self. But from the list of all he said was wrong with him, I frankly doubted he'd be home very soon."

Dusting off her hands, Binney hiked a shoulder. "Sorry, I can't discuss a patient's condition. I do know he had more evaluations scheduled for this morning. You could phone him later and get an update. Uh, it's nice to meet you, Mr. Montoya, but I won't keep you. You may or may not see me again, depending on whether or not I become part of Mr. McNabb's recovery team. However, let me say this is a beautiful ranch."

Pausing, Binney let her gaze roam over the scenic valley. She pictured what it might have been like growing up here, and felt a twinge of regret she always felt when forced to remember how she'd never had a real home or family.

Waving goodbye, she called, "It definitely wouldn't be a hardship to take an assignment here." She left the property with a greater appreciation for Rio's ranch than when she'd first turned off the main highway onto the lonely road.

Rio finished his lunch of cream of tomato soup and custard, wishing again for something more substantial. But he was being promised more for supper. The orthopedic doctor had come to see him after the MRI. He said he thought the cracked vertebrae would heal by themselves if Rio minded his p's and q's and didn't do anything to reinjure his neck. In fact, Darnell wrote an order to move him out of ICU into a two-bed ward later that afternoon. He planned to recheck Rio at the end of the following week, and said if nothing changed he'd discharge him, providing he use something called a TENS Unit, designed to promote faster bone repair. Darnell also said he'd have a tech order up a better-fitting neck collar.

All in all Rio was feeling pretty good. Especially since he'd also asked about cutting back the pain medication, and Dr. Darnell said they'd try less potent pills instead of shots.

His cell phone rang. Picking it up off his tray where the nurse had set it, Rio saw the call was from JJ.

"Hi, buddy. How goes everything at the ranch?"

"Funny, I'm calling to ask how it goes at the hospital."

"Some better." Rio launched into telling his ranch hand all he'd learned.

"So, you think you'll get to come home next weekend? Then you've settled on hiring yourself a home nurse?"

"I haven't decided. Why?"

"Well, now," JJ drawled, "Binney Taylor came out to take a gander at the ranch. She's some looker, boss. Tag liked her so much if she'd been a burglar he'd have invited her in and showed her the silverware."

"Binney drove out to the ranch?"

"Drove isn't the right term. Not only is the lady damned pretty, but she rides a Harley like a pro."

"She what?"

"You got hearing problems? The gal showed up here astraddle of a big old hog. She won over your dog, who usually bares his teeth at strangers. Oh, and before she left she said you have a nice ranch and it wouldn't be a hardship to work here."

Someone came into his room and removed his lunch tray, but Rio didn't acknowledge her. His brain had stalled out picturing the tall slender nurse with soft, soft hands and gorgeous eyes, riding a motorcycle. He then imagined her legs clamped around one of his horses. That image quickly morphed into one where, whole again, he reclined in his king bed, and those same long, luscious legs straddled his hips with just the right amount of pressure.

"Rio, you still there?" JJ whistled into the phone.

Barely managing to say "Yeah" in gruff tones, Rio reined in derelict visions he chalked up to pain and forced inactivity. "Listen, I'm gonna have to call you back later, JJ." He hit disconnect and willed away the all-too-enjoyable snapshot lodged in his head.

Chapter 3

Dr. Layton stopped by Rio's hospital room and told him he'd turned over his care to the orthopedist. "My job as your surgeon is finished. Your lung remains inflated. All else are bone injuries that are Dr. Darnell's field of expertise. I hear he's moving you from ICU. He'll be the one you'll be fighting with about going into rehab."

Rio screwed his lips to one side then said, "Since I'd rather recover at home I'm going to hire Nurse Taylor. Do you have any idea how long I may need her help? Or is that something I should ask Dr. Darnell?"

"Just judging from your initial injuries, I'd say you'll need a month to six weeks to get you moving under your own power. Darnell can pinpoint that better after he sees follow-up X-rays of your broken wrist and clavicle."

Layton turned to the computer and pulled up Rio's

chart. "I see he ordered a TENS Unit to help heal the vertebrae. That requires removing the cervical collar to sit with the electronic device on your neck for a speci- fied time each day. Getting the collar off and on prop- erly will take assistance. Frankly, I still don't get what you have against going to rehab. They're staffed for maximum therapies."

Rio puffed out a disgusted sigh. "I like being in con- trol of my life. Isn't that true of everyone?"

"Yes, unless you're sick or injured. I notice you listed your parents as next of kin. Can they help you at home?"

"If they weren't on their dream trip to Australia they would be my go-to people. Worrier that my mom is, I hope they don't hear of my accident. They'd cut their trip short. You may think I'm unreasonable. As a rule I'm not."

"I see a lot of you cowboy types. Don't blame me for thinking you all have more guts than sense. I do wish you luck." The doctor closed out the computer, shook hands with Rio and then left the room.

Rio barely had time to gather his thoughts when the team scheduled to move him to a ward arrived. Two burly guys dressed in green scrubs transferred him, mattress and all, onto a gurney, while an aide gathered his personal belongings. She'd headed out when Rio called to her. "Did you pick up a business card for a private duty nurse?"

"I left it in the drawer. I heard Gertrude Murphy and Janet Valenzuela talking. I thought they said you weren't going to hire…uh, never mind. I'll grab the card." She turned back and slipped past the gurney.

Rio would have liked to know what he'd said to give the ICU nurses the impression he wasn't going to hire

Binney. If word got back to her, she might take another job. He thought he'd been clear to everyone about wanting to recuperate at home, but weigh his options. As soon as he got settled in a ward he'd phone her and ask about her fees.

He did just that as soon as the transfer team left.

Binney sounded surprised to hear from him. "I charge the going daily rate for in-home nursing care unless I do household chores. There's a greater daily charge if I do cooking, laundry or other housework." She named both amounts.

"Which one includes taking care of a pet? I know you went out to my ranch and met my dog. JJ said you and Tag hit it off. I'm sure he was mistreated before I found him. He's not usually trusting of strangers, so you're an exception."

"I hate hearing he may have been mistreated. Goodness, he seemed such a loving dog. Care for him would be included in either rate." She paused then added, "Mr. Montoya was nice. What I viewed of your ranch was lovely. I hope you aren't annoyed that I went to check it over. It's something I do if the opportunity presents itself before I decide to take a job."

"Has a preview caused you to turn any job down?"

"Once. The old guy raised goats and lived in a one-room shack back in the hills. He had pneumonia and needed care, but a requirement of mine is to have my own bedroom. I never asked the size of your home. Wait…didn't you indicate it's where you grew up, so it'd be a family home layout, right?"

"It is. You'd have a bedroom. I bought the ranch from my folks. They wanted to retire to San Antonio. At the moment they're on a trip out of the country. What about you? Does your family still live in Abilene?"

"I live there. I rent an efficiency apartment downtown. Tell you what, Rio. My contract spells everything out. I work a late-late shift in ER tonight. It'll be past visiting hours when I get to the hospital. But I'll leave a copy at the unit desk and tomorrow you can ask a nurse to bring it in for you to read over. I want you to be satisfied."

"We both need to be satisfied." Rio couldn't help flashing back to his earlier thoughts of the two of them in his big bed. Shoot, not only wasn't he in any shape for monkey business, keeping hands off was probably listed in her contract. "So you know, I'd require some cooking and other stuff. I hope if Dr. Darnell sees I have home care, he'll release me quicker."

"Murph told me two things you balked at were renting a hospital bed and going home by ambulance. Both are most apt to impress Dr. Darnell."

Rio grunted, then said, "I'll see. So, we'll touch base soon?"

"Roger that."

Noting that she'd disconnected, Rio set his phone on the tray table. He tried to find a comfortable position as he closed his eyes and pictured all five foot eight inches of Nurse Taylor.

He woke up, not knowing how much time had passed, to a high-pitched feminine voice exclaiming, "Eew, Sugar Bear! You look awful. How do you feel?"

He smelled Traci Walker's signature perfume before she came close enough to identify. He failed to escape before she bent and brushed a damp kiss on his lips.

"Just what I want to hear, how bad I look, Traci. As to how I feel, I've been better."

She straightened away. "Daddy and Mama told me about your accident. I just got home last night from visiting Samantha in the Big Apple. We saw Ryder ride in Madison Square Garden." She pouted, a sulky face Rio knew she'd long perfected as they'd grown up together and had even dated a few times.

She continued discussing her trip. "We tried talking Ryder into hitting a few nightclubs with us. He's so focused on amassing points, he told Sammi he had to ride the next morning. You know she used to always wrap him around her finger. Ryder's changed. But we snagged Ben Jarvis and still danced the night away." Traci spun away from the bed and peered around, wrinkling her nose. "So when can you leave this horrid, smelly place?"

Rio managed a brief inspection of her expression of distaste. She hadn't changed since she'd unexpectedly popped in to see him at the Fort Worth rodeo in the spring and tried to steamroll him into renewing their long-dead relationship. Her daddy, Weldon Walker, owned the biggest ranch around Abilene. He was a leading patron of the PRCA. Traci, a six-time rodeo queen, dabbled in charity work with her mom. It surprised Rio to hear that his brother had skipped going out with her sister, a New York model. In high school Ryder had dated Samantha longer than he'd stuck with any girl.

"Before I check out I need to hire nursing care and the services of a chief cook and bottle washer at the ranch," Rio said. "Any chance you're in the mood to volunteer?" he asked in jest, knowing her family had always employed a cook themselves.

True to his expectations, she rolled her eyes. "I might lend a hand if you didn't live in the sticks. You need to sell and buy a ranch closer to town. You and I could be good together if you didn't bury yourself miles from civilization. I need to be near town, because Daddy's buying me a boutique."

"What do you mean, we could be good together?"

She wiggled her ring finger. "Daddy says it's time you pop the question and we get married, Sugar Bear."

"What?" Rio knew he was guilty of gaping.

"You're so stubborn, but I can wear you down."

"Don't count on it. You're a partier and I like solitude. And I'll never sell the Lonesome Road. Raising horses out there is all I've ever wanted to do."

"How can you say that when you've been on the rodeo circuit for years? Daddy said Abilene might be your last rodeo, though. I predict you'll get bored soon enough. Oh, but starting tomorrow I'm helping Mama arrange the country club's harvest ball. Heavens, Sugar Bear, can you even get out of bed? From my observation you'll need more help than anyone I know can give. Maybe Lola Vickers. Shall I have Mama call her?"

"Lola's retired." Suddenly recalling how tight the area ranch teens used to be, he blurted, "Do you remember Binney Taylor from high school?"

Traci assumed an annoyed expression. "Why ever would you ask about her? Surely you know she got her name because she was left on the doorstep at the orphanage in one of those green vegetable trash bins. Iona Taylor found her. She assigned the little nobody her last name. Mama said Binney lived in different foster homes, but she never fit in and never got along. By high school they sent her to a group home run by Catholic nuns."

Traci's diatribe left a sour taste in Rio's mouth. "Well, she's a registered nurse now. Sometimes she works here, but also does private nursing jobs. I plan to hire her."

Traci swiveled her head around as if searching for the woman they were discussing. "Land sakes. You can't get mixed up with the likes of her. Mama would bar you from the country club. And what would your folks say? Binney Taylor's not like us. Why, nobody knows her roots."

Disliking the turn of this conversation, Rio couldn't have been happier when a ward nurse came in, interrupting Traci's rant about Binney.

"Visiting hours are over," the nurse announced. "It's time for Mr. McNabb's meds. You'll have to come back later this evening, or tomorrow."

At first Rio thought Traci would throw her wealthy weight around and refuse to go. As it was she merely tightened her grip on her designer purse and said, "I only had a few minutes to spare on my way to a mani-pedi appointment anyway. I'll call you, Sugar Bear. If you're up and around in time for the Harvest Ball the first of October, I'll arrange a ticket. I'll even drive out to the boonies and pick you up."

Rio laughed. "Have you really looked closely at me, Traci? I won't be doin' any boot scootin' boogying by October. Oh, tell your dad I'm glad his horse is okay even if Diablo Colorado did his best to kill us both in the arena."

She paused at the door. "Don't you forget how important Daddy is in the rodeo/ranching community. He could help you build your horse trade if you don't do something foolish like let a person in your home that Lord only knows her background." She blew Rio a kiss and swept from the room on her red spiked heels.

The nurse stared for a moment at the empty door-way then set a small cup of pills on Rio's tray table. She poured him a glass of water from an icy pitcher. "Our ward has strict rules for visitation. We sometimes make allowances for relatives," she said pointedly, again eye-ing the door.

"She's not a relative." It was all Rio could do to hide a smile when the nurse appeared relieved. "What are these for?" he asked when the woman, whose name tag read Suzette Ferris RN, dumped three pills into his hand.

"One is an antibiotic. I'm about to unhook your IV. The other two are painkillers. Dr. Darnell replaced the shots you were receiving. If these keep your pain at bay, he'll likely order them for a couple of weeks. Be sure to tell us if they aren't strong enough. I heard you'd rather be off everything, but truthfully, hurting isn't good."

"Are they addictive?"

"They could be if you were on them for an extended period of time. Our physicians are careful about that."

Popping all three pills in his mouth, Rio swallowed them down with one gulp from the glass. He took the spoon and container of custard she'd opened. "How long before I can have real food?"

"If by real food you mean steak, probably not until it's easier for you to get up and around."

"Not necessarily steak, but even a sandwich. If all I get is baby food, won't that delay how soon I have the strength to get up and around?"

There was a rustling at the door and Rio raised his head, fearing Traci had returned. But Binney Taylor walked in. She wore jeans, boots and a plaid blouse. Her small waist was circled by a two-inch-wide leather belt. Her smile stretched from ear to ear. For the first time Rio noticed a smattering of appealing freckles on her creamy cheeks. He found it difficult to swallow.

"Is he giving you a hard time, Suzette? Knock it off, McNabb. She's one of the best darned nurses on this ward."

Nurse Ferris rushed to hug Binney. "Look who's talking. If you're a friend of this guy, you're far superior to his last visitor," she said, lowering her voice.

Appearing a tad confused, Binney waved an envelope. "I'm bringing Rio one of my private duty contracts to go over. I intended to drop it at the ward desk since I'm working the late shift in ER. But I got a call from Mabel in administration. She said if I'm slated to accompany Rio home, Dr. Darnell may release him soon. He needs time to decide between my services or going to Baxter Rehab."

Suzette wrinkled her nose. "No contest to my way of thinking. Especially as he's bugging me for *real* food." She made quote marks in the air when she said real. Facing Rio, she added, "When Binney worked here full-time she often brought casseroles to our lunch room. All of the nurses fought to see who'd get there first."

Her pager went off. Excusing herself, she air-kissed Binney and dashed from the room.

Binney covered the distance to the bed, set the envelope on Rio's tray table and relieved him of the empty custard container he still held. She stepped on the lever to open the waste container, then stopped. "Are they monitoring what you eat and excrete?"

"What? I'm not getting enough food to excrete anything," he said, turning red.

"They'll give you something more substantial tomorrow. You have to prove your intestines work well before you can go home, you know."

His eyebrows dived together. "I actually don't know. I was only in a hospital ER last time I was thrown from a horse." He tried casting his eyes elsewhere, but he was hampered by the cervical collar.

"I told you modesty flies out the window when you're dealing with extensive injuries. If you turn red as a tomato whenever it's time to shower, get a lotion rubdown or at other pertinent times, it's pointless for us to try to work together."

He studied her for a long moment. "It'll be hard for me to put aside long-held proprieties, but I want to hire you." He hurriedly added, "I'll sign the contract now."

"But you haven't read it," Binney said.

"With all the recommendations you've had from staff here, I shouldn't have waited this long. Do you have a pen?" He didn't say there was someone who hadn't recommended her. But Traci Walker's comments were one reason he wanted to sign on the dotted line and show folks like Traci and her family that not every area rancher gave a damn about their view of someone's roots.

Binney took the papers out of the envelope. "I'll run out to the nursing station and grab a pen while you go over this. Have you compared home care to what all is offered at Baxter Rehab?"

"I'm not going there. Call it plain pigheadedness. Initially I held out hope I could handle healing at home on my own. I'm stubborn, but not stupid. I'll need help."

"In that respect you aren't a lone wolf, Rio. Just since I took over private duty nursing from Lola, virtually every rancher who hired me has shared your feelings about being tended to by a strange woman. Some called me a wet-behind-the-ears kid. At first I resented it. Now I understand. There's a loss of dignity attached to needing help with the basics of one's life. Keep in mind it's temporary."

"I hope so," he said, sounding so unsure Binney hesitated at the door and peered back over her shoulder.

"Did Dr. Darnell downgrade your prognosis? I thought Janet said he's fairly sure you won't require fusion of the vertebrae."

Rio tried to shrug, but was assailed by a pain so sharp in his back that it took his breath away.

Binney rushed back to his side. "What is it, Rio? Not your lung again?"

"No." He ground his back teeth and took a slow breath. "Higher and in my back." He raised his right hand up to his left shoulder and discovered the cast wouldn't allow him to rub where it hurt. "Dammit," he growled, dropping his arm to his side again. Closing his eyes, he took a deep breath as Binney ran her cool fingers under the neck of his dressing gown.

"Sorry I swore. Bad habit," he admitted. "Wow! That feels better, whatever you did."

"I'm guessing the brace for your fractured clavicle is twisted. Maybe in transferring you from ICU. While I'm at the desk picking up a pen I'll ask one of the orthopedic nurses to see if Dr. Darnell will order a fresh one." She lightly massaged the skin under the scrunched material.

"Man, that's nice. If I was a cat I'd purr."

"I'm happy to hear it didn't restrict your sense of humor." Smiling, she said, "Hang in there. I'll be right back."

It was Suzette and another nurse Rio hadn't seen before who next entered his room.

"Why didn't you tell me we needed to check your clavicle brace," Suzette scolded, motioning for the second woman to help her sit Rio up with his feet dangling over the side of his bed. "Dr. Darnell left standing orders to change your cervical collar and clavicle brace anytime you got uncomfortable."

They'd shut the door, but he still felt exposed when Suzette untied his dressing gown and let it fall to pool around his waist. The newcomer steadied him while Nurse Ferris *tsked* and began to unfasten straps passing behind his back. "Removing the sling completely will cause pain," she warned. "Can you hold your breath until I can slip you into a fresh brace? By the way, this is Lacy. She's a fourth-year student nurse training here."

A sharp stitch stabbed Rio's back. "Where's Binney?" he asked, barely able to move his lips.

Suzette spoke from behind him. "She went downstairs to find a brochure on Baxter Rehab for you."

"Why? I said I want to sign her contract." He jerked his head up and unconsciously squared his shoulders. The pain nearly stole his ability to huff out, "Does she not want the job with me?"

Finally Suzette answered. "That's our Binney. She wants a patient to understand all choices." Dropping the old sling, she let her coworker steady Rio while she unfurled a new one.

Binney sped silently into Rio's room and immediately pulled up short as her gaze honed in on the broad, muscled, bronzed chest of the man being propped up in bed. She nearly choked trying to take a breath, and her mouth went dry of its own volition.

In spite of wearing a cervical collar and having a wrist and ankle all casted or taped up, he represented a fabulous specimen of manhood. Wide chest tapering to slender hips, but with corded muscle in all the right places. Why had she ever thought his twin was more alluring?

But, she shouldn't be smitten by Rio, either. There were definite rules in a nurse-patient relationship. It was probably the main reason she pushed him to consider going to Baxter Rehab. Boy, howdy, she hadn't made allowance for possibly ministering to someone so near her age. Someone she'd once had on a pedestal along with his twin, until Ryder fell off.

She forced herself to quit gawking, but because she remained flustered, she dropped the pen and the brochure she'd gone after fluttered from her hand. The noise attracted the attention of the two nurses working behind Rio. And he attempted to check out the commotion.

"Oh, you're back," Suzette exclaimed. "I shouldn't ask, but can you give us a hand? Lacy's never done this before. In surgery they put him in this sling, but didn't add a strap at the back to hold his arm steady. Dr. Darnell won't want his arm flapping and causing him pain." She explained all of that for the sake of the student.

Binney rescued the pen and brochure, set them on Rio's tray table, and hurried over to the sink to wash before pitching in.

The two professionals made short work of getting Rio into the harness, but Binney's fingers had felt unsteady from unusual nervousness.

"Puts me in mind of bridling a horse," Rio grumbled. "Although, it sure feels better. Uh, but can you guide my arms into the gown thing?" He scowled. "How long do I have to wear it? Can I wear regular clothes at home? Even to go home," he stressed. "I'd hate for any rodeo fans to see me going out of here in what amounts to a dress."

Suzette winked at Binney. "And people call women vain." She assisted Rio into the sleeves of the striped gown, tied it securely and Lacy eased him back against the elevated head of his bed.

Binney took pity on Rio. "With your hand and wrist in a cast, you'll need loose-fitting, short-sleeved shirts. Until the doctor says you can quit taping the sprained ankle, I recommend two sizes too large pajamas, and later ripping a pair of jeans up several inches from the bottom. That way you'll look your old self for visitors."

"Thanks for easing my mind on that score. I knew a guy who went to Baxter after he got stomped on steer wrestling. They didn't let him wear jeans until he'd totally recovered. Just hand me the pen and your contract."

Suzette smiled, but because she still stood by his bed, she moved the tray table closer and slid him the items Binney had brought. "Here you go, tough guy. If wearing your own clothes is the criteria for hiring Binney instead of going to rehab, your decision seems made." She gathered up the discarded brace and restored both bed rails. "You know to press this button if you need us," she said, pointing to an area inside the rail.

"Got it." Lifting his eyes, he asked, "Why two copies of the same thing?"

"One is yours, and I get one," she said. "Like any contract. Did you read it?"

"I'm too tired after all the fuss changing my brace.

I want to go home, and you're the best, if not the only, game in town." Rio scribbled his name on the second set of papers and dropped the pen. He shut his eyes. "If someone has time they can put my copy with my personal belongings. I'll find out what day I can leave when Dr. Darnell makes his rounds. I'll call you, Binney. Er… do I need to call you Nurse Taylor now?"

"No." Binney accepted her copy of the contract and watched Suzette store Rio's in a zippered bag with his boots and clothing he wore from the rodeo. "Home care is more relaxed about some things. However, with your extensive injuries, you will need that hospital bed we discussed. Plus, I know you argued against going home in an ambulance. But I've made one trip down the graveled road to your ranch, so book the ambulance, Rio."

Suzette seconded Binney's edict. "You don't want to jar any bones out of place rattling around in a pickup truck. I assume that was your original plan."

"It was. Okay… I'll call about an ambulance. But my ranch hand and I both own king-cab pickups." Opening one eye, Rio pinned Binney. "I imagine my ranch road would be jarring to someone riding a Harley. I hope you can drive a pickup in case JJ's tied up and you need to go for groceries or dog food."

"Of course," Binney said.

Suzette and Lacy gaped at her and gasped. "Really, you travel by motorcycle?" The older nurse whooped. "I'm impressed."

"Me, too," Lacy said as the three women headed out.

"I bought it when gas got so expensive," Binney acknowledged. "I like it, and I can pack everything I need medical-wise and my clothing in the saddlebags."

They exited the room and the door swished closed behind them.

In the hall the student nurse dashed off to join a floor nurse who'd beckoned her. Suzette leaned over and confessed to Binney, "I envy you getting to work outside the hospital setting."

"Private duty is great if the people you work for are pleasant. Some can be overly cantankerous and if you're the only nurse there's no respite."

"Rio McNabb hasn't caused us any angst so far. Of course I can't say the same if you have to deal very often with his rich-bitch girlfriend."

Grinding to a halt, Binney's jaw dropped. "Who? I didn't know he had a girlfriend." She bit her lip. "Actually no one's ever said he didn't. Do you know her?"

"No, thank heavens. I know her type. Everything she had on screamed money. And she skirted me like I was dirt. You'd know how rich she is, too, because she talked to Rio about picking him up for the country club's October ball. I've heard those tickets are five thousand dollars each."

Binney nodded. "A youth center I do some counseling at was their charity one year. I think most of their funds go to local good causes." For some reason her stomach still pitched at the thought of Rio having a girlfriend of privilege. But why wouldn't he? His family had owned a big ranch, and now he did.

"You're so bighearted. I'm not as magnanimous when it comes to rich snobs."

"Having wealth does go to some people's heads." Binney thought back to her school days, when certain girls had been especially cutting and mean. "I hope Rio isn't seriously involved with a woman like that. I can believe that, though, of his twin," she mused. "Oh, maybe you aren't aware that I knew them growing up. Rich girls, poor girls, all girls in school were enamored of both. Ryder dated a super-rich girl, I know. Maybe Rio's trying to outshine his brother." She winked as she said it, and Suzette laughed.

"I've gotta run. If I don't see you again until after you wind down your tenure at McNabb's," the ward nurse whispered, making sure no one else heard, "let's get together for lunch. Should you meet Ms. Rich Witch, I'll be anxious to hear if you concur with my assessment."

"Sure. I may go by St. Gertrude's and light a couple of candles to hopefully ward off the possibility." Binney took her leave, dwelling on what a seemingly down-to-earth cowboy like Rio might see in a woman of the type Suzette had described.

When it came down to it, why did she care what type woman either McNabb twin dated? It was past time she killed and buried a decade-old crush that had ended badly for her. Although she'd be first to admit the way Ryder had treated her had long-affected her willingness to trust men.

Chapter 4

Three days later, Binney hadn't heard from Rio and so was considering a different private duty job in Sweetwater, which was farther afield than she normally traveled, when the call from Rio came. Even though she'd more than half hoped to hear from him, when she saw his name on her cell phone she had to take a deep breath before answering, and hoped she sounded normal. "Hi, Rio. Sorry I haven't been up to the ward to see you again. I've worked double shifts in ER. Truthfully, I'd about decided you'd changed your mind and decided to go to Baxter Rehab after all."

"Gosh, no. Doc Darnell finally said I can go home tomorrow afternoon. It's short notice, but are you available to start working for me then? Please say yes. I'm going stir-crazy."

"I thought your release was imminent the other day. I hope you haven't developed additional problems."

"Not that I know of."

"Okay, so you're totally set?"

"Yep. Yesterday JJ rented a hospital bed. And he got one of those shower seat things Nurse Farris suggested. He said a medical supply place delivered that electronic gadget that Doc wants me to wear an hour or so every day."

"It's the TENS Unit."

"Right. And this morning Doc Darnell said I can leave anytime after one tomorrow. Once you say what time you can meet me at the ranch I'll book an ambulance and finally get home and breathe some fresh air."

Binney laughed. "You can't fool me. I know the aroma around a ranch is rarely fresh."

"Maybe it's an acquired preference," he drawled. "It's no worse than the antiseptic odors around here."

"Touché! It so happens the ER nurse I'm filling in for starts back tomorrow. So, if Discharge starts your paperwork right after lunch it'll probably be one thirty or so by the time they complete everything and transport you downstairs. How about if I plan to meet the ambulance at the entrance and follow you to the ranch?"

"Perfect. I'm so ready to blow this place and get back to normal."

"Rio, you do know you're trading all nursing done at the hospital for pretty much the same routine at your home? I mean, the kind of injuries you sustained take time to heal regardless of where you park your body."

"Yeah, I know. But Dr. Darnell said, depending on your evaluation, maybe in a week or so I can go out to see the horses. Is it dumb for me to think that'll be better for me than any medicine?"

"Not dumb, but it may prove discouraging for someone like you."

"Someone like me? What's that supposed to mean?" His tone vibrated with hurt.

"Nothing bad. Anyone can see you're a true cowboy, Rio. The genuine article. I doubt that in the past you've ever walked by anything at the ranch needing attention that you didn't stop and take care of it. Until all of your injured bones knit well, you simply can't do normal chores. Trying will set you back."

He was silent for so long, Binney thought maybe the call had dropped. "Rio?"

"I hear you. Can you just let me be excited about going home?"

Binney tightened her hold on her cell phone. She'd rained on his parade and he was pouting. Possibly it was a bad idea for her to take this assignment. Either he was more thin-skinned than she'd imagined, or she was more on edge thinking about riding herd on him.

"I didn't mean to snarl at you," he said. "Truce? I know I have to let you call the shots."

"I'm not an ogre, Rio. But I do take caring for my patients seriously."

"So I've heard. Believe it or not, it's why I want you for my home care."

"Okay. I accept your truce. We'll start our relationship tomorrow. Uh, our w-working relationship," she stuttered. Feeling heat climb her neck and cheeks, she disconnected the call without waiting for his response. Afterward she stood in the middle of her bedroom, holding the phone for a long time. *Why was she so darned nervous?* Having anticipated his call, she had packed medical supplies she figured to need for him. After previewing his remote ranch, she'd set out jeans and shirts. In essence she was ready to take the job. *But was her heart ready?*

Maybe a million times since he'd signed her contract she'd stared out her front window in the direction of his ranch and had given herself pep talks centered on spending weeks alone with him.

Binney used her last shift in ER to double down on professionalism. She did every assigned task by the book. When her shift ended, all of the ER docs told her how sorry they were to see her go. The chief of ER made a special point of saying he'd hire her back full-time in a heartbeat. His assertion provided her the grounding to face any challenge, including a too-handsome bronc rider who made her think of herself as a woman, not just a nurse.

Mulling that over, riding home on her bike she blamed her wonky feelings on how many of her impressionable years she'd given both of the McNabb twins a special spot in her lonely heart. While Rio had never paid her any attention, he'd never been cruel like a lot of other boys—like his brother. A lot of guys and girls had made fun of her hand-me-down clothes and the fact she lived in a group home, or they'd rudely joked about the fact no parent had ever wanted her. At first she'd gone to each foster home thinking it would be her forever family. All had disappointed her. She did still long for a family, but shift work and erratic hours stood in her way of making time to date. Really she had yet to meet anyone special enough to make her dream of marriage.

The next morning Binney finished her minimal packing then took items from her fridge that would spoil if left until her job ended. She lugged the box of perishable foods over to her elderly neighbor.

"Mildred, I'm glad you can use my leftover milk, eggs and cheese."

"I'm happy to get these things, girl. Grocery prices keep rising. For those of us on a fixed income it means we sometimes have to give up items like eggs and cheese. You say you'll be working out on another ranch? I miss the good old days my husband, may he rest in peace, and I raised cattle south out of Robert Lee. Hard to believe Bill's been gone thirty years." The woman shifted the sack of food and filtered a pale blue-veined hand through white locks. "I'll keep an eye on your apartment, Binney. Only place I go these days is to church. I know your job as a nurse is to take care of somebody sick, but try to grab some time to enjoy the wide open spaces. Even our medium-sized town keeps growing. With more people comes more pollution. There are times I wish my brother-in-law hadn't sold the ranch and moved me here."

"You're sounding a bit maudlin. Are you feeling okay? I have an hour before I need to meet the ambulance that will be taking my patient to his ranch. Can I run to the store for you? You're not out of the vitamins your doctor wants you to take, are you?"

"Bless you, child. I still have half a bottle. I will sorely miss you popping by to sit a spell and talk. Or bringing your guitar to play tunes for me. I know that will cheer up your new patient, though."

"I hadn't set my guitar out to take. Did you see on TV a couple of weeks ago about the rodeo bronc rider who had a horse fall on him? That's who I'll be taking care of. Guys like that spend a lot of evenings on the road in cities where there are top Western bands and singers performing. I'm self-taught and only mess around for my own pleasure."

"And mine. You sound real good to me. I recognize all of the songs you play. Take it, Binney. If that poor cowboy is as stove-up as they said on TV, he'll be restless. I recollect hearing somebody say that music soothes the savage beast. My Bill always sang to our cattle to calm 'em down."

"You talked me into it." Binney gave the frail woman a gentle hug. "Take care and watch that you don't fall on our stairs. If you need something, call me. I'm staying in the country and won't be able to run over here, but I have a list of friends I know will help."

"The world needs more young folks like you. If that cowboy doesn't have a lady at home, and if he's blessed with half a brain, he'll charm you into sticking around his ranch. Not that I'm anxious to lose you as a neighbor. But a nice, pretty girl like you ought to be settled down with someone to love and be loved by."

Binney laughed, but knew she'd blushed. "Don't hold your breath, Mildred. A nurse on the hospital ward where he's currently being treated told me he has a girlfriend." From the way Suzette spoke, she crossed her fingers that the woman wouldn't drop by to see him at the ranch. But as big as his ranch was, she could make herself scarce. She could always take his dog for a walk, or go see the horses.

"My hope is you'll marry someone who appreciates you, Binney. I'm going to light a candle for you at church. So there."

Binney's smile was weaker. "You do that. Yikes, we've talked half my time away. I have to go. Bye, Mildred." She gave the woman another hug then darted across the hall into her apartment, where she collected everything she thought she'd need at the ranch, including hanging her guitar case across her back.

Fifteen minutes later she rolled into the turnaround in front of the hospital right behind the ambulance.

Binnie knew Jorge, the EMT who hopped out of the vehicle and came to the back to remove the gurney he and the driver would take inside to receive Rio.

Jorge saw her, because he handed off the gurney to the driver and walked back to speak to her. "Hi, Binney. Are you going out on this case?"

"I am. How's your family?"

He beamed. "Good. Real good. Thanks for asking. I have a week's vacation coming. My wife booked a hotel at Padre Island."

"Your kids will love it. It sounds wonderful. Mine are always working vacations." She chuckled.

"The ranch where you're going is out in the sticks. The hot, dry sticks."

"I visited it. It's pretty. There were trees, wildlife, and his ranch is situated at the foot of rolling hills. A nice change from the city."

"You always look on the bright side of things. Hey, I gotta go help Leo get our patient. Since you've been out there, how about if we follow you?"

"Sure, but will you tell the patient I'll be leading the way so he knows I'm here? Most of the ranch road is dirt or gravel. By leading I won't be eating your dust."

The man signified he'd heard by giving a two-fingered salute before jogging off. Binney kick-started her Harley, donned her helmet and pulled to the front of the ambulance, where she waited until they emerged with the rolling bed.

This time it didn't seem so far out to the Lonesome

Road. Binney figured that was because she didn't have to keep consulting her GPS on her cell phone. The hot September sun had shifted in the sky into the western sector enough to send its blistering rays over the stone house and outlying barn and sheds by the time they arrived.

After removing her helmet, Binney hung it on the back and shook out her sweat-damp hair. As she squinted at the shimmering sun, she was thankful she'd managed to get her natural curls cut shorter for however long she'd be out here.

Even though she could feel the sweat beneath the leather guitar case lashed across her back, she didn't unbuckle it when she wheeled her bike over to park it in a slim section of shade.

Leo had turned the ambulance around and backed as close to the three steps leading up to the wide porch as possible. Binney joined him, introduced herself, and they walked to the back of the vehicle where Jorge had already flung open the door.

She'd barely greeted Rio when out of nowhere came a snarling, barking dog that leaped at Leo and nipped his arm.

First to recover from the shock, Binney grabbed the animal's collar. "Tag, Tag," she said softly, but firmly. "We're friends who have brought your master home."

Seeming to recognize her, the big fuzzy Labradoodle released the stranger's shirt sleeve and nuzzled his head against Binney's thigh. That only lasted until Jorge called to Leo for help lowering the heavy gurney out of the ambulance. Then either because he sensed or smelled his favorite human, Tag wrenched loose from Binney. In a single bound he set his paws on the rolling bed's metal frame and amid happy yelps proceeded to lick Rio's ear and face.

"Whoa, whoa. Hold it, Tagalong!" Rio scrunched up his face, but he couldn't escape the swath of the long pink tongue the way he was strapped down and hampered from moving his head aside by the cervical collar.

"I'm so sorry I lost my hold on him." Horrified, Binncy rushed over to again try to curb Rio's enthusiastic pet.

"Binney, thanks for grabbing him. Tag is just happy to see me. But he's on my wrong side, my bad side, so I can't even pet him."

A thundering horse rounded the corner of the house. Rio's ranch hand yanked hard on the reins of the powerful palomino, stopping short of the gurney and the shocked men trying to shield their patient from another onslaught. Binney clamped both hands around Tag's collar, but she couldn't drag his feet down from his master's arm.

JJ Montoya vaulted off his mount's bare back, removed his stained cowboy hat and shoved the big horse back a few steps. "Geez, Rio. I had Buttercup's colt on a lunge line in the arena behind the barn. I totally lost track of time until Tag bolted and cleared the fence. By the time it dawned on me where he was headed, I had to release the colt and toss a bridle on Nugget here. Tagalong, heel," he ordered. "He didn't hurt you, did he?" JJ asked as the dog acted confused, but did drop to his belly, tugging Binney along as he flopped across JJ's boots.

The ambulance driver took the opportunity to signal to Jorge, who still braced the foot of the rolling gurney. "Let's get Mr. McNabb into the house before any other

animals show up. Delivering him safely is our obligation. We'll let his nurse and the other guy sort out the
menagerie."

"I'll have to unlock the front door," JJ announced.
"Ms. Taylor…that's right, isn't it? Can you hang on to
Tag and steady Nugget?" He dug a key ring out of his
jeans pocket.

"Is the hospital bed you rented prepared and set up
to receive Rio?" she called to the man charging up the
porch steps.

He turned and moved aside to let the men maneuver
their patient up to the porch. "The rental bed came with
a sheet and pillow. I opened it up but just set it in the
middle of the living room. I'd better come spell you, so
you and Rio can decide where you want it moved." He
unlocked and opened the house door.

She sighed as he jogged back and took over animal control. "It's up to Rio where he wants to spend
the majority of his days and nights for a while. It'd be
nice to have an area with a lot of natural light. However, for your convenience," she said, pausing next to
Rio, "with as few steps as possible to at least a three-
quarter bathroom."

"Then the living room, but toward the back patio.
Anywhere, really. I'm just damned glad to be home."
Rio gestured with his hand not confined in a cast.
"When my folks remodeled, they added a bath by the
patio doors so people coming in from the pool or the
gardens could change clothes or shower."

"Perfect." Binney hurried inside, quickly took measure
of the room then dragged the rental bed toward a set of
sliding glass doors. "It really is perfect," she said to the
men following her. "Setting his bed here gives me a choice

of chairs to use where I can keep an eye on him. And this way the bathroom is on the side of his uninjured leg."

Jorge locked down the wheels on the rental then he and Leo moved Rio off the portable.

Binney made sure he was comfortable before pulling up the side rails.

"What's that on your back?" Rio asked when she turned to thank the men and walk them out. "A guitar? You play guitar?"

She made a face. "Play is a stretch. More like plunk around on it. My neighbor said I should bring it and claims she likes my music. But she's almost ninety so is likely hard of hearing." Sliding the strap off her shoulder, she set the case by the door.

"I have an electronic keyboard in my travel trailer. You could say I plunk around, too. Sometimes Tagalong likes my tunes. Sometimes he growls, and I swear he puts his paws over his ears." Rio cracked a smile. "How long do you suppose it will be until I get this cast removed so I have use of my fingers again?"

"Did no one provide you with follow-up instructions before you checked out?"

"Come to think of it, Dr. Darnell folded some papers into an envelope he tucked under my pillow. He wants X-rays in three weeks. The good news is that he said by then I might be able to get in and out of JJ's pickup for the ride to the lab."

"I'll find the envelope in a minute. I want to run out and get my saddlebags with my clothes and miscellaneous medical supplies. Shall I ask if JJ wants to come in to talk to you for a few minutes? I see he's still standing out there holding his horse and Tag. I imagine he's waiting for the ambulance to leave."

"He can come in anytime. Will you bring Tag in? He's used to being with me unless I rode in a rodeo event. Then he was confined to my trailer. I hope he won't keep on acting upset about not being able to climb up on this bed. I suppose you'll say it's wrong how I share my bed with the mutt."

"Not up to me to judge. Pure curiosity," she said from the doorway, "How does your girlfriend feel about that? Tag's a pretty big dog."

"Girlfriend?" Rio gave a belly laugh. "It's been three years since anyone even remotely fit that description. And I honestly can't recall if she ever met Tagalong."

"My mistake." Binney opened the door, but Rio's next statement stopped her.

"To call something a mistake insinuates you had reason to believe such a person exists. Or are you fishing?"

Swamped by old feelings she hadn't navigated in years, Binney's breath hitched. "One of the ward nurses said your girlfriend visited you in the hospital. I frankly have no reason to care one way or the other since you're just my patient," she said, digging up a grin. But she lost her hold on the screen door and it slammed, leaving her unfinished thought trailing in the air while she completed her exit from the house.

Rio's jaw flexed hard enough to radiate pain down his neck. He knew he shouldn't be developing feelings for her, but some had sneaked in. As she'd plainly admitted that she'd once hoped to date his twin, he wondered if that interest also stood as a barrier between them. If that were the case he needed to back off. There had always been rivalry between Ryder and him even though everyone tended to think they were alike. Nothing could be further from the truth.

Damn, now he wondered if the nurse he needed for the duration of his incapacitation maybe accepted this job hoping Ryder might drop in on him so they could reconnect. The possibility disappointed him and caused a hole to crater in his chest. Should he tell her that wasn't bloody likely?

JJ had told him he sometimes imagined slights and blew innocent remarks out of proportion. Was that what he was doing with Binney?

Thinking of his ranch hand, in he walked with Tag bounding ahead, and Binney at his heels. So if she was always around it'd be a long time before Rio would get the chance to voice his question to JJ.

It was JJ who directed Binney to the guest room she'd use while staying at the Lonesome Road. That, too, left Rio feeling helpless and useless.

He could see into her room as she'd left the bedroom door open. As a result he kept his conversation with JJ strictly on ranch matters.

"Why all of these orders suddenly? You haven't been gone from the ranch as long as you sometimes are at rodeos, Rio. Nothing's changed. My workload is the same unless you buy that pregnant mare from the guy out of Pecos." JJ snapped his fingers. "That reminds me. Here's a check from the local rodeo association. Seems a bunch of people who witnessed your accident contributed in your name to the benevolence fund." Unsnapping the pearl button on his shirt pocket, JJ extracted a folded check. He read off a sum that had Rio whistling through his teeth.

"Should I accept it? I'm not down-and-out like some guys who get hurt."

"The note said this money was given in your name. And you do have hospital bills."

"True. Did they include a list of people who donated?" Rio asked. "I should send thank-you notes. My orthopedic doc said I can sit in my recliner every day to use that electronic device he says will help heal my cracked vertebrae. Unless it clashes with our Wi-Fi or something in my laptop, maybe I can type notes with one hand and you can print them off and get 'em in the mail."

"I don't know diddly-squat about how to even turn on your printer." JJ made a face. "Maybe Rhonda can operate your setup. Or Nurse Taylor," he added when she reentered the living room.

"What about Nurse Taylor?" she asked.

JJ started to apprise her of what he'd said, but Rio interrupted. "She's only here to take care of my medical needs. There's no reason for her to mess in ranch business."

"Well, *excuse* me," JJ strung out, climbing to his feet. "I assumed she'd have to help in the office, too, since you're stove-up."

The dog, who'd flopped down between Rio's bed and JJ, lumbered up and over to Binney, nudging her until she rubbed his ears.

Pursing his lips, JJ stomped past her and on out of the house.

Approaching a sour-looking Rio, Binney asked lightly, "What was that all about?"

"Nothing. He…just…nothing!"

She arched an eyebrow. "Okay. It's time for your afternoon pain pill. If you point me to the kitchen I can bring you water to take it with, or make some iced tea. I brought tea bags in case you don't stock those."

"I do." Rio released a sigh. "I owe JJ an apology. I just snapped at him and said you were here only to take care of my medical needs. Obviously I need you to handle other things, such as..." He waved the check. "I hate to ask, by chance can you make a deposit to my ranch account, and help print off thank-you notes if I'm able to type them?"

"Probably. I presume you bank in town. Was JJ objecting to taking it there? Just so you know it will be at least a week until I'm comfortable leaving you alone."

"I bank online. JJ claims he can't work our computer."

"Do you know Bob Foster? When his wife was laid up after surgery, I took care of her, their home, prepared meals and handled their ranch bookkeeping on a computer."

"Great." Rio pointed to an archway with the flopping check. "Kitchen's that way. I'd like iced tea. Until it's brewed I'll phone JJ and mend fences. I'll have him bring my laptop from the office and we'll deposit this later."

Binney smiled and squeezed Rio's wrist. "I like a man who's willing to admit that he needs to say he's sorry."

She left the room and Rio glanced down where he fancied he still felt her warm touch. The thing he was sorriest about but couldn't admit to her was that his brother stood like a brick wall between them.

Chapter 5

"You have a dream kitchen," Binney said, returning a short time later with Rio's iced tea and his pain pill, and Tag not letting her out of his sight. "It opens out into the most fantastic screened patio. Do you entertain a lot?" She placed the pill in his unbandaged hand and elevated the electronically operated upper bed while still holding his tumbler of tea so it wouldn't spill.

Rio took the pill and swallowed it down with her assistance. He gave a dry laugh. "JJ's fiancée says I only have a kitchen because it came with the house." He drank more tea. "This hits the spot. But in ten minutes it's gonna need to hit you-know-what. I guess we'll soon see if the two of us can get me into the john."

Setting the glass down, she let him lean back against the pillows again then spared a moment to study the room. "This Saltillo tiled floor makes for easy walking.

We don't have as far to go as you did in the hospital." She made the trek herself and peered in the bathroom before returning to his side. "Nice, Rio. With that large, walk-in shower you have plenty of room for me to help you get in and out, dried off and dressed."

He screwed up his face and she took his hand. "Are you fighting modesty again? Think of me as a robot, not a woman."

His grating half laugh revealed what he thought of that notion. "Maybe if you wore feed sacks from head to toe." He broke off talking as she picked up the glass and once more offered him a drink.

He could get used to having her support his head and neck. And he loved the play of the afternoon sun shining through the tall sliding glass doors to burnish Binney's smooth skin. A bright beam left her short red-blond curls a fiery halo.

His mouth suddenly dry, and other parts of his body reacting, Rio blindly reached his uninjured hand out for the glass, or her, but the clavicle brace restrained him and pain caused him to miss the glass, drop his arm and howl.

Binney hurriedly bent over him, concern carving lines around her mouth. "No sudden moves, Rio. For at least the next couple of weeks you have to speak up and ask me for anything you want." She held the glass to his lips and lightly rubbed between his shoulder blades as he drank his fill.

"You have magic hands. I'm positive no robot matches that. And," he added, "in the sunlight you look like an angel."

Gaze tripping lightly over his earnest face, Binney shook her head. In a no-nonsense voice she said, "No flirting with your nurse allowed. I know that's how you and Ryder cut wide swaths through the female population in high school. Very probably through female rodeo fans, as well. We learn in nursing school to be immune to flattery."

"But you weren't immune in high school. You've said as much. On the other hand if it's true you never dated Ryder, it's hard for me to believe." He deliberately eyed her up and down. "Ryder brags that he dated every pretty girl in the county and left them heartbroken after he dropped them—which he always did." Rio brightened. "Are you trying to tell me you're the exception even though you admitted you wanted to go out with him?"

"Stop it!" Binney stepped away from his bed, set the glass down again and rubbed her upper arms. "If you must know, Ryder asked me to one of the school dances. He never came to pick me up, nor did he bother to call and cancel. Other girls delighted in telling me he'd taken Samantha Walker to the dance instead."

Rio stared at her. "I can't imagine why he would've done that."

Binney's laugh was brittle. "Yet you didn't even remember that we went to the same school. Much of your crowd probably never knew I existed. Those who did looked down on me because I started life as an abandoned baby. I wasn't adopted, and I bounced around foster homes. There may be loving foster families, kind of like how you've cared for and adopted a foundling dog. I was never more than a pair of extra work hands for my foster folks. At sixteen I asked to live in the Catholic group home. I still had chores, but also time to study and take a paying job at a nursing home. It let me save money to attend college. Now you see why someone like your brother wouldn't feel a need to call and dump me."

"I'm sorry. I'll apologize for Ryder. I know he had his pick of girls, but still…"

"You act as if he was an anomaly. You had your share of adulation. Back then the majority of girls didn't distinguish between you two."

"And yet you did," Rio noted, sounding disgruntled. "At least at the hospital you said it was Ryder you worshipped from afar."

"Did I? Since I was applying to be your employee it would've been unseemly to suggest anything different. May I ask now for a big favor? Can we put this pointless line of discussion to rest? High school was ages ago. Life goes on. People mature. I certainly did, and I'm in your orbit for one reason. To help you recover from a bad accident. Can we agree on that?"

His gaze slowly cruised over her from head to foot and back again for a while. His ultimate response was little more than a grunt.

"I'll take that as a yes." She helped him finish the tea before asking in a normal tone, "What sounds appetizing for supper? You know better than I what's stocked in your kitchen."

"I don't have any idea what's left from last time I was home. Rhonda, that's JJ's fiancée, has a key. She comes in after I leave for a rodeo to clean out my fridge."

"I haven't seen a woman around. Does she live on the ranch?"

"She rents a place in town near where she works. Weekends she spends in JJ's house here on the property. If I leave anything they can use, she's free to take it. Otherwise she bags it for the trash that gets picked up out on the main road every Thursday. All I know is I'd like some real food instead of that hospital crap."

Binney set the empty tea glass on a small table near Rio's bed. Tag bounced eagerly up.

Feeling around under Rio's pillow where he'd said Dr. Darnell had tucked an envelope with discharge instructions, she found it and extracted a page. "This says you can gradually get back to a normal diet and taper off opiates. Suzette gave me enough pain pills to last you today and tomorrow. And a script for another week."

"That's the pill you just gave me? I assume so since I'm already feeling loosey-goosey. I prefer to switch ASAP to whatever over-the-counter pills are in the medicine cabinet in my private john. Before you go find it, will you help me to the closest one?" He started to move on his own and rattled the bed rail.

"Hold on a minute." Binney dropped the paper she'd been reading, snatched up one crutch JJ had set by the bed and quickly let down the rail. "Easy does it. I intended to find you real clothes to put on at your first excursion. As that requires altering your jeans, we'll do that tomorrow. Do you have pajamas someplace that I can get?"

"I…uh…no. I sleep in my underwear."

"Ah."

"Can we hurry? But don't let me slip."

"You're still wearing the slipper socks they gave you at the hospital." Binney secured an arm around his waist, lowered the electric bed and helped him stand. "You're really wobbly. Next time, make this trek prior to getting a pain pill."

He leaned more heavily against her slight frame. "We

can solve that by stopping the damn things." His sharp response had Tag whining in concern.

"Tag, sit," Rio ordered.

"I've heard that big talk about quitting painkillers before," Binney said, carefully navigating past the dog, who'd sat as Rio directed. "I want you to cut back, too, but not until your pain is tolerable." They entered the bathroom and he immediately told her to leave.

She blew out an exasperated sigh. "Sit your ass down and quit being one." She guided him to the commode.

"You sound tough, but I'm the boss. Now out."

Ignoring him she eyed the glassed-in shower. "It's going to get old fast if we have this fight every time you need to pee or shower. Ward nurses said you liked lotion rubdowns before bed. Nothing's different here."

"There's a lot different," he fumed. "Those nurses were my mom's age. They've all raised kids. Unlike you, I figure they'd all powdered a lot of bottoms. Now out. Please," he begged, gazing at Binney with pleading, pewter eyes.

"Okay. I'll step outside the door. But I'm telling you straight, if you fall off the pot, I'm calling an ambulance to take you straight to Baxter Rehab. Unless you do damage enough to need to go back to the ICU."

Waiting impatiently outside the door, Binney rubbed Tag's ears. He'd scooted up to her on his belly. She did take pity on Rio. His feelings weren't anything new. Younger men often requested older nurses. In San Antonio where she'd trained, many male patients came from the oil fields, agriculture or ranches. Those types frequently objected to young trainees. It took her a while to realize their qualms had little to do with her not yet having an RN on her name tag. Supervisors joked that youthful nurses should buy gray wigs and granny glasses.

She heard the toilet flush, peeked in and was stunned to see Rio standing up, balancing on one foot, bracing his hips against the sink while he washed the hand not in a cast.

"All right. You've proved you're gutsy. But let's get you back to your bed before you run out of gas," she said, bursting in to wrap an arm around him again.

He treated her to a winsome smile. "I swear I'm feeling better. Maybe simply because I'm home. Any chance you can rummage in my closet and get me some of those real clothes?"

"Sure, I guess. Gosh, those pills usually knock you for a loop," she said as she settled them hip to hip and guided him across the room. "Once you're in bed you can tell me what to fetch and where."

"Shirts and jeans in the closet. Underwear in the top dresser drawer. I'll put those on by myself, but you'll have to help with the jeans."

"Where will I find scissors to rip out a seam?" She eased him down onto his bed, but he seemed reluctant to let go of her.

"I have wire cutters out in the barn," he said cheekily.

"Great. I think I have a small pair of scissors I brought to cut tape."

"Tape?" Rio's eyelids fluttered and closed as Binney slipped loose and engaged the bed rail.

"Yes, I have to tape plastic wrap around your cast and your cervical collar each time you shower. I brought a second clavicle brace we can trade out while one dries."

"You know best." He punctuated that with a yawn.

"I'll go see what I can find for you to put on. Then I have to get something started for supper."

Rio didn't answer. Binney noticed he'd fallen fast asleep. She smiled down on him, and murmured, "Zonked. Come on, Tag. Let's go see what we can find to eat. He won't be ready to have those clothes for a couple of hours. And you, my friend, are probably hungry and thirsty, too. I hate to rummage through Rio's cupboards, but I don't know any other way to find what we need." She went into the kitchen and Tag followed. He padded across the tile and sat in front of two ceramic bowls, both were licked clean.

Binney chose one and filled it with water. Tag immediately woofed and bent his head to lap up the contents.

She opened a cupboard that might be a pantry and was rewarded with shelves of canned goods. Two bags of kibble sat on the floor. One was open and held a scoop. Only guessing, because she'd never owned a pet, she dumped two scoops of pellets into Tag's second bowl.

He gave her a damp lick of her hand, which she accepted as a happy response. When she returned the kibble sack to the pantry she scanned the shelves and found several boxes of macaroni and cheese. "Perfect for Rio," she muttered. She also discovered bread mixes, and on the counter a bread machine exactly like one she owned. Pleased, she washed her hands and hummed while preparing the dough and setting the maker to rise and bake the herb loaf.

Seeming replete, Tag stayed glued to her side.

"It's time to go find your master some clothes," she said, marveling at how quickly she'd begun talking to the animal as if he were human. Oddly, as if he understood, he led the way to Rio's bedroom.

Tag jumped up and lay on the foot of the big bed. *Giant bed*, Binney thought, judging there'd be room for three people and the lanky dog to sleep side by side.

Feeling guilty for having any such thoughts about an employer's bed, she went to a tall dresser and in the top drawer as Rio had indicated sat stacks of white briefs and cotton undershirts. She left the shirts, considering it wasn't cold even in the air-conditioned home.

She felt a bit uncomfortable opening a closet that wasn't hers, but compared to a couple of ranchers she'd worked for, Rio's closet was neat. She selected a chambray short-sleeved shirt and a pair of worn jeans.

Although it felt nosy, it was difficult to not check out his bedroom. What struck her first was a lack of anything on the taupe-colored walls. His dresser and nightstands were also devoid of anything personal like family photos. Two lamps and an alarm clock left her a bit sad to think of anyone's life this barren. Especially a man she knew for a fact had grown up in what she'd always heard was a caring family.

Leaving the room after Tag hopped off the bed to join her, she scrolled back in her mind to a time she had cut shots of families out of magazines and carried them in her wallet just to pretend she had folks who loved her. She no longer did anything so pathetic, but reflecting on Rio's bedroom she thought about all the framed prints on her walls. She had knickknacks, too, and baskets of dried flowers. Stuff in home-goods stores that she'd seen moms with children buy. Family was an area in her life with hurtful gaps, still incomplete. Yet she still dreamed big. She pictured one day having a loving husband and three or four kids.

In the living room, her patient slept on. Feeling domestic she got out her scissors, ripped the seam out of one pant leg almost to the knee so it would go over his bubble-wrapped injured foot and ankle. Afterward she set his clothing in one of the recliners and curled up in the other with one of many ranch magazines tucked in a rack attached to a floor lamp.

Tag nosed his way up on her lap and attempted to make himself a lap dog. Binney scooted to one side to give him more room. Laughing softly so as not to wake Rio, she hugged Tag and kissed him between his furry ears. Then lifting her head, her gaze lit on Rio. His almost black hair had a lot of natural curl she hadn't noticed before. Even sporting the scruff he'd shaved off once in the hospital, he was still darned fine-looking. His high cheekbones, straight nose and narrow jaw with the slightest cleft in his chin presented too much of an enticing picture.

She forced her focus back on the article about cattle ranchers who loved the land in beautiful but rugged places. She wondered if that applied to horse ranchers, too. Probably so. She imagined the hard work and long solitary days that must be a part of life out here on the Lonesome Road.

Before she could find another short read, the bread machine dinged, letting her know the bread she'd been able to smell for a while was done. Hating to disturb Tag, who'd also gone to sleep, she nevertheless needed to rescue the loaf.

She roused the dog and he trailed her to the kitchen, where she washed her hands and brought the round out to cool. There was butter in the fridge. And she'd set out a pot to fix the macaroni and cheese. It wouldn't take long to throw supper together once Rio woke up.

Going back to the living room Tag again settled on her lap. She picked up her magazine and chanced to see Rio open his eyes. For an elongated moment he gazed at her as if confused to see her seated in his recliner.

She witnessed the slow lifting of his fog. His slightly off-kilter, sweet smile that followed sent her heartbeat drumming in her chest.

"FYI," he said. "Tag's a bed hog. Since these bed rails won't let him jump up here with me, don't be surprised if he sleeps with you tonight."

"I don't mind. Unless you object. I mean, will that play havoc with his training?"

"I haven't really trained him. I admit I'm surprised by how fast he took to you."

"Gee, thanks."

"I didn't mean that disparagingly. It's that JJ claims Tag whines and stays by their front door the few times I've had to leave him at their cottage overnight."

"I was teasing."

Rio suddenly sniffed the air. "Something smells good. Did you fix supper? Whatever it is makes my stomach growl."

"I baked herb bread." Binney moved Tag and stood up. "I fed Tag. Guessed at giving him two scoops of dry food. I plan to make mac and cheese to go with the bread if it sounds okay to you. I'll bring you a plate and set up the bed's tray table. Tomorrow, after you shower and put on the clothes I found, we'll see if you can sit at the kitchen table to eat breakfast."

"I'm ready to try that now. And Tag gets three scoops of kibble." He pushed the button and raised the head of his bed.

"I'll give him another to chow down on while I fix

supper. Rio, I know you want to jump straight into your old life. Dr. Darnell's notes say to go slow. In the morning we'll see how you tolerate sitting on the shower bench. Like at the hospital, it will require finessing around your casted hand, neck collar and cervical brace. The former I'll cover with plastic wrap. The latter we'll let get wet and change out when you're done. Likewise I'll remove the Ace wrap on your leg and restore it after you dry off."

"Yeah, I know I'm anxious to be well." He tried to touch his face, but his arm was restricted by the support clipped to the clavicle brace. "Damn, how's a guy supposed to eat? Or shave? My face itches under these whiskers."

"Patience. I can relax the brace provided your back is fully supported by the bed or eventually we'll try one of these recliners. You can shave yourself if you have an electric razor."

"I do in my bathroom. It probably needs charging."

"I'll take care of that." She left the room, unearthed it in his bathroom and plugged it in. "That's done," she said as she returned. "I'm going to feed Tag more, then cook our meal. So don't foolishly try to lower the bed and get out without assistance."

"You'd make a good military drill sergeant. How did you end up in nursing?"

"How did you end up a patient? You found something you loved to do and were good at. Loving horses and riding. For me it's liking to see people be hale and hearty, and being good at caring for them when they're not."

Binney reached the kitchen archway expecting a comeback. As she left the living room he still hadn't said anything. A quick glance back showed his eyes trained on her, steady and somber, but with an added expression she couldn't name. She had no idea what he was thinking, but she maybe ought to avoid further verbal sparring.

She returned twenty minutes later, and he'd fallen asleep again.

"Rio," she called softly. "I have your supper."

He blinked awake.

"I need to balance this tray on your lap and raise you into a sitting position. Then I'll unhook the support so you have greater motion with your good arm." She went through the steps methodically, giving him time to adjust to each.

"Comfort food," he said after savoring his first bite. "Did you already eat?"

"I'll have mine later. This is more solid food than you ate in the hospital. I want to be handy in case you have trouble swallowing."

"Your food will get cold. I'm fine. Go dish up a plate."

"You have a microwave. I can warm something up later."

"Quit being stubborn. I hate eating alone."

She threw up her hands. "Who's stubborn? You want me to stand by your bed and eat my supper?"

"There's room on my tray. And you can drag over a bar stool."

"Okay, but don't you dare choke while I'm gone."

He shot her a toothy smile. "Patient one. Nurse nothing."

"Is everything a competition with you?" she grumbled. Her query didn't get an answer until she returned carrying her plate, and pulled over a bar stool.

"I had to think on your last question about competition. Frankly I'm surprised, but maybe you're right. I am pretty competitive."

"I suppose that comes from all the time you've spent bronc riding." She broke a piece off her bread and ate it slowly.

"Actually I think it goes back to the cradle. Or the womb. You're a nurse. Have you seen evidence of sparring in ultrasounds of twins?"

She laughed. "Not that I recall." She watched Rio scoop in several forkfuls of mac and cheese. "I only did one rotation in OB, but you've brought up an interesting theory about competition and twins. I have my laptop. I'll do some research online. What did you two compete over?"

"Everything. From toys, to cupcakes, to boots, to…" He chewed his bread and gazed into the distance before he swallowed then admitted, "…horses, and even friends." Their eyes met and he added with fervor, "I can assure you that if I'd been the one to ask you to a dance, I'd have taken you come hell or high water."

Binney's mouth fell open at hearing his last pronouncement. "Uh, I have to say in high school anytime I passed either of you, you were in a circle of other popular kids."

Rio stopped eating. "To me, high school and early rodeo weren't fun. My brother had to win or he'd pitch a fit."

"I always thought you were best friends. Certainly you were both popular and both excelled at sports." She idly dragged a fork through her food. "I would've loved having a sibling of any age. I hope you and Ryder have put petty envy behind you."

He shrugged. "The past four years we've gone our separate ways."

"So you don't own the Lonesome Road together?"

"No. He says he hated this backwater spot. If you're hoping he'll drop by, it's not gonna happen. He's gone for good."

She frowned then rolled her eyes. "The only reason I might hope such a thing, Rio, is that you're injured. I should think a visit by family would mean a lot. Will your folks visit?"

"They're vacationing in Australia. I hope they don't get wind of my accident. This trip is something Mom's wanted forever." He polished off his mac and cheese and sank back against his pillows.

"You seem distressed. Are you in pain? I don't want you to lie flat this soon after eating, but you've sat up fairly straight for quite a while. Let me clear away our plates and ease the head of your bed into more of an incline."

"You're still eating. I'm okay. We can talk about something else. I'm not big on revisiting my past."

"That surprises me." She started to ask what could possibly be bothersome about what she'd always judged the McNabb twins' storybook life to be like, but there was a sharp rap at the door.

Binney scrambled off the stool and quickly gathered their plates. She set them aside and rushed toward the door only to see it open, and JJ and a gorgeous woman with long black hair walked in. They were loaded down with grocery sacks.

"We got here too late to fix you supper," the woman said, sniffing the air. "I'm Rhonda Lopez, JJ's fiancée," she added, smiling at Binney. "I know your name, and that you're Rio's private nurse. After JJ explained the extent of Rio's injuries, I told him we needed to pick up supplies. Shall we take these to the kitchen and chat while the men discuss horsey stuff?" Rhonda quickly turned to JJ. "Be nice. Tell Rio not to worry about the bookkeeping. If I can't figure out the ranch system, my sister works at a bank and I'll ask for her help."

Rio gestured with his good hand. "It's settled. I left a message on your house phone, JJ. Binney handled Bob Foster's ranch accounts. But gosh, guys, thanks for the supplies. While you're here, JJ, let's discuss that pregnant mare we talked about buying."

"Give me a minute to adjust the head of Rio's bed," Binney said, brushing past the other man. "He's sat up long enough. You two can still talk if he lies back a bit." In a few short strokes she'd straightened his bedding, fluffed his pillows and let the bed down halfway from what it'd been. "Better?" she asked, deftly refastening the loose strap on his clavicle brace.

Even if he hadn't sent Binney a smile that reached his eyes and lingered on her through several heartbeats, his expelled breath would have conveyed his relief. Going one better, he caught her hand before she slipped away. "Just so we're clear, hiring you is the smartest thing I've done recently."

Sensing his friends' curious expressions trained on her, she tucked her chin down. "I…ah…hope you're still of the same mind once I start getting you up and about two or three times a day." Freeing herself, she backed away from the bed and took the sacks JJ still held.

The dog seemed unsure who to follow. He ended up flopping down between where JJ sat on the empty bar stool and Rio's bed.

In the silence that fell over the room, Binney's boot heels clicked loudly on the tile floor as she zipped into the kitchen behind JJ's fiancée.

Thankfully, Rhonda didn't probe into what that last exchange had been all about. But she mentioned not remembering Binney from high school.

"You probably wouldn't if we didn't have any classes together. I worked after school, and never took part in any extracurricular activities." Binney opened the pantry and they began unloading groceries.

"Makes sense, then." Rhonda carried one sack to the refrigerator. "We bought standard supplies." She took out eggs, milk and cheese. "The only meat we picked up was hamburger. Although JJ says Rio complained about not being able to eat steak, from the sound of his injuries I wasn't sure he could cut steak." After closing the fridge door, Rhonda folded bags together.

"He'll work up to a regular diet once he's up and around more. The doctor had him on a soft diet because of his collapsed lung."

The other woman winced. "JJ says he's never seen Rio hurt this bad."

"Rhonda? Are you ready to leave?" JJ called from the arch.

"Yes, I think we're finished here." Turning to Binney, she said, "Anything else you need from the store or anywhere, tell JJ."

Binney impulsively hugged the other woman. "I appreciate having milk and eggs for morning." She straightened and murmured to JJ, who'd come into the kitchen. "I'd like to surprise Rio with a wheelchair if you can swing it. He'd benefit from getting out in the sun. You can find one with outdoor tires where you rented the bed."

"Sure thing. I can pick it up when I go to Pecos after the mare Rio's buying. I know he's already antsy to see the new horse I'm set to pick up next week. Think you can wheel him out to a corral by next Thursday or Friday?"

"We can shoot for that." The three walked back into the living room. "Our first order of business is bathing, shaving and sitting for a treatment with the TENS. By the way," Binney continued, "these recliners are soft. Any chance we can come up with a wooden rocking chair?"

Hearing them, Rio hollered from his bed. "Any chance I can get a shower and shave tonight? Twist JJ's arm to stick around and help me."

Binney almost laughed at the ranch hand's visible panic. "It's really not hard. He doesn't want me to see him naked," she confided. "Would you mind assisting tonight? He'll get over his modesty in time. But a shower tonight will be beneficial."

Rhonda excused herself to Binney and waved goodbye to Rio. "I'll see you at the cottage," she told JJ, and the two brushed lips.

Binney felt the love radiating between the pair and her heart lurched with envy. Detouring to the door that led to Rio's bedroom, she addressed JJ, "I'll bring his robe and slippers. You can help him shave while I set up for his shower."

The men had Rio clean-shaven when she later emerged from his bedroom. JJ had rolled up his shirt-sleeves. He and Binney jockeyed Rio out of bed. After they walked him to the bathroom, one on either side, she got out the plastic wrap to keep Rio's cast dry. "Once he's showered and you have him dry and in his briefs, JJ, we'll take him back to bed. I'll remove the plastic wrap and rub on lotion designed to stave off bedsores." Smiling at Rio, she added, "Then we'll get you into a fresh clavicle brace and restore the ankle and foot wrap."

"What about my shirt and jeans? Won't JJ already have me in those?"

Binney taped the last of the plastic around his casted hand. "Trust me. I have loads of experience dressing stubborn guys like you."

JJ laughed. "We men are the opposite. We're good at undressing you gals."

Rio scowled at his friend. The minute Binney had finished wrapping the plastic, he was plainly anxious for her to go.

Hovering outside the bathroom along with Tagalong, she blocked out the men's chatter and listened as the shower went on and the shower door closed. Subsequent sessions would get easier. The first one at home for a patient was most difficult. Especially for a male patient who had a female nurse. Some never let go of their modesty. She hoped Rio could.

It seemed a long time after the water shut off that JJ summoned her. "I'm going home. He's all yours," the very wet man stated. He was out the front door before Binney could say goodbye.

"I'm worn out," Rio fretted. "Can we just get the rest of my clothes on so I can go to sleep?"

Binney tucked the single crutch under his bare arm and slipped her arm around his damp waist. "I'll be quick with the lotion. Move, Tag," she told the dog.

It took them a while to make it across to the bed, where Rio sank back with a groan.

Totally unprepared to experience a punch in her gut from merely looking at him sprawled on his bed in nothing but briefs, lotion she usually warmed between her hands sizzled. Averting her eyes, she started at his feet and worked up his legs, and felt his slumberous gaze track her every move. A duty that normally didn't feel intimate to her, suddenly did.

Privately she chanted a mantra over and over. *You're a nurse. He's a patient. You're a nurse. He's a patient.*

One fine-looking patient who showed by his grin that he'd begun to enjoy the whole process way too much as she smoothed lotion over nicely rippled muscles along his lower abs and his manly chest.

Chapter 6

Almost two weeks after his first night at home, Rio's life had settled into a comfortable routine. Every day that passed he'd grown more at ease having Binney around helping him, cooking for him, talking with him, laughing together, playing guitar for him and. yes, he thought, running her soft hands and warm lotion over most of his body. His heart kicked over and his chest tingled as he lay there imagining it. He'd started dreaming about her when he slept. That was new for him.

Midweek JJ had hauled in the wooden rocker Binney had requested. Its seat and back cushions were made of foam and yet the chair was sturdy enough to support his back when Binney hooked him up to the TENS Unit. He didn't know if the treatments he took twice a day were helping his neck. Binney said they'd find out when he had his X-ray the following week. They both came to realize that he wasn't good at being idle. Binney brought in his electronic keyboard. He could only make music with one hand, but Rio relaxed more when they laughingly made bad music together.

Today she'd gone outside after lunch and had taken Tag. As a rule she didn't hike to the end of the lane for mail until later in the day. But she and the dog hadn't yet returned. Her lengthy absence let Rio's restless mind travel a meandering path. He couldn't say when he'd started missing her if she wasn't around, but now he wondered exactly what that meant. Did it mean she'd gotten under his skin? He definitely felt a growing closeness toward her. He thought...hoped...she shared his feelings.

Silent though the house was, his musings were interrupted and his attention diverted to a commotion coming from outside at the front of the house. A loud engine. Gravel spewing. And Tag barking up a storm.

That's when Rio remembered JJ had gone to Pecos to buy the new mare.

He chafed, wishing he could get out of bed to go see the horse he'd spent his money on. *Why couldn't he?* His crutch was within reach if he shifted his butt and grabbed the handrail with his good hand. Oh, but how many times had Binney cautioned him to wait for help? Too many times to count. However, before she'd always been within calling distance.

Yesterday she'd said he was moving better. In fact he'd walked alone from his bed to the rocking chair. And she really only guided him to and from the bathroom. Once there he shaved, showered, dried off and tugged on sweatpants she'd had JJ pick up at the store.

Man, he hated being dependent. If he didn't start taking some initiative, wouldn't his muscles go to hell?

Doubling down on a determination to show he could be more independent, he managed to drop the side rail and swing his legs around. That was a mistake. He realized at once the move would land him on his bum ankle. Plus, the crutch now stood where he'd need to grab it with his casted hand.

In attempting to roll over on his belly to rectify the problem, his lower body and legs dangled half on, half off the bed. That's when the front door flew open with a bang. A sound that made him jerk, which shot pain up his spine.

He heard Tag lope across the tile, his toenails tapping loudly until he leaped up and hit Rio in the butt with both his feet. "Dammit!" Rio couldn't see what was happening to make all that rattling at the door.

All too soon there was no mistaking the panic in Binney's voice when she yelped, "Rio, what in heaven's name are you doing?"

Giving up, he lay still, and was glad when she shooed Tag away and he soon felt her secure grip steering him to his feet. Her hands were touching him, magically but dependably.

"I heard JJ drive in. I figured if I could make it to the porch he might stop and let me see Contessa."

"Who?" Binney gathered him close and turned him until he bore his weight on his good leg.

"That's the mare we acquired. I've only seen her photo and read up on her bloodline and that of the stallion to whom she was bred. All of that is essential to retaining a pure palomino registry. Nearly as important to me is how well she shows. How she holds her head. JJ's the best when it comes to weaning and breaking stock, but I have a sixth sense when it comes to choosing horseflesh."

"Well, then, I have a nice surprise for you." Binney tucked his crutch under his arm and moved him in a circle. "I shouldn't reward you for bad behavior," she scolded and gave him a little shake. "If you'd fallen it would've set back what progress you've made. And you scared me. Can you feel my heart pounding?"

He could, but it wasn't bad in his estimation. Still, he bit his upper lip between his teeth. "I know. I'm sorry."

She brightened again. "Because you've done so well, I thought you deserved a treat. I asked JJ to pick up a wheelchair. Ta da!" She pointed to where Tag sat thumping his tail on the floor as if also eagerly awaiting his master's reaction.

Rio let out an excited whoop. He squeezed Binney tight and awkwardly dropped a kiss on top of her head. "I think I love you," he blurted. "I've been dying to see the horses, and get out around the ranch. Let's go. What are we waiting for?"

His oh-so-casual declaration of love rattled Binney even though she knew it didn't mean a thing. And yet, hearing words she used to long for someone to say and mean, but no one ever had, welded her feet to the floor.

"Come on. Come on. What's wrong, Binney? I didn't hurt you, did I? I forget this cast on my hand and wrist isn't soft." He loosened his hold a bit.

The dog dropped down and whined.

"I'm fine," she assured Rio and calmed her giddy equilibrium. "Okay, so if the wheelchair runs well on gravel, we can get you outside for a while every day." Escorting him the short distance to the chair, she bent and locked the wheels. It took muscle to balance him so he didn't sit too fast.

"Why wouldn't it run on gravel?"

His face seemed all too close to hers. Their eyes locked and felt like a soft caress. Trembling, Binney jerked back and almost fell over Tagalong.

"Hey, hey. Careful." Rio grabbed her forearm. "Ah, damn. I only realized we, uh…you, have to get me and this contraption off the porch. There're only three steps, but still… Can you hold me while I hop down? Then I'll sit in the chair again."

"Rio, hopping down steps would jar your injured bones. And there's no need. I had JJ build a ramp. That's where I was while you weren't minding me about not getting out of bed by yourself. I was tugging the ramp into place." She unlocked the wheels and pushed Rio's chair out onto the wide, shaded porch.

Tag ran back and forth between the wheelchair and the ramp, all the while whimpering and uttering short, nervous barks.

"Come here, Tag." Rio snapped his fingers and the Labradoodle scooted toward him. "We have to trust Binney," he declared with confidence as he rubbed Tag's ears. "Both of us," he added, although he wasn't able to glance back and show his appreciation to the woman now edging him onto the ramp. "Binney, forgive me. I knew when I tried to get out of bed alone that it was risky. You're right to be mad at me."

"I'm not mad." She stopped and knelt to be sure his slippered feet were solidly on the footrests. Rising, she began moving him again. "You worried me, though. I'd be hard-pressed to pick you up off the floor if, say, JJ wasn't on the premises?"

"Yeah." Rio sounded repentant. "I haven't thanked you nearly often enough for all of the extra stuff you do. Like the ranch books, typing thank-you notes for the folks who donated to me, playing tunes in the evening on your guitar to help me relax. And now for this wheelchair and ramp. That's... I can't even find the words."

Done negotiating the incline, Binney aimed the chair with hard rubber tires toward the lane. "Honestly, Rio, the variety offered by home care is what I like most about private duty nursing. Speaking of variety, I noticed you have flower beds on each side of the porch steps that need weeding. If it's okay, one of these days when you're napping, I'd like to clean the beds and show off your lovely marigolds."

"My mom planted the flowers. Last time they visited, she nagged me about the weeds. But don't feel you have to pull them. I didn't see weeding listed in your contract."

She laughed, ruffled his hair then swerved around a pothole. "It falls under other duties that may crop up. I gardened some at the Fosters'. I like digging in the dirt."

"Knock yourself out, then. Hey, I see JJ at the small corral. He must not have taken Contessa to the barn. Do you think we can leave the road and go to the corral? The dirt may be rougher, though."

Tag, who trotted close enough to the chair that Rio could keep a hand on him, barked wildly and tore after a rabbit hopping across the road.

Binney called to the dog. "Get back here and leave that poor rabbit alone."

Rio chuckled. "He's always after rabbits and squirrels. As far as I know he never catches them. Do you, boy?" he asked as his pet slunk back acting guilty.

JJ apparently noticed them. He cupped his hands around his mouth and yelled, "Do you need help?" He jogged toward them. When he got closer, he said, "I can move the mare to the barn if it's easier for you to wheel Rio there. The horse was cooped up in the trailer on the drive from Pecos, so I figured she'd like to stretch her legs."

Binney shook her head. "We're doing fine, aren't we, Rio? I should've thought to ask if you were getting bounced around too much."

"I'm great. The only thing that would be better is if I could get outside under my own power and go back to riding."

"That won't be for a while." Binney squeezed his shoulder. "I hope bringing you out here isn't depressing. We discussed how long it'll take you to heal."

"Don't you go in for another X-ray soon?" JJ asked.

"Next week. I hope the doc says I can lose the hand cast and clavicle brace. It's the most restrictive. I'm sure he'll find my ankle has improved. I can't wait to toss these slippers out and get back to wearing my boots so I'll feel like a cowboy again."

When the men's conversation lagged, Binney said, "Oh, look. Your new mare is coming to the fence to greet you, Rio. She's beautiful. I've only ever seen palominos in old Western movies. How did you happen to decide to raise them? Don't most area breeders raise quarter horses?"

She wheeled Rio right up to the fence. The broad-bellied horse stood in grass and watched Tag, who flopped down, panting in a patch of sunlight.

"I have apples in a pack," Binney said. "JJ suggested I bring some." She leaned down and pulled a few from a basket under the seat of the wheelchair.

Rio took one. "JJ, help me walk to the fence."

The ranch manager, used to taking orders from Rio, slanted Binney a questioning glance.

"This ground is fairly level," she said, setting the brake. "I've got the chair as close to the corral as it'll go. So if you feel weak, Rio, you can sit again quickly."

Without his crutch he needed both JJ and Binney's support to walk over the lumpy ground. Still, he leaned on the top rail, fed the mare an apple and rubbed her narrow nose. "You asked why I raise palominos," he remarked. "From known history they're the chosen horses of kings and queens. By the way, palomino is a color, not a true breed. So they may be registered in one of several associations. We follow guidelines set up by the American Saddlebred Horse Association. Palominos generally have calm dispositions. They're good show horses. We've sold a lot to women and girls who do bareback riding or belong to groups who ride in parades." Rio fed the mare a second apple Binney passed him, then he asked to sit down.

She eased him into the chair, but he didn't let go of her, instead he stroked her arms.

Rio's ranch manager cleared his throat. "Rio likes the challenge of raising a genetically perfect palomino herd. Not all horses with palomino characteristics are true palomino. Some are cremellos. They have more of the champagne gene. Some with darker coats are called chocolate palominos. The true color has brown eyes, not blue. Cremellos often have blue eyes."

"All that's interesting," Binney said, slow to disengage herself, but fussing again over Rio, making sure he sat solidly in the chair. "I don't know a lot about horses, but yours are definitely pretty." She stretched out a hand to pet the mare. "When will she have her foal?"

"Late October," the men said in unison.

"Do you think I'll be fit as a fiddle by then?" Rio asked, catching Binney's eye.

She shrugged. "You'll know more after the X-rays. Which reminds me. JJ, I'll need to drive him into the hospital lab in his pickup. Is it gassed up?"

"I'll check. Are you guys going up to the barn?"

She deferred to Rio.

"I'm proud of our setup. I'd like you to see it. The rest of the herd will be grazing in the big field behind the barn. That's a sight. And I should go over some things with JJ in my office."

Nodding, JJ strode off ahead of them.

Enjoying seeing Rio happier than he'd ever appeared, Binney leisurely picked a smooth path to the barn.

Tag hitched himself a ride on Rio's lap.

"I swear that dog is smiling," Binney remarked.

"For an animal that a few years ago didn't trust any human, he now loves being attached to people he trusts."

"Poor thing. He hasn't had many opportunities to sit that close to his most favorite human—you—since we can't let him on your hospital bed, or in your lap when you're taking the TENS treatments."

"Lucky dog's been sleeping with you, though." Rio looped his unfettered arm around Tag, who turned his head and happily licked Rio's face, making the man sputter.

Not knowing whether to laugh at his comment or take Rio seriously, Binney let his remark slide. "If Tag gets too heavy say so and he'll have to walk."

"Actually he keeps my back pressed to the chair so I sit straighter. That's good because we're traveling over rough terrain."

Binney stopped. "I'm trying to go slow. Is this outing hurting you?" she asked anxiously.

"No. No. I'm happier than a pig in slop to get out of the house. It's not enough to thank you. You deserve way more. Probably candy or flowers—things women covet."

Binney couldn't tell him that his earlier, off-the-cuff *I love you* and even the brotherly kiss on her head would stay with her far longer than any words of thanks he might offer. What she said was: "My job is to get you well."

They'd reached the barn, and JJ, who waited for them there, slid open the big entry door. "Rio's pickup gas tank is nearly full."

"Great. I'm not sure how long he'll be at the hospital clinic. Are you able to keep Tag while we're gone, JJ?"

"Sure thing." He knelt and scrubbed the dog's furry head. "I'll be planting winter grass all week, but he likes to ride on the tractor."

"I should be helping with that," Rio said, sounding glum again.

Binney touched his cheek. "None of that. Your only duty is to take it easy until you heal. What did you want me to see in the barn?"

"The stalls, the tack room, the office. Is the main herd out back?" he asked JJ.

Bobbing his head, the other man moved aside and gestured for Binney to wheel Rio on in.

"Yep, it's a barn," she said, laughing. "Cleaner than most I've seen. But remember for the past year I've done nursing jobs at cattle ranches."

"Since you brought Rio out here, and as barns are old hat to you," JJ said, "I need him to sign Contessa's registry transfer." He pointed to a side door. "Binney, you can take a gander at the rest of our stock. I promise I won't wear Rio out."

She glanced at her watch. "I planned for his first outing to be no more than an hour. I'll give you fifteen minutes. And I'll take Tag." She tugged on the dog's collar. He obediently hopped down from Rio's lap. As they moved away she heard the men talking about seed and fertilizer. It all seemed so natural to her.

Out back the view opened up on a truly beautiful vista. Flat grassy fields were dotted with frolicking golden horses ranging from youngsters to adults. And beyond fenced pastures stretched an array of rolling hills graced with lacy cottonwood and elm trees along with unidentifiable low-growing bushes.

Binney couldn't ever recall being so taken by scenery. It was easy to see why Rio loved the Lonesome Road. Years of hard work to clear so much land and make it habitable probably led to his folks wanting to retire elsewhere. She wondered, though, about a comment Rio had made indicating Ryder's dislike of the ranch. How could identical twins hold such opposing views of the great place where they grew up?

She had fostered in homes of ranch couples so she was aware of the extent of backbreaking labor and deep dedication it took to run a successful ranch. Until being here she'd favored living in town, where there were book and music festivals, and a yearly art walk, to say nothing of restaurants and stores. Now she actually thought she could happily live out here. That had her picturing living here with Rio after he got well, and warmth shot up her body.

Stepping up on the lowest fence rung, she petted a young, curious horse that trotted up shaking a nearly white mane and tail. "Sorry I don't have an apple for you, my beauty," she crooned.

JJ shouted her name, breaking her reverie.

"Are you stuck up there?" he asked from the doorway. "I called you three times. Rio and I are finished, and he's beginning to fade, I think. Although he'll never admit it, so don't tell him I mentioned it."

Binney hopped off the rail. "I'm not stuck. I was woolgathering. Hard not to this place is so gorgeous. Is that your cottage I see tucked into the draw beyond the cultivated land?"

"Yes. Wow, listen to you using terms like draw and cultivated land. Rhonda and I pegged you for a city gal. Although maybe we shouldn't have been so quick to judge after you rode out here on a Harley."

She stuck her two little fingers against her teeth and whistled Tag back from where he'd gone sniffing under a creosote bush. "I read a lot," she said as she and the dog hurried past him.

Grasping the handles of Rio's wheelchair, she murmured, "Sorry I didn't keep track of time. I'll blame it on the lovely tranquility of your ranch." That was better than confessing she'd been daydreaming about him.

"I'm going out to bring in the mare," JJ announced. He settled a brown cowboy hat on his head, exited the barn behind them and closed the door.

It wasn't until after Tag jumped up on his lap again that Rio revisited her comment. "Tranquility is a nice word to describe the Lonesome Road. I've always said this is the only place I can relax and be me."

"JJ seems at home here, too."

"He worked for Dad. JJ and Rhonda dated three or four years before they got engaged and she moved out here part-time. All I hear from most folks is how remote we are. I can't tell you how pleased I am that you get some of what I feel. I don't live in the sticks," he said defiantly.

"Definitely not. It's a charming, unspoiled slice of nature."

They'd almost reached the ramp when Rio said, "Traci Walker called it the sticks when she visited me in the hospital. That's Ryder's term for the ranch, too."

Binney almost lost her grip on the chair. Traci Walker had been the meanest of the mean girls in high school. At least she no longer had to puzzle over Suzette Ferris's oblique comment about one of Rio's hospital visitors. "Is, uh, Traci your girlfriend?"

"Geez, no! We have dated. I gather her dad thinks we still should. But she's way too high-maintenance for me. Do you remember her from high school?"

"Uh, yes."

They were in the house before Rio reached back, caught Binney's hand and tugged her around to where he could see her. "There was a world of angst behind that yes. I remember now you said Ryder stood you up for Traci's sister. According to Traci my brother opted out of going out with them on her recent trip to see Samantha in New York. Probably a first, but from my perspective the Walker girls were raised as queen bees. As a result they both possess a death sting. I hope you know you're ten times the woman, Binney."

"Thanks." Her voice quivered. "Listen, do you need to use the bathroom before we get you back into bed?"

"Yeah. Wheel me to the door and wait while I use the facilities. I loved the outing, but suddenly I'm beat."

"Fresh air can do that." She delivered him to the door, lifted Tag off his lap then assisted him through their routine with practiced ease. But the camaraderie between them had definitely cooled.

Settled in his bed a short time later, Rio yawned. "I'm really sorry I mentioned Traci. She called the other day when you were out after the mail. She thinks I should be healed enough to go to the charity ball at the country club October 1. In case she phones again and you hear us talking, I want you to know I wouldn't go with her if I was well."

"I'm glad you and Ryder both see through her." She smiled down at him, but thought he appeared unhappy. Possibly Rio liked Traci more than he let on. She had visited him in the hospital, after all. And she'd phoned, too, which was more than his brother had done.

"I'm going to feed Tag then go after the mail. I'll fix supper later." Getting no response, she checked back and noted that Rio had fallen asleep.

All weekend Rio was extremely nice to her. He held her hand as she read to him during his TENS treatments. He tucked her under his good arm every time she got him up to walk. And he paid her compliments over her guitar playing and other things to the point she was embarrassed.

"Tomorrow are my follow-up X-rays," he said right after Binney finished rubbing in his after-shower lotion. "How about a bedtime good-luck kiss?" He clung to her hand when she went to adjust the head of his bed for sleeping.

She laughed, but leaned down and brushed a kiss over his forehead.

He latched on to the back of her neck with his unbound

hand and tugged until their lips met. His mouth teased at first, then hardened into something more serious.

She flattened her palms on his chest, and returned the pressure until he coughed and had difficulty catching his breath. Straightening quickly, she fussed with his pillow. "We got too carried away. Are you all right?"

"I'm fine. Listen, if Doc gets rid of most of these troublesome bandages, and if he says I can start taking care of myself, I still want us to keep seeing each other."

"You don't mean…date?"

"I do. I want you to stay in my life, Binney."

"I'd like that, Rio. A lot." She ran a finger lightly over his lips. Anticipation of joy like none she'd ever experienced flowed through her as she eased away. That night she couldn't sleep. She curled around Tag, but pictured a time when Rio would lie between them.

Returning to the ranch after Rio's appointment the next day, Binney watched him slump silently in the passenger seat. The visit hadn't gone as he'd hoped. His vertebra showed some improvement, warranting a less chunky collar. But his clavicle hadn't formed enough callus. A nurse cut the cast off his wrist and massaged his hand. She said Dr. Darnell wanted Binney to carry out daily PT for at least two more weeks. And Rio needed to continue using crutches and have help walking until his next visit for a follow-up set of X-rays.

Her attention on the road, Binney tucked her bottom lip between her teeth. "You have made progress, Rio." She tried to return to the closeness they'd shared over the weekend.

He stared ahead, letting his chin rest on the smaller neck collar.

"I know you'd hoped you would no longer need my services. Dr. Darnell said you probably only require my assistance for three more weeks. That's not long."

"Maybe not for you. My life's still stuck in limbo. Can we not talk about this anymore? I'm exhausted after all that poking and prodding."

Worried that she didn't know what more to say to help him, Binney pulled up next to the house.

JJ met them with the wheelchair and an excited Tag. "I wasn't sure he'd still need this chair."

Shooting him a warning scowl, Binney pressed a forefinger to her lips and jerked her head toward where Rio still sat, stone-faced.

"Gotcha," JJ murmured, going around to the passenger door, where he assisted Binney in boosting Rio down. It took both of them to get him into the house and lying flat in the rented hospital bed he'd told JJ that morning they could probably return.

"You two can go," Rio grated, his voice husky with pain Binney judged was emotional.

"I'll stay until he falls asleep," she whispered to JJ. "Dr. Darnell ordered an opiate because of the jarring ride in the pickup. Once I know he's zonked, I think I'll go out and tackle weeding those flower beds by the front porch. I need to do something physical." She continued to speak softly as she trailed Rio's friend to the door. After closing it behind him, she fed Tag and got out Rio's pill.

"I don't want the damned medicine," Rio insisted, tightening his lips when Binney brought the pill and a glass of water.

"Doctor's orders. You're tense. Take this and unwind. We'll talk about a schedule for your hand therapy after you have a nap."

Tagalong emerged from the kitchen, whined and paced back and forth near the bed.

"Rio, you're even upsetting your dog."

At that he opened his mouth and took the pill.

He was sawing logs by the time she came back from taking the glass to the kitchen. Tag, too, had settled his chin on his paws and he snored softly.

She sighed, but decided to prepare a casserole for dinner.

Because Rio hadn't stirred by the time she finished, she dug out garden gloves she'd had Rhonda buy, left the front door ajar and set out to pull weeds.

In half an hour she'd unearthed two rosebushes and rows of marigolds. Hearing a vehicle traveling the ranch road, she sat back on her heels, assuming it was Rhonda. But looking around she was surprised to see a dark blue car instead. In her time at the ranch, no one had come to visit Rio. *Oh, boy, she hoped it wasn't Traci Walker.*

The car braked a foot from where Binney knelt. Dust rolled over her. She sputtered and got to her feet as the vehicle made a sweeping turn heading out toward the highway again. Probably someone was lost.

She shed her gloves and dropped them in the bucket of weeds as a well-dressed woman perhaps a few years older than her emerged from the still-running car.

"Is this where Rio McNabb lives?"

"It is, but he's sleeping. He was injured at a rodeo several weeks ago." Binney walked toward the woman. But the driver hurried around to the passenger side, where she opened the door and removed a wicker basket and two large totes.

Curious, Binney figured someone had belatedly sent Rio get-well gifts. However, she was rendered mute when the woman plopped both totes at her feet and shoved the bulky wicker basket so solidly into her midsection that Binney nearly lost her breath.

"That's Rio McNabb's son," the woman stated in a no-nonsense voice. "He's a month old. My sister birthed him at home with a midwife. Something went horribly, horribly wrong." Her voice cracked as she tottered around the front of the car on spiky heels and paused again by the open driver's door and started to get in.

"Wait!" Binney couldn't take a step as the totes hemmed her in.

"Lindsey bled to death on the way to the hospital or she would have contacted the baby's father. I'm sure she would've wanted me to keep Rex Quintin, but I work erratic shifts at a busy casino on the Vegas Strip. The same one where Lindsey dealt blackjack. Had she lived, we'd have raised her kid, but…" The woman's voice gave out and she dashed at tears. "I had to dig to find McNabb, the scum. If you're the little woman he leaves behind when he rodeos and paints a town red, I'm sorry. I can see you're shocked. I warned Lindsey time and again not to trust footloose cowboys, but she fell hard for the jerk." After piling into the car, the woman slammed her door, gunned the engine and sped toward the highway, leaving a rooster tail of dust and much more in her wake.

The dust had settled around her before Binney recovered enough to peek inside the basket, where a baby slept.

Chapter 7

Waves of shock washed through Binney, welding her boots to a spot next to Rio's porch steps even after the blue car had disappeared from sight. Its dust had totally dissipated by the time she quit reeling enough to chastise herself for not committing to memory the number on the license plate. *It had been a Nevada plate, all right.*

But as her initial stunned feelings subsided, stilling her racing heart, a realization of the impact of what had just transpired kick-started her still-addled brain. Not only had she failed to mentally log the license number, she hadn't asked the woman's name, nor inquired about the last name of the baby's birth mother.

Other emotions coursed through her one after another. Disappointment in Rio. Not just because he'd kissed her and had said he wanted her to remain in his life when he had had another relationship on a not-so-back burner, although that stung her personally. She felt sorrow for the baby, who, like her, would grow up without a mother.

Suddenly cold in spite of standing in the late-summer sunshine, Binney shivered and wished she could hop on her Harley and leave this job right now. She had again let her heart get too invested in a McNabb twin.

Of course she couldn't run off. She had to take Rio his son, and continue doing her job until he was able to make other arrangements.

After what seemed like an eternity of fence-straddling passed, she tamped down the ache in the back of her throat. Telling herself Rio's problems didn't truly matter, she juggled the basket and the two totes and went into the house.

Rio was apparently just waking up. His eyelids fluttered, but sprung wide when Binney kicked the door closed with a loud bang.

Smothering a yawn, he cleared his throat. "How long have I been sawing logs? We missed lunch. I'm starved." Finally noticing that she was laboring under a burden, he blinked a few more times. "What's all that? Did Rhonda go shopping? If so, why isn't she or JJ helping you carry stuff in?"

Binney dropped the totes at the foot of his bed, pressed the button to raise his torso to a partial incline and set the wicker basket across his thighs.

"What's this?" He grasped one of the handles with his newly freed hand, but because it still lacked full mobility he wasn't able to bend down the side to see in the basket.

Tag, who'd also been sleeping below the bed, woke

up and shook himself hard. He whined and leaped up until both feet rested on the bed. Snuffling the basket, he proceeded to bark. And he barked until the occupant of the basket awakened and began to cry.

Rio let go of the basket rim and reared back as if he'd been burned. "Binney...what the hell?"

Urging the dog away from the bed, she ordered him to sit. Fixing Rio with her sternest nurse's glare, she unloaded on him. "Well, Rio, this is your son. He didn't come by stork, but did arrive special delivery. The woman who brought him claimed she's his aunt. He's a month old." Her voice faltered. "I'm sorry to be the one to tell you his mom unfortunately is deceased." Her throat worked and her voice gave out.

As much as Binney wanted to watch Rio squirm, she couldn't bear to let the baby sob. She scooped him out of his makeshift bassinet, held him to her shoulder, swayed and crooned to him until his crying lessened.

"What in the devil are you talking about? Whose kid is it, really?"

"Rio, the woman who drove in and left you this bundle of joy said her sister gave birth to your baby at home. I'm so sorry, but something went wrong and she di...died on the way to the hospital. In Las Vegas. Her first name was Lindsey. The sister said you two met at a rodeo. Were you in Nevada at a rodeo about ten months ago?"

"I've ridden in a lot of Vegas rodeos. But I swear I did not father this baby or any other. Why would you take the kid and let some crazy woman leave without first talking to me?"

"Don't you go blaming me, Rio McNabb. I had no choice. I was weeding. She drove in and turned her car around. It blew dust all over me. I thought she had gotten lost, but she pulled these bags and the basket out of her car and shoved them on me with very little explanation. Before I could catch my breath she drove off like a bat out of hell."

"Well, she lied. Get her back."

"How? She conveniently didn't share her sister's last name, or say who she was." Binney jiggled the baby. "I think he's wet. Or hungry. I need to see if she left anything to solve either of those problems. Can you hold him a minute? Crook your good arm, please."

"Oh, I don't know…" He did follow her edict, but with a sour face.

She moved the basket, setting it aside after placing the crying baby in the curve of Rio's arm. The infant instantly stopped crying and gazed up at the man holding him with huge dark blue eyes.

Seeing the two engrossed in staring at each other made Binney smile. Then Rio looked up and scowled at her, and she quickly dived into the totes. "Ah, diapers, wet wipes and premixed formula. Oh, what have we here? A packet of papers." She pulled them out.

"The top one lists his feeding and sleeping schedules. That's helpful." She flipped to the next page. "There's a certificate from the midwife about his birth. It verifies he was born at home in the state of Nevada."

"What does it say? Does it give the mother's full name?" Rio demanded while trying to peer down over the cervical collar once the baby he held began to suck on one of his own chubby hands. The respite didn't last long and was followed by louder cries, from which Rio recoiled.

Binney set the papers aside. "First things first. Let's

see to it that he's dry and fed. A cursory glance at his schedule shows he's past due for a bottle."

"Dammit, Binney. We have to find out where he really belongs."

Digging into the bag again, she found a puddle pad, which she laid on Rio's lap. Taking the baby, she unsnapped the short rompers he wore, removed the soaked diaper and, while holding the baby's feet, she folded the sticky edges together. Scooting Tagalong away with her toe, she set the wet item on the tile floor between her feet. Deftly she opened a dry diaper and in seconds had restored it along with his rompers. "Here, hold him again," she said, passing the now gurgling infant to Rio. "I need to find a plastic bag for dirty diapers, dispose of this one and wash my hands before I warm a bottle."

"How did you do that?"

"Do what?" she asked, gazing back over her shoulder.

"You changed that diaper so efficiently."

"Yes, I'm a trained nurse," she said, setting out for the kitchen.

"I thought you only took care of old ranchers," Rio called.

"Nurses work with patients of all ages," Binney yelled back. "And I update my skills with professional development courses every so often."

She took care of what needed doing. On returning to the living room, she noticed the baby had grabbed on to one of Rio's fingers. "Hey, cowboy, you sort of have the magic touch yourself. That's good, because I need to put his bottle in warm water for a few minutes."

Rio wasted no time shaking his finger loose. He

glowered at Binney. "Take him with you. By the way, does the kid have a name?"

"The aunt called him Rex Quintin."

"Maybe Quintin is really his last name. I don't know anyone around here by that name, but she obviously left him at the wrong ranch."

Binney leveled a look of sympathy, but shook her head. "She began by asking for you by name, Rio." She grabbed one of the baby's bottles. "Let me take care of readying his bottle then I'll see if I can remember everything she said, which wasn't much. She rocked me back on my heels with her news, too." Clenching the bottle, Binney dashed back to the kitchen. Her legs were still unsteady, and her stomach was one icy pit.

It wasn't long before she returned to take the baby. She sat in one of the recliners, and watched as the infant latched on to the bottle's nipple and sucked greedily.

Binney had draped a clean receiving blanket over her shoulder. Every so often she raised baby Rex up, rubbed his back and waited for him to burp, which he did with gusto.

The second time, Rio said, "What's in that bottle? Beans? The kid burps like a cowboy at a roundup."

"He was hungry and drank too fast. If he didn't burp, gas would build in his tummy. He'd be uncomfortable and cry. Babies cry if they're wet, hungry or gassy."

"Thanks. I can't see why I need to know that. We've gotta find the woman who dropped him off and give him back ASAP."

Binney heard Rio's stomach rumble. "When Rex finishes his bottle I'll go put a tuna casserole I assembled earlier in the oven. We can have it with more of the bread I made into French toast this morning."

"I know I said I was starved, but why are you deliberately dragging your feet about checking the paper you said verified his birth?"

"I'm not deliberately dragging my feet, Rio. A wet, hungry baby in the house takes precedence over adult wants."

"That's my point. A wet, hungry baby does not belong in my house."

His words hit Binney like a punch to her stomach that she couldn't prevent from cramping and churning. She brushed kisses over baby Rex's fuzzy head. Sympathy welled for a poor baby that no one seemed to want. Was that how she'd come to be left on the agency doorstep?

"Why are you staring at me like I'm a horrible person?" Rio asked harshly.

"Perhaps because you took in a stray dog, but seem only too ready to kick an innocent baby to the curb."

Rio retreated into a shell. Rex slurped the last of the milk from his bottle. Climbing to her feet, Binney set the bottle on the coffee table. The baby settled his face into the side of her neck as she marched to Rio's bed and snatched up the papers she'd stuffed back into the tote earlier. Shaking a page in front of his nose she said, "This is a certificate stating the baby was born at home in the city of Las Vegas." She read off a date and time. "It's verified by a midwife. The baby's name is Rex Quintin McNabb."

She held it steady so he could see it. "Lindsey Ann Cooper, age twenty-five, is shown as the birth mother. The aunt said she would have contacted you if she hadn't died."

Taking the fluttering paper in his own shaking hand, Rio hauled in a deep breath. "I'm telling you I don't know any Lindsey Ann Cooper. If the rodeo was in town she must've pulled my name off one of the fly-ers. They're distributed everywhere."

Binney spun the rocking chair around and plopped down. "The sister said she works in a busy casino on the Vegas Strip where her sister dealt blackjack. The aunt called you scum, a jerk and, further, said she'd warned her sister to stay away from footloose cowboys. Think hard, Rio. Were you drinking in a casino, maybe after winning some big event? Although the aunt sounded as if it was more than a one-night stand. But then she ranted on about you painting the town red and leaving me behind, because I guess she assumed I was your wife, so I don't know."

Shutting his eyes, Rio plainly tried to curb his mounting irritation by rubbing his temples repeatedly. "I'm telling you, since I decided to buy the ranch six years ago, all winnings not needed for entry fees and travel went to my dad and to buy horses. Gambling was never my thing, and I don't drink except for a rare beer with buddies after a significant win. I park my pickup and camper on the rodeo grounds so I don't have to pay for a hotel. I can't remember the last time I walked through a casino." He finished speaking and silence filled the living room.

Binney got awkwardly to her feet. "I'm going to put the casserole in the oven."

Tag clambered up as if knowing she'd feed him, too.

Rio picked up his phone. "I hope you have enough for JJ. I want him to come over and talk about this issue since you're sure not on my side."

The chill taking root in Binney expanded. She rubbed the baby's back and turned away, recalling how in high school the twins and many in their privileged crowd skipped out of taking responsibility for even slight indiscretions. Recently she'd started believing that Rio had changed—had grown up. "Rio, for the life of me I can't see why a pregnant woman would lie about her baby's father or pick a total stranger to pin it on. Especially since the poor woman's sister insinuated if her sister had lived they wouldn't have needed you. On the other hand you seem so adamantly opposed."

"I am!" He practically stared a hole through her, then glanced down and punched a number on his cell phone.

Binney left the living room. As she waited for the oven to heat up enough to stick in the casserole, she fed Tag and worried over baby Rex's fate.

She got out plates and silverware using one hand. Since they were having a supper guest she should probably add a salad to their skimpy meal. That required doing something with Rex. While deciding she'd have to prevail on Rio to hold him, she heard the front door open. Maybe she ought to let the men talk by themselves. But she also wanted to listen to their exchange.

"What's all this?" JJ asked. He locked eyes with Binney as she came into the room with the baby in spite of Tagalong bounding between them and playfully butting his head against JJ's knee.

Rio answered from his bed. "Ha! That's almost the exact question I asked. Brace yourself for Binney's tall tale, buddy."

"You tell it, then," she snapped at Rio. "I need to fix a salad to go with supper. Without a front pack, or someplace secure to lay Rex, you'll have to supply your arm again."

Rio balked as if he'd object, but didn't, and made space in the crook of his arm.

"Is that a real live kid?" JJ moved closer. "Cute. But what's a baby doing here?"

After making sure Rio had a good hold on the baby, Binney stepped away from his bed.

"You tell him the story before you go," Rio pleaded. "It's so damned preposterous I'm sure to get something wrong."

Binney pinched the bridge of her nose. "I was out weeding the flower beds."

JJ nodded. "You did a good job. They look nice. Linda's going to love them."

"Who?"

"Rio's mom. Rob and I took care of the cattle, barn and fields. Linda handled the house, garden and flowers before Rio bought the ranch."

"Your dad's name is Rob?" Binney asked Rio. "I guess that makes all the male McNabb names start with the letter *R*."

Rio's brows dived together. "Just tell the damned story."

Binney set her hands on her hips. "Okay. In the middle of my weeding a car drove in and stopped." Gesturing this time, she repeated verbatim the story she'd given Rio.

JJ's mouth fell open. He rubbed the back of his neck and gaped at Rio after Binney fell silent. "You're positive you never met Ms. Cooper?"

"Never!" Rio said harshly. "And because we don't know the name of the woman who dropped the kid here, I think we need to call Abilene's social services and have someone come get him." He reached for his phone.

Binney gasped and the men both reacted with a start. "They won't take him, Rio," she said. "Like it or not, the midwife put your name down as the baby's father. Do you want to be investigated for possible child abandonment?"

JJ broke into the middle of their dagger-tossing match. "She has a point. I know you were at a clinic today, but you need to call and get an appointment for a DNA test."

"I should have thought of that," Binney exclaimed.

Waving his little arms around, the baby started to fuss again.

Tag left JJ's side and trotted over to the bed. Propping his feet on the side rail, he sniffed the baby through the bars.

Rio lifted his arm. "Tag, stop deviling the poor little guy."

JJ scanned the room. "Is this all the woman brought? If you can't return the kid ASAP to the aunt you need some baby furniture and stuff."

Binney picked Rex up, pulled a bottle of water out of one tote and sat in the rocker, offering him a drink.

Tagalong left the bed to set his chin on Binney's knee. It was clear he didn't know what to make of the baby. She let him sniff Rex, which satisfied the dog.

Rio sat eyeing the domestic scene. "I'd go now if I thought the lab was open after five o'clock. I want this settled. Since I have to wait until morning to call, what do you recommend I do in the meantime?"

"You can't do a lot, Rio. I'll take care of him," Binney promised.

"Where will he sleep? Like JJ said, the woman who dumped him off only provided bare essentials."

"True. I cannot believe she drove all the way from Vegas with a baby in a wicker basket. What if she'd been in a wreck?"

JJ sat beside Binney. "You said you have to make a salad. Give him to me. I need practice. Rhonda and I are going to get married soon and we want to start a family."

"You can't get married until I'm a hundred percent," Rio said. "I know Rhonda is planning a big church shindig. I'm not going to be your best man on crutches and wearing this stupid neck collar with my tuxedo."

"You'll be recovered. Rhonda's lifelong dream is having a Christmas wedding. If it was up to me," he said, accepting the baby Binney handed him, "I'd go down to the courthouse and find a justice of the peace. You gals put big emphasis on all the wedding folderol."

"Not me." Binney gave JJ the bottle.

"Why not you?" The question came from Rio.

She stopped at the kitchen doorway. "I don't know. I guess because all of my energies were focused on becoming an RN and then work." She went on into the kitchen, but now her mind seemed stuck on wondering, if most women had long-standing wedding wishes, what was wrong with her? She'd been in nursing friends' weddings and had been happy for them. Really, she'd never spared time to date much even though some interns had hit on her. Her best friends in nursing swore med students and interns were only hunting for a meal ticket until they became docs and made money, then they frequently divorced. She had witnessed the truth to that.

What few thoughts she'd had on wedding folderol, as JJ called the white dress and trappings, took a backseat to her lifelong dream of wanting to belong in a family. She'd dwelled on stepping into a ready-made one with grandparents, parents and siblings. She hadn't envisioned a husband. *How silly was that?*

Brushing aside the images, she tossed a salad. Seeing the casserole was almost ready to be served, she stuck her head in the living room. "Do you guys want me to bring plates to you on trays, or shall I set the table in here? Rio, you traveled to town today, do you feel like sitting in a kitchen chair?"

"I'm okay. JJ and I were just discussing all of us driving in to the big box store after supper to pick up a cradle or crib, that front pack you mentioned and anything else you think we'll need for the little dude until I get his true paternity straightened out. JJ said he thinks DNA tests may take as much as two weeks to get results."

"Maybe. Not my area of expertise." She crossed the room and took Rex from JJ. The baby was wide awake and happily blowing bubbles from his rosebud mouth.

She didn't have to ask JJ to help Rio from his bed. He just did it. And Rio appeared steadier on his feet, moving toward the kitchen on his crutches.

They all sat around the kitchen table, and she and JJ passed Rex back and forth while she dished out food. Then she took the baby back and held him in her left arm, preparing to eat with her right hand until she noticed Rio frowning. "What's wrong? I'm not going to drop hot tuna and noodles on him. Haven't you seen moms do this in restaurants?"

"Mostly their little ones are strapped into high chairs. We'll buy one of those."

JJ stopped shoveling casserole into his mouth and wiped his lips with a napkin. "Are you sure you want

to buy a lot of baby stuff, Rio? You say he's not yours.
With his mother gone, and his aunt not assuming responsibility, you're eventually going to have to turn him
over to local child services. Why get left with a bunch
of baby furnishings?"

Binney sat up straighter. "I wish I was in a position
to apply to adopt him. I know an unmarried nurse who
did that. But she works set hospital shifts. Maybe I could
find a sitter and go back to the hospital," she mused.
Tightening her arm around the bundle, she gazed lov-
ingly down on the infant.

Both men fixed her with disbelieving stares. Rio
broke the tense silence. "I know you have a big heart,
and I can see you care, but you love home nursing."

"I do, but…"

JJ stated the obvious. "You don't own a car. I doubt
any children's court would approve of you hauling a
baby to a sitter's on a Harley."

Thrusting out a defiant chin, she gestured with her
fork. "I can buy a car."

"Why would you?" Rio asked huffily. "You don't
have any connection to his family, whoever they are."

Tears filled her eyes and spilled over. "I know what
it's like to grow up a throwaway child. One committed
parent is better than living among a raft of people who
don't care one iota if you live or die."

"Didn't you live with foster families?" JJ asked. "I
didn't figure that would be much different than having
regular folks."

"Believe me, it is in some cases. If you aren't cute
and sweet enough to be adopted, you may get treated
more like an indentured servant. If the family has birth
kids and they don't like you, everything that goes wrong

is your fault. And I can attest that it's no picnic living in a group home. By then most unwanted teens are cranky and mad at the world. And city cops shake them down at the first sign of trouble."

"Have you ever tried to find your parents?" Rio asked quietly. "Like, I'm wondering how hard it'd be to find the woman who dumped Rex off here."

"I have no desire to find the people who abandoned me. You never met Rex's aunt. She didn't know me from Adam and yet was willing to plop him in my hands. She couldn't make tracks out of here fast enough. I don't want to find her. He needs someone to raise him who cares," she said fiercely.

"This conversation is pointless," JJ said. "If we're going to drive to the store before it closes, we should finish eating."

Binney was gratified to see Rio looked troubled by the turn of their conversation. What that meant she wasn't sure. Just a few days ago he'd said he wanted her to remain in his life. He'd said nothing about that now. She kept returning to the fact he had admitted to riding in rodeos in Las Vegas. It still made no sense to her that a woman of twenty-five would pluck a strange guy's name off a rodeo flyer—why? Because she had a thing for cowboys and found them interchangeable? If not Rio, who was Rex's father? Was it someone Lindsey wanted to keep hidden from her sister, or perhaps from people where they worked? Had she dallied with a boss? Maybe a married one.

She fell silent and they all tucked into their food, but tension in the room didn't dissipate. Finally, Binney said, "We need to chill. All our arguing has upset

Tag. Have you noticed he's pacing around the table? If he senses something's wrong, Rex surely feels it, too."

Rio set down his fork. "Supper was good, Binney. Look, I didn't mean to hit so many of your hot buttons. I'm sorry you had a hard life. You've come a long way all on your own. I just wish we knew Rex's real story is all. He is kinda cute, but little and helpless. I've never been around any babies. This is all unnerving to me."

"I understand that, Rio. I really do. But you can speak out for yourself. Rex has no one to advocate for him."

"I don't know. I'd say you're doing a pretty good job."

Binney wasn't sure from his tone how Rio meant that. Did he want her to get out of their lives?

Rising, JJ cleared the table and took plates to the sink. "Can we load the dishwasher when we get back from the store?"

"Fine by me." Binney handed him the casserole dish. "Will you put this and the leftover salad in the fridge while I change the baby?"

Rio scooted back his chair. "JJ, will you drive? Your pickup bed is longer than mine. We'll be hauling my wheelchair as well as bringing home whatever we buy."

"Rhonda works late tonight. She won't believe any of this if I try and explain over the phone. Binney, do you mind if I have her meet us at the store so I can fill her in?"

"I don't have any problem. But it's not my story to tell. My name's not on the midwife's record."

"Mine shouldn't be, either," Rio charged. "But, Rhonda's not going to broadcast to the world."

Binney sent him a searing glance. Why did he care what the greater world thought?

JJ came back from the fridge and helped Rio stand.

"I'll go bring my pickup down to the house. Binney, can you handle getting Rio and the baby out front?"

"Sister Mary Margaret always told us where there's a will there's a way. I'll manage. I know you'll drive on back roads so I'll sit in back and hold on to the baby's basket until we get a car seat. That's the most important. I'll make a list of what else we need. Shall we take Tag, or leave him here?"

"Take him. He's family," Rio said, as he hobbled across the kitchen to the bathroom.

His touchy tone gave Binney pause. Just where did that leave Rex? Unfortunately it was as if Rio had drawn a very clear line in the sand. Tagalong was family. This poor child who bore his name wasn't.

Chapter 8

They didn't buy out the store, but had put a serious dent in the baby aisle. Rio had generously told her and Rhonda to purchase whatever they thought was necessary.

After checking out, Binney installed the safety-rated car seat in the second seat of JJ's king cab. Now, with Rio in the passenger seat, she drove JJ's vehicle back to the ranch. He had opted to ride home with Rhonda.

While at the store they all kept deferring to Binney. Probably because she was a nurse, but also plainly the one most attached to Rex. It did cross her mind that perhaps she shouldn't lavish so much attention on the baby, because her role at the Lonesome Road was as caregiver to Rio, the man who'd hired her.

In streetlights that shone in through the pickup windows, Binney chanced to see how weary Rio appeared.

His head was pressed tight against the headrest and his eyes were closed. In the flickering light she could see he had dark smudges underneath his eyes.

"Are you okay?" she asked softly, just loud enough to be heard over Tagalong shuffling around in his portion of the backseat. "You've had a long day. How's the left hand doing? We need to work in the therapy session after we get home."

Rio opened his eyes. "Of necessity a rancher puts in long days. Am I really getting better? I don't hurt, but I feel out of sorts, and I'm beyond done in."

"You started the day thinking the doctor would say you'd almost be back to normal. All that got knocked aside before you were handed a baby and that jarring news. I'm really sorry I let the woman from Nevada get away. I was stunned, to say the least."

"I suppose anyone would have been. It's not every day a person gets a baby handed to them. What all do you need to do before lights out tonight? Anything I can help with?"

"I have to assemble the crib and give Rex his night feeding. Will you want a shower, or can you wait and take one in the morning? Baby or no baby, you're my patient and come first, Rio."

"Yeah. I wish that wasn't true, either. Even more I wish you believed me when I say I don't know anyone named Lindsey Cooper."

Chewing on the inside of her lower cheek, Binney let out a sigh. "I believe you're convinced the woman and her sister made a mistake. I also know you recently hit your head hard enough in that rodeo accident to knock you out. I've seen where an injury like that can cause short-or even long-term amnesia."

His eyes narrowed. "You're saying you think I've lost some of my marbles?"

"Not lost forever. But I saw a video on the news of your accident. You were knocked out and they carried you out of the arena before you came to. Furthermore, you claim you don't remember me from high school, yet I can describe your favorite shirt. Blue with white pearl buttons and an applique of a bucking horse on both breast pockets."

"I think you're making that up."

"I'm not. Come on, you wore it two days out of five your senior year."

Rhonda and JJ passed her at the turnoff to the ranch road.

"I've owned a lot of Western shirts with horse appliques," Rio said after a period devoid of talk. "But there is absolutely no way I'd forget in ten or so months what you're accusing me of forgetting."

She shrugged and stopped next to Rhonda's car. "Have it your way, Rio. Tomorrow we'll go get your and Rex's DNA tested." Setting the emergency brake, she vaulted out of the pickup.

Rhonda scurried to unlock the house. JJ dropped the tailgate and muscled out Rio's wheelchair. Binney unstrapped Rex from his new car seat. Tag ran back and forth overseeing the humans. Soon everything was out of the pickup except for Rio and small packages left in the cab.

JJ gestured to Binney. "Let Rhonda take the baby and his basket inside while I see to Rio. You can remove the car seat. You'll need it tomorrow in Rio's pickup."

Rhonda accepted Rex, but hesitated beside Rio's open door. "Now that I've heard the whole story, Rio, it's too ludicrous to not be fiction."

"Binney thinks the crack I took when my head connected with the fence at the rodeo grounds wiped my memory of having sex with a woman in Nevada."

JJ spewed a snort as he helped Rio into the wheelchair. "Convenient, if that was your MO. I've been around you since you competed in junior rodeos. For you to have gone so far off the rails is completely out of character. And I can't believe a woman you'd have had to know very well would be forgettable, Rio."

Listening, Binney fumbled unhooking the car seat. JJ's casual statement left her heart aching. On day one Rio had established how forgettable she was to him. And they had attended the same schools for several years.

However, maybe she was wrong. In the time she'd been caring for Rio, he didn't seem the type of man who'd make love with a woman then drop her like a hot rock. Just things he said about his folks, about the ranch, about his horses, labeled him a good person.

"I thought you said removing the seat would only take a few minutes?" JJ spoke from directly behind her.

Rising up fast, Binney hit her head on the door frame. She let out a yelp and rubbed the spot she'd smacked against the unforgiving metal.

"You okay?" He paused long enough for her to nod, then said, "Sorry, I thought you heard me walk up. I helped Rio into bed. Rhonda left him with the baby. She went on up to our house. I wonder if you should contact social services for Rio. I keep going back to the fact there's no proof the woman, the aunt who dumped off the kid, didn't catch Rio's accident on the news and figure she'd found a patsy. It's devious, but some people are."

The car seat came loose with a force almost causing Binney to fall. "Really, JJ? Why? She cried in front of me. She drove here from Nevada. And there's the midwife's note stamped with a date commensurate with the baby's age. You suggested DNA tests. Are you changing your mind?"

"No, but something feels fishy to me."

"Your truck is ready, and I've removed the car seat."

He accepted the ignition key, but heaved a sigh. "I feel sorry for Rio."

"Me, too, JJ. But..." Her thought trailed and she trudged on up to the house. She, too, sighed before opening the door. If she put herself in Rio's shoes, she did see how he could be emotionally drained.

It surprised her to see him sitting with the head of his bed elevated to where he could stare at the baby inside the basket on his lap. "I thought you'd be asleep," she said, leaving the car seat near the door.

"At the store, women who passed us went on about how cute the little guy was, and everyone assumed I was his dad. One even said, 'Oh, your daddy is all banged up.' I remember a bronc rider and his wife showing off their new baby at a rodeo. Some guys said the baby resembled his wife, others swore he was the spitting image of Owen, the papa. This fellow has dark curly hair, like mine. Outside of that he looks like a million other babies to me."

Just then Rex opened his eyes and stared up at Rio. His eyes were huge and black or midnight blue. "Look at his eyes, Binney. Mine are gray. Honestly, I'm going crazy making useless parallels. If you bring me a bottle I'll feed the kid while you start putting the crib together. I wish I could do that, but obviously I can't."

"The kid has a name," she snapped in exasperation, but crossed to dig a bottle of premixed formula from one of the totes left by the baby's aunt.

"Yeah. But I know a guy, a rodeo clown, who named his dog Rex. Seems more fitting than sticking a boy with that handle."

She cracked a smile. "Actually Rex is Latin for king. Maybe Lindsey Cooper had lofty ideals for her son and that's why she chose you," she said, softening her tone a lot.

Squalling came from the depths of the basket.

Tag jumped up and trotted up to the bed, whining first at Rio, then Binney. She took the baby out of the basket and put him in Rio's arms then wiggled a new bottle. "I'll go warm this."

"What about the crib assembly?"

"I'll bring back a knife to open the box."

From the kitchen she could hear Rio either trying to calm the baby or talking to his pet. She thought baby Rex was winning over the not-so-tough cowboy. She returned quickly and opened the crib box, trying not to smile over how the infant had quieted just being held against Rio's muscular chest. She wouldn't mind laying her head there, either.

"I thought you'd decided to buy a full-sized crib," Rio said when she leaned the narrow mattress against one of the recliners.

"I debated between this one and a travel one that was more like a playpen. It cost less, but had a playpen bottom and mesh sides. It would've served him far longer than it'll take to get results from a DNA. Besides, it'll be months before he crawls and needs a playpen."

She noticed Rio staring into space for a few minutes until he focused on the directions she placed in his weaker hand. Wondering what was going through his mind, rather than risk asking and opening another discussion about calling social services, she went after the bottle.

Relieving him of the directions, she put a burp cloth over his arm and settled him with the baby and the bottle. At times she sneaked a peek at him as she assembled the crib. Her feelings remained jumbled with the advent of the baby in their lives. Rex was wonderfully uncomplicated. Grown men, not so much.

"Check this out, Binney. Is he trying to hold his bottle? Is that common?" Rio asked.

She almost said *your son is precocious*. Canceling that comment, she met Rio's steady gaze and chuckled. "He's trying, but he's a little young to have a firm enough grip. It'll be six or seven months before he can be left to drink on his own."

"Last year JJ and I hand-raised a foal the mother refused to nurse. At the time I wondered how a mother who gave birth could turn her back on her baby."

Thinking of her own life, Binney swallowed a lump. "Yeah, it defies reason."

"Damn! Shame on me," he said with genuine regret. "I forgot your circumstances."

"It is what it is." She got up and helped him burp Rex, because plainly it was a struggle for him. His remark did make her feel teary-eyed over a circumstance she hadn't cried about in years.

With the bottle empty, and because she still battled shaky insides, she turned her back on Rio and set the empty bottle on the coffee table. Crossing the room she detached the infant seat from the car seat base and brought it back to place it in the recliner. "I'll change his diaper since you probably can't manage that yet, and put him in sleepers I saw in one of the totes. That way you won't have to hold him on your lap while you direct me in the final crib assembly."

"I can't unsay what I said, Binney. I'd never purposely hurt you."

"I know." Except for the crinkling tote bag and the gurgling baby, the room remained oppressively quiet. Finally as she changed Rex, she said, "I shouldn't be so sensitive over something that happened a lifetime ago. And technically Rex's mom didn't turn her back on him, her sister did that."

Rio said nothing until she went to buckle Rex in his seat. "I know we determined you aren't in any position to adopt him, but you'd be a good mother, Binney."

The sadness merely thinking of Rex being adopted by strangers, or growing up without a real home as she had, weighed heavily on her heart. "Your saying that means a lot to me, Rio," she said, letting their gazes connect and hold.

Time stretched like a rubber band. Tag woofed, and Binney shook off an odd longing that she and Rio could, together, make a perfect family, a perfect home for Rex.

The feeling persisted, not dimming in the least as with Rio's concise directions and her mechanical ability, they got the crib assembled, and even managed to negate the earlier tension with a few self-deprecating laughs along the way.

"I hope I can get this through the door to my bedroom," Binney said, critically eyeing the finished product.

"Why not leave it out here?" Rio asked around a yawn. "I'm a light sleeper, but Tag will also sound an alarm so I can send him to wake you. That way I won't have to lie here listening to the baby cry, and not be in any shape to do anything about it."

"I would never sleep through his crying, but it's your call," she murmured, carefully shifting the sleeping baby into the crib. That settled, she turned out lights, said good-night to Rio and went to her bedroom pondering if any of what just happened meant he had mellowed toward his son. She still thought some kink in his brain following his horrific accident must be causing him to not recall Lindsey Cooper.

Chapter 9

Awakened around 2:00 a.m. by Rex crying, Binney crawled out of bed to take care of his feeding. She almost tripped over Tag, who came whining at her bedroom door. Sashing a robe around shorty pajamas, she stopped at the kitchen to put a bottle she'd stashed there on to warm then hurried over to calm the baby and change his diaper before Rio shouted for her.

She soon laughed, because in spite of Rio saying he was a light sleeper, he apparently hadn't heard the baby's cries or Tag's signals. After completing the comfort routine with still no movement from Rio's bed, she went over to see that he was all right.

The rise and fall of his broad chest as he lay on his back was easy to identify in moonlight streaming through the patio sliding glass doors. Binney was oh so tempted to smooth back a lock of dark hair that flopped appealingly over his forehead. Her fingers itched to do so.

Reminded of the stress Rio had endured throughout the over-long day, she juggled the baby and resisted touching or waking him. "Your daddy needs his rest," she murmured in the baby's ear on her way to collect his bottle.

As if he understood, Rex waved his arms and gurgled, even blowing a few bubbles that made Binney smile and kiss his soft dark hair. He was so sweet it gave her physical pain to think tests might prove Rio wasn't his dad. He needed one reliable parent. She knew she was falling in love with Rex and Rio. Her head told her that wasn't wise. Her heart didn't listen well.

Tag yawned, but he shadowed her in and out of the kitchen. And when she later took a seat in the rocker, he sniffed the baby then flopped down at her feet. Twice during the feeding, Rio stirred restlessly. But he didn't wake up.

In the still night, while Rex happily sucked down his formula, Binney used the quiet time to plan for the next day. But her mind kept veering off to a dream of the family she and Rio and Rex could be.

Rio slowly woke up to sunlight and the smell of frying bacon. He blinked a few times and experienced some new body aches after he pressed the button to raise the head of his bed. He didn't hear Tag shuffling around. And the baby's crib stood empty.

He rattled the side rail trying to slide it down. It didn't budge.

"Binney," he called, loudly since she had to be in the kitchen.

She appeared in the archway at once holding a spatula. Rio realized she had the baby strapped around her in the front pack they'd bought the night before. For some reason it made him smile.

"Good morning, sleepyhead."

"What time is it?" Rio stifled a yawn. "Did the baby sleep the whole night through?"

"It's six fifteen. He roused Tag and me at two, but you snored through it."

"I do not snore. Do I?"

"Actually, no. But you slept like the dead. Can you give me a minute? I'm putting waffles in the warming oven along with bacon. Decide if you want breakfast first, or a shower."

"I can wait." She disappeared and Rio ran his right hand over his prickly jaw. His stomach growled so it wanted food. But as discombobulated as he felt, he needed a shower and shave to come fully awake.

The next time Binney showed up, he'd won his battle with the side rail and sat dangling his legs over the side of the hospital bed. "Will the food keep if I shower and get rid of my fuzzy face first?"

"No problem." She passed him his crutch and slipped her shoulder beneath his opposite arm. He wobbled a tad so she tightened her hold around his waist. Her fingers had slid under his loose shirt. "Steady there. Rio, are you okay? Did you overdo things yesterday?"

"I'm good." He brushed his lips over Binney's hair. "You're cute. Do you feel a bit like a kangaroo wearing that pouch?"

She laughed, rubbing her cheek against the flannel of his shirt. "At the store I said wet wipes were the best invention known to parents everywhere. Today it's a toss-up between them and this front pack. I gave Rex a bath this morning in his new tub. I wish you could have seen him kick and coo. He loved it."

He stopped and pressed his forehead to hers. "Binney, you shouldn't get so attached to him. Before I fell asleep something hit me that none of us brought up. Someplace, Rex has a real dad. After those DNA tests today we need to track down his aunt and wring more information out of her."

"She swore you were his father, Rio. Since it's obvious the midwife thought so, too, the only other person who'd really know is…dead. I know you're sure in your mind, but I can't imagine two women would cook up a scheme to…to do what? Later show up and scam money out of you? Are you secretly rich?"

"Lord, no. Do I need an appointment for the DNA test? I definitely want it done today if possible." Rio held back again at the bathroom door. Binney had yet to cover his cervical collar in plastic wrap.

She did that efficiently even with the baby kicking his feet and moving his arms. "No appointment needed as far as I know. After breakfast we'll go to the drop-in lab near the hospital. I was thinking, too, after I went to bed—" she passed him his shaver, but met his eyes in the mirror "—while we're in town I think we should visit the family clinic next door and have Rex checked by a pediatrician. I combed through the notes left by his aunt. Lindsey's midwife pronounced him in good condition. That's no more a bona fide exam than her note of birth is truly legal. I'll pay for it, Rio," she rushed to say.

"How would that look? I'll pay. Now let me get cleaned up so we can eat."

"Okay. You seem testy today. Be extra careful getting in and out of the shower," she said and ran her hands down his chest after she tucked the ends of the plastic wrap under the fat neck collar.

"I'm not testy at you." He looped his arms around her and the baby. Pulling her close, he brushed yet another a kiss across her bangs. "None of this mess is your fault," he said through a big sigh. "I am doing better, but stick close outside. I'll holler if I need you. After those exercises you did with my hand yesterday, it feels more limber. But my grip's still not a hundred percent."

She couldn't resist rubbing his prickly whiskers. "Your full strength will come back. Keep working that hand with the squeezy ball Dr. Darnell gave you."

As she always did, Binney left the door ajar and paced outside. This time she hummed to Rex, trying not to place too much importance on the couple of casual kisses Rio had delivered. One, after all, was to the top of her head. The other on her forehead—like an uncle with a favored niece. Not at all like a lover.

Soon, though, as happened with more regularity of late, her heart stumbled when Rio finally emerged scrubbed clean and shaven. No matter how many times she warned herself to view him as just as another patient, she too frequently experienced an unravelling of once tightly controlled emotions. Especially because he still needed her to button his shirts, and in doing it for him her fingers brushed his sculpted chest, sending her stuttering heart into overdrive.

From the smug gleam in his eyes, she knew he felt it, too.

Except for a couple of haphazard kisses, Rex's arrival had stalled the earlier ardor that had been developing between them. Binney feared she could be mostly to blame, because she wasn't able to believe Rio's denial. Rex seemed tangible proof that he'd tomcatted around. And it harkened back to the old days when every girl in their high school fawned over the McNabb twins, and they'd both cut a wide swath she knew for a fact. At least it'd been widely reported by those in the know.

After breakfast they went outside to Rio's pickup. From the passenger's seat, he phoned JJ. "We're leaving for the lab as soon as Binney installs the car seat in my truck. We left Tag in the house. I've no idea how long we'll be gone. Binney thinks we should have Rex checked by a doctor while we're in town."

"I feel for your predicament, Rio. Good luck with the test. Touch base when you get back."

"I will." Closing his cell phone, Rio dropped it on the console. He didn't need good luck for a test for which he already knew what the results would be. He just needed results ASAP. And then he needed to get the baby to his rightful relatives.

"Isn't this a glorious morning?" Binney asked a few minutes after they were under way. "I love how the first pop of sunlight filters through all the live oak trees around here and turns your private road into pure fantasyland."

"I'd like it better if I viewed the sun rising over the foothills while I'm out at dawn breaking a new horse."

"Rio, you can't think of climbing on a bucking horse for at least a year after Dr. Darnell releases you. Released won't mean your bones are as good as new. Not for a long time. Maybe I shouldn't be so blunt, but you hate the help you need now. Another accident akin to the last might leave you paralyzed."

"Dr. Layton was clear about that the first day he examined me. But JJ and I gentle our horses from the time they're foals by care in handling so they don't grow up to buck."

"Sorry, I just assumed…"

"It takes longer because a horse's inclination is to fight a bit and saddle. The most stubborn ones we take out into the pond where they can't buck when we're teaching them to bear our full weight. It's an old-time method true cowboys prefer."

"I like the sound of that practice. See, that's why you'll be a great dad. Kids do better with patience and understanding rather than criticism or punishment, too."

"I'm not going to be a dad, Binney. At least not anytime soon."

His flat denunciation ended their conversation.

On arriving at the lab some fifteen minutes later, Binney loaded Rex into the front pack again. Then she assisted Rio into the wheelchair she had muscled out of the pickup bed.

"I wish I could walk in on my own power."

"I know you do. I'm sorry the sidewalk is cobblestone."

Because she was familiar with the lab, they bypassed several steps and were soon ushered in to see a technician.

"That's quite a story," Sam Hartman, the lab technician, said, ending with a soft whistle. "Okay, so here's the deal. I'll swab the baby's saliva. But if you want the best, most accurate results, sir, I'll take a drop of your blood," he told Rio. "I recommend having a forensic

DNA even though there are cheaper models. Forensic reports stand up in court."

"Court?" Frown lines gathered between Rio's eyebrows. "Do the best one, but I don't see why it'd come to that. Uh…how fast can I expect results?" he asked as Sam swabbed a spot with alcohol then pricked his finger.

"If we weren't backed up with police department work you'd have results in three to five days. Because Binney is a hospital employee I'll do my best to expedite this. However, be forewarned, it'll likely take seven to ten days."

Rio glanced at Binney. "That's better than my ranch hand thought. He figured two weeks. As you might guess I'm anxious about the results."

"You said the aunt didn't give you much pertinent information on the baby's mother. Have you checked online to see if anyone posted her obit?" Sam asked, stripping off his gloves and donning a new pair before running a sterile cotton swab inside Rex's mouth.

The baby made a face, and Binney put him on her shoulder to rub his back. "I never thought about an obituary. We stopped here first, Sam, but next we're going over to the walk-in clinic to have the baby seen. His aunt didn't indicate whether he'd been checked at birth by a pediatrician. She came and left so fast I admit I never asked a lot of questions I should have."

Sam broke the swab off, corked the tube, labeled it, then rubber-banded it with Rio's small vial of blood. "If I were in your shoes I'd move heaven and earth to track the woman who left the baby. I think she could be charged with neglect for leaving him with a total stranger. I mean, you two have no idea, for instance, if he's had the hepatitis shot they give at birth now."

"I trust his birth date is correct, so he won't start routine shots for another month." Binney sounded confident as she tucked Rex back into his pack and secured him with the Velcro straps.

"Hep is now given at birth and again at one month." Sam walked with them to the door and then touched Rio's shoulder. "I saw your rodeo accident on TV. Add this problem, you're having a helluva year, man."

Rio pursed his lips. "I've definitely had better."

Outside, Binney asked him how he was holding up after she bumped his wheelchair over the lip of the door as they left the lab. "I'd suggest you wait in the pickup while I go down to the clinic, except I have no authority to have Rex examined."

"And I do?"

"By virtue of your name at the bottom of the midwife's delivery note, I think so. I brought it." She patted her pocket.

"Even if it's total bullshit?" He huffed out a breath. "I know you've no more hand in this mess than me, so let's just go get him examined, okay?"

"Rex isn't to blame for any of this, either. Quit looking at him as if he's poison."

"I'm not. He's a cute tyke. But he's not my son," Rio said for the umpteenth time.

Following that exchange they covered the distance to the clinic in total silence. A sign on the door read Mother and Infant Care Clinic. Binney struggled to open the door and back in with Rio's wheelchair. This time she jarred him twice.

"I wish we'd brought my crutches. I hate people thinking I'm a complete invalid."

And once inside, Rio turned out to be the only male in the waiting room. His condition earned sympathetic glances from other moms and staff, which he seemed to abhor.

In as much as it was a clinic for low-income families and those without insurance, it took a longer-than-normal consultation with several clerical staff to register Rex. Even as quietly as Binney tried to speak after explaining her role in being the one to fill out the paperwork, clerical questions caused many in the room to eye them with interest.

"I'm glad to be away from prying eyes," Rio muttered once they were shown into a room, and the nurse who'd undressed, weighed and measured Rex left them alone.

"I know you hate all of this," Binney said. "This won't be the last time you have to tell the story even if the DNA comes back in your favor."

"What do you mean, if? When it shows I'm not related, I'm done. Like it or not the next step will be to contact county social services. Are you prepared for that?"

Binney glanced away. "You've no idea the grilling we'll both be subjected to from their social workers." She would have fleshed that out further, but a doctor swept into the room, cutting off their private conversation.

"I'm Dr. Bernard." She nodded to each of them. "You two and this little guy have quite a tall tale, according to our intake staff," she murmured. Warming her stethoscope on her lab coat, she set it on Rex's chest. He kicked and waved his arms throughout his examination.

"I understand you're a registered nurse," Dr. Bernard said, casting an eye toward Binney after she sat down at a desk computer, where she struck a series of keys.

"I'm currently doing private duty nursing for Mr. McNabb. Anytime I'm between field jobs I schedule shifts with City Hospital. Mostly in ER."

The doctor studied Rio a moment, but her scrutiny again shifted to Binney. "How much longer will your current position last?"

Her heart dived. "I don't know for sure. Maybe a couple of weeks." She slanted her gaze toward Rio.

"I hope to lose the clavicle brace at my next doctor's visit," he provided. "That only leaves wearing the collar part-time for a once-cracked vertebrae that my orthopedic doc said is knitting. My broken left hand is weak, 'cause they just removed the cast. But I have a therapy ball that should help."

Binney quickly added for him, "He'll be able to get around his house once he has strength enough in that wrist to fully operate his crutches." She smiled at him and slipped her hand between Rio's neck collar and shoulder, pressing lightly. "I'll be at the ranch until his orthopedic doctor releases him," she said to the pediatrician.

"I was just wondering who'll handle the baby's care when you're gone. Also, who will bring him in for his immunizations?" As she talked, the doctor got up again and examined Rex's eyes, ears, throat, fingers and toes. Then she went back to the computer and typed some more.

"Someone will," Binney said with all the assurance

of a person who knew when actually she didn't. "Just write down the date you want him brought in again."

The doctor nodded. "For all it sounds like he's been through, he's a fine boy. The formula you listed provides essential vitamins. Add rice cereal at six weeks. Routine shots begin at two months. I think we'll skip a hepatitis shot today since we don't know if he had the first in the series. They're recommended at birth and four weeks, but can be started later. Pick up a copy of my report at the desk and schedule his next visit. It's easy to cancel if things change." The last statement she made directly to Rio. Then she hit Send on the computer, closed out the screen and walked to the door. "I hope whatever happens, he ends up in a loving home."

Binney's lips trembled as she restored Rex's clothes. She avoided Rio until she lifted the baby to strap him in her front pack and their eyes collided. It surprised her to note Rio's gray eyes were cloudy as if sad, and his mouth appeared pinched with concern. "What's wrong?" she asked, crossing to him.

"Just because he's not my son doesn't mean I want him tossed into a stream of unwanted kids." He scraped his right hand through his hair, leaving it standing on end. "We need to track down his aunt. She's the only one with answers."

"We don't have her name. Maybe she's a Cooper, but who knows. I know she abdicated all responsibility. Frankly, I don't understand how locating his aunt tells us anything more than what she already said to me."

"We'd better go," Rio said unhappily. "They probably need this room."

They left and Binney swung past the window bearing a sign that read Check Out Here. Since it was essentially a free clinic, there still seemed to be a suggested amount for a visit along with a recommended payment on a sliding scale for those who could afford something. She swiped her credit card and typed in the full amount.

"Thank you." The clerk smiled and tore off a receipt she gave Binney. "Here's the baby's report. Dr. Bernard wants to see him when he's two months old." The woman scrolled to her calendar and offered two possible dates.

Binney pocketed the receipt, passed Rio the report and blindly chose the first date knowing it was unlikely she'd be the one coming back.

"Why did you pay the bill?" Rio grumbled as they headed out.

"It didn't amount to a tenth of what you laid out on his supplies." Wedging open the outer door she somehow managed to get the wheelchair, herself and the baby out without assistance even though she banged her elbow hard enough on the door frame that for a moment it went numb.

At Rio's pickup she boosted him into the front passenger seat then buckled Rex into his car seat directly behind Rio. She rushed to the rear of the pickup and nearly fell over backward trying to lift the heavy wheelchair up and over the tailgate.

A Good Samaritan exiting an insurance office detoured to help.

"Thank you." She set blocks under the wheels so the chair wouldn't slide, and offered a head-bob again when the stranger closed the gate and shook it to make sure it was shut tight.

"I saw you put your husband and baby in the truck.

Little lady, you need to install a lift or you'll end up needing one of these yourself."

His perfunctory smile blunted the warm rush of pleasure Binney felt hearing Rio termed her spouse and Rex her child. "Uh, his injury is only temporary," she stammered, thanking the man yet again before fumbling pickup keys out of her pocket.

He tipped his cowboy hat, walked away, and she dropped her keys twice on the way to climb in the driver's door.

"Who's the dude who stopped to yak? I hope he's somebody important enough to leave me with a crying baby I can't turn around to check on?" Rio was plainly miffed.

"Only a nice man who took pity on me. He helped me with your wheelchair. Sorry, I didn't hear Rex." She twisted over the console and gave the baby a pacifier she'd bought the previous night with all the other baby items. "He's due for a bottle, but I'm sure you're hungry, too. It won't take that long to get back to the Lonesome Road." She started the pickup and jockeyed out of the parking space.

"That woman who dropped him off has made us snipe at each other, Binney. I hate it. We got along great before," Rio declared.

"If we credit her with recognizing that she couldn't raise her sister's baby, Rio, it might be easier. I don't see any reason for us to have cross words over this. Should I have thrown him and the tote bags of stuff back at her?"

"Of course not." Reaching across the console, he traced Binney's arm with fingertips of his once-bad hand. "You've assumed the lion's share of my care and his. I'll pay you extra."

"That's not necessary. Dogs, cats and kids are all factored into the price you're already paying me." Her eyes leaked tears. She didn't want extra money. She wanted Rio to accept Rex. And if she was honest, her.

"Well, when we set the contract it was just me and Tag."

"I know, but you forked out a lot at the store. And you're going to be slow assuming ranch duties for quite a while after you no longer need me."

"That reminds me. JJ said we have a buyer coming today for a colt and filly. Half of our mares are due to foal any day. If I get in shape to help train them, sales will be better than we've ever seen. It's what I've dreamed of since I bought the ranch."

"The doctor said you've done fantastic for the scope of your injuries. I realize it's hard not to get impatient, but keep following your doctor's orders. Don't overdo."

"It is hard when I watch you put together a crib, that swing thing, a car seat, and you're forced to lift my wheelchair. Darnell said I'd have to wear this stupid neck collar for a year if I return to light work around the ranch. He and Layton said I shouldn't think of ever competing in a rodeo again. Not even on the working cowboy's circuit, which I'd hoped to do."

"So what? Is competing and winning so important?"

Rio screwed up his face. "Watching you work while I'm sidelined isn't manly."

Amid a full-throated laugh she couldn't contain, Binney braked in a cloud of dust in front of the house. "Rio, I promise if you only stand by a corral, anyone looking at you will call you manly." She hopped out, took down the wheelchair and hustled everyone into the house, where they were greeted effusively by Tag. It pleased her all the same when she caught Rio smiling for the first time that day.

She started to help him to his bed, but he stayed her with a hand.

"I want a TENS session to hopefully hurry the healing process on my neck. Then if you'll hand me my laptop, I'm going to take Sam Hartman's suggestion and hunt for Lindsey Cooper's obituary."

"Okay. I'll feed Rex and then decide what to fix for our lunch."

Not long after they'd both settled silently in opposite chairs, Rio called to Binney. "Success! I found it. The obit. Come read it with me."

She set aside Rex's empty bottle and tucked him into his bouncy swing. She started its music box and stepped over Tag to go sit on the arm of Rio's rocker. "It's not very helpful," she said, squinting at the screen. "We already knew her name, age and that she has an unnamed older sister. Clever how whoever provided this information really didn't give particulars. It doesn't even say she died from complications of childbirth, or say where she worked."

"Yeah." Rio pinched his lower lip. "Also there's an unnamed parent, their dad, who apparently lives in an Alzheimer facility in Arkansas. With no city listed. Not that he could be of any assistance if he has dementia. Look, there is a photo of her... Lindsey." He scrolled to a black-and-white headshot. "Too grainy to be of any use." Rio started to hit delete.

"Wait. Print it," Binney urged. "It's clear enough to see she has long dark hair and is pretty."

"She's a liar," Rio declared emphatically.

Binney traced a finger along Rio's rock-hard jaw.

"One day it may be Rex's only connection to his birth mother. Something like that would have meant the world to me," she said, gazing over at the baby with shimmering eyes.

Relaxing his shoulders, Rio pressed her palm against his cheek. "I remember one of my mom's favorite sayings—the Lord works in mysterious ways. Maybe that daft woman brought Rex here so you would be his spirit guide through the system."

"His what?" Binney sat near enough to inhale the scent of Rio's aftershave, and it rattled her. She removed her hand and scrubbed away tears.

"A friend, a Native American bronc rider, claimed his grandfather sent him a spirit guide to watch over him on the rodeo circuit. I guess I'm mixing religious beliefs. Spirit guide, guardian angel or whatever we want to call it, you're the one with experience to take care of Rex, and you've gone through losing your parents at his age. I figure no matter what happens you can maybe stay in touch and help him understand."

"I rather like the idea of being Rex's spirit guide. Most likely it's you, though. I keep pointing out, you're the one Lindsey apparently named as his father. Send that article to print and I'll clip it to the copy of his birth record. If it comes to tracing his roots further, every snippet of information will help." Suddenly an emotional mess, she leaned down and kissed Rio. She aimed for his cheek, but being tippy on the chair arm, hit his lips, which made her hot and tingly all over.

He tried to deepen the kiss, but Binney slid off the arm of the chair. "Uh, sorry. I wasn't making a move on you, Rio. It's all the comparisons between how Rex and I were both abandoned. I just want you to want him." She quickly changed the subject. "Do you see how Rex is loving his swing? I...uh...will run in and fix us some lunch."

Rio attempted to maintain a hold on her arm, but she disengaged easily from his still-weak left hand.

Throughout the next few days Binney took real heart in Rio's sprouting interest in Rex. Where in the beginning he'd acted gruff, now she often caught him talking to the baby as if he were explaining things to Tag. He took turns feeding Rex without complaint and grinned watching him kick his legs and gurgle in the swing. Rio also seemed to love how Rex intently stared at Contessa, the pregnant mare, when the three of them took daily walks out to the corral.

Binney couldn't help it, her feelings for Rio expanded, too. To the extent that one afternoon she blurted without thinking, "In high school most of my girlish daydreams centered on Ryder before he dumped me. Before that he stood out larger than life. But you're a good man, Rio McNabb."

Rio started to speak, but Rex cried his *I-need-changing* cry, and she hurried off with a dry diaper, neglecting to confess that it was hard to understand now, how back then Rio flew under her radar. Thinking back, Ryder had always had smug arrogance she'd misconstrued as charm.

Rio sat in his recliner with the electronic unit intended to heal his vertebrae. Since he had the use of both hands to type now, he worked on ranch records. His fingers stilled and he thought about telling Binney why he and his brother weren't speaking. But his folks thought he should forgive and forget the incident even though they, too, placed more blame on his twin. But did he really want her to feel sorry for him, or take his side against his twin?

No, that wasn't his way even if he was on the verge of falling in love with his private duty nurse. What he really wanted was for Binney to see him as a whole man. Not as an invalid who needed her nursing care.

Starting that moment, Rio redoubled his efforts to do more to help himself. He spent extra time getting around using only his crutches. Whether he wanted to or not, he needed to prepare for the day Binney would leave the ranch. But he honestly didn't know if he wanted it to be sooner rather than later. And if she left before he turned Rex over to someone else, he couldn't care for a baby alone. But as it stood, no way could he share his deepest feelings for her until he was able to offer himself on equal ground.

Anytime Binney left the house to go after the mail, Rio phoned Las Vegas casinos personnel offices, asking if they'd employed Lindsey Cooper. With so many casinos and so little time, he hadn't so far made any inroads at all.

On Friday, Rex was napping and Rio and Binney were in the middle of exercising his left hand when a call from the lab popped up on Rio's cell phone. They both tensed while he answered.

"Yes, this is Rio McNabb. Oh, hi, Sam. You have my test results already? Fantastic, give me the good news." Rio flashed Binney a grin.

As quickly, he frowned. "You can't give me the results over the phone? Ah… I don't see any reason why we can't come to the lab now." He waited for Binney's nod. "We'll head out ASAP and be there in half an hour or so."

"It's odd he couldn't provide you a simple yes or no." She capped the cream she'd been rubbing into Rio's wrist and hand.

"I agree. But he said they have to show me the graphs. I trust they have good reason."

Tag wasn't happy to be left behind, but Rex didn't appear to mind being awakened and hauled out to the pickup. He loved slapping the string of rattles attached to his car seat.

In spite of the baby's happy gurgles, tension arced between Binney and Rio.

"It's almost over, Rio," she said haltingly, her hands flexing around the steering wheel. "If you'd like after we finish at the lab we can stop and see if Dr. Darnell thinks you're able to shed the clavicle brace, providing you continue to use the neck collar for limited tasks around the ranch. That way I can leave and you'll be free again."

"How do you figure?"

"Well, you expect the tests to absolve you of father-hood. You'll call social services, and once you no longer need anything except the neck collar, you won't need me underfoot."

A coldness gripped Rio. Binney had taken hold of his heart, and so had the cute baby with the chubby cheeks and sparkling dark eyes. That came as a shock to him.

"I know Rex and I won't share DNA," he finally said, not venturing that until Binney motored up to the lab and found a parking spot. "It'll still take time to work out handing him over to social services. I'll still need your help with him. So you won't be leaving right away, Binney."

Even as they left the vehicle and he was able to walk into the lab using his crutches, he was seized by a moment of panic where he wanted to grab Binney and Rex and go home. His steps slowed markedly. He stopped altogether when he heard Binney give his name to a receptionist.

She glanced around, her arms steadying the baby in the front pack. "Rio, are you okay? They said Sam's expecting you, so we can go straight on back." She returned to where he sagged on his crutches.

He stroked the pudgy hand of the happily kicking boy. "Suddenly I'm not sure I'm ready to hear that some unknown man is Rex's father."

Binney rose on tiptoe and brushed a kiss across Rio's trembling lips. "More than all the other times you've denied the possibility, your sadness now convinces me you've told the truth about not knowing Lindsey Cooper. If that's any consolation, I guess it comes too late since Sam's waiting for us at the door."

Hauling in a deep breath, Rio hobbled past her.

Inside the lab workroom, Sam directed them past a couple of other technicians to a waist-high table, where he spread out a set of papers. "Examine these four lines closely, Rio. Placed side by side they show that you and Rex share several specific genetic markers."

"Impossible." Rio huffed out a massive breath. At the same time his body bucked and he dropped one of his crutches.

Binney moved quickly to his side. She circled his waist with one arm, murmuring, "Rio, your heart is galloping and I can feel your legs shaking. Sam, he needs to sit down." Looking around, she pulled over a stool.

"Good. You sit, Rio. I'm not finished," Sam said, drawing their attention to two new papers he laid on the table.

Binney guided Rio to be seated as Sam continued pointing at lines. "These graphs show variants." His finger tracked four lines that didn't intersect with matching segments marked with Rio's name.

"You're saying those aren't differences due to his mother?" Binney asked.

"These outliers are female chromosomes belonging to his mother." The technician traced green lines that did align with those of the baby.

An older man with graying hair and glasses came from across the room to their table. "I've been doing this work for thirty years, Mr. McNabb. And I'm the second geneticist Sam had go over these results. Have you had cancer?" he inquired abruptly of Rio.

"Never."

"He's recently been in the hospital after a bad accident he sustained at a rodeo," Binney supplied. "With as many MRIs, blood work and X-rays as he's undergone, his doctors would have spotted cancer. Is there another lab, say in a bigger city, where Rio can be retested?" she asked.

Sam pinched his lower lip as he eyed Binney. "Any forensic technique has limitations. Of course you're free to go to San Antonio or Dallas. But we had three experts study these tests. All were puzzled by the anomalies. One of our geneticists said it might be a result of their age difference or other family discrepancies."

"Ryder," Rio said, reaching out to grip Binney's arm.

The older technician had walked away, but turned back when Binney said excitedly, "You may be onto something, Rio. Now I remember. In my last year of nursing school I had a lab class where the instructor showed us slides on cutting-edge blood studies being done on identical twins. That was a few years ago, but I'm sure he showed samples of variations they'd found when it had been commonly thought identical twins' blood bore exactly the same properties." Binney threw up her hands. "Is it likely? Why wouldn't the mother have had Ryder's name?"

"This screwup is damned sure something my brother would do."

Sam Hartman broke in. "If you'd told me you have an identical twin we would have had a probable explanation for the marker variations. You need to contact him and ask him to be tested. Or, if he's the little guy's biological dad, maybe he'll just tell you."

Rio gritted his teeth. "I don't have his phone number. I'm sure my mom does. I think she and Dad are due back from their trip this week. I have no idea how to begin trying to explain this to her. Maybe I can just ask for Ryder's number. Let's go, Binney." He struggled to stand. "I could wring Ryder's neck."

Although she appeared a bit dazed, she assisted him.

"Will you get back to me if you learn anything from your brother that explains the marker differences? Or someone could send us a sample of his blood to test and compare." Sam pressed Rio. "I can tell Binney's still puzzled. However, if true it'd help us to ask more questions on our future DNA application forms."

"I'll call you. It's definitely possible," Rio said testily.

Chapter 10

Binney hurriedly thanked Sam for the speedy way they'd returned the tests before she dashed after Rio, who made a beeline out of the lab.

She caught up to him and begged him to slow down before he tripped and fell. "I am as confused as ever. Why would Lindsey not have given her sister and the midwife Ryder's name?"

"I know you used to think he walked on water. You'd believe this if you knew why he and I haven't spoken for almost four years in spite of my parents doing their best to smooth things over."

He pulled away from Binney on the way to the parking lot. Propelling himself ahead of her, he threw his crutches into the back of the pickup, and swore when he couldn't climb into the passenger seat without her assistance.

"Rio, stop it. Please. You're going to hurt yourself

again." She tried unsuccessfully to calm him and ended up boosting him up into the passenger seat in an ungainly fashion. Then when he stubbornly said nothing, she quietly buckled Rex in his car seat and made sure he had his pacifier. It didn't take a genius to read Rio's stormy countenance as she backed out and began the drive to the ranch. What did it all mean for Rex? It hurt to think of the possibilities.

"Listen, Rio, I'm sorry I mentioned you and Ryder being identical twins. I lampooned both of you in front of Sam and the other techs. You traded identities as kids to prank the teachers. You're both grown up now."

"One of us is," Rio countered. "Let me tell you about our last dispute." His lips turned down as he rubbed his chin. "We were both at a PRCA rodeo in Denver. Ryder and some buddies shared a ritzy hotel suite. Someone in the group had won high points and big money bull riding. They threw a party and trashed the room. I'd gone on to Wyoming when I got served a summons for a court date in Colorado. It turned out my dear brother used my name on the hotel registration form. I denied being there, but the manager picked me out of a photo lineup. I was forced to pay damages and a fine in order to have my case acquitted. My folks contacted him, and Ryder paid me back, but he thought it was funny. He said he did it because he was afraid the party would get rowdy and he didn't want to reflect badly on bull riders and the PRC. So…do I put it past him to lie to a woman about his name? Hell, no!"

Binney digested his story bit by bit, but she didn't know what to say, because it sounded so terrible.

Rio slumped in his seat. "My brother has always been brash and arrogant, and more so once he started getting a big name in the PBR. He's a hard-charging partier and a womanizer. He'll never change."

Letting the reverberation of his words fade, Binney probed gently, "Rio, you admit you haven't seen each other in almost four years. Maybe he was egged on by his friends to pull that stunt at the hotel. You've matured. Until you talk to him you can't be positive he's involved in this. Remember the older geneticist said health reasons could cause DNA anomalies."

"Why are you standing up for Ryder?" Rio growled. "I tell you there is no other explanation. In fact, I should have thought of him myself."

Binney opened her mouth to refute that her hope about the truth had anything to do with Ryder. Really she didn't want sweet baby Rex to land in the center of a family squabble. And she didn't want Ryder to be Rex's biological father, because everything Rio said about his twin being arrogant and brash was true.

But before she could tell Rio, she pulled into the ranch and noted a strange vehicle, a dusty green SUV sitting where she usually parked. "Hey, maybe Rex's aunt had second thoughts and had someone bring her back here."

Straightening, Rio followed her finger. "That's my dad's Range Rover. I wonder what they're doing here." He flung open his door before Binney had shut off the engine.

A pretty, vibrant woman Binney recalled having seen at the twins' high school sports events rushed out of the house and down the steps followed by a tall man only slightly gray at the temples. *Rio's dad.*

A suddenly shy observer, Binney spared a moment to appreciate how much Rio resembled his father. She

cataloged how handsome Rio would still be in his re-
tirement years.

"Mom," Rio shouted. "When did you get back from
Australia? And why are you here?" He slid out of the
cab and teetered. It forced him to hang on to the door
so he didn't fall.

Linda McNabb rushed to steady her son. "We got
home and our neighbor gave us several news articles
about your terrible accident. I was so worried we came
to see how badly you'd fared. We've only been here a
short while. Your dad was just going out to the barns
to see if that's where you and JJ were."

"Hand me my crutches and I'll explain a few things.
I'm really glad you're here."

His mother took the crutches her husband had lifted
out of the pickup bed. "We've been inside." She passed
the crutches to Rio. "What else has happened while we
were gone? Care to fill us in on all of the baby stuff
strewn around the living room?"

Rio stopped at the front fender. "Uh, will you get the
baby from his car seat? It's behind where I sat. We'll
go inside and talk about a bunch of stuff." He still felt
rocked by the news from the test, and let down by Binney's willingness to abet Ryder.

His mother turned and opened the back door. Plainly
shocked, she nevertheless leaned in and unbuckled the
baby. In doing so her curious gaze strayed to where Binney remained unmoving in the driver's seat.

"Ah, hello." Grabbing Rex, his mom whispered a tad
too loudly, "Rio, is she the baby's mother? It appears
you have a whole lot of explaining to do."

"What? No, that's Binney Taylor, my home care nurse.
She's been taking care of the baby, too. Now, though,

if you and Dad can stay on a couple of weeks until I get cleared by the orthopedic doctor, Binney can leave ASAP. I know that's her wish, because she mentioned it."

"Sure, honey." Still wearing a confused expression, his mother shut the back door of the king cab. She cradled the baby and stepped around Tag, who'd bounded out of the house with them. "If you need us, Rio, of course we'll stay awhile. Right?" She deferred to her husband, who shrugged and nodded.

Binney emerged around the hood only to have Rio say, "Hear that? Earlier you sounded more than ready to be on your way. Now you can go. I'll cut your check while you pack."

Shock over the rapidity of how everything was ending stole Binney's breath. She slowly trailed Rio and his family to the house feeling worse than a fifth wheel as she heard him pouring out the story of how he came to have Rex.

Once inside, Rio's mute father stood behind the chairs where his wife and son sat. Linda in a recliner still holding the baby, Rio at the desk, where he took out the ranch checkbook.

Binney circumvented the group and went straight to her bedroom. It was with a leaden heart that she began folding clothes into her saddlebags. As yet she hadn't heard Rio mention Ryder.

Tag loped into her room, rubbed against her and whined.

She hugged him before she hefted her things, went out and snatched the check Rio waved at her. "Dad's going to call Ryder and put him on speaker phone, but you don't have to stay. No matter what he says you'd take his side." Impatiently, Rio waved her away.

"I didn't, I wouldn't…" She tried to deny that by suggesting he give his twin a chance to answer questions meant she was favoring Ryder. "Okay, think what you will. For Rex's sake I hope Ryder has changed," she said, eyes passing over Rio and his silent folks. "In the time I've cared for you and the baby, believe me, I've completely shed any rose-colored glasses when it comes to your brother."

Tightening his lips, Rio muttered, "Not fifteen minutes ago you tried counseling me that he's matured. You know what, I'd rather not discuss Ryder with you anymore. Goodbye, Binney. Uh, thanks for all of your help. If you need references I'll provide them, of course."

She hadn't reached the outer door when Ryder's voice boomed into the room. She badly wanted to stay and hear what he had to say for himself. However, staying would only make Rio more certain she still had some lingering interest in his twin.

She'd cried while packing, but now her tears ran unchecked. At the door she had to shove Tag back with a quick scratch to his chest so he couldn't follow her out. Wiping at her eyes, she stumbled to the barn to get the Harley that she hadn't ridden in the five weeks she'd been at the ranch.

She heard JJ out back working with the horses, and was thankful he didn't emerge to chat. Blotting her eyes, she secured her saddlebags, picked up her helmet and wheeled her bike out to the lane. Once there, she gazed again at the ranch she'd come to love. Before she became overwhelmed with sorrow and regret, she donned her helmet, slung a leg over the Harley and stomped down on the kick-starter. She was very thankful her bike roared to life and ran smoothly without choking. She wasted no time in peeling away.

Twice before she reached the main highway she had to stop and soak in the scenery. The second time she remembered she hadn't kissed the baby goodbye. And Rio—darn it all, he filled her hurting heart. True he had blustered and had ordered her to leave, but she would bet all she had in the world it was because he was hurting, too. Probably there was nothing to be done about that. At least not now. Maybe never.

Inside the ranch house Rio's dad spoke to his other son, letting him know they'd returned from Australia and were currently at the Lonesome Road.

Moving closer to Rio, his mother touched his arm. "Did you notice your nurse's red, puffy eyes? I think your sending her away so abruptly made her cry. Now you don't look so good, either. What, besides thinking Ryder falsely used your name and got some woman pregnant, is going on?"

"Nothing! Dad, ask Ryder about Lindsey Cooper. That's the name of the baby's mother. Her sister told Binney something went wrong in her home birth and Lindsey died on the way to the hospital. See if Ryder knows that."

Rex started to fuss. Rio's mother swayed with him, but he only sobbed louder.

"There are diapers in one of those bags. And he may be hungry, Mom, although I've never heard him fuss so much." Rio cupped a hand around the baby's head and it did lessen his sobs.

Tag ran over, set his chin on Rio's knee and whimpered. Then he ran back and forth to the door as if wanting someone to bring Binney back.

"Stop it, Tag. Uh, maybe I was too hasty in sending Binney away," Rio stammered. "Mom, can you take Tag and Rex into the kitchen? There's premixed formula in the cupboard. And kibble for Tagalong. I need to hear what Ryder tells Dad."

She obliged, although it was plain she wanted to stay and listen. She herded the lop-eared dog into the kitchen.

Rio heard his father ask if Ryder knew a woman in Las Vegas named Lindsey Cooper.

Rio fidgeted through his brother's lengthy pause. So long he wondered if his twin had hung up.

Finally the man on the other end of the call responded. "Why? Geez, has she turned up at the ranch? Tell Rio she's a leech. I never thought she'd go so far as to hunt him down. I swear it."

"Rio had a horse buck over on him. Did you know that? And what about this Cooper woman? What's the story, Ryder?"

"I only recently heard about his accident when I was in Florida. I'm in Kansas City now. My next event is in Corpus Christi. I planned to swing by the ranch to see how he's doing. We're in the final phase leading up to the world championships, you know." He coughed. "Obviously Lindsey tracked Rio down. Warn him to not get mixed up with her. She's trouble with a capital *T*."

"How so?" asked the elder McNabb.

"Well, it's kind of convoluted. The best friend of a fellow bull rider dated her. He had filed for divorce from his wife, but they decided to get back together. Lindsey kept bugging him, threatening to call his wife to insist he really loved her. Our mutual friend Troy Pritchard wanted to help. Both guys insisted Lindsey was only in love with the idea of being attached to a rodeo cowboy. Troy asked if I'd invite her out and bust up her fixation on his pal. She was pretty, so I flirted some and then asked her out."

"And you used your brother's name?" his dad charged.

"No. I didn't claim to be Rio. As it turned out he'd just ridden in Vegas the previous week. Lindsey had watched his event and his win. Her casino and others, plus my hotel still had flyers all over with Rio's picture. She immediately thought I was him. I didn't tell her any different. We went out a few nights. The last evening we had dinner and drinks in my room. By then it was plain she was hell-bent on marrying a cowboy. Any cowboy. You all know I'm not the marrying kind. She did her best to wrangle my phone number, but I never gave it to her. If she's found Rio, I didn't help her."

Rob McNabb's voice hardened. "So, you did pretend to be him, though."

"Ah…yeah, in a way I did, because I never corrected her error." He laughed. "Rio was long gone to another event. I was blowing Las Vegas, too, so I figured what the hell!"

"The hell is, Ryder, you got Ms. Cooper pregnant. She had the baby and her sister and the midwife assumed he was the baby's dad. I hate to be the one to break the worst news. Lindsey died from complications and her sister dumped the baby in Rio's lap."

For several moments there was nothing but crackling on the speaker phone.

"She's dead? That's awful. I'd never wish that on her or anyone. Geez, you guys, it's not my kid. I don't like talking to my parents about my sex life, but the one night we did it, I used condoms. I always use protection."

His fury building, Rio shouted, "You dumb ass, your

so-called protection failed. I had DNA testing. I knew I'd never met the woman. There were aberrations in the results, because while we share a lot, we don't have identical DNA."

"God, Rio, I had no idea. I'm sorry," Ryder said in a raspy voice. "Listen, I was going to leave here in the morning. I'll take off now. I can be at the ranch by daylight. We have to talk. This can't happen. For the first time ever I'm high enough in the point standings that I'm within striking distance of being the next world bull-riding champion. Tell Mom I'll be there for breakfast."

The elder McNabb frowned at his phone. "Ryder. Ryder?" Looking up, he shook his head. "He hung up. No use calling him back, he won't pick up. It's good he's coming. But this is your ranch now, Rio. Are you okay with seeing him?"

"I don't know. I'm mad as hell, but I have the baby. The midwife wrote my name on her record. So, let him come. We have to get this resolved, Dad."

Linda McNabb entered the room having finally calmed the baby. "I heard some of that. Ryder needs to step up and take responsibility."

"Has he ever?" Rio asked bitterly, struggling to get out of the chair.

His dad pocketed his phone. "Linda, how did he turn out so damned self-centered? When the boys were teens, did we help Ryder out of one too many scrapes of his own making?"

"We did what we thought was right, Rob. This is especially egregious, but I can't not love him. He sounded shaken. Maybe this will teach him a lesson."

"I hope so. There's a baby who didn't ask for any of

this. I still carry photos of you boys from about this baby's age, Rio." Rob got out his billfold and peeled out a folder of photographs. "Everyone thought you were cute as could be when you started mutton busting at the Abilene rodeo." He unfurled the packet under Rio's nose.

"Dad, don't. Ryder and I have been growing apart since... I don't really know when. I think that issue at the Denver hotel was the end for me." He sat in the rocker and reached out to take the baby. "This little guy deserves stability," he murmured, borrowing from what Binney said repeatedly. "Ryder didn't sound as if he'd be willing to raise this poor little bugger."

His mother set the now sleeping child in his arms. "You give all appearances of becoming attached, though."

"I guess so. Binney handled the lion's share caring for him, but I've helped." He gazed down on Rex and smiled when the baby cooed. "He's such a happy little guy."

His mom sat on the arm of his chair. "Honey, running a ranch is difficult in itself. You're battling injuries. Frankly I can't fathom what it'd be like to be a single dad on top of that."

"It's true, son. You can barely get around," Mr. McNabb said. "Maybe the nurse you had helping knows of a reputable adoption agency in town. It's not my druthers, but we need to look at what'd be best for the boy."

Rio shifted. His shoulders sagged. "I see you don't remember that Binney attended school with Ryder and me. She was abandoned as a baby and was never adopted. Agencies don't always find families, Dad. And fostering didn't sound ideal in all cases, either. She doesn't like to talk about it, but I know Binney had a hard life. I want better for Rex."

"And so do we," Rob said, walking over to put his arm around his wife. "I say we set talk aside until Ryder gets here tomorrow. Linda, didn't you bring a cooler with some sandwiches?" He returned his wallet to his back pocket.

"I did. There wasn't much in the way of food in our condo after being gone a month. I hurriedly made and packed PB&J. You okay with that, Rio? I can put on a pot of coffee, too," his mother said.

"I can eat a sandwich. Although I'm not very hungry. Binney fixed bacon and waffles for breakfast. I ate a lot knowing we were going to get my lab results. That seems as if it happened ages ago," he said, gazing vacantly into space.

"Rob, if you put the baby in his swing and help Rio make his way into the kitchen, I'll go fix lunch." She hugged Rio and went toward the kitchen.

Rio's father bent down and scooped up the sleeping child. "Hey, tadpole, come to Grandpa."

Rio blinked. "It's true, Dad, you are Rex's real grandfather. Binney would've loved hearing you say that," Rio murmured as his father helped him out of the recliner. "She wanted him to belong someplace with a family who cared about him."

Binney rode straight into town from the ranch. She felt a need to shower away the sweat and dust from her ride. As a rule she would have stopped at the bank to deposit her earnings. Today angry stomach cramps brought on by being summarily dismissed left her too restless to even care about Rio's generous check. Had he paid her more because he felt guilty for the way he hustled her out? He ought to. She'd like to be a fly on the wall back at the ranch. She couldn't help but wonder how the conversation with Ryder McNabb had gone.

It wasn't her problem. It was time she marked the last weeks off as a bad experience.

As yet unable to face Mildred since her elderly friend was so perceptive, Binney got off her Harley a block from the apartment complex and pushed it to her assigned parking spot. Then she hiked up the back stairs, taking care to not jingle her keys lest Mildred hear.

She went straight to her bedroom, stripped off her clothes and stepped under a bracing warm spray. Once clean she wrapped in a big towel, fell back on her bed and stared at the ceiling. She was mad at herself for caring so much about Rio and the baby. For nearly her whole life all she'd wanted was to be a nurse. She was still that. Just because seeing Rio McNabb again had awakened old yearnings she'd had as a lonely teen, it really had no bearing on her future. The few hugs and kisses they'd shared meant nothing.

Sitting up, Binney unwound the towel. She hadn't believed Rio about not fathering Rex and she'd been wrong. She had tried to apologize, but he'd chosen not to listen. She needed to get over him, and fast.

Finally she donned clean clothes, but she chided herself for the way she'd all but fled Rio's ranch as if she was guilty of something. If his parents hadn't been there she would have argued and at least tried to make him understand that she could never back Ryder, not after the things he'd pulled on Rio. She was sorry to learn he was Rex's biological father. Did she wish he had grown up enough to man up? Yes, especially for Rex's sake. And for Rio's. They'd each stolen pieces of her heart.

But, damn it, Rio should have recognized where her

concern and hope had sprung from. Falling for him had been a serious blunder.

Her heart ached as it hadn't ached in a very long time. She thought Rio had seen the real her and thought he liked her. Yet he couldn't kick her out of his life fast enough.

At least it didn't have anything to do with her nursing care. He'd offered her recommendations.

Knowing that didn't ease the pain in her heart.

But hadn't Lola Vickers cautioned her to not let herself get too attached to the people she did home health care for? Yet she'd done just that. Gotten attached to Rio and the baby. Even attached to his dog, for pity's sake. And the ranch. She loved the Lonesome Road.

This might be a wake-up call for her to quit home care and return to work in the hospital. The ER needed another full-time nurse. And with the variety of cases they dealt with, she shouldn't get bored. Nor would she have any patient long enough to develop an attachment.

That's what she would do. And she wouldn't give herself any time to waffle. Scooping up her earnings and the key to her Harley, she left to deposit the check with Rio's name on it and go ask for her old nursing job back at the hospital. That should keep her busy enough to erase Rio McNabb from her mind and her heart.

Once she had secured another job, she'd go back and share the whole impossible-sounding story with Mildred.

Chapter 11

Later that afternoon, Rio and his folks took the baby and Tag on a journey out to see JJ and the horses. The outing didn't have the usual enjoyment for Rio. It wasn't Binney laughing and holding Rex up to see and pat Contessa.

He wasn't hungry for supper, because Binney didn't fix it and she wasn't around to play her guitar to help him and Rex relax and fall asleep that night.

In fact he barely slept at all.

His mom got up for Rex's 2:00 a.m. feeding. Tag padded over to his bed and whined, very likely because he couldn't find Binney. Damn, but Rio missed her and she hadn't even been gone a full day. He missed her smile. He missed her touch. He hadn't expected to feel so bereft.

Everyone rose early the next morning, and Linda had pancakes and scrambled eggs ready when Ryder rolled up in his midnight blue Tesla. It was easy to see where he spent his winnings. Rio steeled himself for the visit.

His brother stalked into the house, removed his cowboy hat, looked around at his family and said, "I've thought about this horrific problem on the entire drive from KC. I hate that my protection failed and Lindsey had a baby. It's awful something happened and she died. But I've gotta be honest here. I've never wanted to be a husband or father. I don't have what it takes to settle down. You know that, Rio." His shifting gaze stopped on his twin.

Their father gestured toward the kitchen. "I suggest we discuss this over breakfast. Your mom has it ready. And Ryder, you shouldn't make a hard-and-fast decision before you've seen your son."

Ryder grimaced, tossed his hat on a chair and caused Tag to growl ominously. "Sorry," Ryder said. "I wanted to get that out from the get-go. Rio, you still don't look so good. You have to believe me when I say I didn't know about Lindsey being pregnant. I swear I didn't hear about your accident until I was at the rodeo in Kansas."

Linda McNabb collected the baby from his swing, put him in his infant seat and let her husband carry him to the kitchen table. He placed the seat where Ryder was forced to face the baby. His baby.

Rio, who'd thought all night about what he wanted to say to his wayward twin, held his tongue and brought up the rear. He waited until he'd had a bracing swig of coffee before he spoke. "I'm healing. Slower than I'd like. Frankly, I didn't expect to hear from you. Given our most recent history I'm surprised I didn't suspect you when the aunt showed up out of the blue and gave the baby to my home nurse, insisting he was mine."

His brother had the grace to look guilty. Only as their mother dished out food did Ryder take time to study the baby. "I probably should feel something for him, but I don't. It doesn't seem real. His mother was only a week's flirtation to me. Pop, can you and Mom adopt him or something? I'll send money toward his keep."

Linda passed her husband hot sauce for his eggs. "Ryder, we're retired. You know we live in a senior community. They don't allow children except for short visits. We're prepared to help out as grandparents, but eighteen years of parenting is your responsibility."

Ryder kept shaking his head and fiddling with his fork. "I can't."

"You jerk," Rio grated, slamming down the syrup pitcher. "I'll raise Rex providing you relinquish all rights. I want something airtight and legal. Oh, and a paragraph swearing you'll never impersonate me again."

"You mean that?" Ryder sounded too grateful, too quick. "I'll see a lawyer after breakfast. Maybe I don't have grounds to ask for anything, but can we keep this under wraps? The PBR doesn't like messy stuff dogging their riders. Rumor says you're leaving the PRCA for the RHAA. That means we'll never land in the same cities at the same time, bro."

"Don't bro me," Rio said through clenched teeth. "Your colossal nerve rubs me wrong. My injuries have very likely excluded me from all rodeo. I'm going to raise horses at the Lonesome Road. Get me custody papers. I'll claim Rex Quintin McNabb as my son, and you'll never be more than his uncle. Be real sure you can live with that."

"I can. I know he'll be better off with you, Rio. I promise I'll stay out of your life except for if we all end up at Mom and Dad's for holidays or something. Are you able to ride in a vehicle? If so, let's go see an attorney together. Not in Abilene, where we're known. We can go to Big Springs and have something drawn up. Dad can drive you home and I'll head on to Corpus Christi."

It was a quiet breakfast thereafter. Once Ryder phoned and booked an appointment with a lawyer for just prior to noon, Linda volunteered to stay behind with Rex and Tag.

Rob drove Rio in his pickup and Ryder led the way in his car. Rio spent most of the drive staring fixedly out the window.

It turned out after listening to the story and seeing the midwife's report, the lawyer had forms where all they had to do was fill in their names and affix signatures.

"Boys, it seems as if this covers everything pertinent," Rob said once they'd all read the document through. "Although, what about this line that says Ryder relinquishes forever all legal, moral and monetary obligations for Rex, who he admits he likely fathered. Shouldn't he have to pay support? This lets him totally off the hook."

"There's no likely about it. I have copies of the DNA tests. But, if I accept support won't that open the door for him to maybe one day change his mind and want paternity rights?" Rio asked.

"I swear I won't," Ryder said quietly. "I'm not currently and may never be father material. Even if I meet someone that I someday want to marry, I can't see it happening for years. Trust me, Rio." Ryder extended his hand.

Rio met his twin's eyes for several protracted moments before he accepted and clasped his hand. "My home care nurse knew us in high school. She went with me to get the DNA results. She said maybe you'd matured. I want to believe you have."

"This has had a sobering effect. You were never footloose like me. If I win this championship I want to travel and see the world." He fidgeted and finally asked, "Does this agreement mean you can't occasionally send Uncle Ryder photographs? Is it wrong for me to at least want to see he's doing okay?"

Rio glanced at the lawyer, who'd tipped back in his chair. The white-haired man pressed his fingers together. "Strictly speaking from my fifty years in family law, it's totally up to the guardian how much to share."

"I didn't think I'd be open to anything like that, but I am."

The elder McNabb smiled at his sons, and Ryder scribbled his name on the copies, followed by Rio, who did the same.

The three men exited the office carrying their respective folders. "Pop, will you keep this for me?" Ryder held out his folder. "I'd like it a lot if you all could come see me ride in the championships. Maybe that's too much to expect. It requires travel."

Rio leaned heavily on his crutches. "We'll see how I am in December. JJ and Rhonda are getting married then. If the wedding doesn't conflict with your event, maybe I can manage both. I do hope you win."

"Your mom and I will try to make it. Let us know

the date." He and Rio watched Ryder climb in his Tesla and drive off before Rob helped Rio into the pickup.

"That was generous of you, son. I'm proud of you, but still disappointed in Ryder."

"You are? I think this time he'll try and make an effort to change some of his wild ways."

"If that wasn't all show for the lawyer."

"He's always wanted to be a superstar. Although that will make him more popular with rodeo groupies like Lindsey Cooper." Rio smoothed a hand over the hollows of his cheeks.

"It bothered me that he didn't ask if you had a significant woman in your life. Anyone who might serve as a mother to Rex. In spite of some softening toward the end, he rushed to absolve himself of any liability."

"That's okay, Dad."

"Your mom and I can stay a couple of weeks and help you out, but we were gone from our condo a month already. We can't stay at the Lonesome Road indefinitely. And the shape you're still in, how can you take care of your home, the ranch and a baby?"

"My orthopedic doctor said by next week I should be able to shuck the clavicle brace. This troublesome neck collar is going to be part of my life for quite a while. If you and Mom stay long enough to make sure the doctor releases me, I should be okay. JJ's used to covering ranch chores. I have to make it work," he said grimly.

They drove the remainder of the distance in silence. Once home they filled Rio's mother in on all that had transpired. He reiterated his vow to handle everything, including being a single dad.

"I believe you'll try," Linda said without hesitation. The baby woke up and started to fuss, causing Tag to shake himself out from beneath the hospital bed. The dog raced into Binney's old room and began barking. Tearing out of the bedroom again, he ran around the house alternately barking and whining.

"I think he keeps looking for your nurse," Rob said.

"Oh, so now you can read a dog's mind?" Linda picked up the baby and jiggled Rex. "A week or so of our help won't be enough. Rio, if you can afford it you need to hire a nanny. Which of you wants to hold the baby while I fix his bottle? By the way, did his doctor say when to start cereal? He's a big boy. I don't think this formula is holding him between those listed feeding times someone taped to the cupboard door. Who wrote those? Was it the pediatrician?"

Both Rio and his dad reached out their hands for Rex. Because Linda stood nearer to her husband, she passed the baby to him.

Rio answered her question. "Binney must have taped up the feeding sheet that his aunt left. I think the doctor said to start some kind of cereal, but not right away. She typed findings from her exam and listed information on when to begin his shots. A clerk gave Binney the copy of his record when we checked out."

His mom returned from the kitchen, where she'd warmed the baby's bottle. "Seems to me you relied a lot on her. On your nurse."

"I did." Rio averted his eyes to break his mother's intense scrutiny. "I admit I was clueless. She and Rhonda knew what a baby required and what I needed to buy. Of course, then I didn't expect to keep him. I never would've thought to have Rex seen by a pediatrician the day we went in to have our DNA tested. That was Binney's idea. She knew the midwife who helped deliver Rex probably only gave him a cursory exam."

He let several blank moments tick past then said in a low voice, "On day one when I said I wanted to call social services, Binney swore if she could, she'd apply to adopt him. Then she found the midwife's birth note with my name on it in the tote bag. After that she assumed I was lying about not knowing Lindsey Cooper. But the day we went to get the DNA results, before the tech showed them to us, she said she believed me. Later I screwed up and got all peeved when it seemed she backed Ryder."

Rob stood up. "The baby is wet and smells like maybe he did more than tinkle. I haven't changed a baby in over thirty years, but like they say about never forgetting how to ride a bicycle, I'm sure I can handle this. Where are his diapers, Rio?"

Rio struggled a bit, but got up, too, and hobbled his way into the living room, where he sat heavily in the rocker. "There are packages of diapers stacked under his crib, and a garbage can in the main bathroom that Binney told me should be lined every day with disposable liners and emptied in our Dumpster at the end of the lane."

"Rob, you should let Rio change the baby," his mother called. "If he can't handle that simple chore he'll need to find a nanny right away. Your father and I are only here temporarily," she reminded, framed in the kitchen door, appearing plainly worried.

Rio started to get up out of the rocking chair, but his dad shook his head. Ignoring his wife, Rob completed the task and placed a much happier infant in Rio's lap while he hurried on to the bathroom.

Linda McNabb emerged from the kitchen and passed Rio the bottle. "I'm not being hard-nosed about this to be mean. You're injured and this is a situation of your brother's making. I'm happy to hear you two sort of buried the hatchet. On the other hand he ducked out free again. I wish you'd have demanded some monetary assistance. You shouldn't have to shoulder the entire burden." She reached out and stroked a finger over Rex's dark hair and huffed out a sigh before plopping down in a recliner. "Shoot, it's wrong to imply our first grandchild is a burden. He's sweet as can be. It's you I'm worried about, Rio. But I'd better just shut up."

Rob returned and set both hands on his wife's shoulders. He massaged the back of her neck for a minute, then bent and kissed the top of her head. "Sweetheart, I'm sure Rio knows the origins of your concerns. First reading about his bad accident then walking into this shock after we broke all speed limits to get here caused you a lot of heartache, and that was before we learned what Ryder did."

Setting the partially finished bottle of formula on a side table, Rio lifted Rex and bent him over his broad hand and rubbed his back with the other. "Wearing this cervical collar I can't burp him on my shoulder. Binney showed me this way."

Rex let out one of his loud, classic burps. "See, it works," Rio said grinning at his parents. Tipping the baby back in the crook of his arm, he again offered him the bottle.

"Okay, I'm convinced you aren't completely inept," his mother murmured and smiled.

"Well, there's a world of space between not being inept and being an able-bodied dad. I need both crutches to stand up. I can't do that while holding Rex. I haven't yet showered without some assistance from Binney. She bathed the baby in the kitchen sink in a tub she bought the other night, but I didn't watch. I could probably wash him, but until I'm free of the clavicle brace I probably can't lift him in and out of a tub."

"Don't stress over those things," Rob said, standing between where his wife sat and where Rio still sat rocking the baby. "We're staying until after you have your next doctor's appointment. Your mom can give you tips after you get rid of the brace and crutches. You can carry him around in that front pack. Whoever designed that was genius."

"I still vote for hiring a nanny," Linda stated firmly. She got up and collected the empty bottle, and took it into the kitchen, leaving the men alone.

"I notice every time your mom mentions hiring a nanny you flinch. Why is that? It's pretty plain to me you're going to need help, son. Is it money?"

"No. JJ and I tried to hire a housekeeper for either full-or part-time while I was off at rodeos and he was left to deal with my house, his and the horses. We interviewed a bunch of suitable women, but they all turned down working for us because of how remote the Lonesome Road is. Finally no employment agency in town would send us prospective applicants."

"Hmm. That is a problem. Yet you had a home care nurse."

"Yeah. Binney liked the ranch." Rio left his response at that, but for the remainder of the evening he brooded, wishing he hadn't sent her away. He missed her cheerfulness. He missed watching her blow on Rex's tummy. He missed her joy whenever they trekked out to see

Contessa and the other horses. He knew she had wanted to see the new mare's foal, too. He felt like a damn fool.

Over the ensuing three days he found himself turning, expecting to see Binney anytime the front door opened. Or at night when Rex cried and his mom helped him out of bed to change and feed the baby, he detected Tag searching for Binney. The dog padded to the door of her old room, whimpered and turned accusing eyes on Rio.

It was possible, too, that Rex cried more than usual. Plus, it took longer for the baby and him to go back to sleep in the middle of the night.

Midmorning of day four Rio ran across Binney's phone number in his cell phone, and he considered calling her to apologize. He wondered what she was doing. Mostly he worried whether or not she'd gotten another job with some fellow rancher. How often did home health care jobs come up, though? He ought to let her know what all had transpired with Ryder. Would she care that he'd assumed full custody of Rex? He thought she would.

The next day his mom wanted them to go buy a few things at the grocery store. "You need to see if you can handle hauling Rex in the front pack," she said.

He did fine, but women shoppers, even grand-motherly ones, stopped and engaged him in conversation as they cooed over Rex and offered him sympathy.

"Babies attract women of all ages," Linda said around a grin. "You won't have any problem hiring someone to take care of him. That is, if an agency will send you applicants. Your dad said that was an issue."

Not until after they were in the pickup headed home did he say, "I don't want just anyone to move in and care for Rex, Mom." It was at that moment Rio realized exactly who he did want. *Binney.*

His mother shrugged and dropped the subject while he continued to meditate.

Rob met them outside and helped unload the groceries. Less than an hour later they all sat at the table eating tomato soup and grilled cheese sandwiches. Out of the blue Linda stopped eating and said, "Rio, I knew you'd bought an electronic keyboard and were teaching yourself to play a couple of years ago. When did you take up the guitar?"

"What?" He dropped his soup spoon. "I haven't."

"Then is the guitar case propped against the far end of the baby's crib JJ's or Rhonda's? It's been in the same spot since we got here."

"Huh?" Rio shifted as much in his chair as he could. "Binney plays guitar. Oh, no, she must have forgotten to take it with her when she left."

"Why do you suppose she hasn't called about it?" Linda asked.

"Probably because I acted like a jerk sending her away the way I did." His response sounded stilted.

"Is she the reason you've been moping about for days? I told your dad it's so obvious I've been concerned you may be having second thoughts about keeping Rex."

"I miss Binney," Rio admitted, plucking at his napkin. "I only figured out how much when you drove down the lane from our grocery shopping trip. Binney's the only person I know who could get excited over seeing the sun stream down through the live oak tree branches. She cared about the horses. She weeded your flower beds even though that really wasn't one of her listed duties."

"Do you think her abrupt departure is why Rex and your dog have been extra fretful?"

"I don't know, Mom. Probably. We all depended on Binney. Me most of all if you want the truth. She worked for me, so I kept telling myself not to fall for her. I did and thought it was mutual until we got the baby. For a while that put us at loggerheads. Then we fell into a routine caring for Rex and things picked up again. The DNA results came back. I was steamed at Ryder and got steamed at her for seeming to give him a pass. Remembering what all was said after you guys showed up, I think she maybe just wanted me to calm down."

His mother engaged his father with a quirked eyebrow. "Did you not hear her say before she left that she saw through Ryder, and her concern was for the baby?"

"Yeah, I heard. It didn't fully register because I was so ticked off." Rio ate a few bites of his sandwich, but he struggled to meet his mother's steady gaze.

"I thought maybe you missed her explanation since your dad was phoning Ryder. You handed the nurse her check and told her she didn't have to stay to hear your brother since she'd stick up for him anyway, or something to that effect. To me she sounded sincere when she said after coming here and taking care of you she'd seen through him. I remember it so clearly, because at the time I was totally confused about what the heck was going on."

"I only listened with half an ear. By then Dad had Ryder on the phone. I really, really miss her. I care for her more than a lot."

Rob McNabb, who sat listening to the conversation

swirling around the table, squeezed his son's shoulder. "Care for her, or love her? You have that lovesick, sad expression. Hey, I have an idea. Let's let your mother babysit the baby and Tag. I'll fetch that guitar and drive you back into town. You can unburden yourself and beg her to come back."

"I do love her," Rio conceded, sounding awed by his own revelation. "But I screwed everything up, big-time. I was rude. I can't face her, Dad."

"You won't know unless you try. Maybe it's time to cowboy up."

Rio's gaze drifted to Rex, whom his mother had lifted out of his infant seat. "What if she thinks I just need a nanny?"

"You said she was smart," Linda said. "We women can tell when someone is giving us a snow job as opposed to when love is real. Give her credit. Be honest about the hole she's left in your heart."

"I have her phone number. I could just call her."

Linda rolled her eyes. "Phoning, texting, those don't have the same impact."

"You're right. If my name came up in her caller ID, she probably wouldn't answer. Whether or not she wants to come back I don't want her to go on believing I'm a freakin' toad."

"That's the spirit," his dad said, collecting their dishes and carrying them to the sink.

"Don't think I'm dragging my heels, but I'm not sure where to start hunting for her. Maybe her apartment. I remember the address was on the contract we signed. It's lying on top of the desk in the living room. Dad, it'd be quicker if you go grab it while you pick up the guitar."

"Okay. You head on out to the pickup. Is there anything else you need?"

"Outside of luck being a lady today, nope."

Rio's parents laughed at him, but he didn't think it was so funny. Binney would have every right to toss him out on his rear. He should have told her after they'd kissed that he was falling hard for her. He hadn't given her much to indicate his true feelings.

His dad came out to the pickup carrying an envelope and the guitar. He put Rio's crutches in the backseat and helped him settle in before he climbed behind the wheel and passed him the contract. "Plug that address in your phone GPS, and we'll get this show on the road."

"Thanks." Rio dug out his phone. Within half an hour they sat outside an older apartment building in the heart of Abilene's historic district.

"Her apartment number is three ten. If she lives on the third floor I hope there's an elevator. I haven't tried climbing stairs using crutches. JJ built the ramp for when I relied on a wheelchair. That was all Binney's idea."

"I wondered about that," Rob said. "This building is far from modern. I'd offer to help you, but if it takes effort on your part, son, that will show her you're serious. I'll come into the foyer with you and carry the guitar that far."

Inside it was plain the wide steps leading up were the only means of accessing upper floors. "Showing you have guts is one thing. You shouldn't try navigating stairs carrying a guitar," Rob said, gazing up.

Agreeing, Rio tightened his grip on his crutches. "I'm getting better at using these, and I hope after tomorrow's appointment I'll only need to wear the collar when working out around the ranch. Then I can start building strength and soon I should walk normally."

"I'll take the guitar back to the pickup. Bring her down to get it. I'd like a chance to do more than say hello in passing."

Rio agreed. There was a sturdy handrail and the stairs weren't too steep. He figured out it'd work better if he left one crutch in the lobby and traversed the stairs utilizing the aid of one crutch and the railing. Still he was out of breath when he hobbled to Binney's apartment. Taking a deep breath, he pounded on her door.

And waited.

He knocked again, feeling from the silence it was futile. His heart dived. Her door remained closed, but then the door directly across the hall sprang open. A tiny, very elderly woman peered at him. Rio felt he was being doubly measured.

"Binney's not home. She's at work," the woman said. "You a friend? Or a future client?" she asked, her eyes on his crutch.

"She was working for me until several days ago. I'm Rio McNabb."

"Oh, you're the fella who was injured at the rodeo. Humpf! What do you want? I think you broke her heart."

Rio flinched. "Will you tell me where I can find her if I promise I want to rectify that? By the way, are you the neighbor she plays guitar for? If so, she left her instrument at my ranch. I need to get it back to her. I left it out in my pickup with my dad. I couldn't carry it and climb the stairs."

"Only today did she say she'd left her guitar at your ranch. She's gone back to working full-time at the hospital. In the emergency room. Today her shift is three to eleven, so you've missed her by an hour or so."

"Thanks. Like I said, my dad drove me here. I'll have him swing by the hospital. I hope she won't be too busy to see me." He turned away, walking slowly, guiding himself with his injured hand pressed to the wall.

"You take care. Don't be falling down our stairs. I'm too old and feeble to help you up. And don't you be making Binney cry again or I'll find a way to crack your knees with that crutch."

Stopping at the head of the first set of steps, Rio laughed. "I believe you will. I swear my intentions are honorable."

His dad was pacing around the lobby. "You didn't call. I couldn't stay double-parked out front. I found a spot down the street. I hate to ask how it went since she hasn't come with you to get her guitar." Rob picked the case up from where he'd propped it against the wall and passed Rio the crutch he'd left in the lobby.

"She's working today at the hospital emergency room. I talked to her feisty neighbor. If I remember right, Binney said the woman is ninety. She threatened to break my kneecaps if I make Binney cry. So I hope our next stop goes well."

"Like I said, you can only do your best. Selfishly I hope it works. Your mother and I have a grandson now, and we always wished for a daughter. The Lord didn't bless us with more than you boys, but maybe He will grace us with a daughter-in-law."

Rio chewed that over as his father went to retrieve the pickup. He hadn't known his folks had wanted more children. Standing there on the sidewalk, he mulled over how nice it'd be to give Rex a brother or sister. And got hot all over picturing him and Binney getting around to that the old-fashioned way.

It was a short drive to the hospital. Rio directed his dad where to park. "I've been here so often now it feels like my home away from home. I even know some of the staff. Surely somebody will help me have a word with Binney."

"Good luck," Rob called after rolling down his window. He gave Rio a thumbs-up.

Unable to stop the smile that spread across his face, he entered through the patient door leading into the emergency room. It seemed a slow day. Several staff dressed in blue scrubs stood around chatting. A couple of them glanced up when the pneumatic door swished open. A tall red-haired woman approached him.

"May we help you? Or direct you to a clinic office?" She eyed his neck collar and his crutches.

"My name is Rio McNabb. I'd like a word with Nurse Binney Taylor. She was my home care nurse for an accident I recently had," he added for good measure. "She, uh, left her guitar at my ranch. I have it out in my pickup. She'll probably want it, but maybe she can walk out with me to get it."

The woman studied him thoroughly as if assessing the validity of his statements.

After some deliberation she said, "Binney's on break. The breakroom is three doors down that hall on your left." She pointed.

"Thank you." Rio shuffled away not nearly as fast as he'd like since he felt all eyes tracking him.

He opened the door, hoping he'd find Binney alone. But no, she sat at a table drinking coffee with four other women all wearing various colors of uniforms. All stopped talking and gave him the same kind of once-over he'd received down the hall. He zeroed in on Binney's lovely face. A face with a glow that made his heart ache.

"Rio!" Binney gaped at him.

He took note of how her hands tightened around her cup.

"I'm here for a couple of reasons. My dad drove me. We…uh…have your guitar in the pickup. You left it at the ranch."

"I only missed it today when my neighbor Mildred asked if I'd play for her sometime this week."

"I met Mildred. She's a pistol. Promised me bodily harm if I make you cry. So please don't."

She frowned slightly and her hands fell to her lap. Rio hurried to fill her in on what she hadn't stayed to hear; his brother admitting Rex was his baby. "He signed over full custody of Rex to me."

She stood then and gripped the back of her chair. "Congratulations on gaining full custody. Are you happy about that?" she asked, hesitantly meeting his eyes.

"I'd be much happier if you'd consent to be my wife and, by virtue of that, Rex's mother. I love you, Binney," he blurted, giving her a lopsided smile. "I don't deserve it, but I hope you can forgive all I said in a fit of anger at Ryder. I've let him get in the way too much in my life. He came to the ranch and we kinda made peace. I regret so badly not taking you at your word when twice you told me you saw through him. I'm sorry." He lifted a hand off one crutch and extended it toward her.

Her mouth had fallen open about the time he said

he loved her. Now she cast a hurried glance around at her grinning coworkers. "Talking about Ryder seemed safer than admitting how I was falling for you, Rio. You were my patient. Ryder already meant nothing to me before I spent time with you at the ranch and fell head over heels. Did I hear right? Did you propose to me?"

"I did. I am." It wasn't easy, but Rio tried to bend and kiss her over the cervical collar he still wore. "I don't have a ring to give you. I'll get one. Or you can pick out what you'd like. And we'll have a fancy wedding and invite everyone you want. Really what I want with all my heart is for us to make a family. You, me, Tagalong and Rex, for starters," he said huskily. Then, when most of the women at the table chuckled, he felt himself blush.

Binney rose on tiptoe and kissed him soundly and for so long a cheer went up behind her from her friends. That made her go red in the face, too.

But after she dropped back on her heels, she traced a finger along Rio's jaw. "I don't need a ring. I don't want a fancy wedding. You've offered me what I've most longed for my entire life. A family. To be part of a real family. I accept, Rio. I accept."

Their next kiss blocked out the noise of her coworkers clapping and whistling.

Lifting his lips, Rio said, "Do you have time to go out to the parking lot and say hello to my dad? He felt bad that he never got properly introduced. He said now that he and Mom have a grandson, he hopes they'll soon have a longed-for daughter-in-law."

Binney laughed with joy. Turning to her friends, she said, "You heard. Cover for me until I get back? It's not every day a woman gets to meet her prospective father-in-law."

"We'll cover," called the woman who'd sat across from Binney. "But only if you promise you'll have a wedding and we're all invited. You've been raving about this guy and his ranch ever since you came back to work. It's only fair that we all get to judge for ourselves. The ranch, that is." The woman winked. "Your cowboy passes muster."

Rio hugged her again, although awkwardly, and laughed a deep, rich sound. "A ranch wedding it is, sweetheart," he said. "You have only to pick a date."

"The sooner, the better." She slid an arm around his waist and moved them toward the door.

* * * * *

USA TODAY bestselling and RITA® Award–winning author **Marie Ferrarella** has written more than three hundred books for Harlequin, some under the name Marie Nicole. Her romances are beloved by fans worldwide. Visit her website, marieferrarella.com.

Books by Marie Ferrarella

Harlequin Special Edition

Matchmaking Mamas

Coming Home for Christmas
Dr. Forget-Me-Not
Twice a Hero, Always Her Man
Meant to Be Mine
A Second Chance for the Single Dad
Christmastime Courtship
Engagement for Two
Adding Up to Family
Bridesmaid for Hire
Coming to a Crossroads
The Late Bloomer's Road to Love

Visit the Author Profile page at
Harlequin.com for more titles.

THE RANCHER
AND THE BABY

Marie Ferrarella

To
Michael & Mark,
who were once my
younger brothers,
but through the
miracle of creative math,
are now my
older brothers

Prologue

"Mind if I cut in?"

Instantly pulled out of her mental wanderings—a defense mechanism she employed when whoever she was with was boring her out of her mind—Cassidy McCullough looked up, focusing on the man who had just tapped her dance partner's shoulder.

Not that she really needed to.

Despite the fact that he had been absent from Forever for the better part of four years, she would have recognized that voice anywhere.

It popped up in her nightmares.

Will Laredo.

Will had been her brothers' friend for as far back as she could remember—until his estrangement with his father had taken him to parts unknown, simultaneously bringing peace to her own corner of the world.

As she looked back, it felt as if her peace had been far too short-lived. Especially since, for reasons that were beyond her understanding, all three of her brothers liked this six-foot-one-inch, dirty-blond-haired irritant on two legs—which was why Cody had not only invited him to his wedding, he'd made Will one of his groomsmen.

To her surprise, Ron Jenkins, her fawning partner on the dance floor, seemed all too ready to acquiesce to Laredo's casual query. Under normal circumstances, she would have celebrated getting a different partner—but not this time.

Ron might be willing, Cassidy thought, but she damn well wasn't.

"He might not mind," Cassidy retorted defiantly, "but I do."

Rather than taking his cue and backing away, Will remained exactly where he was. Not only that, but his mouth curved in that annoying, smug way of his that she had always hated.

"Your brothers seemed to think I should dance with you."

"Maybe you should dance with one of them since they all seem to be so keen on the subject of dancing," Cassidy informed him.

Looking increasingly more uncomfortable, Ron seemed ready to fade into the shadows. "No, really, it's all right," he assured both her and Will nervously. A slight man, he appeared more than ready to surrender his claim to her.

Cassidy's eyes narrowed as she froze her partner in place. "You stop dancing with me, Ron Jenkins," she warned the man, "and it'll be the last thing you'll ever remember doing."

Rather than slow down, Cassidy sped up her tempo.

Instead of being annoyed or embarrassed at this obvious rejection, Will laughed. "You'd better do as she says, Ron. Most men around here would sooner cross an angry rattlesnake than Cassidy. I hear that her bite is a lot more deadly."

Struggling to hold on to her temper, Cassidy tossed her head. Several blond strands came loose and cascaded to her shoulders. She ignored them.

"If I were you, Laredo, I'd keep that in mind the next time you think about cutting in," she informed him, her eyes blazing.

Will inclined his head, the same amused smile slowly curving his lips. "There's not going to be a next time," he assured her.

Cassidy turned her face up to her partner's and said in a voice intentionally loud enough for Will to overhear, "Dance me by the champagne table, Ron. Now I've got something else to celebrate besides my brother Cody's wedding."

"I would," Ron told her dryly, "if you'd let me lead for a change."

Cassidy could have sworn she heard Will laughing in the background.

She wasn't going to cause a scene, she promised herself. Not here. This was the first wedding in the family, and it was Cody's day. But the moment it was over, she was going to find out which of her three brothers had put Will Laredo up to this, and they were going to pay dearly for it. They knew how she felt about him.

She'd been incensed when she found out that Cody

had gotten in contact with Will and asked if he would come and be in his wedding party. When he'd told her about it, she'd almost withdrawn herself, but Connor had talked her out of it, appealing to her sense of family.

"Cassidy," Ron said, raising his voice.

She realized by the look on the man's face that this was not the first time that Ron had tried to get her attention.

"What?" she snapped, then cleared her throat and repeated the word in a more subdued tone—silently damning Laredo. The man had the ability of messing with her mind and ruining any moment just by his being there. "What? Am I leading again?"

"I don't care about that," Ron said, which told her that she was guilty of doing just that. Again.

"Then what?" she asked.

"You're crushing my hand." He looked positively pained.

Embarrassed, as well as annoyed, Cassidy released Jenkins's hand. A more accurate description would have been that she threw it aside and out of her grasp.

To the casual observer from across the floor, had Ron's hand been detached, it would have most likely bounced on the floor and gotten wedged somewhere.

"Man up," she ordered Ron through gritted teeth and then walked away from him just as the band began to play another song.

Out of the corner of her eye, she saw Laredo shaking his head. He made no effort to hide the fact that he was observing her. She felt herself growing angry. Had they not been at her brother's wedding, she would have marched right up to him and demanded to know just what he thought he was shaking his head at.

But they *were* at Cody's wedding, so she couldn't cause a scene, couldn't hold Will accountable or wipe that smug look off his pretty-boy face. It wouldn't look right for the maid of honor to deck one of the grooms-men at her own brother's wedding.

That didn't change the fact that she really wanted to.

Cassidy squared her shoulders and went to get a glass of punch.

Hang in there, she told herself. Come tomorrow, Will Laredo was leaving Forever, going back to wherever it was that he disappeared to when he'd initially left. And then life would go back to being bearable again.

Twelve more hours, she thought. Just twelve more hours.

It felt like an eternity.

Chapter 1

Noise had never been a distraction for Olivia Blayne Santiago. She had learned how to effectively tune it out long before her law school days.

Rain, however, was another matter.

While noise, from whatever source, had always been an ongoing part of her day-to-day life and as such could be filed away in the recesses of her mind and matched later to an entire catalog of different sounds, rain demanded immediate attention.

Because rain in this part of Texas could sometimes come under the heading of being a life-or-death matter.

As the first lawyer to open a practice in Forever, Texas—a practice she now ran jointly with Cash Taylor with an eye out for further expansion—Olivia put in rather long hours. This despite the fact that she was married to the town sheriff and had a young, growing family. Between them, she and Cash handled all the legal concerns for the residents of Forever, be those concerns large or small. For the most part, Olivia could do that in her sleep.

But rain was something that always made Olivia pause, especially when it seemed to give no indication of stopping. What that meant was that a downpour could turn into a flash flood—often without any warning.

Olivia had learned to be leery of the sound of rain on her roof. It had been raining since early morning and gave no sign of stopping.

"This storm looks like it's going to be a bad one," she commented, looking at Cassidy.

Cassidy McCullough had been interning at the law firm for close to four months now, and she saw a great deal of herself in the young woman. Granted she was the firstborn in her family while Cassidy was the last, but Cassidy possessed a spark, a drive to become someone. She wasn't one to just allow herself to float along through life, enjoying each day but never having any sort of an ultimate game plan other than making it through to the end of another week. A go-getter, Cassidy was working for her as an intern even as she was taking online courses at night to complete her postgraduate degree.

They had instantly hit it off, and Olivia had taken an interest in Cassidy from the first day she had walked into the law office.

Since Cassidy hadn't said anything in response to her comment, Olivia raised her voice to get the young woman's attention. "Why don't you call it a day and go home?" she suggested.

Stationed at a small desk in the corner of Olivia's office—a desk that was piled high with stacks of paper—Cassidy glanced up from the report she'd been compiling since she'd come in that morning.

Her brow furrowed slightly as she replayed Olivia's words in her head.

"I can't leave now. I'm not anywhere near finished with this." It wasn't something she would have normally advertised since she took pride in being fast as well as thorough, but if Olivia was considering sending her home, it was something the lawyer needed to know.

Olivia listened again to the rain as it hit the windows. Was it her imagination, or had the rain gotten even more pronounced in the last five minutes? If it got any worse, she wondered if the windows could withstand it.

"If you don't leave now," Olivia warned her, "you may have to sleep on that desk, and I promise that you won't find it very comfortable."

"Why?" Cassidy asked, puzzled. "I mean, I can see why the desk wouldn't be comfortable, but why would I have to sleep on it if I went on working?" She glanced at her watch. "It's not late."

"It's later than you think," Olivia responded, then looked at the younger woman seriously. "Don't you hear that?"

"Hear what?" Cassidy asked uncertainly, scanning the room.

"That." Olivia pointed toward the window when she saw she wasn't getting through to her intern. "The rain," she added for good measure just in case she wasn't making herself clear.

Enlightened, Cassidy nodded. "Oh, that. Of course I hear the rain," she acknowledged. As far as she was concerned, a storm was no big deal. There was always going to be another one. "It was raining when I came in this morning."

"Not like this," Olivia insisted. "This sounds like it's only going to get worse, and you know what that could mean."

Cassidy nodded. "Yeah. Connor's going to be stomping around the ranch house, muttering that he can't do any of his work because it's raining too hard."

Olivia shook her head. Her intern was misreading the situation. "I think you should go home," she said.

Cassidy still saw no need for her evacuation. "To watch Connor stomping around?"

"No, to keep from being washed away," Olivia insisted. "You should know better than I do just how quick these flash floods can hit."

"I know," Cassidy agreed, "but there hasn't been one in a couple of years and even that one was over before it practically started." She waved away what she felt was Olivia's needless concern. "Besides, I can take care of myself."

Olivia sighed as she rolled her eyes. "Lord, did you ever pick the right profession. Someday, you are going to make one hell of a lawyer, but in order to do that, Cassidy, you're going to need to stay alive. Now, I might not be a native to this area, but I've seen what a flash flood can do—"

"I can swim," Cassidy insisted stubbornly.

"All well and good," Olivia replied patiently as she began to pack up some things on her desk, "but your truck can't. Now, I'm not going to spend the next hour arguing with you. I'm your boss and what I say goes. So now hear this—go home."

Cassidy retired her pen and the stack of papers she'd

been going through with a sigh. "Okay, like you said, you're the boss."

Olivia smiled at her. "Yes, and I've been arguing a lot longer than you have. Although, given what your brother said to me at the wedding a few weeks ago, you were born arguing."

Cassidy paused to give her boss a penetrating look. "Which brother was that?" she asked conversationally.

Olivia wasn't being taken in for a moment. Finished packing her briefcase, she snapped the locks into place. Behind her, the wind and rain were rattling the window. "I never reveal my sources."

"Isn't that what a journalist usually says?"

"Where do you think they got it from?" Olivia asked with a smug smile. Packed, she rose from her chair. "I'm not sure if my kids can recognize me in the daylight. Although…" She glanced out the window again. The world outside the small, one-story building that housed her law firm had suddenly become shrouded in darkness. "There's not all that much daylight to be had, and it's getting scarcer by the minute."

Raising her voice, Olivia called out to her partner. "Cash, we're locking up."

The words were no sooner out of her mouth than the lights overhead went out.

"None too soon, if you ask me," Cash Taylor commented, poking his head into the office. "Is it just us," he asked, flipping the light switch off and on with no change in illumination, "or do you think the whole town's lost power?"

"Lord, I hope not," Olivia commented with feeling. "The only thing worse than cooking over a hot stove is *not* having a hot stove to cook over."

"You have a fireplace, don't you?" Cassidy asked as she gathered a selected stack of papers together so she could review them that evening.

As far as Olivia was concerned, a fireplace was good for one thing and one thing only. "Yes, but that's for cuddling in front of with my husband after the kids are asleep in bed."

Cassidy grinned at this human glimpse into her boss's life. "In a pinch, it can also be used for cooking dinner as long as you're not trying to make anything too elaborate."

"Elaborate?" Olivia echoed. "I'd just settle for it being passably edible."

Now that she thought of it, Olivia had never made any reference to a meal she'd taken pride in preparing. The woman's talents clearly lay in another direction.

"Maybe you should stop at Miss Joan's on your way home," Cassidy suggested tactfully.

Cash seconded the suggestion. "It'll give my step-grandmother something to talk about."

"No offense, Cash, and I obviously haven't known her nearly as long as either one of you have, but I've never known Miss Joan to ever be in need for something to talk about. She's everybody's go-to person when it comes to getting the latest information about absolutely *everything*."

There was a sudden flash of lightning followed almost immediately by an ominous crack of thunder, causing all of them to involuntarily glance up.

"Well, if we don't all get a move on, this rain just might turn nasty enough to give *everybody* something to talk about—provided they're able to talk and aren't under five feet of water," Cash observed.

With one hand at each of their backs, Cash ushered

the two women out of the main office and toward the front door.

The moment she opened the front door, Olivia knew that she'd made the right call to have them leave early. The rain was coming down relentlessly.

It was the kind of rain that placed raising an umbrella against the downpour in the same category as tilting at windmills. Olivia turned up the hood on her raincoat. Cash did the same with his jacket. Cassidy had come in wearing her Stetson, a high school graduation gift from her oldest brother, Connor. She held on to it with one hand while pressing her shoulder bag with its newly packed contents against her with the other.

Locking up, Olivia turned away from the door. She was having second thoughts about her estimation of the rain's ferocity.

"Maybe you should come stay at our place," she suggested to Cassidy.

"And interfere with your plans for the fireplace? I wouldn't dream of it," Cassidy responded with a grin. "I'll be fine. See you in the morning, boss."

The rain seemed to only grow fiercer, coming down at an angle and lashing at anyone brave enough to venture out of their shelter.

Taking two steps toward her vehicle, Olivia turned toward her intern. "Last chance!" she called out to Cassidy.

Rather than answer her, Cassidy just waved her hand overhead as she made a dash for her four-by-four. Reaching it, she climbed in behind the wheel and pulled the door closed behind her.

Utterly soaked, Cassidy sat for a moment, listening to the rain pounding on the roof of her vehicle. This really was pretty bad, she silently acknowledged. Half of her expected to see an ark floating by with an old man at its helm, surrounded by two of everything.

Well, she couldn't just sit here, she told herself. She needed to get home. Pulling the seat-belt strap up and over her shoulder, she tucked the metal tongue into the slot.

"I better get going before Connor and Cole come out looking for me," she murmured. Connor got antsy when he didn't have anything to do.

Starting her vehicle, Cassidy turned on her lights and put the manual transmission into Drive before she turned on the radio.

Apparently music wasn't going to be on the agenda that afternoon, Cassidy realized with a sigh. The reception was intermittent at best—and hardly that for the most part. When a high-pitch squawk replaced the song that kept fading in and out, Cassidy gave up and shut off the radio.

With the rain coming down even harder, she turned the windshield wipers up to their highest setting. The blades all but groaned as they slapped against the glass, fighting what was turning out to be a losing battle against the rain.

Exercising caution—something, to hear them talk, that all three of her brothers seemed to believe she didn't possess—Cassidy reduced her speed to fifteen miles an hour.

Three miles out of town, her visibility went from poor to next to nonexistent.

At this rate, it would take her forever to get home, and the rain was just getting worse. She needed to hole up someplace until the rain subsided. Remembering an old, empty cabin she and the others used to play in as kids, Cassidy decided that it might be prudent to seek at least temporary shelter there until the worst of the rain let up.

The cabin was less than half a mile away.

If the rain *didn't* let up, she thought when the cabin finally came into view, then she would be stuck there for the duration of this downpour with nothing to eat except for the half consumed candy bar she had shoved into her bag.

Her stomach growled, reminding her that she had skipped lunch.

Leaning forward in her seat, she looked up at the sky—or what she could make out of it.

"C'mon, let up," she coaxed. "The forecast specifically said 'rain.' It didn't say a word about 'floods' or the end of the world."

Cassidy sighed again, even louder this time. She held on to the steering wheel tightly as she struggled to keep her vehicle from veering off the trail. Ordinarily, veering off wouldn't have been a big deal, but just as Olivia had predicted, the rain had become ferocious, turning what was normally a tiny creek into a rapidly flowing river.

One wrong turn on her part, and her truck would be *in* that river.

And then, just when it seemed to be at its very worst, the rain began to let up, going from what had all the characteristics of becoming a full-blown monsoon to just a regular fierce downpour. Even so, Cassidy knew she needed to get her truck onto higher ground before she found herself suddenly stuck and unable to drive—or worse.

The cabin was still her best bet. From what she remembered—and she really hadn't paid all that much attention to this aspect when she was a kid—the cabin *was* on high ground.

Most likely not high enough to enable her to get a signal for her cell phone, she thought darkly. What that meant was that she wouldn't be able to call Connor to assure him that she was all right. As much as she talked about being independent and being able to take care of herself, she didn't like doing that to her big brother. Connor had been both mother and father to the rest of them for the last ten years. What that had entailed was giving up his own dreams of a college education and a subsequent career. He'd done it in order to become their guardian when their father died three days after Connor had turned eighteen.

While she was grateful to Connor for everything he had done and appreciated the fact that he cared about her and the others, she was equally convinced that Connor needed a family of his own—a wife and at least a couple of kids, if not more—to care for and to worry about.

About to turn her truck in order to get it to higher ground, Cassidy thought she saw something out of the corner of her eye. It was bobbing up and down in the swollen water.

She thought it was rectangular—and pink.

You're losing your mind, Cassidy silently lectured herself.

The next second, her body went rigid as she heard something.

She couldn't have just heard—

No, that was just her imagination, getting the better of her. That was probably just some animal making that sound. It couldn't have been—

A baby!

"Damn it," Cassidy bit out, "that couldn't be—" And yet, she really thought she heard a baby crying.

You're really letting your imagination run away with you, she silently lectured.

Even though she was convinced she was wrong, Cassidy knew she couldn't just shrug it off. She had to look again—just in case.

It wasn't safe to turn the truck on a saturated road. Cassidy did the only thing she could in order to give herself peace of mind.

She threw her truck into Reverse.

Driving backward as carefully as she was able, she watched the road to see if she could catch sight of the bobbing pink whatever-it-was.

And then, her eyes glued to her rearview mirror, Cassidy saw it.

She wasn't crazy; there *was* something bobbing up and down in the water. Something rectangular and, from what she could make out, it appeared to be plastic. A plastic tub was caught up in the rushing waters and, for some reason that seemed to defy all logic, it was still upright and afloat.

If that wasn't miraculous enough, Cassidy could have sworn that the baby she'd thought she'd heard was in the bobbing pink rectangular plastic tub.

With the truck still in Reverse, Cassidy stepped on the gas pedal, pushing it as far down as she dared and prayed.

Prayed harder than she ever had before.

Chapter 2

The rear of Cassidy's truck fishtailed, and for one long, heart-stopping moment, she thought the truck was going to slide straight down into the rushing floodwater.

Everything was happening at a blinding speed.

Cassidy wasn't sure just how she managed it, but somehow she kept the truck on solid ground. Not only that, but with her heart in her throat, she backed up the vehicle far enough so that it was slightly ahead of the approaching bobbing tub—all this while the four-by-four was facing backward.

She knew what she had to do.

If Cassidy had had time to think it through, she would have seen at least half a dozen ways that this venture she was about to undertake could end badly.

But there *wasn't* any time to think, there was only time to react.

Throwing open the door on the driver's side, Cassidy jumped out of the truck and hit the ground running— as well as sliding. The ground beneath her boots was incredibly slippery.

The rain was no longer coming down in blinding sheets. Although it was still raining hard, she barely noticed it. All she noticed, all she *saw*, was the crying baby in the plastic tub. And all she knew was that if she couldn't reach it in time, the baby would drown.

It still might.

They very well could *both* drown, but Cassidy knew she had to do something, had to at least *try* to save the baby. Otherwise, if she played it safe, if she did nothing at all, she would never be able to live with herself. Choosing her own safety over the life of another—especially if that life belonged to a baby—was totally unacceptable to her.

Cassidy wasn't even aware of the fact that as she rushed to the water's edge and dove in, she yelled. Yelled at the top of her lungs the way she had when she and her brothers would engage in the all-too-dangerous, mindlessly death-defying games they used to play as children. The one that came to her mind as she dove was when they would catapult from a makeshift swing— composed of a rope looped around a tree branch—into the river below. Then the ear-piercing noise had been the product of a combination of released adrenaline and fearlessness. What prompted her to yell now as she dove into the water was the unconscious hope that she could survive this venture the way she had survived the ones in her childhood. Then she had been competing with her brothers—and Laredo. Now she was competing against the laws of nature and praying that she would win just one more time.

The water was strangely warm—or maybe it was that she was just totally numb to the cold. She only had one focus. Her eyes were trained on the plastic tub and its passenger as she fought the rushing water to cut the distance between her and the screaming baby.

The harder she swam, the farther away she felt the tub was getting.

Keeping her head above the water, Cassidy let loose with another piercing yell and filled her lungs with as much air as she could, hoping that somehow that would help keep her alive and magically propel her to the baby. There was absolutely no logical way it could help; she only knew that somehow it had to.

Will Laredo had no idea what he was doing out here. Ordinarily he wasn't given to following through on dumb ideas, and this was definitely a lapse on his part. For all he knew, the colt he was looking for could have found his way back to the stable and was there now, dry and safe, while he was out here on something that could only be called a fool's errand.

It was just that when that bolt of lightning had streaked across the sky and then thunder had crashed practically right over the stable less than a minute later, it caused Britches to charge right out of the stable and through the open field as if the devil himself was after him.

Seeing the colt flee, Will ran to his truck and took out after it as if he had no choice.

Will knew it was stupid, but he felt a special connection to the sleek black colt. Britches had been born

shortly after he'd returned to take over his late father's ranch, and he'd felt that if he lost the colt, somehow, symbolically, that meant he was going to lose the
ranch—and wind up being the ne'er-do-well his father
had always claimed he was destined to be.

It was asinine to let that goad him into coming out
here, searching for the colt, when the weather conditions made it utterly impossible to follow the animal's
trail. Any hoofprints had been washed away the second they were made.

Hell, if he didn't turn around right now, *he* would
wind up being washed away, as well.

His best bet was to take shelter until the worst of this
passed. These sorts of storms almost always came out of
nowhere, raged for a short amount of time, did their damage and then just disappeared as if they'd never existed.

But right now, he was wetter than he could remember
being in a very long time and he wanted to—

Suddenly, he snapped to attention. "What the hell
was that?"

The yell he thought he heard instantly propelled him
back over a decade and a half, to a time when estrangement and spirit-breaking responsibilities hadn't entered
his life yet. A time when the company of friends was
enough to ease the torment of belittling words voiced
by a father who was too angry at the hand that life had
dealt him to realize that he was driving away the only
thing he *did* have.

There it was again!

Will hit the brakes with as much pressure as he
dared, knowing the danger of slamming down too hard.
He didn't feel like being forced to fish his truck out of
this newly created rushing river. Opening the door, he

strained to hear the sound that had caused him to stop his truck in the first place.

He waited in vain.

The howl of the wind mocked him.

He was hearing things.

"You don't belong out here anymore, Laredo," he said, upbraiding himself. "What the hell are you trying to prove by going out looking for a colt that probably has more sense than you do? Go home before you drown out here like some damn brainless turkey staring up at the sky during a downpour."

Disgusted as well as frustrated, Will leaned out to grab hold of the door handle—the wind had pushed the door out as far as it would go. Just as he began to pull it toward him, he heard it for a third time.

That same yell.

"Damn it, I'm *not* hearing things," he swore, arguing with himself.

Getting out of the truck, he squinted against the rain and looked out at the rushing water. Yesterday, this entire length of wet land hardly contained enough water to qualified being called a creek; now it was on its way to becoming a full-fledged raging river.

Will's square jaw dropped as he realized that he wasn't looking at debris being swept away in the center of the rushing water. It was some sort of washtub, a washtub with what looked to be a doll in it.

That wasn't a doll; that was a baby!

He was already running to the water's edge when his field of vision widened and he saw her. Saw that Cassidy was fighting against the current and was desperately trying to reach the baby.

It hit him like a punch in his gut.

That was what he'd heard!

He'd heard Cassidy screaming out that yell, the one that Cole had come up with so many summers ago. It had something to do with making them band together, giving them the strength of five instead of just one. They'd been kids then.

She wasn't a kid anymore and there were all sorts of things he wanted to yell at her now, all of them ultimately boiling down to the word *idiot*.

But that was *after* he got to her.

And before that could happen, he had to save Cassidy's damn fool hide. Hers and that baby she was trying to rescue.

Where the hell had it come from?

He had no time to try to figure that out now. Later, that was for later.

Will gave himself a running start, using the increasing speed he built up to propel him as he dove into the water.

He swam the way he never swam before—as if his life depended on it.

As if *her* life depended on it.

Hers and that baby's.

Divorcing himself from any other thoughts—from anger, fear, astonishment—Will focused entirely on the goal he'd just set for himself. Rescuing the woman who took special delight in filleting him with her tongue whenever the opportunity arose, and the baby he'd never seen before, both of whom had just one thing in common: they had absolutely no business being out here under these conditions.

And they had one more thing in common: both of them were going to die here if he didn't reach them in time.

* * *

Her arms were getting really, really heavy, but she knew that if she gave in to the feeling, gave in to the very thought of how exhausted she felt, both she and most likely this baby were not going to live to see another sunrise.

Hell, they weren't going to live to see another half hour if she didn't find a way to save them.

Her lungs aching so much that they hurt, she still somehow managed to tap into an extra burst of energy. She stretched out her arms as far as they would go with each stroke, and she finally managed to get close enough to the baby to just glide her fingertips along the lip of the tub.

C'mon, just a little farther, just a little farther, she frantically urged herself.

"Gotcha!" Cassidy cried in almost giddy triumph, her fingertips securing just the very rim of the tub. Her heart pounding madly, she pulled the tub to her. "I've got you, baby," she all but sobbed. "I've got you!"

The problem was, she'd used up all of her energy, and, while she'd finally, *finally* managed to reach the baby, both she and it were still in the middle of the rushing water.

The situation didn't exactly look hopeful.

And then Cassidy felt something snaking around her waist and holding her fast as it grabbed her from behind. Exhausted beyond belief, unable to turn to see what had caught her, Cassidy still frantically cast about for some way to free herself and the baby before whatever it was that was holding her dragged them down to the bottom of this newly formed river.

With no weapon within reach, Cassidy frantically

pulled back her arm and struck hard at whatever was holding on to her with her elbow. Her only hope was to use the element of surprise to drive off whatever creature had ensnared her.

"Ow! Damn it, Cassidy, I should have my head examined for not letting you drown instead of trying to save you," the deep voice behind her grumbled.

She could *feel* the words as they rumbled out because the man behind her had such a tight hold on her; his chest was pressed up against her back closer than the label on a jar of jam.

"Laredo?" she cried, absolutely astonished even as she struggled to keep the very last ounce of energy from seeping out of her body. Confusion vibrated through her. "What the hell are you trying to do?"

"I thought that was rather obvious," he bit off coldly, both his breath and his words grazing the back of her head. "I'm trying to save you from drowning in this damn flash flood." Before she could offer any sort of a protest, he turned the tables on her. "What the hell are *you* doing out here?"

She had a death grip on the baby's tub, which in turn kept the baby from being swept away by the river. "What does it look like I'm doing?" she challenged angrily.

"Proving me wrong," he answered, still keeping one arm firmly secured around her torso as he continued to slowly, powerfully, make his way back to the bank.

"Okay, I'm waiting," Cassidy retorted weakly, mentally bracing herself.

Whatever was coming was not going to be flattering. She knew him too well to expect anything else. She also knew him well enough to know he was bound to save her because of the same ingrained sense of honor they all shared.

"Why are you wrong?" she gasped when he didn't say anything.

"Because you *can* still find new ways to mess up, just when I thought you'd exhausted all the available possibilities."

Anger appeared out of nowhere, giving her an unexpected surge of energy. She knew it wouldn't last, so she talked quickly.

"There was a baby in the river. What was I supposed to do?" she demanded weakly. "Wave at it?"

"No, but drowning with it wasn't exactly going to help anything," Will snapped as he finally managed to reach the riverbank with both of them in tow.

The baby was still crying. It was loud enough to almost drown out the sound of their voices.

"I wasn't drowning," she informed him.

She meant to snap the answer at him, but all she could manage was an indignant gasp. Her last surge of energy was all but gone. But he had a way of making her so angry, she still felt compelled to argue.

"I had everything under control. I didn't need your help."

Exhausted himself from fighting against the current, Will fell back against the bank. It was still raining, but at this point, he was hardly aware of it.

"Right." The single word mocked her.

She would have peppered him with biting rhetoric if she only had the energy. As it was, taking in a full breath was about all she could manage. She couldn't remember *ever* being this exhausted.

The moment she had at least an ounce of extra energy to spare, she would direct it toward the baby whose cries had turned into subdued whimpers—and that, in reality, worried her more than the cries did.

So, for the moment, all she could say in response to Will as they both lay on the bank, getting wetter and silently grateful that neither one of them would become a statistic today in this latest battle with Mother Nature, was, "Thanks for the thought, though."

"Any time," he murmured.

In the distance, as the rain began to swiftly retreat, he could have sworn that he heard a horse whinnying.

Or maybe it was a colt.

His mouth curved ever so slightly.

Britches was safe after all.

Chapter 3

Cassidy hated to admit it, even if it was just to her-self, but there was no getting away from it. Laredo had a great smile that warmed up a cold room and could easily set even the coolest heart on fire, at least mo-mentarily. It was exactly for this reason why she would never even allow him to suspect that she felt this way.

Ever since she could remember, Will Laredo at-tracted the female of the species as if they were thirsty jackrabbits and he was the only watering hole for more than two hundred miles. Cody and Cole—and even Connor on occasion—seemed to think that was one of Laredo's attributes. She, on the other hand, viewed it in an entirely different light.

It just gave the man an even bigger head than he al-ready had.

When she saw the corner of his mouth curve just

now as they both lay on the bank, gasping for breath, all these other thoughts came crowding into her head. Like how this resembled the aftermath of a marathon lovemaking session with the two of them lying so close together, breathless and grateful.

She was delirious, she angrily upbraided herself.

Cassidy squelched her thoughts. She was exhausted and consequently—although she would have rather died right here on the spot than admit it—vulnerable. This was *definitely* not the time to have thoughts like that marching through her brain.

People did stupid things when they felt vulnerable—even her. Stupid things that would go on to haunt them for the rest of their lives.

Well, not her.

"What are you smiling about?" she demanded breathlessly, expecting him to say something about getting to play the superhero to her damsel in distress—or something equally irritating.

She braced herself to lash out and put him in his place.

But Laredo surprised her by saying, "Britches made it."

Britches? Her eyes narrowed into probing slits. Right now, the baby they had saved was quiet, and she was beyond grateful for that.

Was Laredo referring to the baby?

"Is that some kind of a nickname?" she challenged.

Was this yet another way to talk down to her? Even so, she had to admit that she was glad Laredo had showed up when he did. Despite her defensive words to the contrary, she really wasn't 100 percent convinced that she would have been able to make it back to the bank with the baby without Laredo's help.

But if she even hinted at that, he would never let her live it down.

"No, it's a name," Will told her mildly, "for my colt."

"Your colt?" she repeated.

Was he talking about his father's old gun? As she recalled, Jake Laredo had kept an old Colt .45 that he claimed had belonged·to his great-great-grandfather, handed down to him by Stephen Austin, the man who'd founded the Texas Rangers. There was more to the story, but she'd always pretended to be disinterested whenever he mentioned it. In her opinion, Laredo's head was big enough. She didn't need to add to it by acting as if she cared about anything he had to say.

"A colt's a male horse under the age of four," he told her patiently.

Some of her energy had to be returning because she could feel her back going up. Heroic endeavors or not, Laredo was talking down to her again, Cassidy thought, annoyed.

"I know what a colt is," she snapped, or thought she did. Afraid of scaring the baby again, she lowered her voice. "I just didn't know you had one."

"It's a horse ranch," he reminded her, referring to the property that his father had left to him—something she was aware of since she was in Olivia Santiago's office when he'd been called in and told about his father's will. The fact that his father had left it to him had rendered Will speechless. She'd almost felt sorry for him--almost. "What else am I going to have?"

"Debts."

The answer came out before Cassidy could censor

herself. It was Laredo's fault. He had that sort of effect on her. The next moment, remorse set in. He was the bane of her existence, but he didn't deserve that.

"Sorry," she mumbled, "I didn't mean to say that."

"Sure you did." Instead of being annoyed, he let her words pass. "Because it's true," he admitted matter-of-factly.

Everyone in town knew that his father had had money troubles. They'd only gotten worse over time. There was no reason to believe that anything had changed just before he died. Jake Laredo had sought refuge in the bottom of a bottle, drinking to the point of numbness, after which he'd pass out. Subsequently, the ranch had fallen into disrepair and ruin. When he'd gotten the letter from Olivia about his father's death, he'd returned only to put the old man into the ground. He'd been surprised that the ranch was still standing and that there were a couple of horses—rather emaciated at that—still in the stable.

Will saw it as a challenge.

"It's probably why he left the place to me," Will was saying, more to himself than to her. "It was his final way of sticking it to me."

Still lying on the bank, Cassidy turned her head toward him. She decided it had to be what she'd just gone through. The experience had to have rattled her brain to some degree because she was actually feeling sorry for Laredo—a little, she quickly qualified. But the feeling was there nonetheless.

"Someone else would just walk away," she pointed out to him.

"Someone else isn't me," he told Cassidy. "Besides, I can't walk away. If I did, that old man would have the last laugh."

The last laugh would have meant that he couldn't do the honorable thing, couldn't pay off his father's debts, couldn't make a go of the ranch. In effect, it would have made him no better than Jake Laredo had been. Or at least that was the way Will saw it.

"I don't think he's laughing much where he is now," Cassidy said quietly.

Meaning hell, Will thought. He almost laughed at that but checked himself in time. "Well, I see you haven't lost it."

Her eyebrows drew together in a puzzled look. She was actually trying to be nice to the man. Served her right. What the hell was he talking about?

"Lost what?" she asked.

"That knack of saying the first thing that comes into your head without filtering it," he told her.

Cassidy had to admit that she felt more comfortable sparring with the cocky so-and-so, receiving stinging barbs and giving back in kind.

She could feel the adrenaline starting to rush through her veins again. She was definitely coming around, Cassidy thought.

"Hey," she cried, bolting upright as the realization suddenly hit her. "It's stopped raining."

"And that baby's stopped crying," Will added. "It's like Nature's taking a break."

The moment he said it, Cassidy's head snapped back around. What had struck her subconsciously now hit her head-on. Laredo was right; the baby in the tub was no longer crying.

Was that because…?

Her heart froze as she looked down at the infant in

the tub again. And then she exhaled the breath she'd just sucked in and held a second ago.

Wonder of wonders, the baby was sleeping. For a moment, she'd thought the worst.

"I guess all that crying took everything out of him— or her," Cassidy added as an afterthought.

"Him or her? You don't know if it's a boy or a girl?" he asked her incredulously.

Rather than answer him directly, she said, "Well, it was crying so hard I couldn't think, so it's probably a male," she speculated.

He was trying to nail Cassidy down, something that had never been easy to do. "Then you've never seen this baby before?" he questioned.

"Well, I haven't been to the new-baby store recently, so no, I've never seen this baby before. Not until I saw it floating by in that flash flood that used to be a creek," Cassidy added.

Laredo looked at her skeptically, which indicated that he didn't believe her. But then, she supposed that just this once she couldn't really fault him. If she were in his place, she wouldn't have believed him, either.

"No, seriously, I've never seen this baby before." She looked at the sleeping infant and shook her head. The whole thing seemed almost macabre as well as incredible. "Who sticks a baby into a plastic tub?" she asked.

"Someone trying to save its life would be my guess," Will said, speculating. "Maybe it was someone who's new to the area. They were driving through and got caught up in the flash flood—this could have been their last-ditch attempt to save the baby."

She had a question for him. "Who drives around with a plastic tub in their car?"

"Someone who had no place to live," he guessed. The expression on her face told him that she thought he was stretching it. "Hey, I don't have all the answers, but it's a possibility."

"It's also a possibility that the kid's mother or father is looking for him or her right at this very minute," Cassidy said, thinking how she would feel in that person's place.

Scared out of her mind.

The baby began to stir. Any second it was going to wake up and start crying again, she thought, looking at the infant intently.

And then it was no longer a speculation.

The baby they had rescued was awake again. The next moment, it began to cry.

Will recalled something he'd overheard a young mother saying. "At this age, they only cry for a reason. It's either hungry or wet," he told her, getting up.

"Or maybe it just doesn't like being crammed in a little plastic tub." Speculation aside, she lifted the infant out of the confining tub. And as she did so, she also quickly drew back a section of the diaper and took a peek. "He's also wet," she pronounced, although that could have been the result of being caught up in the flood.

"He?" Will echoed as he stood up.

"He," Cassidy repeated. "It's a boy." Holding the baby to her chest, she started to get up only to have Will reach down for the infant. She tightened her hold. "What are you doing?"

"You don't want to risk falling over with the baby as you get up," he told her as if it was a common occurrence for her. "I'm already up."

"Good for you," Cassidy commented sarcastically. Grudgingly she let Will take the baby, then popped up right beside him and reached to take the child back.

But Will didn't release him. "What are you planning on doing?" he asked.

"Well, I certainly don't want to have a tug-of-war with this child if that's what you're thinking." It came out like an accusation.

Will didn't rise to the bait. "No, what I'm thinking is that this baby needs to be seen by one of the doctors at the clinic." It wasn't a suggestion.

Okay, Cassidy allowed, so maybe Laredo was capable of having a decent thought once in a blue moon. But she wasn't about to let him think that he'd gotten the jump on her.

"That's just where I'm taking him," she informed Will coolly.

But he wasn't budging.

Now what? she thought, exasperated.

"You planning on tossing him in the back of the truck?" Will asked.

Her eyebrows drew together like light blond thunderbolts, aimed right for his heart. "Of course not," she snapped.

He continued to hold on to the infant protectively. The baby was beginning to fuss. But Will's attention was focused on the woman who stood in his way. "Okay, then what?"

"Um—"

To Cassidy's surprise, he relinquished his hold on the infant, who was now beginning to cry. "C'mon, you hold the baby, I'll drive."

It really irked her when he took the lead this way,

as if he was in control of everything, including her. "I don't need you to drive us."

Standing right in front of her, Will drew himself up to his full height. Although Cassidy would have never admitted it out loud, he did make a formidable obstacle.

"You planning on holding him in one arm while driving with the other hand?" he asked, then challenged, "On these roads?"

She knew he was right and hated giving him that. But unless she was willing to stand here, listening to the baby crying progressively louder—possibly even endangering this baby—she had no choice.

"Okay, fine," she bit out, "*you* drive—but we're coming back for my truck."

He nodded absently. "I've got no problem with that," he said, leading the way back to his vehicle.

"What's that supposed to mean?" Cassidy asked.

He made her crazy. It felt as if everything out of his mouth came with a hidden meaning. Plus, Cassidy found she had to really lengthen her stride in order to try to keep up with him. But there was no way she was going to ask Laredo to slow down. She'd never done it with any of her brothers—all of whom were taller than she was—and she sure as hell wasn't going to do it with Laredo.

Instead, Cassidy glared at the back of his head all the way to his truck.

When they reached it, Will opened the door directly behind the driver's seat and held it open for her.

She immediately took it to mean he regarded her as subservient to him. "What's wrong with the front seat?" she asked.

Will continued to hold the door open for her. "Backseat's safer for the baby."

Cassidy blew out a breath. Damn it, Will was right, and she hated that.

When he took hold of her elbow, she pulled free and nearly jabbed him with it. "I can get into the truck on my own."

Unfazed, Will said, "I'm just looking out for the baby."

Cassidy scowled at him. "Just because you *helped* save him doesn't automatically make you his fairy godmother."

"I kind of see myself more like a guardian angel than a fairy godmother," he deadpanned. "They've got bigger wings." He added that with a sly wink that made her desperately want to punch him if only her arms weren't full.

Cassidy bit her bottom lip to keep from saying something caustic. The next moment, as she seated herself directly behind the driver's seat, she felt Laredo reaching over her.

So much for silence, she thought, giving up. "Okay, what the hell do you think you're trying to do?" Cassidy demanded.

"I *think* I'm trying to get this seat belt around you and the baby. We're liable to hit a skid in this weather, and I don't want the two of you suddenly flying out the window—or worse," he added with deliberate emphasis.

"Since when did you become so damn thoughtful?" Cassidy asked coldly.

Her eyes widened. Was it her imagination, or had Laredo's hand just slid over her lap as he stepped back after fastening the seat belt?

"I've always been thoughtful, Cassidy. You've just been too mean-tempered to notice," he answered mildly.

Before she had a chance to snap at him, Will shut her door and went over to get into the front seat.

"I am *not* mean-tempered," she informed him, struggling to hold on to that same temper.

Will shut the door and secured his own seat belt before starting the vehicle. Only then did he raise his eyes to the rearview mirror to look at her. "I've got a town full of people who might argue with you about that," he replied mildly.

Her eyes met his in the mirror. She could feel her temper heating, but there was no time to give Laredo a piece of her mind or take him down. The baby had begun to cry in earnest now. Even if the infant was just wet and hungry, she had no dry clothes, diapers or food to offer him, so the sooner they got to the clinic, the better.

"Just drive!" she ordered.

"Yes, ma'am," Will responded.

She didn't need to see his face to know that his mouth had assumed that all-too-familiar smirk she knew and hated. She could hear it in his voice.

Okay, Laredo. I need you to help me get this baby to the medical clinic. But once we do and this little guy is someone else's problem, I am going to become your worst nightmare.

She paused for a moment, savoring that thought. And anticipating.

Even worse than I already am.

Chapter 4

The infant hadn't stopped crying since before they'd gotten into the vehicle. The wailing noise was making it hard for Will to think. That, added to the fact that the rain had picked up again, was enough to really put him on edge.

"You sure he's not hurt?" Will asked, glancing at Cassidy over his shoulder.

She raised her eyes to meet his.

"I have no idea, but I know that he will be if you keep taking your eyes off the road like that. It's starting to rain harder again," Cassidy pointed out. Her nerves were getting the better of her.

"Gee, really?" Will asked, feigning surprise. "I hadn't noticed."

He hated the way Cassidy treated him, as if he was totally oblivious to things. She'd done that for as far back as he could remember, and at times he had to admit it almost amused him. But right now, with the baby crying and the roads growing progressively more hazardous, he was having a rough time staying calm.

Although he did his best to pretend otherwise, no one could get to him the way Cassidy could. There was just something about the way she talked, the way she tossed her head, the smug, superior gleam in her eyes, that just made him want to get back at her and teach her a lesson.

Just what form that lesson would take he hadn't worked out yet. But if he was going to remain in Forever, even for a little while, he had a feeling that day would come —and most likely sooner than either one of them reckoned, most of all her.

"That doesn't surprise me," Cassidy told him, acting as if she'd taken his words at face value. "But do us all a favor and try to pay attention. I've got way too many things to do to die out here with you today."

He laughed shortly. "Funny, I was thinking the same thing."

"Funny," she said, mimicking his voice, "I didn't know you *could* think."

He'd almost reached the end of his supply of patience. "You really want to get into this now?" Will asked, his voice becoming ominous and foreboding.

"What I *want*," Cassidy informed him, "is to get into town while I still have any hearing left." She'd tried everything in her rather limited arsenal of tricks with this baby—rocking him, trying to talk to him, patting his back—all to no avail. "How can something so little make such a loud noise?"

Will focused his attention back on the road—just in

time to avoid driving into a large branch that had broken off a nearby tree. Another casualty of the storm.

Heart pounding, he drove around it. "Maybe his crying like that is a good thing. At least it means he's got healthy lungs."

Laredo was doing it again, she thought. Acting like a know-it-all. He wasn't here in the backseat with the baby blowing out *his* eardrums. "Where did you get your degree, Dr. Laredo?"

"Same place you learned to be a shrew—no, wait, you just came by that naturally, didn't you?"

Okay, she'd had enough, Cassidy thought. "Stop the truck," she ordered.

Thinking that something was seriously wrong, Will did as she asked. His thoughts immediately zeroed in on the baby.

"Why? What's wrong?" he asked, twisting in his seat.

They were right on the outskirts of Forever. The clinic wasn't all that far off. Rain or no rain, she could walk from here.

Cassidy began to undo her seat belt. "I can't listen to you blathering on like this. I can walk to the clinic from here."

Biting off a curse, Will started the vehicle again. Gravity had Cassidy falling back in her seat. Because she'd inadvertently squeezed him, the baby was wailing even harder than he had been before.

"Damn you, Laredo," she cried. "What the hell do you thinking you're doing *now*?"

"Driving a crazy woman and the baby she's holding to the clinic," he bit out. "Now shut up and hold on."

She didn't want to give him the satisfaction of thinking that she was obeying, but by the same token, she didn't want to get into another fight with him when he was this angry already. So she did as he told her.

She really didn't have any other choice.

Cassidy remained in the truck and counted off the minutes in her head until they reached the clinic.

Rather than park the truck in the lot—which was the emptiest he could remember ever seeing it since he'd returned to Forever—Will parked directly in front of the medical clinic's front door.

Just in time, he judged.

Daniel Davenport, the doctor who had reopened the clinic when he'd arrived in Forever several years ago, was just locking up.

"Hey, Doc," Will called out, raising his voice in order to be heard above the crying baby and the howling wind. "Got time for one more?"

Dan turned. For the first time since he'd begun to run the clinic, the facility was entirely empty. He'd sent his partner and the two nurses who worked with them home over half an hour ago. Just in case someone did come by, he'd hung back, giving it another half hour.

Thirty minutes had come and gone. He wanted to get home to his family. Dan figured there was no point in waiting any longer. But obviously there was, he thought, looking from the man who'd just called out to him to the young woman who was emerging out of Will's somewhat battered truck holding what appeared to be an infant in her arms.

Dan caught himself thinking that they were as unlikely a couple as he had ever seen. For the most part, Dan was oblivious to most of the gossip and the personal details that made the rounds at gathering places like Miss Joan's Diner and Murphy's Saloon. His attention was exclusively focused on helping and healing the people who sought him out at the clinic.

But even *he* knew that whenever the newly returned Will Laredo and Cassidy McCullough were within spitting distance of each other, they usually did. Neither could keep their temper holstered, especially not Cassidy.

His eyes narrowed slightly as they focused on the smallest player in this group. There was no way in God's green earth that baby was theirs.

"Caught me just in time," Dan said, addressing Will as he unlocked the door he had just locked. Pocketing the key, Dan pushed the door opened with the flat of his hand. "I take it that 'one more' you're referring to is the baby?"

"It is," Will answered.

"Where did you find it?" Dan asked, ushering in the trio. He didn't waste time asking if the infant belonged to either one of them. He knew it couldn't.

"Bobbing up and down in the creek, except it was more like a rushing river at the time," Cassidy told him.

Once inside, she pushed back her wet hair and turned to face the doctor. "I'm thinking of calling him Moses," she quipped, looking down at the squalling baby, "since I pulled him out of the river."

"More like out of a rubber tub in the river," Will corrected.

"Okay, maybe you think we should call him Rubber Ducky," Cassidy retorted sarcastically, turning to glare at Will.

"Back up. The baby was in a rubber *tub*?" Dan questioned, looking from one to the other, waiting for enlightenment.

Cassidy nodded. "It was probably the only floatation device his mother—"

"Or father—" Will pointedly interjected. Although he had enjoyed neither, he knew by watching the Mc-Culloughs that parental feelings were not the exclusive domain of the female population.

Cassidy ignored him and continued with her narrative "—could find. It was obvious that she was trying to save him."

"Then you didn't find either of the baby's parents?" Dan asked, again looking from Cassidy to Will for an answer.

Cassidy shook her head. "I just saw the baby—and almost missed seeing him at first. He was in the middle of the rushing water, crying." She winced as a particularly loud cry pierced the air right next to her ear. "Kind of like he is now. Could you check him out, please?" She held out the infant to Dan. "See if there's something wrong with him. I'll pay for it," she quickly added, not wanting the doctor to think that just because the baby wasn't related to her that she expected him to do the examination for free.

"I'll take care of it, Doc," Will assured him. Finances were tight, thanks to what he'd found himself walking into when he took over his father's ranch, but he still had a little cash to work with if he did some artful juggling.

"I'm not worried about that right now," Dan told both of them.

When he'd first arrived to reopen the clinic in Forever, Dan had viewed it as a temporary assignment until another doctor could be found to take over the practice on a more permanent basis. But even then, monetary compensation had never been his goal.

What he hadn't counted on was the emotional rewards that went along with this job.

"While I'm giving this little guy the once-over, one of you should call the sheriff and tell him about what happened," Dan suggested. "Could be his parents are stranded somewhere right now and need some rescuing themselves."

Will's eyes shifted toward Cassidy, and she could hear the question as if he'd said it out loud.

"I didn't see anyone. That doesn't mean they weren't there," she admitted, then frowned. "But it could also mean that they could be dead." Cassidy thought for a moment. "Last really bad flash flood we had, Warren Brady's nephew pulled his car up on the side of the road and got caught in it before he even knew what was happening. He was gone before anyone could reach him, and that was in a matter of moments."

Dan sighed. He hated hearing about senseless losses like that. It made him that much more determined to do as much as he could for those he *could* help.

"This is going to take a while," he told the two people in his waiting room. "Why don't you wait out here until I can determine if this little guy's got a problem beyond missing parents?"

It wasn't so much a question as politely voiced instruction.

Will nodded toward the phone on the reception desk. "Mind if I use your phone to call the sheriff?" he asked Dan. "I can't seem to get any reception on my cell phone. The storm wreaked havoc on the signal."

"Go right ahead. I'll be back when I'm finished with the exam." The baby let loose with another lusty wail. Dan glanced toward Cassidy, an amused smile on his face. "Sure sounds like he's got a healthy set of lungs on him, though," he noted with a laugh.

She didn't have to look in his direction to know that Laredo had a smug expression on his face. Just like she knew he was going to rub it in.

She didn't have to wait long.

"Told you," Will said, clearly vindicated.

Cassidy had no intention of going down without a fight. "Even a broken clock is right twice a day," she pointed out.

"Set your standards that high, do you?" Will asked with a smile as he began to tap out the sheriff's number on the phone's keypad.

Cassidy curled her fingers into her hands to keep from grabbing the first thing she could find to throw at Laredo's head. If she was going to kill him, she knew she would have to do it when there were no witnesses around. And if she gave Laredo what was coming to him, she knew that Dan would come out to see what the noise was all about.

Restless, agitated, not to mention concerned about the infant she'd rescued, instead of sitting, Cassidy paced around the waiting room.

Well, this day wasn't going the way she'd thought it would when she'd gotten up this morning, she thought in frustration. She'd planned on getting a number of things done in the office today. She was really determined to prove herself an asset to Olivia.

Instead, here she was, killing time in the clinic's waiting room, sharing space with Will Laredo of all people.

Why did both of them need to stay here, waiting for the doctor to give them the results of his examination?

Laredo had two ears, she thought. At the very least, he could hear whatever it was that Dan had to say. Meanwhile, she could—

She could wait right here, she thought darkly. Her truck was still out where she'd left it. As much as she hated to admit it, she needed Laredo to drive her back to it.

Cassidy blew out a frustrated breath. More than anything else, she hated being backed into a corner like this.

Damn it, maybe if she called one of her brothers?

Out of the corner of her eye, she saw Laredo holding out the phone receiver to her. She eyed him quizzically. Couldn't he talk?

And then he did.

"Sheriff wants to talk to you," Will said.

She made no move to take the receiver. "Why?"

"Do you have to question everything I say?" he asked, annoyed.

There was as close to an innocent look in her eyes as possible as she replied, "Yes."

Laredo did what he could to hang on to the last of his composure and told her in carefully measured words, "He's got a couple of questions."

"What did you tell him?"

Will never missed a beat. "That you're a royal pain, but he wants to talk to you, anyway." With that he pushed the receiver toward her again.

Cassidy took it grudgingly. But when she spoke, nothing but pure honey dripped from her lips. Will entertained thoughts of strangling her.

"Hello? Sheriff? This is Cassidy McCullough. Laredo said you wanted to ask me something."

"Hi, yes. Will said you were the first one to dive into the floodwater to save this baby you saw."

Well, at least Laredo hadn't made himself the hero of the little drama—but then, in her heart, she knew he wouldn't have. He wasn't like that around other people. It was only when they were together that he went out of his way to drive her insane and contemplate justifiable homicide with every breath she took.

"Yes, I was," she answered.

"Did you see any other vehicle around, on either side of the rising water, or *in* the water?" Rick Santiago asked.

She was completely honest with him. "I really wasn't looking for another vehicle," Cassidy admitted. "But as far as I remember, nothing else caught my eye. It looked like the baby was alone."

"And it was in a plastic tub? Did I hear Will right?" Rick questioned uncertainly.

No matter how many times she said it or heard it, Cassidy had to admit that it still sounded weird. "Yes. Like the kind they give you when you get discharged from a hospital. Maybe the mother had just come home from the hospital. Or maybe she was a nurse," she added suddenly as the thought occurred to her.

"More likely the patient," Rick said in speculation. Although at this point, anything was possible. "Exactly where was this?"

A product of the area, Cassidy gave the sheriff the location as close to where she first saw the baby as she could, given that she'd been entirely focused on saving the baby and that some of the road she'd traveled on had been traversed backward in order to get parallel with the infant's makeshift sailing vessel.

She gave the sheriff every detail she could remember, holding nothing back.

"Okay, that helps," Rick commented when she was finished. "I'll have Joe and Cody check it out."

"Sheriff?"

He'd been about to hang up. It took him a second to respond. "Yes?"

"What happens to the baby if you can't find his parents?"

"Well, these aren't the best conditions and who knows how long that baby was out there, so locating his parents might be very difficult."

"And if it's impossible?" she pressed. "If you can't locate either of his parents, what happens to him then?"

"Someone would have to take him to Mission Ridge," Dan said grimly. "That's the closest social services office in the county."

"Oh." Everyone viewed social services as the last resort. For the most part, the people in Forever found a way to take care of their own, no matter how distant that match was. "Okay. Let me know if you find anything."

Disturbed, Cassidy frowned as she hung up. It only occurred to her after she'd replaced the receiver in the cradle that she'd forgotten to say goodbye.

The conversation had upset her that much.

Chapter 5

"Something wrong?"

Cassidy realized that Will was asking her a question, and from the sound of his voice, this wasn't the first time.

"Sorry. For a moment, I forgot you were here." Not wanting to seem as if he'd caught her off guard, she added, "Best moment of my life." An exasperated expression came over his face. Okay, he'd just expressed concern. Maybe she should have gone easier on him. She flashed a grin. "Sorry, couldn't help myself."

"We do seem to bring out the worst in each other," he commented. "Why do you think that is?"

Because everything you do rubs me the wrong way. And because sometimes just having you this close is way too crowded for me.

"Oh, I don't know," she said out loud. "You have a good moment every now and then."

Rather than say anything in response, Will went to the bay window and looked outside.

He'd aroused her curiosity. Had something outside caught his eye?

"What are you looking at?" Cassidy asked, joining him.

Will took his time answering her, making her wait. He figured she owed it to him. "You said something nice to me. I figure The Four Horsemen of the Apocalypse should be riding up the street anytime now, signaling the end of the world."

Cassidy slanted a glare at him. "Very funny. I had no idea you had a sense of humor."

Will pinned her with a penetrating look. The kind that went clear down to her bones. "You don't know a lot of things about me."

Although she'd never backed away from going toe-to-toe with him, there was something about standing close enough to feel his breath on her face that Cassidy found completely unnerving.

"And we're keeping it that way," she announced glibly, turning away.

"Round two," Will muttered, then shrugged. "Okay, have it your way."

"What other way is there?" Cassidy asked, knowing this would antagonize him. Then, just to drive her point home, she raised her chin, silently daring him to make some kind of a response.

She was deliberately goading him, and she knew it.

Damn it, what was it about this blond-haired witch that pulled him in like this? If he had a lick of sense, he'd just turn his back on her and be done with it. Yet here he stood, smack in the middle of her war zone.

It had to be some sort of insanity, like when a salmon felt compelled to swim upstream to mate even though death lay waiting for it just beyond that finish line.

"Someday," Will warned her quietly, his voice barely a low growl, "you're going to find out."

Her chin rose a fraction of an inch higher as she smugly asked, "And you think you're going to be the one to show me?"

She was challenging him, and he knew he should either put her in her place with a couple of choice words or, better yet, just ignore her because he had a gut feeling that got to her more than anything.

But it was hard to ignore that face and that mouth when they were right in front of him like this.

Taunting him.

Daring him.

Before he could think his actions through—something he had *always* been able to do, even in the worst moments, even when his father would push him almost beyond the brink—Will caught hold of Cassidy by her shoulders.

His eyes searched her face, trying to understand the woman who was driving him crazy. Trying to get underneath the layers.

"You don't even have the sense to be afraid, do you?" he asked incredulously.

"Afraid?" Cassidy echoed, even as her heart did a quick little summersault that she damned herself for. "Why? You can't throw me off a cliff because we're standing on flat ground. And you can't strangle me because the doctor's just one scream away."

"You're right. I can't throw you off a cliff—whatever the hell that means." What went through her mind, anyway? He didn't begin to have a clue. "And I can't strangle you."

"See?" Her eyes challenged him as she tossed her head again. "Nothing to be afraid of," she declared, as if she'd proved her point.

It was that smug look that came over her face that was her undoing, because it got to him as surely as if he'd just been shot straight through the heart with an armor-piercing bullet.

Before he knew what he was doing, still holding on to her shoulders, Will pulled her almost a full inch off the floor.

And then he kissed her.

It was meant to put her in her place and to frighten her.

What it did, instead, was frighten the hell out of him.

Frightened him because he didn't stop kissing her. He continued. Continued kissing Cassidy as he gradually allowed her feet to touch the floor, gradually leaned further into the kiss and found her responding to it.

At the same time, a whole host of things suddenly went off within him, things he couldn't put into words. The closest he could describe it was that it felt like someone had thrown a match into a shed full of Fourth of July fireworks.

Rockets went off everywhere.

Cassidy found herself melting like candle wax even as something in her head screamed, *This could be very dangerous!*

It wasn't screaming that because he was kissing her but because she was *responding* to his kissing her. Responding with every single part of her in a way she had *never* done before.

Other words failed to form in her head as sensations she couldn't begin to describe suddenly sprang up and mushroomed within her, scrambling for a foothold, desperately searching for more even as a part of her viewed the entire episode in mounting horror, as if she was watching some sort of a disaster movie unfold on the screen, all happening to someone else.

The last shred of what could only be termed as survival instincts finally rose and had her wedging her hands against his chest in a desperate bid to create some small sliver of space.

Or maybe what she actually felt was *Laredo* pulling back.

For the life of her, she couldn't distinguish which of them had made the first move to pull apart or begin to understand why such a feeling of bereavement was washing over her.

Cassidy's eyes blazed like blue flames as she ground out, "I should kill you."

"Don't bother," he told her coldly. "I think I'm already dead."

Why else, Will silently asked himself, would he have gone on kissing her that way? As if he wanted to. As if he couldn't draw another breath if he didn't.

It didn't make sense.

Before she could say anything else to him, coherent or otherwise, she heard Dan clearing his throat behind them. Her head all but swiveled as she turned to see who it was and realized that the doctor was standing right behind them.

Had Dan just walked in, or had he been there long enough to see what had just happened?

What *had* just happened? she silently demanded in complete confusion.

And why had she *let* it happen?

The expression on Dan's face gave her no answers. He looked as if he was taking this whole incident in stride. She certainly couldn't, she thought, irritated and disoriented.

"You'll be happy to hear that the baby is none the worse for his joyride on the floodwater this morning," Dan told both of them.

Will appeared mystified. "Then why was he crying like that?"

Dan lifted a shoulder in a casual shrug and then let it drop. "The usual reason babies this age cry. He was hungry and wet. Very wet." Dan laughed softly. "I've had patients who sounded a lot worse when they were hungry and wet. I changed him after my exam. We've got some spare baby clothes just for these occasions. And I fed him, as well. He seems rather happy now." Since Will was closer to him, he looked to him for an answer. "What's the status with his parents? Did the sheriff say anything?"

"I called it in, and the sheriff said he was sending out a couple of his deputies to look around, see if they can locate either one of the baby's parents, or find any sign of an abandoned vehicle."

Dan nodded. "Guess that's the best we can hope for now." And then he looked at the duo in front of him, as if he was waiting for one of them to speak up. When neither did, the doctor took the lead again. "Seeing as we don't have the parents yet, which one of you are going to take the baby?"

Cassidy blinked, feeling a little confused. "Take him where?"

"Well, home would be my first guess. I'd take him home with me, but Tina called a little while ago to say that one of the kids was running a fever. I wouldn't feel good about bringing this little guy into that kind of atmosphere. After what he's gone through, his resistance might be down," he explained in case they weren't following his argument. "It's not something I'd want to test."

"No, you're right," Will agreed. There was nothing to do but step up. He didn't even hesitate. "I guess since I rescued him, he's my responsibility."

That was all she needed to hear. "What d'you mean, *you* rescued him?" Cassidy cried. Did he think he could just dismiss her out of hand like this? As if she'd been some sideline observer?

"Okay," Will amended patiently. Then to her great outrage she heard him say, "Technically I rescued both of you."

Cassidy's mouth dropped open as she glared at him. "What?"

He did his best to hold back a few of the more choice words that rose to his lips. Instead, he reworded his previous statement.

"I rescued you rescuing him, does that suit you?" he asked.

"What would suit me is if you—"

When he'd gotten his medical degree, Dan had never thought that he was going to need one in mediation, as well.

"I think what we're all forgetting here is that this little guy needs a place to stay," Dan told them calmly, forcing their attention back to the baby. "So one of you decide which of you it's going to be—now."

"I'll take him," Cassidy announced. And then, as she heard herself say the words, she glared at Laredo and was forced to incline her head, grudgingly giving the man his due. He was better than she'd thought. "You planned it this way, didn't you?"

The expression on Will's face mimicked pure innocence.

"Don't know what you mean," Will responded. The look in his eyes told her otherwise.

Cassidy forced her thoughts to center on the baby she'd pulled out of the rushing water. And she remembered the drawer that her brother Cody had improvised to use as a bed for the baby he'd helped deliver a while back. The one he'd wound up bringing to the ranch, along with the baby's mother, Devon. Devon, Layla and Cody had gone on to form a family.

Cassidy abruptly shut down that line of thinking. This wasn't like that.

There was only one important thing to be gleaned from all this. The baby the doctor was holding in his arms looked as if he would have no trouble fitting into that drawer—at least until the baby's parents could be found or someone could come up with an alternate plan for this little nomad.

"Well, at least I have somewhere I can put him for the time being," Cassidy told the doctor. She spared Will what amounted to a dismissive glance. "Knowing you, you'd probably put him in the feed bin."

Instead of responding, Will looked at the doctor. "See what I have to put up with, Doc?"

But Dan quickly shook his head. "Oh, no, I'm not getting in the middle of this," he told both parties adamantly. "My only concern right now is to find a place for this little guy right here."

Cassidy spoke up and reminded the doctor, "I said I'd take him."

He waited a moment for her to back down. When she didn't, Dan nodded. "All right. I can give you some formula to take with you. I heard that the general store was closing down for the day, hoping to avoid the worst of the storm's damage."

He glanced from Will to Cassidy. "By the way, either of you have a name for him? I realize it's just temporary until we find his parents, but I need at least a first name to put down on my records, and I've always thought that 'Baby Boy Doe' sounds incredibly sad."

Will looked at the infant's face for a long moment. "How about Adam? Seems kind of fitting if you ask me—unless you've got some kind of an objection against it," he stated, looking pointedly at Cassidy.

She managed to surprise both him and Dan when she shook her head and said, "No, actually, I think that's kind of a nice name. 'Moses' was never really going to work," she added, referring to the name she'd first pinned on the baby.

"Well, Adam," Dan said, addressing the child in his arms, "I think you and I have just witnessed history being made. I don't recall hearing that these two *ever* agreed on anything before. Looks like you just might be having a good influence on them, what do you think?" He asked the baby as if it was a serious question.

Will glanced in her direction before saying, "Kind of nice, isn't it?"

There it was again, that damn sexy grin of his, she thought angrily. And now—heaven help her—she had something else to couple it with: that mind-blowing, toe-curling kiss of his, which was every bit as earth-shaking as all his female conquests claimed it was. And she was *never* going to give him the satisfaction of letting him know her reaction to either.

Not even on her deathbed.

So, retreating to form, Cassidy blew out a breath as she tossed her head again, doing her best to revert to a smug expression.

"Yeah, well, don't get used to it. I really doubt it's ever going to happen again because, odds are, you're not going to say anything smart again for a really, really long time."

"Okay, you two call a truce, and see about getting this baby to your ranch," Dan instructed Cassidy, "before this storm decides that it's not through with us yet." So saying, the doctor handed the baby to her. "I'll get that formula for you and a few disposable diapers as well until the general store opens again, hopefully tomorrow. Last I heard, it intended to open again in the morning."

Turning toward Will, Dan asked, "You want to come with me and help bring out those supplies?"

"Sure." He glanced in Cassidy's direction. "You'll wait?"

He didn't put anything past her, no matter what he assumed was the logical course of action. Cassidy and logic were hardly ever on good terms.

"Where am I going to go?" she asked. "You're my ride—at least until you get me back to my truck."

"I know that—but with you I'm never sure just what you're going to do," he told her honestly. "You just might get it into that fool head of yours to show me just how independent you are and suddenly set out on your own."

Cassidy pressed her lips together as she glared at him. She even glared at the back of his head as Will followed the doctor to the rear of the clinic.

"Do you two ever stop?" Dan asked wearily.

"I would if she would," Will responded.

"Then in other words, no," Dan concluded. Shaking his head, he laughed softly to himself.

"What's so funny?" Will asked as the doctor unlocked a couple of cabinets in the storage area.

"Oh, nothing," Dan said dismissively. And then he surprised the hell out of Will when he said, "Just picturing the wedding, and the aftermath."

Will's eyes had grown huge. "Whose wedding?"

Dan decided that, for now, he'd said enough.

Opening the cabinet door in the first exam room, he took out a supply of disposable diapers he kept on hand for his littlest patients. After stacking them on the exam table, he took out several cans of formula as well, plus a blanket. He put them all into a sack and handed it to Will.

"This should be enough to last Cassidy for at least a couple of days. By then, maybe she can get some from the store, or if that's still closed, Cody's wife might be able to spare some," the doctor suggested.

"This is more than generous, Doc," Will told him. Rather than argue with the doctor, which he knew Dan was wont to do if he raised the point about payment again, Will discreetly left a twenty on the exam table when he took the bag Dan gave him and then followed the doctor out of the room. It didn't begin to cover everything, but for now, it was all he could spare.

Chapter 6

"Ready to go?" Will asked Cassidy as he walked back into the reception area directly behind the doctor.

Cassidy was slowly pacing the room, gently rocking the baby in her arms and hoping that the ongoing motion would continue to keep him quiet and calm. She'd taken care of Cody's little girl on several occasions, but she felt way over her head right now—and was determined not to show it.

"Oh, more than ready," she answered.

Will nodded. "Okay, just let me load these baby survival supplies into the truck, and then I'll come back for the two of you," he told her. The next moment, he walked out of the clinic.

"Well, this has to be a first," Dan commented, almost more to himself than to the other adult occupant in the room.

Cassidy looked in the doctor's direction. "What is? A possibly homeless baby?"

Dan shook his head, his eyes crinkling in amusement. "No, you and Will working together."

Given her feelings toward Laredo, Cassidy was not about to admit to something like that. "We might just be occupying the same space, Doc, and we might have the same general goal. But I guarantee that we are not 'working' together."

"There, that's what I mean," Dan told her. "Everyone in Forever is accustomed to seeing the two of you at odds with each other the second you're within in the same half-mile radius. But this—" he nodded at the dozing baby she was holding "—is bringing out something different from the two of you than your normal mode of behavior."

Dan had always been very nice to her and her family. The man probably didn't have a mean bone in his body, so she didn't want to pay him back by offending him. But she really found it difficult to go along with his view of what was going on.

"Yes, well, as soon as Laredo gets me back to my truck, life will go back to normal again," she promised with a little too much conviction.

Dan heard her out and smiled. "You go right on thinking that, Cassidy."

She raised her chin, the way she always did when she anticipated a fight, or at least an argument. "I will, because it's true." Because she didn't want to come off as combative with the doctor, she decided to redirect his attention toward something far more important than some artificial truce between her and Laredo. "How old do you think Adam is?"

He looked at the boy, quickly reviewing the exam in his mind. "Best guess is about two to three months old."

"And you've never seen him and his mother or father before?" Cassidy pressed. After all, a lot of patients came through this clinic every day. How could he remember every one of them?

But looking at the baby's face, Dan shook his head. "No, I'm afraid not."

"Maybe Dr. Alisha saw them?" she suggested. Granted, a few people did pass through Forever now that there was a hotel in town, but if they did, they did it during the summer months, not this time of year. It was nearing the end of November; nobody came here in the winter.

"It's not that big an office," Dan pointed out, looking down at the sleeping baby. "I would have recalled seeing this little guy and his mother or father if they ever came in here."

"Well, if you don't recognize him, I guess Adam and his parents were just passing through," Cassidy decided.

"There's another possibility," Will stated as he came back into the clinic. He was almost directly behind Cassidy.

She almost jumped. She hated when Will caught her off guard like that. "Okay, what?" she asked, sparing him a disdainful glance.

Will addressed his answer to the doctor rather than to her. "It's possible that he could be from the reservation. They've always had their own way of dealing with things. If this little guy was born on the reservation, there would have been no reason for you to have ever seen him or his mother before."

They all knew that the residents of the reservation

rarely sought out the doctors at the clinic. They did on occasion, but those occurrences were few and far between. Nothing short of an outbreak of some sort of contagious disease brought the reservation residents to the clinic, seeking the help of the medical staff.

As if to contradict Will's theory, Cassidy pointed out, "He has blue eyes."

"Maybe one of Adam's parents wasn't Native American. Who knows?" Will looked at Cassidy. She was stubborn to a fault, and what she was the most stubborn about was admitting that he might be right. "It wouldn't hurt to ask around."

Cassidy frowned. She supposed Laredo might have a point. If anyone else had suggested that possibility, she would have readily agreed. But every word out of Will's mouth just seemed to irritate her beyond belief.

She pulled the blanket a little tighter around the baby.

"I'll mention it to Cody when I see him," she said dismissively. And then, glancing over her shoulder at Dan just before she left, Cassidy said, "Thanks again for everything, Doc."

"That's what I'm here for," Dan told her.

Grabbing the rain slicker he'd discarded when he'd let them in, Dan now followed the couple out of the clinic and locked up for a second time.

Will's truck was still parked directly in front of the clinic where he'd first left it. Cassidy hurriedly made her way over to the vehicle. But Will's stride was longer, and he beat her to it without even trying. He proceeded to open the door behind the driver's just before she reached it.

Cassidy pressed her lips together, biting back the desire to tell him that she could have opened her own door, thank you very much. Instead, she muttered a barely audible, "Thanks."

Will greeted the choked out verbal offering with a grin. His eyes were almost dancing as he asked, "Almost hurts you to say it, doesn't it?"

Cassidy got on without so much as looking at him. "Just get me to my truck," she ground out.

Rather than getting into the front seat, Will leaned over her to help her with her seat belt, just as he had the first time. But this time Cassidy was faster than he was. She grabbed the end of the belt from him.

"I can buckle my own seat belt, Laredo," she informed him.

"Just trying to make things easier for you," Will answered cheerfully.

Cassidy never skipped a beat. "That would involve disappearing off the face of the earth."

Will climbed into the cab of the truck behind the steering wheel. "Your brothers would miss you," he said.

He knew damn well what she meant. "I was referring to you."

"Maybe later," he replied glibly, and then he turned the key, starting his truck.

The next moment, they were back on the road.

The rain was starting again, Cassidy noted, but the sky didn't look nearly as foreboding as it had earlier, so she crossed her fingers and hoped for the best, praying that history didn't repeat itself. The last thing in the world she needed right now was to become stranded somewhere with the baby and with Laredo.

Neither one of them spoke for the first few minutes,

with only the rain cutting into the silence. But the stillness within the truck was very short-lived.

Will was the first to break it.

"Are you sure you're up to this?" he asked.

She should have known the silence was too good to last. That she actually welcomed the break was something she would have gone to her grave before ever admitting it to him. "Was that supposed to be some kind of a crack?"

"No," Will replied mildly, his eyes all but glued on the road in front of him. He was taking no chances on driving into an unexpected sinkhole; they had been known to occur after a heavy rain. "That's just a question. I mean, quite honestly—" he raised his eyes for a second to meet hers in the rearview mirror "—I can see you wearing a hell of a lot of hats, but I *never* thought of you as the maternal type."

She frowned. It *was* a crack. Not that she had any driving need to have him think of her in any sort of a positive light, but she didn't particularly care for what she viewed as his put-down.

"Just because I have this constant, overwhelming desire to hit you over the head with a two-by-four doesn't mean I don't have any maternal instincts. I do." Her eyes narrowed as she glared at him in the mirror. "Just not any toward you."

"Which, don't get me wrong, I'm very grateful about." Had Laredo stopped there, she could have accepted it, giving it no more thought than she would have given another bad, incorrect weather forecast.

But he didn't stop there.

Will continued, saying, "I never wanted you to think of yourself as my mother."

She was having a hard time not saying what was on her mind, but she knew an explosion would have the kind of consequences she was *not* looking for—it would have set off the baby. Any moment that the baby wasn't wailing was another moment to be savored and enjoyed—even if Will was there to share it with her.

"I don't know if you accidentally meant that as a compliment," she told him, "or if it was another crack, so I'm just going to leave that alone."

She heard him laugh shortly to himself. At her expense. She was starting to suspect that just the sound of his breathing was enough to set her off.

"Good thinking," Will commented.

"Is that another accidental compliment?" Cassidy challenged.

He undoubtedly hadn't meant it that way, but she wanted to needle him, and this was her only opportunity. He owed her after having ripped through the foundations of her world with that kiss he'd laid on her earlier.

That she owed him because he had jumped into the water when he didn't have to and thus could have, very possibly, saved her life, not to mention the life of the baby who she in turn was trying to save, was beside the point and not something she wanted to dwell on at the moment.

That was something she'd reexamine some sleepless night—or maybe the reexamination of that would turn it *into* a sleepless night. She didn't really know, but in any event, she didn't want to think about either case right now.

"No, just another observation," Will replied.

He was really getting under her skin now, and while

she couldn't exactly explain why, she knew she wanted him to stop doing it. Now.

"Yeah, well, I don't need you to 'observe' anything with your running commentary if you don't mind. All I want is for you to get me back to my truck so we can both go our separate ways."

"Not a good idea," he told her mildly.

Didn't the man ever just say yes and let the matter go? Cassidy wondered in exasperation.

"*What's* not a good idea?" she demanded. "Getting me back to my truck?"

"That, and you driving off on your own," he added mildly.

That really got her angry. "I drive better than you do," she retorted.

"That is a matter of opinion—although you don't," Will said. "But either way, that's not the point right now."

"And what is the point?" she asked him in a tone that could only be described as haughtily angry.

If she was trying to get him to lose his temper, she was failing miserably. He seemed determined to remain on an even keel as he spoke with her, no matter how much she poked the proverbial stick at him.

"Same thing that was the point when I drove you to the clinic," he told her, his tone mild, as if he was talking to someone who was slow-witted and had trouble following him. "You can't drive and hold on to that baby at the same time. It's not safe for either of you, although I'm more concerned about the baby than I am about you."

If he said that to get a rise out of her, she wasn't

about to let that happen. Instead, she murmured, "At least you're honest."

Will nodded, again never missing a beat. "Always. I also have a point," he told her, stressing the words as he glanced up into the rearview mirror again to catch her eye. "You can't just stick the baby in the backseat and drive."

If he wasn't driving, she would have hit him. But as it was, she had to work at keeping her temper—at least for now.

"I know that. What about my truck?" she asked.

He tried to recall where she'd left it. "Barring another flash flood, it should be safe," he told her. "After you get everything set up for the baby and do whatever it is you have to do to make that happen, you can go with one of your brothers to bring it back.

"Or I could just take Connor there now after I drop you off." Except for the time he'd left Forever, he and Connor, as well as her other brothers, had been friends for as far back as he could remember. "I expect he's probably pacing around right about now, looking for something to do."

Although he was right, she didn't like what he was saying about her oldest brother. It made Connor sound like some sort of wimp.

"You were out in this," she reminded him. "The rain didn't stop you."

"I was out in this *because* of the rain," Will reminded her.

"Oh." The matter of the baby had driven the information out of her head, but she remembered now, remembered what he'd told her. "That's right, you were looking for that colt."

For just a brief moment, Cassidy's guard came down and she experienced concern for the animal's welfare. What if something had happened to the horse because he'd stopped to help her?

"I'm sorry. Do you think you'll still be able to find him after all this time?"

"I'll find him," he told her. There was no bravado in Will's voice, much as she might have wanted to accuse him of that. There was just confidence in his own abilities. "I can be stubborn if I have to be, just like you."

She raised her eyes again, expecting to meet his, but Will was once again strictly focused on the road ahead. She felt something weird for a second.

"Are we having a moment here?" she asked him.

Will wasn't able to read her tone of voice and decided that the wisest thing was just to acknowledge her words in the most general possible sense.

"I suppose that some people might see it that way," he said.

Cassidy shook her head. "Typical."

"Come again?"

Cassidy raised her voice. "I said your answer's typical. You're a man who has never committed to anything."

"Not true," Will contradicted before he could think better of it.

"Okay, name one thing," she challenged.

She was not going to box him in if that was what she was looking to do, he thought. At least, not about something that was way too personal to talk about out loud with her. Besides, he did just fine having everyone think that he was only serious about any relationship he had for a very limited amount of time. That way, if he brought about the end himself, he never had to publicly entertain the sting of failure.

"I'm committed to restoring my father's ranch, making it into the paying enterprise it should have been and still could be with enough effort," he told her.

"You mean that?"

Rather than say yes, he told her, "I never say something just to hear myself talk."

"There's some difference of opinion on that one, but—"

"Look," he began, about to tell her that he didn't want to get into yet another dispute with her over what amounted to nothing, but he never had the opportunity. The one thing that Cassidy admittedly could do better than anyone he knew was outtalk everyone.

"—if you're really serious about that," she was saying, "I can probably manage to help you out a few hours on the weekends." The way she saw it, she did owe it to him for helping her save the baby, and she hated owing anyone, most of all him.

Will spared her a glance before he went back to watching the road intently. Cassidy had managed to do the impossible.

She had rendered him completely speechless.

Chapter 7

It took him a minute—more like two—but he finally found his voice.

"Wait, did you just actually offer to *help* me?" Will asked incredulously.

Cassidy was beginning to regret the offer already, although she knew what he had to be facing—exactly what Connor had faced when their father died suddenly, leaving them all orphaned and in debt.

"Don't sound so stunned. I didn't just say I'd marry you," Cassidy said brusquely. "I said I could give you a few hours on the weekends to help you get the ranch back on its feet. It's what neighbors do, right? They help each other. You're not the only one who can come through," she informed him. "As a matter of fact, I *have* to help you."

"And why is that?"

"Because I refuse to be in your debt."

"Oh." She was talking about his diving in to rescue her and the baby. This was her way of admitting that he'd saved her, he realized. "Okay, well, now it all makes sense," he allowed. "For a second there, I thought maybe I'd slipped into some alternate universe. You know, one where we're actually friends," he said with just a touch of sarcasm, even though he was smiling.

"Like I said," she told Will, "don't let your imagination run away with you."

His eyes met hers briefly as he thought of their moment in the clinic when who-knew-what had possessed him and he had done what he knew a lot of other men in the area all yearned to do. In his opinion, he had already gotten carried away, and once had to be more than enough. Because he might wind up being seriously doomed.

Cassidy McCullough had a body made for sin and a temperament that would make a shrew envious. That was *not* a combination that he would fare well with.

Any way he looked at it, it spelled trouble, and he intended to live a long, prosperous life. That meant avoiding, as much as humanly possible, having his path cross hers.

And yet, she was offering to help. If he turned that down, who knew what sort of consequences he would wind up reaping? Cassidy became insulted easily, and her wrath was not the sort to be taken lightly. Besides, there was no denying that he could use the help.

"Wouldn't dream of it," he told her, thinking that might call an end to the exchange.

Something in Laredo's voice challenged her, but that was for another time. Right now, there was a small human being depending on her. A small human being whose parents were probably frantically looking for him right at this very moment.

She knew she would be if she were in their shoes.

"As long as we're clear," Cassidy replied. The next moment, she leaned forward as far as she could in the backseat.

"There's the house," she said, pointing to it.

"I know what your house looks like, Cassidy," he replied. "I was just away for a few years. I wasn't strapped to some gurney, having my brain wiped clean by some evil scientist."

The latter was a reference to the superhero comic books they had all read as kids. Back then, they had pooled their money together to buy one each month as it came out, and then they'd pass it around, each taking their turn reading about whatever adventures were taking place in the current issue.

By the time she would get her turn, the pages had been folded countless times, not to mention faded. Consequently, some of the lettering was hardly legible. Being the youngest definitely had its drawbacks, she recalled.

"Eric Smith was a lot handsomer than you," she recalled, mentioning the hero he was referring to by the character's secret identity.

"He was a comic-book hero," Will reminded her. "He was drawn that way."

"I know. Makes the truth that much sadder, doesn't it?" she asked, looking at him pointedly.

He could almost feel her eyes boring into the back of his head.

The next second, he was calling her attention to something else.

"Looks like you've got a welcoming committee," Will observed, nodding at the front door. It was opening, and the next second, Connor came out.

The oldest McCullough didn't exactly look happy, Will observed.

"Where the hell have you been?" Connor demanded the moment Cassidy opened her door. Connor walked over to the truck quickly. "Why didn't you call, and why are you so wet? It's raining, but you look like you've been swimming in the river."

Reaching the truck, her brother saw the baby in her arms just as he was starting to cry. His brow furrowed. "What are you doing with Cody and Devon's baby?" he asked.

"Nothing," Cassidy answered. "Because this isn't their baby." She passed the baby to him before getting out of the truck. Once her feet were on the ground, she reclaimed Adam.

Somewhat dumbfounded, Connor turned toward Will.

"You make sense out of this for me?"

Will merely shrugged. "Hey, she's your sister. I haven't understood a thing she's said since the day I met her."

"Come in before it starts raining again," Connor ordered. The sky had darkened again, and there was every indication that it would pour despite a short, promising break in the weather.

He waited until they were all inside the house. Will brought in the supplies the doctor had given them for Adam. Closing the door behind him, Connor faced the two of them. "Now, whose baby is this?" he asked. And now that he'd gotten a closer look at Will, he must have noticed that the latter was in the same condition as his sister. "What the hell were you two doing out there, and how does it involve this baby? You *both* look like you've been swimming in the river."

"There's a reason for that," Cassidy told her brother, shifting the baby to her other arm. Adam was small, but he wasn't exactly weightless.

"I'm listening," Connor said, waiting.

She glanced at Will, thinking that he might jump in and interrupt her. When he didn't—there'd always been something about Connor that put Will on his best behavior, she thought grudgingly—Cassidy went on to answer her brother's questions.

"I saw the baby caught up in the flash flood, and I dove in to rescue him."

"I rescued her rescuing him," Will added, filling in his part in the story.

Connor's eyes went from his sister to his friend, speaking volumes even as he remained silent and continued to wait.

Connor could always make her squirm, she thought, annoyed. She shrugged. "Maybe he did at that."

"I look forward to hearing the details," Connor told them. "But right now, why don't you both change out of those wet clothes? I've got some clothes in my bedroom that'll fit you, Will."

As he spoke, Connor took the baby from his sister with the confidence of a man who had expertly taken care of his three siblings over the years, as well as, most recently, his niece. "I'll just wait for you down here with the baby. Whose is it?" he asked again as they both began to head for the staircase.

"That's the big mystery," Cassidy replied, starting to take the stairs two at a time.

"Wait, what?" Connor asked. Babies didn't just appear out of nowhere like in some fairy tale. Babies had parents and a definite entry point.

"We brought him to the clinic to get checked out," Will told him. "But the doc didn't recognize him. Couldn't tell us who he belonged to. Then I called the sheriff about it—"

"—and he's having Cody and Joe look into it," Cassidy concluded as she hurried the rest of the way up the stairs. Her clothes were starting to feel clammy as they stuck to her, and she welcomed the thought of changing into something dry and more comfortable.

"Will," Connor called to him, stopping the other man for a moment. Will turned and looked at him, waiting. "Thanks." He didn't elaborate any further.

He didn't have to.

Will shrugged away Connor's words. "Couldn't exactly let her drown, now, could I?" he asked glibly. "Wouldn't do that to my worst enemy—come to think of it…" Will's voice trailed off as he grinned.

"Right," Connor replied, knowing the game that went on between his sister and the man he and his brothers had known—and liked—all of their lives. "Just go change."

Left alone, Connor gazed down at the baby in his arms. Bright blue eyes looked back up at him, as if trying to absorb everything in the immediate area and make sense of it.

"Well, you look none the worst for the experience,"

Connor observed. "Want to give me a clue?" he asked. "Just whose baby are you?"

The baby just went on looking up at him.

He was still wondering that several minutes later when both Will and his sister came back downstairs.

Cassidy, he noticed, might be trying to assume an air of complete disinterest and nonchalance, but she'd dried and combed out her hair rather than just catching it back in a wet ponytail the way she might have when they were a lot younger. And she'd put on a light blue blouse, one that brought out the color of her eyes.

She'd gone to some trouble to look good for a man she claimed not to be able to stand. He wondered how much longer she was going to continue to play that game.

"What do you plan to do about this baby?" Connor asked once they were both downstairs.

"Do?" Cassidy echoed.

"Yes, do. A baby takes a lot of work," he reminded her.

She didn't like being put on the spot, especially with Laredo witnessing all this. "I know that. I thought that we could all take turns."

"And just when would your turn come up? As I recall, you're normally putting in some pretty long hours at the law firm. Cody's got a full-time job—not to mention a wife and baby to take care of—and Devon's teaching," he reminded his sister, referring to Cody's wife. "Cole's working at The Healing Ranch now, and that leaves me running the ranch here."

Cassidy felt overwhelmed for a moment. She glanced in Will's direction, but rather than say anything about him, she asked, "What about Rita?" Connor had recently hired the young woman on what amounted to a part-time basis. She did some light cleaning, and occasionally cooked dinner since all of them had taken on more responsibilities in the last few months. "She comes from a large family. A baby should be a piece of cake for her."

"Having a large family doesn't immediately qualify her to take care of a baby," Connor pointed out. The baby was fussing, so he shifted the infant to his other arm, then began to slowly rock the child.

"Why don't we just ask her if she'd like to pitch in? Between all of us, we'll be able to handle one little baby," she told her brother with confidence. "Besides, this could all be just for a short duration, just until Adam's parents can be found."

"Adam?" Connor repeated somewhat uncertainly. "You know his name?" If that was the case, then locating the parents shouldn't be a problem.

"No," she admitted, quickly adding, "We thought it might be helpful to have something to call him while we try to find his parents and take care of him. The name was Will's idea."

Connor wasn't sure if she was giving the other man credit, or blaming him. He looked at Will. "So it's a boy?"

"You can't tell?" Will asked, feigning surprise.

Connor looked at him as if his friend was kidding. "It's a baby," he said pointedly. "At this age, they all look alike."

Will laughed, amused.

Cassidy wasn't. "If you ever get married and wind up having one of these little people yourself, make sure that your wife never hears you say that," she warned her brother.

"If I ever do get married—" something Connor highly doubted, given that his life was almost always all about work and, until not that long ago, about watching out for his siblings "—and have one of these, I'll know what it is when it's born. There'll be no reason to say that they all look alike."

"Look, why don't I just take him with me?" Will offered.

Cassidy turned to stare at him as if he'd lost his mind. "You?" she questioned, looking at Will incredulously. What did he know about taking care of a baby?

"Yeah, why not?" Will asked, taking offense at her tone. "I know I can take care of a baby as well as you can."

Connor sighed. "As entertaining as this anything-you-can-do-I-can-do-better refrain might be, why don't the two of you put aside this competition thing you've had going on since forever and join forces to take care of this little guy until we find out just what his future is going to be?"

"Join forces?" Cassidy echoed as if her brother had suddenly lapsed into a foreign language. "You mean like, live together?"

Connor nearly choked at the very mention of the idea. "I don't think the world is ready for that kind of warfare just yet. I was thinking more along the lines of you two each pitching in a few hours a day."

"Laredo's got a ranch to run by himself, remember? He can't very well strap the baby onto his back," Cassidy protested. "I've got a better idea. I'll take the baby into work with me tomorrow."

Both Connor and Will stared at her as if now *she* was the one speaking in a foreign tongue. "What?" Cassidy challenged. "Olivia's a mother. She can appreciate the problems that arise with having a baby."

"This isn't your baby," Will pointed out.

"Doesn't matter whose he is," Cassidy insisted. "The point is that he is *a* baby, and he needs to be taken care of. She's got a couple of her own—as does Cash," she reminded them. "They'll probably be very helpful."

There were times when her optimism astonished Will, given her usual personality. No doubt about it. Cassidy McCullough was a mystery on two legs. Two very long, shapely legs.

"She's good when it comes to volunteering other people, isn't she?" Will asked her oldest brother, amused by the liberties she assumed.

"Always," Connor agreed. "But maybe you have something there," he told Cassidy. "And who knows? Maybe by then Cody or Joe will be able to find out who Adam's parents are."

"Or at least what happened to them," Will added grimly.

"You think they were lost in the flash flood?" Connor asked him.

"It is a possibility," Will acknowledged.

"That would make this little guy an orphan." Connor looked at the infant with new interest. "Maybe you came to the right place after all, little guy," he said, addressing the baby.

"Are you going to be here for a while?" Cassidy suddenly asked her brother.

"Why?"

"Because I still have to get my truck, and if you're

okay with watching Adam here for a little bit, Laredo can drive me back to where I left it."

She turned toward the other man. "Right?" she asked him pointedly.

"Nothing would give me greater pleasure than to drop you off somewhere," Will answered, forcing a smile. It appeared utterly fake.

"That okay with you?" he asked Connor.

"Go, take her." One arm securely around the baby, Connor waved his sister away and toward Will with his free hand. "The sooner she gets her truck, the sooner she'll be back herself."

"You heard the man," Cassidy said to Will. "Let's go."

Will sighed, following her out the front door. "Somewhere in the world," he commented, "there is a small country missing its dictator."

Chapter 8

Neither one of them spoke as they got into Will's truck. Nor were any words exchanged once they got back on the road. The silence seemed only to grow louder and more encompassing as they continued to travel back to the site where she had left her truck.

After a few minutes, the silence almost seemed deafening. Cassidy leaned over and turned on the radio. Despite the fact that she turned it up as far as it could go, no sound came out. Cassidy tried again, turning it off and then on again. Still nothing.

Biting back a few choice words, Cassidy tried pressing a few of the buttons, thinking that perhaps a couple of the stations were down, but, obviously, the radio itself wasn't connecting.

In response to the frustrated sigh she exhaled, Will told her, "It's dead."

"I kind of figured that out," she answered curtly. "Can't you fix it?"

The radio, like the truck itself, had had its share of problems. "Not worth fixing," he replied.

How could he stand driving around without a radio? In her opinion, music made everything more tolerable. "Then get a new one."

He didn't even spare her a glance. "Not exactly high on my priority list right now."

There was an entire host of expenses facing him. He didn't have the money to waste on a new radio, and he wasn't handy enough to bring the car radio back from the dead.

Cassidy contemplated lapsing back into silence, but the idea was just not appealing. Even arguing with Laredo was better than riding along in this all-encompassing silence.

Desperate for some sort of noise, Cassidy decided to try her luck at getting him to talk. "You know, I didn't think you'd stick around after Cody's wedding."

"You didn't think I'd stick around, or you *hoped* I wouldn't stick around?" he asked, glancing in her direction.

They knew each other better than either of them was really willing to admit. "Both," she answered. "When my brothers told me you had that big, knock-down, drag-out fight with your father and then just rode out of town, I really thought we'd seen the last of you."

She'd almost slipped and made it more personal by saying, "I," but she'd caught herself just in time. That was all she needed, to have Laredo think that she had some sort of personal stake in his being around.

"Well, you were the one who sent that letter from

Olivia's firm, notifying me about my father's will, telling me that he left the ranch to me. I wouldn't be here if you hadn't." He'd always figured that his father was too ornery to die and would go on living on the ranch forever. The letter he'd received had knocked him for a loop. It took him a while to reconcile himself to the facts. "How did you track me down, anyway?" he asked.

"I had nothing to do with it," she informed him. Then because he was looking at her, waiting for her to own up to the deed, she said, "Connor knew where to find you. And anyway, that notification wasn't from me personally. As I already mentioned, I was told to draft the letter on behalf of the law firm." Thinking he might need more of a background than that, she said, "Your father had Olivia draft the will leaving the property to you."

Will heard the words, but he still couldn't really make any sense out of what he was hearing. He shook his head. "That doesn't sound like the old man. Leaving all his debts for me to pay sounds more like him," he had to admit, "but not the ranch."

She knew what he was saying was right, but facts were facts, and Jake Laredo had indeed come into the office and dictated his will. Not a word had been changed.

"Some people have a change of heart when they know they're dying," she told him.

Will laughed shortly. For as far back as he could remember, there had never been any love lost between his father and him. For some reason, his father always blamed him for his mother leaving. It was easier that way than to blame himself.

"To have a change of heart, the old man would have had to have one," Will told her. He kept his eyes on the road, not trusting himself to look at her. He didn't want her glimpsing what he was trying to bury. "That man was as cold-blooded as they came." He paused, then added, "I never blamed my mother for running off."

"Not for running off," Cassidy agreed. "But she should have taken you with her, not left you behind."

All that had happened years ago. He'd been only seven at the time. He remembered crying himself to sleep for weeks. That was something he'd never shared with anyone. "Wanted to be rid of me even then, is that it?"

"Hey, you were always giving me a hard time," she reminded him, playing along for the moment. "But for the record, I meant that if she knew your father was such a mean-spirited son of gun, she shouldn't have left you. Your mother should have tried everything she possibly could to take you with her. Mothers have a responsibility to look after their children's welfare."

Damn, she hadn't meant to sound as if she was preaching. If he was okay with what had happened, then who was she to rail against it? She had no stake in this. But even so, she couldn't help feeling for the boy Laredo had once been, abandoned by his mother and mistreated by his father. It had been a hard fate.

Will deliberately shifted the conversation away from himself. "Think that's what Adam's mother was trying to do?" he asked. "Putting him into that pink tub to save his life?"

Cassidy didn't doubt it for a second. "It did the trick, so I guess the answer to that is yes." The alternative to that was that Adam had been abandoned, but as far as she could see, that was highly doubtful. "It's not like she—if it was his mother—had exactly planned all this. That flash flood today came out of nowhere. The forecast I heard was for rain, not sudden storms and flash floods."

She paused for a moment, then, because her conscience goaded her, she forced herself to stumble through an apology. She was totally unaccustomed to rendering one unless absolutely necessary, and while she had no problem when it came to slicing Will Laredo down to size, bringing up painful memories of his less than happy childhood was in her estimation a low blow. She hadn't meant to remind him of it.

The childhood she and her brothers had shared was by no means a happy-go-lucky one. She'd never known her mother, and she and her brothers had had to work long and hard for everything they had, but there was always love in the family. That was something she knew that Will never had in his.

It was also why, she knew, that he'd always been so drawn to her own family. While her father had been alive, he'd treated Will with respect and decency—and her brothers regarded him as one of them. They never clashed with Laredo the way she always did. But even that had come out of a sense of competition that existed between her brothers and her. In a way, she'd regarded Will as another brother herself.

"Look, I didn't mean to bring up any bad memories," she told him, trying to find the right words to convey that she'd made a mistake and for that, for dredging up any painful memories, she was sorry.

Will shrugged. "Don't worry about it," he told her in a completely dismissive tone. It irritated her, but she knew why he sounded like that. In his place, she had to admit that she would have spoken the same way. Vul-

nerability was not something either one of them really
owned up to.

"There's your truck." He pointed to the vehicle just
up ahead.

She breathed a sigh of relief. "At least it didn't wash
away," she murmured.

The truck had been secondhand when she'd gotten it,
but it got her to and from town, which was all that really
mattered. Someday she would get a new truck. Maybe
even a new sedan instead. Trucks were far more prac-
tical given the terrain, but she had to admit she found
a sleek sedan very appealing.

But all that was a long way away. First she had to get
her final degree and join Olivia's firm in earnest, as an
associate, not just an intern.

Will pulled up right behind her truck. Cassidy lost
no time in getting out.

"Thanks," she tossed over her shoulder as she went
to the driver's side of her less than pristine vehicle. If
anything, the rain seemed to have made it dirtier, not
cleaner.

Opening the door, she was about to get in when she
realized that Will hadn't pulled out the way she'd expected him to. She'd taken up almost half his day. What
was he waiting for?

"Something wrong?" she asked.

He inclined his head. "That's what I'm waiting to
find out."

That made no sense to her, and her expression indicated as much. "Just what is that supposed to mean?"

He put it into plain English for her. "I thought I'd
wait to see if your truck started up again."

"Why shouldn't it?" she asked suspiciously. What

did he know that she didn't? Had he done something to her truck before diving in to help her save Adam?

"'Cause your truck is over twelve years old, and you can never tell with these old trucks. I just don't want to have you on my conscience if you wind up being stranded out here after I leave."

Her eyes narrowed as she regarded him. "Since when did you develop a conscience?" she asked.

"I've always had one," he informed her. "You were just too busy trying to find new ways to torment me to ever notice."

"As I recall, you were the one trying to torment me."

"Cassidy…" There was a warning note in his voice.

"Yes?"

He couldn't tell if she was getting ready to go another round with him or just waiting for him to go on talking. He waved at the vehicle up ahead. "Just start the damn truck."

"Since you put it so sweetly," she said, swinging into the driver's seat.

The next moment, Cassidy put the key into the ignition and turned it. The truck seemed to sputter once, then again. On the third try, the engine finally turned over and the truck came to life.

She turned to tell him he could go home now and saw that he was already doing just that. Will was backing up his truck and then turned it around, heading, she assumed, to his own ranch.

Cassidy gunned her engine and tore out.

She left for town early the next morning. Cassidy felt she had a stop to make before she went into work. She was heading for Miss Joan's.

Miss Joan's Diner was the only restaurant in Forever. It had been that way as far back as any of the local residents could remember. The woman who ran the place was not a local herself, but it seemed as if she had been running the diner for as long as there had been a diner to run. As far as the town was concerned, both were beloved fixtures.

"Want you to meet someone," Cassidy told the baby as she took him, along with the car seat she'd borrowed, out of the backseat of her vehicle.

The tall, thin, redheaded woman, who always seemed to be somewhere within the diner, was looking in her direction when Cassidy walked in.

There were times, like now, Cassidy thought, that Miss Joan's hazel eyes seemed to look into a person's very soul.

The moment she walked into the diner, Miss Joan beckoned her over to the counter. She was looking directly at the baby.

"Is that the baby you and the Laredo boy rescued?" Miss Joan asked.

There were times when the woman took her breath away. It was obvious that Miss Joan already had the answer to the question she asked, but Cassidy said, "Yes," just to be polite.

She'd gotten the car seat that Adam was in from Cody. Her brother had an extra one, thanks to the baby shower that Miss Joan had thrown for his wife. Miss Joan could always be counted on to come through in any emergency. Right now, Cassidy was hoping the woman could come through with some information, as well.

Cassidy put the baby and the car seat on the counter so that Miss Joan could get a better look at the boy.

"Looks pretty healthy for someone who'd gone through the kind of ordeal he just did." And then she raised her eyes to Cassidy's and told her, "No, I don't recognize him."

Cassidy could only stare at the older woman. This was unnerving, even for Miss Joan. "How did you know I was going to ask you that?"

"Why else would you bring him here this early? Unless you were hoping one of the girls could watch him for you," she suggested. "We're not busy right now, so if you'd like to drop him off for a few hours…"

But Cassidy shook her head. She wasn't about to impose on Miss Joan like that unless she had no other option. "No, that's very generous of you, but I just—"

"Hell, I'm not being generous, girl. Don't you know everybody likes seeing a cute baby? Customers'll stick around a little longer, eat a little more while they're here, just to look at him. Only makes good business sense to have the kid around," Miss Joan told her matter-of-factly.

Cassidy merely nodded. She knew better than to argue with the woman. She also knew that Miss Joan enjoyed playing the part of a "tough old broad," as she liked to refer to herself on occasion. But everyone in town knew that the woman had a heart of gold, and anyone in trouble could always rely on her to come through.

They also knew better than to thank Miss Joan profusely for her help. She and her brothers would forever be indebted to the woman for being their surly guardian angel in more than half a dozen different ways when their father died suddenly. Even with Connor taking over as their guardian, they were faced with some really hard times. Miss Joan always found jobs for them to do, playing the hard taskmaster. She always made sure that they were never hungry.

Cassidy had no idea how they would have been able to make it without the woman's help.

"I'll keep your offer in mind," she told Miss Joan. "But I'm going to take him with me this morning." Despite Miss Joan's statement that she didn't recognize the boy, Cassidy looked at her hopefully. "I was just hoping that maybe you recognized him so that the sheriff and Cody could try to find his mother."

Miss Joan shook her head. "Don't know who she is, but I'll have my girls ask around," she promised Cassidy. She paused to look down at the baby again. "Can't see somebody not recognizing that face once they've seen it." She leaned closer to the baby. "We'll find your mama for you, little man."

One of the waitresses approached Miss Joan, leaving a small bag, neatly folded on the top, in front of her on the counter. Miss Joan, in turn, pushed the bag toward Cassidy.

Cassidy didn't take the bag immediately. Instead, she asked, "What's that?"

"That's for you," Miss Joan replied brusquely. Her manner silently indicated, *Who else would it be for?*

"But I didn't order anything," Cassidy politely pointed out.

Miss Joan's thin eyebrows narrowed over her nose. "I didn't say you did, did I? You haven't changed a bit since you were a little girl. Always arguing. You better hope that he's not like that," Miss Joan told her, nodding at the little boy.

"Won't matter one way or another," Cassidy replied. "He's either going with his mother when we find her, or if she doesn't turn up, I guess that social services'll take him."

"Is that the same social services your big brother worked himself to the bone to keep you, Cody and Cole away from?" Miss Joan asked pointedly, already aware of the answer to that question, as well.

That was a sharp jab to her conscience, Cassidy thought. But then, Miss Joan had never been one to pull her punches.

Picking up the car seat, Cassidy reached for the paper bag that Miss Joan had had prepared for her. She made no effort to answer the rhetorical question that had been put to her.

Instead, she nodded at Miss Joan. "Thanks for the coffee and whatever else is in here," she said as she began to leave.

"Could just be your conscience," Miss Joan said, addressing the back of her head as Cassidy made her way across the diner to the front door.

The woman still knew how to deliver a well-aimed remark to skewer her, Cassidy thought as she made her way back out to the street.

"And that," she told Adam as she brought him to her truck and secured his car seat to the restraints that were built into the truck, "for future reference, is Miss Joan. Don't let her scowl scare you. Woman's got a heart of gold. You just have to mine through a lot of hard rock to get to it. But it's well worth the effort." She checked the ties to make sure they held. "Okay, next stop, reality," she quipped.

Cassidy started her truck and headed off to the law office.

Chapter 9

"Well, I must say, the clients seem to be getting younger and younger these days," Olivia commented when she saw Cassidy walking in with Adam. Crossing to her, Olivia took a closer look at the baby. "This isn't Cody's little girl, is it? As a matter of fact, it's not a little girl at all." Olivia looked at her intern, her curiosity aroused. "Cassidy, whose little boy is this?"

For the moment, because it felt as if the baby was getting heavier by the second, Cassidy placed the car seat on the floor next to the chair in front of Olivia's desk. "That's just the problem—we don't know."

"We?" Olivia questioned.

"She means her and Will Laredo," Cash Taylor told his partner as he walked in on the exchange. Surprised, he looked at Olivia. "You mean that you haven't heard?" he asked.

"I had my hands full last night with a couple of kids who were convinced we were all going to float away at any minute—and Rick didn't get home until late, which just made things worse in their minds. When he did get home, he fell into bed, face-first. He was up and gone again before I was awake." Olivia shook her head. Being a sheriff's wife took a great deal of understanding and patience. "The storm did a lot of damage at the south end of town." Olivia looked from her partner to their intern. "Heard what?"

Cash answered before Cassidy could say anything. "We're in the presence of a hero—or at least one of them," he amended. Cash willingly filled in the details as he had heard them related by his stepgrandmother, Miss Joan.

"Seems that our intern here saw this little guy smack in the middle of what used to be the creek that runs by the Laredo place, being swept away. Miss Joan said she'd heard he was in some kind of a plastic container. Cassidy dove in to save him."

"How does Will Laredo fit into all this?" Olivia asked.

"Story is that he dove in to save Cassidy saving the baby," Cash replied.

"I would have been fine," Cassidy protested for what felt like the hundredth time. And then she shrugged. "But Laredo likes taking charge of things."

"Those kinds of things can get ugly really fast," Cash said. "Maybe it was a lucky thing that Will was there."

Cassidy couldn't bring herself to agree outright. The closest she could come was to vaguely echo the word Cash had just used.

"Maybe," she allowed. "All I know was that I had

the baby and I was heading for the bank when Laredo grabbed us both from behind, so I'll never really know if I needed his help or not." She conveniently left out the part where her arms felt like lead right about that time.

In her opinion, that was enough talk about Laredo. She had something more pressing on her mind right now. Since the firm had been initially started by Olivia, she felt it only right to put the question to the woman regarding the baby. "Is it all right if I have him stay here today? I know I should have called and asked you first, but—"

Olivia nodded knowingly. "But it's better to ask for forgiveness than for permission, right?" Not waiting for an answer, Olivia crouched beside the car seat and smiled. The baby returned her smile by looking at her with wide, wide eyes. "I think we can set something up to keep this little guy happy and out of the way." For a moment, Olivia watched as the baby seemed content to play with his toes. Rising to her feet, she commented wistfully, "This really takes me back."

"Thinking of having another one?" Cash asked her, amused.

"Thinking of borrowing one on occasion, maybe," Olivia corrected her partner. "I've had my share of diapers and staying up all night just to come into the office the next morning so groggy and beat that I could hardly sit up in my chair."

Cassidy thought of last night. She'd kept the baby in her room, not wanting to disturb Connor or Cole, but as it turned out, she needn't have worried.

"I guess that Adam must be ahead of the game because for the most part, he slept all through the night."

"Adam?" Olivia questioned.

"The baby," Cassidy explained, realizing that she hadn't used the name before.

"How do you know his name?" Olivia asked.

"I don't," Cassidy confessed. "But we felt we had to call him something until we could find his family, and 'Adam' seemed like the logical choice." She paused and then felt somewhat obligated to add, "It was Laredo's choice."

"Adam," Cash repeated in his resonant voice. The baby stopped playing with his toes and looked in the lawyer's direction. "How about that? He seems to respond to the name." Cash grinned at her. "You and Will might be on to something."

Not wanting to be lumped together with Laredo, Cassidy changed the subject. "It might have partially been my fault that your husband didn't get home until late last night," she told Olivia.

"Your fault?" Olivia repeated. Amusement curled the corners of her mouth. Enrique Santiago was as honorable a man as she had ever met, and she trusted him implicitly. She wasn't one of those women who jumped to conclusions even under the worst of conditions—and this was not one of those occasions, even though her intern had worded her sentence rather badly. "Why's that?"

"I reported where we first saw Adam, thinking that maybe his parents might be around there somewhere, looking for him," she stated.

Olivia nodded, filling in the missing pieces. "Knowing Rick, he probably went to check it out and scoured the area himself." She shook her head, a fond expression slipping over her face. "My husband delegates but also can't help getting involved. He takes a lot of pride in saying that this is his town, and he can take care of whatever needs doing."

Olivia went around to the other side of her desk and took her seat. "Since he didn't get in touch with you, my guess is that he couldn't find any sign of the baby's parents or their car."

"Maybe there was no car," Cash suggested, turning the thought over in his mind.

"Adam's too little to have walked to the creek," Cassidy pointed out. "According to Dr. Dan, he's maybe three months old."

"But it wasn't a creek yesterday, was it?" Olivia said, picking up on what her partner was driving at.

"No," Cassidy agreed. "Yesterday it was more like a river," she recalled. She tried not to think about it. It had all been rather frightening how quickly everything had evolved.

"How far back did the 'river' go?" Cash asked her. "Did you happen to notice?"

Cassidy shook her head. "All I noticed was the baby. I was about to take shelter in that old run-down cabin on Laredo's property when I heard Adam crying. Once I realized it wasn't my imagination—that I was actually hearing a baby—I really didn't take any notice of anything else," Cassidy confessed.

"Consciously," Olivia stressed. When Cassidy looked at her curiously, the woman went on to say, "But we notice more things than we realize."

"What are you getting at?"

"I think that this little guy just might be from around here after all," Olivia suggested. She exchanged glances with Cash. "You go out far enough from town, you wind up at the reservation."

"You think that this is a Navajo baby?" Cash asked.

"I think that it's possible he might be from around

that area." She looked at Cassidy. "Why don't you go talk to Joe Lone Wolf?" she suggested, mentioning her husband's senior deputy.

She thought of checking in with the sheriff later, during her lunch break. This was hardly past breakfast. "But I have work to catch up on," Cassidy protested.

Olivia smiled. "Honey, it's not that I don't appreciate your dedication, but we're a small firm in a small town. There's nothing here that can't wait for a few days if it has to. But his mother might be beside herself if she has to wait that extra time," she pointed out.

"As long as it's all right with you," Cassidy said, picking up the baby and his car seat from the floor.

"It's my suggestion. Of course it's all right with me." She waved Cassidy out of her office. "Just let me know what happens," she called out after Cassidy.

"Absolutely," the younger woman promised.

Cash went out in front of her to hold open the door as she carried Adam out in the car seat. "Thank you," she told him as she passed by.

Cassidy could feel her arms aching in protest as she went back to her vehicle. "I am going to have really large biceps by the time we find your mama," she told the baby. Opening the door to the truck's rear seat, she felt as if she'd only taken the restraining straps off the baby seat a minute ago, and here she was, putting the straps back around the car seat as she got Adam situated again. "I guess that comes in handy when you're working on a ranch, but it doesn't look all that attractive for a legal intern working at a law firm."

Adam gurgled, as if he was making a response to her observation. Bubbles cascaded from his tiny lips, making Cassidy laugh. She closed the rear door and then got in behind the steering wheel.

"I'll take that as a compliment," she told the baby cheerfully.

It took Cassidy next to no time to arrive at the sheriff's office. The latter was located several streets down from the law firm.

After getting out of the vehicle again, she went through the tedious process of removing the restraining straps and then taking the baby and the car seat out for the second time in half an hour. She thought of her sister-in-law and wondered how Devon could put up with having to do that over and over again without going crazy.

Some women were cut out for motherhood, but she didn't think she numbered among them.

Cassidy used her back to push open the front door to the sheriff's office, which was why she didn't see him immediately. But once she and the baby were inside, she not only saw the bane of her existence, she heard him, as well. The sound of his deep voice cut straight to the bone.

On any other day, she might have just turned and walked right out, but this wasn't any other day. And besides, this wasn't about her. This was about the baby. A baby who needed answers more than she needed to avoid Will Laredo.

"What are you doing here?" she demanded the moment she crossed the threshold and noticed Will talking to both her brother Cody, as well as Joe Lone Wolf. From the looks of it, the sheriff wasn't around.

"Last I checked, this was a public office," Will replied. "And not that I need to answer your questions, but I came in to find out if any progress was being made in locating Adam's mother or father."

"I just saw Cody last night," she reminded Will, waving a hand impatiently in her brother's general direction. "If any headway had been made, I would have known about it."

"Yes, but you're not exactly inclined to share that kind of information with me, are you?" Will asked. "And since I'm involved here, I have an equal right to know, same as you."

Joe frowned as he looked at the squabbling duo. "You two keep going at it, you're going to make this kid cry, not to mention me," he told them in his low, calm voice.

He nodded toward Will and said, "Will here thinks that maybe the baby might be from the reservation."

Cassidy made no comment about Will's thinking one way or another. She certainly didn't like sounding as if they were on the same side, but she had to ask, "Is he?"

"If you're asking me if I recognize him, I don't," Joe said. "But I haven't been up around the reservation for months, so I really couldn't say for sure. What I am willing to do is go up there and ask around." He looked at the baby and just the barest hint of a smile crossed his lips. "Might not be a bad idea to take this little guy with me, see if anyone recognizes him. So whenever you two feel like calling a truce, I'm ready to go with you and your foundling to the reservation."

Cody laughed as he shook his head. "If you're waiting for them to call a truce, the kid'll be ready for college by that time. Maybe even older."

Cassidy gave her brother a dirty look. "You're supposed to be on my side."

"There aren't supposed to *be* any sides," her brother informed them matter-of-factly. "The only thing that's supposed to matter here is finding this baby's parents—

or at least one of them," he reminded the couple he was looking at.

"He's right, you know," Will said to her.

Cassidy found it rather difficult to be agreeable or even docile when she could feel her back going up because of something Will was saying to her. "So now you're lecturing me?"

"No, what I'm trying to do is bring about that truce," Will told her.

Right, she thought, like he thought he was going to accomplish that by talking down to her in front of the others.

"You've got a funny way of showing it," she informed him coldly.

Will bit back a few well-chosen words. Getting into it with her wasn't going to do any of them any good, and he was tired of squabbling with Cassidy. Besides, they were wasting time.

"Why don't I just start over again and say I'm sorry?" he said.

The offer caught her off guard. She just stared at him. Exactly what was he up to? "Sorry about what?"

"Sorry that I keep setting you off all the time. Look, we can pick this up later if you want," Will said. "But right now, since Joe's free, why don't we take him up on his offer and bring Adam up to the reservation? Who knows? Maybe we'll finally get some answers about who he is and what happened."

In Cassidy's eyes, agreeing with Will was like capitulating. She turned toward Joe. "I'm ready to go anytime you are."

"Hallelujah," she heard Will murmur behind her.

Chapter 10

All four of them rode to the reservation in Joe's all-terrain vehicle. He felt it kept things simple—having two to three vehicles arrive on the reservation at the same time would call undue attention to them and definitely put the local residents on their guard.

Because he was a representative of the law in the area, there were those on the reservation who viewed Joe as an outsider despite the fact that he had grown up there. They felt he had turned his back on his people. Those were the ones who refused to accept any help from anyone who lived outside the reservation's borders.

However, not everyone thought that way, and conditions on the reservation were improving. Not fast enough in Joe's opinion, but at least they were better now than they had been when he was growing up there. Homes were no longer in disrepair, and the reservation school had been built up over the last decade, going from a small, old-fashioned single room facility to one where all the grades, from the first to the twelfth year, were now being taught.

Just recently a kindergarten had been opened, along with a small day care so that working mothers who were employed both on and off the reservation had somewhere to leave their children while they worked.

"It looks better than the last time I was here," Will commented as he looked around.

"It has taken a lot to improve things here," Joe said honestly. "Efforts to help the locals aren't always welcomed with open arms. Some see an extended hand as a handout and take it as an insult."

"Can't you say anything to change their minds?" Cassidy asked. To her, Joe represented a success story, as did the two brothers who ran The Healing Ranch, a ranch that used horses as a way to get through to troubled teens.

"Not easily," Joe said quietly. "A lot of people on the reservation think I've sold out."

In those people's opinions, there was no such thing as being able to walk in both worlds. It had to be either one or the other, and since he was a deputy sheriff, that meant that Joe had made his choice and turned his back on his heritage.

Cassidy was surprised to hear the deputy admit to that. She knew him to be a decent, hardworking man who was always ready to lend a hand, but he was also very private and closemouthed when it came to his personal life. To have him say that some of the same people he'd grown up with now took a dim view of him was surprising.

She also knew it had to hurt.

"Do these people even *know* you?" she asked incredulously, becoming indignant on Joe's behalf. It really didn't take much to arouse the crusader within Cassidy.

"Apparently not," Will commented.

"They're not all like that," Joe told them, and then was forced to admit, "But enough of them are."

Joe pulled up in front of a small, single-story wooden building that, although relatively new-looking, seemed to have come out of a bygone era, one that clearly belonged in the middle of the last century. The building was what passed for a general store on the reservation.

Joe got out, explaining, "I thought I'd ask Smoky if he's heard anything about a missing baby."

"Smoky?" Cassidy repeated uncertainly. It seemed to her like an odd name for someone who lived on the reservation.

"It's obviously not his real name," Joe told her. "But he likes it. To tell the truth, I don't remember what his real name actually is. As far back as I can remember, everyone always called him Smoky."

Getting out, Cassidy rounded the back end of the vehicle in order to get Adam out of his car seat more easily. But by the time she got to the other passenger door, Will had beaten her to it and had already taken out the baby.

Cassidy stopped short. Her eyes swept over the rancher and child. Although she wanted to find some kind of fault with what Will was doing, she couldn't. "You don't look awkward holding Adam," she told him grudgingly.

He was accustomed to hearing nothing but criticism coming out of her mouth. Her compliment threw him off balance. Recovering, he responded, "You say that like it's a bad thing."

"No," she was forced to admit, "it's just that most bachelors hold babies as if they were holding a sack full of rattlesnakes."

Will's eyes crinkled at the corners. "Maybe being around you has taught me to be unafraid around everything else."

Cassidy didn't take that as a compliment. "Give me Adam," she ordered.

"Don't worry, kid," he told the baby, "she doesn't bite. Usually," he added as he handed Adam over to Cassidy.

"I take it the truce is over," Joe observed.

"It never fully went into effect," Will answered. "Cassidy can't bring herself to be civilized around me for more than a couple of minutes at a time—and even that's hard for her."

"That's because I can ignore you for only a couple of minutes at a time," Cassidy countered.

Joe gave her a long, penetrating look. "Well, for the sake of the kid, you two might want to consider giving it another shot while we're inside the general store talking to Smoky."

Will offered her a wide grin. "You heard the man, 'Sweetness,'" he said, placing one hand to the small of Cassidy's back as he ushered her and the baby into the general store.

Cassidy stiffened. Because she was holding the baby, she was forced to go along with Will's behavior. But it didn't keep her from fervently wishing she could elbow him in the ribs just once.

The man stacking a new inventory of wax beans glanced up when he heard the front door opening.

Recognition brought with it a welcoming smile, but Cassidy thought he looked a little wary, as well. "Hey, Joe, what brings you here?" Putting down the can he was about to arrange, Smoky wiped his hands on the apron tied around his waist and came forward. "Haven't seen you in a long time. Crime waves keeping you busy?" he asked with a dry laugh.

The man everyone called Smoky was shorter than Joe by a few inches. He was also heavier than the deputy by a good twenty pounds or so. His face appeared to be somewhat weathered, but taking a closer look at him, Cassidy guessed that Joe and the general-store clerk were probably around the same age.

"Same old stuff," Joe replied noncommittally. "How's your mother?" he asked politely.

"Still complaining because I'm not married," Smoky answered with a good-natured shrug. Midnight-black eyes swept over the two people and the infant beside Joe. "Bringing your friends around on a tour of the rez?" he asked.

Cassidy was about to tell the man why they were there when she felt Will's hand, which was still up against her back, press against her spine lightly. He was signaling for her to remain silent.

Ordinarily that would have the complete opposite effect, but they weren't on their own territory right now. Though it had always been there, the reservation was considered to be a different world, and, as such, she and Will were there as visitors. It was up to Joe to conduct the conversation, so, hard as it was for her, Cassidy bit her tongue and kept quiet.

"Actually," Joe told the shopkeeper, "we're here to ask if you heard anything about a baby going missing from the reservation."

It wasn't difficult to put two and two together. "Your question have anything to do this little guy?" Smoky asked, nodding at the baby that Cassidy was holding.

"Yeah." Joe kept his eyes on the other man's face. "You recognize him?"

Smoky returned the deputy's gaze. "Nope. Afraid I can't say that I do. I could ask around if you want," he offered.

Joe nodded. "I'd appreciate it."

"So what's the kid's story?" Smoky asked, apparently curious—or at least he seemed to feel the need to appear to be.

"He was found him in the creek yesterday—it had swollen up to a river by then," Joe said, still closely studying his childhood friend for some sort of indication that he recognized the baby—or knew more than he was saying.

"Swimming?" Smoky asked mildly.

The man couldn't be serious, Cassidy thought. She just couldn't keep quiet any longer. The words all but burst out of her mouth. "No, floating. Someone had put him in a pink tub."

Rather than act surprised, Smoky seemed interested and asked, "Where?"

"Halfway between town and the reservation," Will answered.

Smoky gave no indication that the story rang any bells for him.

"Like I said, I'll ask around." Just then, someone else walked into the general store. "I've got a customer," he told Joe. It was meant to signal the end of the conversation between them.

Taking out the card that the sheriff had printed for all of them, Joe placed it on the counter before the shopkeeper and tapped the bottom of the card. "That's my number if you find out anything."

Cassidy saw the storekeeper pick up the card and absently tuck it into his back pocket. She had her doubts about the card's fate.

The next minute, she felt Will's hand at her back again, this time he indicated that he was ushering her out. Although it annoyed her that he felt she needed clues in order to know what to do, she didn't want to cause any sort of a scene. She did her best to hold her tongue as she allowed herself to be guided out.

Her silence lasted only for so long.

"I know how to go in and out of a store," she informed Will between gritted teeth.

"Yes," he agreed amicably, "but you usually don't know *when*," he pointed out. Once outside, Will turned toward the deputy. "You want to ask around anywhere else, or is that it?"

"One more stop," Joe answered. "I thought we could stop by the church and see if Father Tom knows anything about this baby. He doesn't pick sides," Joe added as he drove them to the church.

Father Tom was a slight man, standing about five-seven or so. He'd run the church and ministered to those who chose to attend for close to fifteen years now. Unlike the shopkeeper, there was no wary expression in the priest's eyes when he saw Joe and the others entering the church.

Approaching Joe quickly, Father Tom embraced the

deputy before extending a hearty greeting to the two strangers Joe had brought with him.

And then the priest smiled warmly at the baby in Cassidy's arms.

"Is this yours?" Father Tom asked the deputy.

"No, my two are home," Joe told the man who was the sole reason for his conversion as a young man. "We were hoping that you might recognize him." He nodded at the baby.

But the priest shook his head, looking somewhat chagrined. "Unless they happen to have a distinct look that sets them apart, until they begin to take on personalities, I'm afraid that all babies look rather alike to me. Was this one abandoned?" he asked sympathetically.

The word *abandoned* raised red flags for Will. "What makes you ask that?" he asked.

The explanation seemed relatively simple to Father Tom. "Well, it's obvious that you don't know who the parents are. Why else would you bring him here, asking if I recognized him?"

Cassidy was studying the priest as he spoke, and while he didn't sound as if he was closed off the way the shopkeeper had been, she had a feeling that there was something that the priest wasn't saying. Or maybe he felt he wasn't at liberty to say.

"Good guess, Father," Cassidy told the priest. "So no one came seeking forgiveness for having given in to temptation and now had no idea what to do with the end result of that moment of weakness?"

"No matter how general the terms are, if you're asking me about someone's confession, you know I can't say anything one way or another," the priest told her good-naturedly.

"Even if it means reuniting this baby with his mother?" Cassidy pressed.

"You're assuming the mother's from the reservation," he replied, still carefully navigating the line between admission and denial.

"Guessing, not assuming," Will interjected, correcting the priest.

"All I can do is ask around," Father Tom said as he escorted them to the small church's entrance. He held the door open as they left.

"Well, that went well," Cassidy said with a sigh as they made their way back to Joe's all-terrain vehicle.

Joe shrugged. "I didn't really expect anyone to jump up and down, waving their hand or pointing someone out for us."

Then what was the point of coming? Cassidy wanted to ask. But because she liked Joe and he was helping them, she tempered her question to sound a bit more sedate. "Then why did we come here?" Cassidy asked him.

"We came," Joe replied quite frankly, "to plant the seeds."

"Seeds?" Cassidy repeated, looking at the deputy and waiting for more details.

"Sometimes it takes a lot of patience to get someone to step forward with any information around here," Joe informed them matter-of-factly. There was no judgment in his voice. That was just the way things were around here. They had very little, so they guarded what they did have—their secrets. "People like to play things close to the vest. If this baby does belong to someone on the reservation, I wanted the word to get out that we have him and that the baby is perfectly well."

"Maybe that's all they wanted," Will pointed out, "to be reassured that the baby's all right. Now that they know that, they can just go on with their lives without saying anything or claiming him."

"Maybe," Cassidy allowed, surprising the two men she was with, especially Will. "And maybe, after a while, that won't be enough."

"What do you mean?" Joe asked.

Will knew what she was saying. "Maybe now that she knows we have the baby, the baby's mother will have second thoughts and want to reclaim him."

"That's a possibility," Joe agreed. "Another possibility is that now that his mother knows that her son is safe and with some people who risked their lives in order to rescue him, she's found the right parents for her baby."

"Right parents?" Cassidy almost choked on the term. "You mean us?" she cried, startled. She barely spared Will a glance before protesting the scenario that Joe had just come up with. "Wait a minute, there are no 'parents' in the wings here. There's just me and there's just Will. In no known universe does that translate into the right 'parents' for this baby." She was barely able to keep her voice down.

Will laughed shortly. "Don't hold back, Cassidy. Tell us what you really think."

"What I think is that this was just a waste of time," she informed the two men. "Even if the priest acted like he was holding something back, nobody is going to come forward and suddenly cry, 'That's my baby, please give him to me.'"

She deliberately scanned the area, taking note of every woman who had even momentarily turned in their direction. What she saw was mild curiosity, if that. What she didn't see was any expression of longing, secret or otherwise.

Adam's mother wasn't here.

"So what's next?" Will asked.

"That's easy. Next we go back into town so I can change Adam's diaper before someone comes along and decides to cite us for polluting the air," Cassidy quipped.

She was about to shift the baby to her other side so that she could open the vehicle's rear door and get in when Will reached around her and opened it for her. She slanted a glance at him, then muttered a perfunctory, but less than enthusiastic, "Thank you."

She could hear the smile in Will's voice as he replied, "You're welcome."

Cassidy didn't bother to look at her childhood adversary. The next moment, she more than had her hands full. Adam had decided that he had been quiet long enough. Filling his small lungs full of air, he let loose with a loud wail, making his displeasure heard by everyone within what had to be a half-mile radius.

Chapter 11

Olivia was hanging up her landline when she saw her intern returning. Since Cassidy still had the baby with her, Olivia came to the logical conclusion, secretly hoping she was wrong.

"No luck?"

Cassidy had intended to go straight to the cubbyhole she usually occupied when not working in Olivia's office, but since the latter had called out to her, she stopped and stepped into the woman's office. She really wished that she had better news.

"No, no luck," she confirmed. There was no point in hiding her disappointment. "I thought for sure we'd find at least his mother on the reservation." The more she had thought about it, the more it seemed to have made sense to her.

"Well, maybe he's not from the reservation," Olivia

suggested. After all, it wasn't as if they had any proof. At best, it was just one possible assumption.

"I've just got this gut feeling that Adam's connected to the reservation in one way or another."

"Well, the truth has a way of coming out if you give it enough time, so if one of his parents *is* from there," she said, nodding at the baby in Cassidy's arms, "we'll find out eventually."

"Hopefully sooner than later," Cassidy added. She looked down at the baby. Adam was scrunching up his face again, which she had already learned could only mean one thing. She wasn't certain just how much one diaper could hold. "Right now, I've got to change Adam's diaper before it gets toxic."

Olivia laughed, waving Cassidy on her way. "Good idea," she agreed. "Meanwhile, you've given me something to think about."

By now, the aroma from Adam's diaper was definitely competing with the oxygen in the room, but Cassidy couldn't bring herself to just walk away with that open-ended comment hanging in the air.

"What have I given you to think about?" she asked.

"Getting an investigator," Olivia said bluntly. "Up until now, I didn't think our firm really needed one, but now, with this coming up, I'm beginning to think it might be a good idea to have an investigator working for the firm, or at least having one on retainer. We need someone who could look into things for us, make sure all the details are straight if we have any concerns to the contrary. Or, in this case, someone who could find out if this baby's parents can be located."

Yes, Olivia nodded to herself as Cassidy hurried off

to the ladies' room with Adam, hiring an investigator was definitely something to think about.

Cassidy was determined to put in as long a day as she could to make up for the time she'd missed. Olivia, however, was equally determined that she leave early with the baby. Cassidy made a counteroffer, insisting on taking at least some of the work home with her so she wouldn't fall any more behind than she already was.

It was all part of not just the learning process at the law firm, but part of making her feel useful.

In the end, it was a draw. Cassidy left earlier than she'd intended, but she did leave with a satchel full of papers to work on during those snatches of time when Adam didn't need her.

When she finally arrived home, Cassidy still felt as if she'd put in a day and a half at the office even though that was far from the case.

"How do mothers do it?" Cassidy asked her small passenger as she undid his car seat from its restraints in the backseat. "I feel like I'm ready to crawl into that crib Cody lent us for you, and it's not even six o'clock yet. Must be some vitamin supplement I don't know about."

In response, Adam whimpered. He seemed ready to launch into another crying jag, but then apparently changed his mind. And just like that, the baby began to play with his toes again, which had become his newest form of fascination.

"Lucky thing I can't misplace those," Cassidy commented. "Hope you keep on playing with them until we can locate your mama."

That that might never happen was an idea she didn't want to even remotely begin to entertain—even though part of her had to admit it was a viable possibility. Although not a regular occurrence, flash floods did happen near and around Forever. Thinking about it now, Cassidy could remember hearing about at least five flash floods during her lifetime. However, she could only recall hearing about one fatality in all those instances. Since those odds were in her—and Adam's—favor, she fervently hoped that they would continue to hold.

Busy trying to carry the baby as well as bring in her satchel, Cassidy took no notice of the truck that was parked off to the side of the house. At least not until she walked into the house.

Before she could call out to Connor to announce that she and Adam were home, Cassidy stopped dead. There was someone else standing in the living room. He had his back to the front door, and he was thumbing through the album that Connor kept on the secondhand coffee table their father had brought home one year.

Cassidy's breath caught in her throat. She knew that back anywhere.

"What are you doing here, Laredo?" she asked. Wasn't seeing him once today enough? she silently demanded in frustration. "And where's my brother?"

"Which brother?" Will asked as he turned around to look at her. "And to answer your first question, I'm waiting for you."

"Connor," she clarified. And then Cassidy replayed what Laredo had just said to her. She interpreted his response in her own way. A bolt of excitement zipped right through her as her eyes widened hopefully. "You found his mother!"

For possibly the umpteenth time since their very first clash of wills, he wondered why Cassidy McCullough had to be so damn pretty. Why didn't she have a face that made men embrace celibacy instead of nurturing thoughts where purity had no place?

Snapping out of his momentary flight of fancy, Will had to think for a moment in order to remember her question. "No," he answered, "why would you think that?"

"Because you said you were waiting for me, and I just thought—" Why was she even bothering to explain herself to this man? She didn't owe him an explanation. "If you're not waiting here to tell me that you've found Adam's mother, then why are you here?" she asked, running out of patience.

Damn him, Cassidy thought. Laredo could make her temper flare faster than any man alive.

In response, Will calmly smiled at her, which only irritated her further—and she knew that he knew it, but that still didn't change things. "I'm waiting here for you to get back with the baby because I'm here to help out."

Cassidy stared at him. What was he talking about? "Help out with what?"

Cassidy was a great many things, Will thought, most of them irritating. But he had never known her to be thickheaded before. Why was she pretending to be that way now?

Blowing out a breath, Will spelled it out for her. "Help out with the baby."

If anyone else had just said that, she would have immediately, not to mention happily, turned over the baby to them and sank down on the sofa with a huge sigh of relief. But this was Will, and although she couldn't really explain it, it went against her grain to admit to him that she needed his help—or any kind of help for that matter.

"I never said I needed help with the baby," she informed him coldly.

"You didn't have to," Will told her. Looking down at the baby, he smiled warmly at Adam. "Everyone needs help with a new baby."

"He's not a new baby," she said defensively. "Dr. Dan said he was around two or three months old."

"Let me rephrase that," Will said patiently, starting over again. "New to *you*. All babies represent a lot of work, and you're not used to taking care of one."

"Oh, but you are," she retorted sarcastically.

"The man is offering to help, Cass," Connor said in his eternally patient tone as he walked in from the kitchen. "Let him help." Connor was carrying a couple of bottles of beer. He offered one to Will.

Still holding the baby, Cassidy turned her entire body so that it blocked Will from having access to Adam. "I am *not* turning Adam over to a drunkard," she informed her oldest brother.

"He hasn't had anything to drink yet," Connor pointed out. "I just took the caps off the first two bottles. And since when did you become a teetotaler?" her brother asked. Cassidy liked sharing a beer as much as the rest of them.

"Since I brought a baby into the house," she replied, then her eyes shifted toward Will. "You can take the beer and go."

Instead, Will accepted the bottle from Connor and then put it on the coffee table. The indication was that he could have the drink later if that was her objection.

"I'm here to pitch in," Will told her firmly. "I helped rescue him. I want to help take care of him as well—until we locate his parents."

Cassidy drew in her breath.

"You're under no obligation—" she began.

"That," Will said, cutting her short, "is a matter of opinion. I'm not here to argue with you."

"Well, you certainly could have fooled me," Cassidy retorted.

Will went on talking as if she hadn't interrupted him. "I'm here to do my fair share."

Just what was Laredo's game? Cassidy was certain he had something up his sleeve, but what? While she couldn't pinpoint what it was, she knew it had to be something that was meant to get under her skin—just like everything else he said or did.

"Duly noted," she told him crisply. "I'll tell everyone that you're a real prince." Her hands were full, so she couldn't wave him off. All she could do was say, "You're free to go."

"Cassidy," Connor interjected wearily. Will had been gone from the area for nearly four years, but it was as if nothing had changed in that time. The two still butted heads whenever they were in the same area—with his sister the bigger offender.

Cassidy shot her older brother an impatient look. "What?" Her temper was growing increasingly shorter, and she found she had to exert effort not to growl out the word.

"Shut up," Connor said in the same mild-mannered voice he might have used to describe this morning's breakfast.

Stunned, Cassidy could only stare at her brother. "What?"

"You heard me. I love you to pieces, Cassidy, but you

could make a saint lose his temper. Now accept Will's help and stop arguing over the matter."

"Look, Cassidy," Will began, giving it another try. "I didn't come here to cause you any problems, I honestly came here to help. Now for once in your life, will you stop arguing with me and just let me help." It wasn't a request.

In what Cassidy later viewed as a weak moment, she refused to give in, quipping, "But arguing is half the fun."

Will gave her a look she could only interpret as a promise of things to come. Why she felt a strong pull within her very core, she couldn't begin to explain— nor did she really even want to think about it.

"We can have fun later," Will told her. "Right now, I want to help out with the baby. You can go on arguing with me all you want, but I think you should know that I'm not planning on going anywhere tonight. It's only right and fair that I help out with Adam, and I intend to do just that," he concluded, standing his ground.

"I'd listen to the man if I were you," Connor counseled.

Cassidy frowned. She was outnumbered and outmaneuvered—and she knew it. But she had never given up easily. "I really hate to set a precedent—"

"Cassidy," Connor said in a warning voice.

"—but I obviously have to, so okay, sure, give me a hand with him." With that she held Adam out to Will.

Taking the baby from her, Will couldn't help but take a whiff of the less than pleasing aroma that was part of the baby. "He needs to have his diaper changed," he told Cassidy.

The corners of her mouth curved with pleasure. "Good call."

Instead of asking her, Will looked at her brother. "How often does this happen a day?" he asked, unconsciously wrinkling his nose.

"More times than you'd care to think about," Connor answered. "C'mon." He put his hand on Will's shoulder. "I'll walk you through it."

But to his surprise, Cassidy put up her hand to stop her brother. "That's okay, let me," she said.

"You're going to change him?" Connor asked, surprised.

"If you're referring to Laredo, that's not possible," she told her brother.

He gave her a long-suffering look. "I was talking about the baby."

"Nope, not going to change him, either. But I'll gladly walk Laredo through it," she said with a wide grin.

"Why do I suddenly get the feeling that I've just walked into a trap?" Will asked as he followed Cassidy out of the room.

"I have no idea why you think or feel anything," she replied. "Now let's get this over with before Adam winds up getting a rash."

Connor could only shake his head as he watched his sister and his lifelong friend walk out of the room. He dearly loved Cassidy, but he'd be the first to admit there were times that she could try God's patience. He had no idea why Will was putting up with her drill-sergeant temperament. Unlike the rest of them, Will certainly didn't need to. There were no family ties to bind him to her.

As far as Connor could see, there was only one reason in the world why the two fought the way they did and why Will didn't give Cassidy a biting, formal dressing-down once and for all before he finally walked out on her—permanently.

Connor smiled to himself as he contemplated that reason now.

He'd always wanted another brother, he thought as he turned and walked back into the kitchen.

It was time to see about getting dinner on the table. The idea of hiring Rita to cook meals on a more permanent basis was beginning to sound better and better. He had to admit that they had all gotten rather spoiled with all the meals that Devon had made for them when she had first arrived.

Cassidy stood to one side of the bed, her arms folded before her chest as she watched Laredo change Adam's diaper. It was rather full, and the baby required a great deal of cleaning.

When Cassidy didn't offer a running commentary on what he was doing or make any critical wisecracks on his method, Will glanced up at her.

This wasn't like her at all.

"Why aren't you saying anything?" he asked.

She sighed, giving him his due. He hadn't turned green when he first opened the diaper, and he hadn't surrendered, telling her she could finish up. He'd grimly done what needed to be done.

"Okay," Cassidy said. "Not bad."

"What?"

"If you're waiting for me to burst into applause, you've got the wrong person."

He didn't understand half the things that Cassidy said. "What are you talking about?"

Was he even *in* the same conversation as she was? "You just asked why I wasn't saying anything, so I said something."

"What I meant was that I'm not used to you being so quiet. I was sure that you were going to tell me what a bad job I was doing."

"I wanted to," Cassidy freely admitted, then added, "but there's only one problem."

Okay, here it came. Will had thought that since he volunteered to help out, it would have some kind of an effect on her, making her a little more easygoing and less scissor-tongued. He should have known better.

He braced himself. "And that is ‟"

This was hard for her, but not saying it would be too close to lying, so she made the best of it and forced out the words.

"You did a better job than I thought you would. Not perfect," Cassidy said, quickly qualifying her statement. "But better."

Finished cleaning up and putting a fresh diaper on Adam, he nodded at Cassidy. "That sounds more like you—all except for the semi-compliment."

"Yeah, well, don't let it go to your head," she warned. "Although, I guess there's no harm in that. It'll die of loneliness up there."

Will couldn't help laughing. "Now that *really* sounds more like you."

Since Will was apparently finished, she picked up the baby from the bed. Holding Adam against her, she automatically patted the baby's bottom, a gesture that soothed both her and the baby.

"Okay," she told Will, "you changed a diaper. Now go home."

She wasn't going to get rid of him that easily. "I said I was going to help and I meant it, Cassidy," he informed her. "So I'm staying."

"Oh, joy."

She'd turned her back on Will and walked out, so he had no way of seeing that there was a smile on her face as she left the bedroom.

Chapter 12

The knock on the door didn't wake him up—Will had never believed in sleeping in, no matter what time he'd finally gone to bed the night before. Sleeping in was for people who had no life, no responsibilities to meet. But the knock did catch him off guard.

He was just about to go outside to begin working with the horses. He was still trying to settle in after being gone for so long, and settling in was a slow, tedious process. All his time, spare or otherwise, was devoted to trying to make a go of a ranch that had very little going for it.

Even when he was growing up here, Will remembered times always being tough, remembered his father being drunk half the time even though—or maybe because—bills kept piling up. Despite the wolf being at the door countless times, and his father's habit of losing himself in the bottom of a bottle, somehow they managed to make it from one month to the next, usually just one jump ahead of complete ruin. Sometimes it was even less than that.

Part of Will felt that he should just sell the ranch for whatever he could get, use the money to pay off what he could and then just walk away from this part of his life.

The other part of him was determined to dig in and make a go of it, refusing to go under. Refusing to make his father's prophecy regarding his own life come true.

In essence, the ranch represented a challenge to him—a far more serious one than Cassidy did.

If this was a bill collector at the door, Will thought, approaching it, they were going to be disappointed. He wouldn't be able to make a payment until the first of the month—if then. It was the first of the year, actually. This was December, the month of miracles and, appropriately enough, Christmas. Heaven knew he could do with a miracle or two.

It was awfully warm for December, he couldn't help thinking. Recently the days had felt more like June. That was probably the main reason why he hadn't lost the colt that day of the flash flood. The horse had managed to survive until he had finally found him.

Will didn't bother asking who was at his door. Break-ins and thieves were just not common in the area, and if it was a bill collector, well, he'd just have to reason with him.

With all the possibilities that went through his mind, Will had to admit that not once had he considered that he'd find Cassidy on his doorstep when he threw open the front door.

"Something happen?" he asked, thinking only an emergency would bring her here.

Cassidy didn't bother answering his question. "Most people around here still say 'hello' when they see someone standing on their doorstep."

She waited for Will to step back and admit her. When he didn't, she ducked in around him.

"Maybe that's because most people don't see you on their doorstep," Will answered.

Since she'd walked in, he closed the door, resigned to her presence. Will braced himself, waiting for her to say something cryptic about his lack of housekeeping.

"How would you know?" Cassidy asked, looking around. She couldn't recall a single instance when she and her brothers had been inside Will's house. She could see why. The place looked positively depressing, she thought. "Have you asked around?"

What was she doing here? It wasn't as if she was in the habit of dropping by for a friendly visit. None of his friends ever did. His father's ranch had always been off-limits to them. His father always made a point of saying that.

"Is it Adam?" Will pressed. "Did something happen to Adam?" His mind raced through a list of possibilities. It had been almost three weeks since they'd rescued the boy, definitely time enough for word about him to get out. "Did his parents turn up?"

"No, nothing happened to Adam and no, his parents haven't turned up yet," she replied, answering Will's questions in order. She couldn't keep her reaction to herself any longer. "My Lord, it's gloomy in here. You might want to think about having a bigger window put in the front," she suggested, walking over

to the rather small window that was there now, looking out on the front of the house. "Cole could help you
with that. He's good with his hands." She glanced at
Will over her shoulder. "A little more light coming in
could only help."

She was making his head spin, not exactly an un-
common reaction whenever he was around Cassidy. He
hadn't slept much last night after going over his finances
and finding that the ranch his father had left to him
was in even worse shape than he'd originally thought.

Cassidy was only adding to the headache he'd had
ever since he'd gotten up.

Will caught hold of her shoulders, anchoring her in
place so that he could get her to hopefully give him a
straight answer.

"Cassidy, *why* are you here?" As he put the question to her, it occurred to him that she had asked him
the same thing when he'd first gone over to her family
ranch to pitch in with the baby.

But she had no such excuse. The baby wasn't here,
only an ever-growing pile of bills and a mushrooming
sense of impending failure.

"I guess you forgot. I figured you would," she told
him.

He was having trouble hanging on to his temper right
now. It felt as if the walls were closing in on him and
his normal ability to take things in stride was seriously
depleted. "Humor me. Tell me again."

Maybe it was the lack of light within the room, but
he could have sworn there was a hint of amusement in
those blue eyes of hers. Amusement and something else
he couldn't quite read.

Just what was going on here?

"Okay," Cassidy said gamely, deciding to take him off the hook and answer his question. "I told you that I'd come over on the weekend to give you a hand on the ranch. I couldn't come last week or the week before that, but that doesn't mean I forgot about it. I live up to my promises—even if you don't think so," she told him pointedly.

He barely remembered the conversation. It felt almost like a lifetime ago, and while he'd enjoyed the handful of times he'd gone over to her ranch to help take care of Adam, it seemed like a pleasant interlude in an otherwise oppressive existence.

"That's okay. I absolve you of your hasty promise," Will told her, waving her words away. "Go home to the baby."

Cassidy dug in, her body language telling him that she wasn't going anywhere. "I said I'd give you a hand and I—"

"I don't need a hand," Will told her curtly, his patience snapping. "I need a miracle."

She was accustomed to bantering with him. At other times, biting words were exchanged between them as they bickered. But this was something different. His tone was different, almost hopeless, she realized. Cassidy couldn't recall ever seeing him like this. She wasn't about to walk away without some sort of an explanation from him.

"Define miracle," she told him. When he didn't answer her, Cassidy tried another approach. "Okay, what is it that you need done?"

"Go home, Cassidy," Will told her flatly. "There's nothing you can do."

She was used to him underestimating her. What she

wasn't used to was not getting angry over it. Something about his manner kept her calm. What she felt was a genuine concern that he had a real problem.

"You'd be surprised at what I can do," she answered loftily. "Now I said I didn't intend to be in debt to you, and I'm not, so out with it," she instructed. "Just what kind of 'miracle' are you talking about?"

He looked at her as if she had lost her mind—or maybe he'd lost his and he was only imagining her here like this, trying to help him instead of trying to make his life miserable as was her usual custom.

Part of him thought that maybe this was some kind of an elaborate ruse on Cassidy's part to get him to believe that she actually wanted to help—just so she could laugh in his face when he told her what was wrong.

But then apathy came over him. What did it matter if she knew? Nothing was going to change. In the last couple of days, he'd woken up feeling numb, the way a man did when he knew he was going to go down for the third and last time because it was inevitable that he was going to drown.

Exasperated, Will blew out a breath and told her, "If I don't raise this month's mortgage payment, the bank is going to foreclose on the ranch."

Cassidy never took her eyes off his face as he talked. "And you don't want them to."

"Of course I don't want them to!" he shouted at her. Why would he be this upset if losing the ranch didn't matter to him?

Someone else would have backed off, but Cassidy wasn't someone else.

"Why?" she questioned, trying to get him to talk to her, to tell her what he really felt. "Why not let the bank take it? This place only reminds you of your father," she pointed out.

"It also reminds me of other things," he told her. He didn't know why he was bothering to explain this to her. After all, she didn't care. But he still heard himself telling her, "Besides, if I let them foreclose, then he wins. The old man wins," he bit out. "He left this place to me only to yank it away after he died."

Cassidy could see that the bad blood between Will and his father ran deep. "That's giving him a lot of credit for thinking clearly," she said, and then she shook her head because he probably wasn't aware of this. "Your father wasn't thinking clearly toward the end."

Will didn't ask her for details. He didn't want to know. Knowing would only compound the feeling of depression and hopelessness he was trying hard to battle and keep at bay.

He had to find a way to rally, to come up with a way to make the mortgage payment so he could buy himself some time until he could turn the ranch into a paying enterprise again.

Will had fallen silent. Cassidy tried prodding him again. "How much do you need?"

His eyes met hers. "Why?" he challenged.

Since he didn't seem to believe that she wanted to help him—he was, after all, her brothers' friend—she went back to the persona he felt he did know. "Because I want to know what it takes to make you go under."

Will squared his shoulders. It gave her hope. "I'm not going under."

"So back to my question. How much do you need?" she asked again.

He knew that she wasn't going to let up until he finally told her what she wanted to know.

So, grudgingly, he did.

Cassidy nodded. "Okay," was all she said in response as she turned on her heel and headed for the front door.

"I thought you said you came to help," he called after her. It was meant to mock her because he'd never expected her to stay and work on the ranch no matter what she'd initially said to the contrary.

"I did," she told him. And then, just as she opened the door to go out, Cassidy surprised him by adding, "I am."

And with that, she left.

"Right."

Will shook his head. That seemed par for the course, he thought, staring at the closed door.

He didn't have time to think about Cassidy and why she was behaving even stranger than usual. He had horses to feed. At least that much he could do. Coming up with that miracle he needed, however, was another story entirely.

Instead of going back home to share what she'd managed to get out of Will with her brothers, Cassidy went straight to town. Specifically, she went straight to Miss Joan's diner.

The diner was full when she walked in. On weekends, people had a few more minutes to spare on breakfast, or at least their morning coffee, than they did on weekday mornings.

Despite the crowd, Miss Joan spotted her before she had walked more than two feet into the diner.

Their eyes meeting, Miss Joan beckoned her over to

the counter. The older woman had a cup of coffee waiting for her by the time she reached it.

"Light," Miss Joan said, pushing the cup toward her. "Just like you like it. Now take a load off and tell me what's bothering you."

While Miss Joan's voice couldn't exactly be described as inviting, it had been known to coax many a story from a troubled soul.

Cassidy sat down at the counter. She knew better than to hesitate. Miss Joan wasn't a person someone played games with.

She told Miss Joan everything, that she'd come straight from Will's ranch, adding that she'd never seen him like that before. "He was so incredibly disheartened, he was almost like another person."

"Go on," Miss Joan urged quietly.

Cassidy went on to say she thought that Will was almost on the brink of defeat. She'd also told her why. Miss Joan listened and nodded. She waved off another customer when that man called out to her to get her attention.

Her eyes were fixed on Cassidy. "How much did you say he needed?"

Cassidy repeated the sum, remembering when an extra dollar could make all the difference in the world. "I know that in the scheme of things, it might not sound like all that much," she told Miss Joan, "but—"

"But when you don't have it, it's a king's ransom," Miss Joan concluded knowingly. She leaned closer to Cassidy, her words intended for the young woman's ears only. "I've been running this diner a lot of years now, and I've always been a woman with simple needs. I've got more money than I could even spend. If I lent Will the money for his ranch—"

Cassidy shook her head. She knew Will, knew how he thought. "He wouldn't accept it," she told her.

The hint of a smile on the woman's thin lips told Cassidy that she already knew that.

"What would you suggest?" Miss Joan asked, wanting to see if they were of a like mind.

She'd been mulling over possible solutions ever since she'd left Will's ranch. "We could start a fundraiser," Cassidy proposed. "Get everyone to put in a little. That way it's from everybody, not just one person. He couldn't turn that down."

Miss Joan laughed at the certainty she heard in Cassidy's voice. "Do you *know* Will Laredo?" she asked.

"Okay, he could turn it down," Cassidy allowed, then added fiercely, "But I won't let him. If he lets that ranch go, it'll eat at him for the rest of his life—and that's just not going to happen."

Miss Joan nodded, pleased to hear Cassidy take this stand. She was pleased for a number of reasons, not the least of which was that she had a feeling in her bones that all those years that Cassidy and Will had spent feuding and sniping at each other were about to come to a long anticipated end.

About time, Miss Joan thought.

Picking up a thick water glass, Miss Joan began to hit its side with a knife. She kept on hitting it until the noise level within the diner died down and then completely faded away.

"I'd like everyone's attention," she declared in her honey-dipped whiskey voice.

And once she was satisfied that she had it, Miss

Joan launched into the details of why she was holding an impromptu fund-raiser at the diner, explaining that no one was going to be allowed to leave without contributing *something*.

It didn't matter how little, but it had to be something.

She went on to add—without mentioning a name—that this was for one of their own, and that each and every one of them—herself included—knew what it was like to be faced with bills that couldn't be paid on time for one reason or another.

To seal the deal, Miss Joan told the diner patrons that if they could afford it and their contribution was for a decent amount, they would receive a voucher for a free breakfast on the date of their choice.

And then Miss Joan sat back and waited.

She didn't have long to wait.

"You're back," Will said in surprise late that same afternoon.

Cassidy had spotted him in the corral. After parking her truck near the ranch house, she'd walked back to where he was working with the horses that Connor had told her Will had bought earlier in the month. Ironically, it was with the last of his money.

She wasted no time with small talk. Instead, she crossed over to Will and ordered, "Put out your hands."

"Why?" he asked warily, eyeing the sack she was carrying.

Cassidy huffed. "Will you stop questioning everything I say, and for once in your life just do as I ask?"

After a moment, Will put out one hand. The wary look in his eyes, however, remained.

Cassidy frowned. Even when it was a good deed, it

was like pulling teeth with this man. "Both of them," she prompted.

He regarded Cassidy suspiciously, then did as she asked, never taking his eyes off her.

She opened the sack and took out a manila envelope, holding it out to him. The envelope looked as if it was about to burst.

Will made no move to undo the clasp. Instead, he asked, "What is this?"

"The miracle you asked for," she answered very simply.

When he said nothing, only continued looking at it, she scowled at him. "You do have a way of sucking the joy out of things, you know that? Take it. It's the money you said you needed to keep the bank from foreclosing on the ranch."

Instead of accepting it, Will pushed the envelope back toward her. "I can't take your money."

Cassidy pushed it right back at him. "It's not my money."

"Well, then I can't take Connor's money," he said, impatience mounting in his voice.

"It's not his, either." She saw him open his mouth. "And before you go down the list, it's not Cody's or Cole's, either."

She was playing games again. No one he knew had that kind of money to lend him just like that. "Then whose is it?"

"Yours," she answered innocently.

"Cassidy," he warned, "don't play games with me."

"Trust me, the last thing on my mind is playing with you, Laredo," she told him. It was clear that she was not about to tell him the origin of the money. She didn't want anything getting in the way of his accepting the money and saving his ranch. "Consider this an early Christmas present. Now stop being a jackass and take this to the bank. You've got just enough time before it closes to make that payment. Unless, of course, you want your father to be right—posthumously."

Cassidy had always known just what to say in order to goad him.

"This isn't over," Will promised her, taking the money.

"I didn't think it was," she told him, adding with a smile, "I look forward to round two."

Chapter 13

"I don't get it," Will said to Connor.

Several days had passed since Cassidy had brought him the mysterious envelope filled with money, and this was the first opportunity that the two of them had to get together. Connor had come by Will's ranch to volunteer his help, taking his turn the same way that his siblings were doing.

The first thing Will did was tell him about the envelope full of cash that Cassidy had given him.

"I've asked around, but nobody'll tell me where that money came from," Will said, clearly confounded as to the money's origin.

Because Cassidy knew she could trust him—and because she hadn't wanted him thinking that she had bent some laws to secure the funds—his sister had confided in him about Miss Joan's impromptu fund-raiser for Will's mortgage payment.

He and Will were working on replacing several lengths of fencing that composed the corral. It was almost restored.

"You don't have a need to know," Connor told him. "All that matters is that you bought yourself some time with the money."

"I know that," Will answered impatiently, holding the rail steady as Connor nailed the new length to the end that remained on that side. "But, Connor, in all good conscience—"

Finished hammering that end, Connor let the hammer drop before he tested the strength of the replaced rail. "Will, conscience has a place in our lives, a very big place. But sometimes, you just have to close your eyes and go on faith," he told his friend.

Will wasn't sure if he could accept that. Most of all, he wasn't sure just how to interpret Cassidy's actions. "Just what the hell is your sister up to?" he asked.

"Who knows? This is Cassidy we're talking about," he reminded Will. "She's always been rather unpredictable. Maybe *she's* following her conscience." Connor stopped working and faced the other man. "Look, she did a good deed. Let it go at that. You two have spent so much time bickering, you completely lost sight of the two human beings living behind all that rhetoric."

Pausing, Connor stooped to pick up his hammer again. "Now, are we going to spend the rest of the day flapping our gums, getting nowhere, or are we going to get some work done?" he asked. "'Cause I am *not* a man of leisure and this is all the time I can spare for a while."

Will nodded. Connor was right. His father had left the family ranch not just in debt but in complete disrepair, and he was grateful for any help he could get. "Work," he answered.

Connor smiled, patting his friend's back. "Good choice."

"Still want to know where she got that money," Will murmured as he picked up another length of railing.

"I'm sure you do," Connor replied mildly as he began hammering again.

The inference was clear. There were more important things that needed his friend's attention than discovering where the money had come from.

Cassidy was running behind.

Actually, these last few weeks, she felt as if she was always running and always behind, she thought as she hastily buttoned her blouse. She couldn't remember ever feeling this tired.

She supposed that this was what it felt like to be a single mother, always trying to balance taking care of a baby with the demands of a job—except that she wasn't a single mother. She wasn't a mother at all. Any day now, all that would change, and her life would slow down and get back to normal, whatever that was.

What really surprised her was that the thought wasn't nearly as comforting as she'd expected it to be.

Hurrying into the rest of her clothes, Cassidy winced when she heard Adam beginning to cry.

Again.

She stopped by his crib, which was a few feet away from her bed and the chief reason why she wasn't getting anything close to a full night's sleep since he'd taken up temporary residency in her house.

Though she tried not to be, Cassidy was tuned in to

Adam's every movement and was aware of each time he so much as shifted in his crib whether he was asleep or not.

"I've already fed you and changed you. *Why* are you crying?" she asked the baby helplessly.

Cody's wife had volunteered to watch the baby today, but she couldn't very well leave Devon with a crying baby, especially when her own baby had turned into a dynamo who was just beginning to crawl and get into everything.

"Okay, tell me what's wrong?" Cassidy asked wearily, picking Adam up. She had her answer immediately. The baby felt as if he was on fire. "Oh, my God, you're hot. Really hot. You weren't this hot half an hour ago." She could feel herself beginning to panic. "I didn't know anyone could get this hot so fast."

As fear enveloped her, Cassidy felt as if she wanted to run in half a dozen directions all at the same time. She tried to focus and found that she really couldn't.

Grabbing her shoes, Cassidy all but flew down the stairs, holding the wailing baby against her. "Connor," she cried, raising her voice so she could be heard above the baby's wails.

Reaching the bottom of the stairs, she looked around desperately, trying to locate her oldest brother. When she didn't see or hear him, she dashed into the kitchen and all but crashed into him there.

Connor was just putting dishes into the dishwasher.

"What's wrong?" The trivial guess he was about to make to answer his own question faded the second he saw the look on his sister's face. He'd never seen her like that before. "Cassidy?" he asked uncertainly.

"It's the baby," she cried, her voice almost breaking. "Connor, he's burning up."

He was accustomed to hearing his sister exaggerating things, but when he took the baby from her—wanting to comfort both of them—he could feel the heat radiating from Adam.

For once, Cassidy *wasn't* exaggerating. "You're right," he told her, cradling the unhappy baby against him. "He is hot."

"I know I'm right," she answered impatiently. "What do I do?" Connor was the one they all turned to for advice, the one they depended on. "Is it even possible to be this hot without— What do I do?" she repeated, not wanting to complete the thought that had just flashed through her head.

"We need to get him to the clinic," Connor told her.

He was doing his best to keep the urgency out of his voice because he didn't want to make Cassidy any more panicked than she already was, but one look into her eyes and he knew that she saw through his act.

"It's bad, isn't it?" she asked him, trying hard not to allow her fear to get the better of her.

"You ran high fevers all the time when you were around his size. You nearly drove Dad crazy. Turns out you're still here," he pointed out comfortingly. "But it never hurts to have a doctor check him out. At least we won't have to drive fifty miles to Mission Ridge the way we did when you were running high fevers. There was no clinic in town when you were Adam's age.

"C'mon, let's go," he said, walking ahead of her with the baby.

It was all Cassidy could do to remember to grab her

purse before she hurried after him. Her brain felt like the contents of a scattered can of green peas.

"So he'll be all right?" Cassidy asked Dr. Alisha Murphy anxiously, wanting to hear the pediatrician reassure her again.

Alisha smiled. "He'll be fine. Babies run high fevers all the time," she said. There was nothing but sympathy in her voice as she looked down at her little patient. "But just to be sure, why don't I keep this little trouper here today for observation? This way I can check in on him every half hour or so to make sure everything's under control. I'll have Debi give you a call if there's any significant change."

Cassidy was torn.

She thought of all the files she'd allowed to pile up on her desk in the office these last few weeks. She didn't want Olivia or Cash to feel that she was letting them down. She was trying to forge a career, which meant she needed to act accordingly, not appear as if she was just going through the motions when it suited her. But at the same time, she wanted to be here, with Adam. He needed her, and she needed to be reassured that he wasn't going to take a turn for the worse. She was well aware that things had a way of changing suddenly, especially at that age.

Finally, she relented. "All right," Cassidy agreed, then added, "As long as you're sure someone will call me if Adam suddenly starts getting worse."

"He won't, but one of us will definitely call you if anything changes," Alisha promised, then added comfortingly, "Kids are a lot more resilient than we think they are, and this little guy seemed like he was a healthy baby the last time I examined him."

Taking the words to heart, Cassidy finally left the clinic.

She wondered how mothers did it, how they made it intact through their baby's first year. It had to be extremely taxing, not to mention exhausting. How did they do it? And how did they, knowing all this, go on to have more children? It seemed like a mystery to her, she thought, leaving the clinic.

Cassidy couldn't remember the last time a day had gone by so slowly. She checked her watch as well as her phone periodically, afraid she'd somehow missed a call. But other than a call from each of her brothers and her sister-in-law, checking on how the baby was doing as well as how *she* was doing, there were no other calls.

Specifically, there were no calls from the clinic requesting her immediate presence.

Eventually Cassidy calmed down enough to concentrate on her work—at least to a degree.

And the minute that her workday was officially over, Cassidy was out of the office and the one-story building like a shot. Since Connor had driven her to the clinic, she had no means of transportation available. He had gone back to the ranch, leaving specific instructions that she call him the minute she was ready to pick up the baby and come home.

She wasn't about to bother him until she knew what was going on, so she walked to the clinic now, after turning down both Cash's and Olivia's offer to drive her there. She insisted she was quite capable of getting there on her own.

Because the town was small, everything was within walking distance, although she had to concede that some of those distances were farther than others.

Besides, she'd told Olivia, she could use the exercise to walk off her tension. Her boss had decided not to argue the point.

When she walked into the clinic, Cassidy saw that Debi was behind the reception desk. The woman looked up as she entered and waved her into the back.

"Dr. Alisha's just checking on Adam," the nurse told her. "You can go right in."

Wanting to race to the last exam room—which had been converted to an interim hospital room where patients could recover from minor outpatient surgery—Cassidy still hesitated at the closed door. She needed a second to brace herself before entering.

Once she walked in, she asked Alisha, "How's he doing?"

The pediatrician smiled at her patient's "mother," obviously happy about being able to deliver a positive prognosis.

"He's doing better. His fever's almost gone, but it's still hanging in there to some degree."

Was the doctor deliberately keeping something from her? Cassidy wondered. Her stomach had been queasy all day, ever since she'd realized that Adam's fever had spiked.

"Give it to me straight, Doc. Should I be worried?" Cassidy asked.

Alisha met the question with a self-depreciating laugh. "Mothers go on worrying until after their kids turn fifty. After that, they still worry, but I hear not as much," she confided, then went on to say, "Because this is his first go-round with a high fever, I'm going to suggest keeping him here overnight."

Cassidy felt a rush of disappointment. "Then I can't take him home?"

"You could," Alisha conjectured, "but if the fever suddenly goes up again for some reason, you're going to have to drive back here, and I promise you that you'll agonize all the way. This way, he'll be right here, and if his fever does spike for some reason, which is only a possibility, not a sure thing, I can give him a shot to bring it down again."

Cassidy felt as if she needed everything spelled out for her. "But the fever's down now, right?"

"It's down," Alisha assured her.

Cassidy chewed on her bottom lip, undecided as to what to do for a moment. And then she looked up. "How about a compromise?" she proposed. "Adam will stay here overnight, but I'll stay with him, not you. If anything goes wrong, I'll call you or Dr. Dan right away." She could see that the doctor was about to protest the decision. "You need to go home to your own kids, Doc. They probably don't see you nearly enough."

"All right. Either one of us can be here within minutes," she stated.

Cassidy nodded. She really hadn't wanted to leave Adam's side, anyway. She'd spent every night for the last month near him, and she wouldn't be able to sleep at all knowing he was sick somewhere away from her. "Good enough for me, Doc."

Alisha eyed her rather warily. "Are you sure about this?"

Cassidy never hesitated. "I'm very sure," she said firmly.

Alisha asked her the same question a few hours later as she was about to close the clinic for the night. Cassidy gave her the same answer.

"Okay, then I'll see you in the morning," Alisha told her, softly closing the door behind her.

After checking on Adam, who was mercifully asleep and breathing a lot better, at least for the time being, Cassidy noted, she sat back down in the chair.

She wasn't aware of sighing as she tried to find a comfortable position for herself in order to settle in for the night.

Just as she was about to close her eyes, Cassidy heard the door behind her opening again. It had only been a few minutes since the doctor had left her.

"I said I'm sure," Cassidy repeated, hoping that would finally send the doctor on her way to her own family for the night.

"What are you sure about?"

Only extreme restraint kept her for crying out in surprise.

As it was, Cassidy jumped to her feet, almost sending the chair crashing to the floor. Will darted in and caught it just in time.

"What are you doing here, Laredo?" she asked. "It's after hours, and everyone at the clinic's gone home for the night."

"Yes, I know," Will told her. "I passed Dr. Alisha just as she was locking up. She was the one who let me in."

Cassidy pulled him over, away from the sleeping baby before his voice could wake Adam up.

"I repeat," she said to him in an annoyed whisper, "what are you doing here?"

"I'm here so you can get some rest. We can take turns watching the baby while the other one sleeps."

As far as she knew, none of her brothers had called him about Adam's fever. At least, none of them had mentioned it to her. But that didn't mean that they hadn't. She frowned.

"How did you find out he was sick?" she asked. If she had to make a guess, she supposed that Connor had to have told him, but she guessed wrong.

The answer was quite simple. "Miss Joan told me when I stopped by the diner on my way back from the general store."

Cassidy sighed. She didn't bother asking how Miss Joan had found out. Miss Joan *always* found out.

"So how is he?" Will asked, nodding toward the baby.

"Better," Cassidy answered. "His fever's almost gone Look, you don't have to stay here with me, taking turns watching him. I can—"

"I wasn't asking for permission," Will pointed out quietly. "We both rescued him. That means, like it or not, Cassidy, we're both in this together."

Cassidy sighed again. "You're determined to ignore me, aren't you?"

Will watched her for a long moment, so long that she could almost feel her body heating beneath his gaze. Cassidy upbraided herself for her reaction. She did her best not to look at the smile that was slowly slipping over his lips.

"Oh, I wouldn't say that," he said, more to himself than to her. He had finally come to terms with the fact that ignoring Cassidy was just not in the cards for him. "You look like you've been through the wringer. I'll spell you for an hour." He dragged over another chair and positioning it on the other side of the crib that had been brought in for the baby.

He was about to tell her that she could close her eyes now and discovered that he didn't have to. She already had.

Chapter 14

Cassidy's eyes flew open as if someone had shaken her shoulder to rouse her. As far as she could tell, only a few minutes had passed since she'd closed her eyes.

Taking a deep breath, she tried to orient herself a little more. She focused in on her watch to make sure that she *hadn't* been asleep for long.

A moment later, she remembered why she was here—and with whom.

"Sorry," she murmured, certain that he'd noticed that her eyes had closed. "I was just resting my eyes for a minute."

"You were asleep," Will corrected her with a grin. "But let's not quibble over terms."

"I wasn't quibbling, I was 'stating,'" she told him emphatically. "In this case, stating the fact that I wasn't asleep." Knowing Will, he'd take her momentary catnap as an opportunity to ridicule her about it, or something along those lines.

He hadn't come here to argue, Will thought. He'd come here to help—no matter how much she fought him about it.

"Fine, have it your way," he allowed. "I'm really not in the mood for another battle of 'who gets the last word' with you. I'm just here to help."

She couldn't help it. She was very suspicious of this so-called act of kindness on Will's part. She recalled the state of his range.

"Don't you have enough to do?" she asked.

His eyes met hers, and she had that same feeling that he was looking deep into her thoughts, her soul, that she'd had before.

"Well, thanks to the last person in the world I ever thought would volunteer to help me, I seem to have gotten a stay of execution, so right now I have a little extra time to spare, and this is where I want to be, watching over Adam."

She wasn't just going to allow him to take over like that. Cassidy knew him. She'd be pushed over to the sidelines in no time flat.

"I'm watching over Adam," she told him.

He could work with that. "And I'm watching you watching over Adam," he amended.

Cassidy had a feeling that this could go on forever, and she knew it wasn't really getting either one of them anywhere. Besides, she had to admit—if only to herself and certainly not out loud—that she was rather touched that Laredo was so concerned about the boy's condition. Adam had gotten to both of them.

It started her thinking about the whole situation again. And that aroused a fresh set of fears.

"You know, I've kind of gotten used to having him around." She sighed, pressing her lips together. "It's probably a bad thing."

Will's forehead furrowed as he looked at her. "Why would you say that?"

"Because I'm really going to miss him when his parents show up to take him." She felt a pang even as she said the words.

"I'm not so sure they're ever going to." When she looked at him quizzically, he said, "Think about it. It's been a month since that flood hit, and so far, nobody has come forward looking for him. Not even after we took him with us to the reservation."

"Maybe they can't come forward," she suggested. "Maybe Adam's parents are in the hospital, in a coma, recovering from a car accident or some other kind of unforeseen mishap."

There was one problem with her theory. "Are you forgetting the closest hospital is fifty miles away?" he reminded her.

She was still casting about, trying to find a viable excuse. What she couldn't bring herself to believe was that Adam had been abandoned.

"Maybe whoever they were with, or his mother was with, realized how badly they were—or she was—hurt and took them straight to Mission Ridge and the hospital."

"And the baby? How do you explain the baby being out there in the flash flood?" he asked.

She was working hard to try to pull all the ends together. Although she'd always maintained that she didn't have any maternal feelings, she'd been trying to see what happened from her own point of view.

"The flash flood hit suddenly, she wanted to save the baby so she put him into that plastic thing we found him in. Meanwhile, she got swept away and lost consciousness. Then someone found her. When she remained unresponsive, they took her to the hospital."

Listening to her, Will could only shake his head. "Incredible."

"You like that, huh?" Cassidy asked proudly, happy that she was able to come up with a scenario that seemed to account for all the pieces.

He hadn't meant that her explanation was incredible. The word was meant to describe her and the contortions her mind had gone to in order to come up with this convoluted explanation.

"I'll say this for you," he said, laughing shortly, "you've got one hell of an imagination."

It wasn't hard to read between the lines. "So you don't think that's possible?" she asked him, taking offense.

"If you've taught me nothing else, Cassidy, you've taught me that just about anything *could be* possible," he told her.

Cassidy frowned at him. "You're being sarcastic again," she accused.

"No, actually," he stated, "I'm being in awe. I've honestly never seen anyone bob and weave the way you do. Who knows? The sheriff still hasn't found either a body or an abandoned car, so until one or the other—or both—turn up, then I guess that anything *could* be possible in these circumstances."

In light of what she'd just suggested, Cassidy thought

that perhaps another course of action was necessary. "Maybe the sheriff should place a call to the Mission Ridge Hospital."

"Actually, I think he is, first thing in the morning," Will said.

This was news to her. "You talked with him," she assumed.

Will had stopped by the sheriff's office just before coming to the clinic. "Just to find out if he was making any progress locating Adam's parents," Will told her. "He hasn't, so after we talked, contacting the hospital is what he's going to try next."

She nodded, thinking about the possible end result of the sheriff's investigation—either end. "What if he doesn't find anyone?" she asked.

"You're talking about Adam's parents?"

"Right. What if Sheriff Santiago calls all the local hospitals in a hundred mile radius and doesn't find anyone who could possibly be Adam's parents, then what? What happens to Adam?"

"Exactly what would have happened to him if you hadn't stepped up and volunteered to take him until his parents—or mother—could be located. He'll be sent to social services in Mission Ridge—or maybe even one of the larger cities—and then they'll place him in someone's home."

The very suggestion of Adam being taken away to live with someone else made her blood run cold. "And you'd be okay with that?" she challenged, horrified at the thought of Adam being passed from hand to hand, without anyone actually caring for the boy.

"I didn't say that," Will corrected her tersely. "But there's not exactly a lot that I can do in this situation. I can't claim I have some kind of blood relationship with him, and I'm sure that nobody would let *me* adopt him."

She listened to Will, surprised that he had actually thought it out that far. Maybe she'd misjudged him after all.

"Social services wants a stable home environment for any child they place. Considering that I was on the brink of foreclosure, and if I don't wind up selling a few of the horses and start making some kind of profit, no matter how minor, I'll wind up losing the ranch, I'm not exactly a star candidate. Social services doesn't smile upon a prospective adoptive parent living out of his truck."

She pushed aside all that, wanting to be perfectly clear about what he was saying. "But otherwise, you would?"

He'd lost the thread of what she was saying to him. Cassidy had a way of jumping around. "What?"

She tried to be clearer. "Otherwise, if the ranch didn't go into foreclosure and you were making a go of it, you would adopt Adam?"

Will didn't even pause to think about it. He knew what he would do. "Sure, why not?"

Cassidy had to admit that she was having trouble wrapping her mind around this new, improved Will Laredo. "I've got a better question for you—why? Why would you adopt Adam?"

"Maybe so I could give him a home, give him someone who cared about him. And maybe, while we're at it, so I could finally have a family myself." Maybe it was the late hour, or the situation, or just a combination of both. Whatever it was, he found himself admitting things to Cassidy that he had never said out loud before. "I never felt I had one before. The closest I ever came to feeling like I had a family was when I hung around your brothers and you."

That really took her aback. "I understand you feeling that way about my brothers, but about me, too?" she questioned.

Will shrugged. "Sure, a lot of brothers have pesky little sisters. Your brothers certainly did," he pointed out with a grin.

Cassidy drew herself up. "I was never a pesky little sister to them," she protested.

Will laughed. He could think of so many different instances to cite. "Right. You keep telling yourself that."

"I wasn't," she insisted. "We were a team, my brothers and I. We had to be once Dad was gone, we had to work together to make a go of the ranch. Otherwise, the county was going to come in and take us away. At least take three of us away," she amended.

Will nodded, vividly remembering how concerned Connor had been that he might not get custody of his siblings. Never once had he lamented about what he was giving up for them.

"Yes, I remember. I guess, in a way, that gives the three of us something in common," Will said, nodding at the baby and then her.

Ordinarily Cassidy would have protested the comparison, saying that while she and the baby had something in common, when it came to running the very real danger of having the county step in and absorb them, she and Will had *nothing* in common. But it wasn't true. She and Will were both orphans, she because her parents had both died and he because, while his father had remained alive for a lot of years after hers had passed away, Will had been just as alone as they were. His father had died on the inside long before the man was officially pronounced dead on the outside.

Though she would have hated to admit it, she could feel herself empathizing with Will. All she was willing to do was vaguely say, "I guess it does."

Will did his best to suppress a grin. "I guess I must be the one who's asleep."

Cassidy stared at him, trying to fathom his meaning. "What are you talking about?"

He tried again. "Well, I must be asleep because I'm definitely dreaming."

Still nothing. "Again, *what*?" Cassidy said impatiently.

"I'm dreaming," Will repeated. "You're being much too agreeable for this to actually be taking place. The Cassidy McCullough I know enjoys vivisecting me with her tongue. The one I think I'm talking to is being sweet, kind and understanding."

Was that a backhanded compliment—or a backhanded insult? She wasn't sure. "I can start vivisecting again if you'd prefer."

"No, that's okay," he quickly assured her with a laugh. "Let me go on dreaming a little longer."

Cassidy could only sigh. "You're crazy, you know that, don't you?"

"For what I'm thinking?" His eyes slid along the length of her, saying things to her that were better left unsaid—for both their sakes. "Yeah, probably," Will agreed.

Cassidy couldn't explain why, but she felt this warm shiver undulating up and down her spine like a garden snake uncoiling and staking out its territory while it was familiarizing itself with its new surroundings.

She did what she could to block the sensation, but for some reason, that only seemed to reinforce it.

"I'm not interested in what you're thinking," she finally said in a last-ditch effort to make Will think that his words—and the intent behind them—left her completely cold instead of the exact opposite.

"That's good," he replied, his voice mild. "Because I'm not about to tell you."

And that simple declaration aroused her curiosity. "Why not?"

"Because it wouldn't be safe."

"For me?" she challenged. Only she was the best judge of what was—or wasn't—safe for her to hear. He had no right to make that judgment call, and she was about to make him know it—never mind that something was warning her that she was heading into dangerous territory.

The smile that was teasing the corners of his mouth—and consequently her—made her stomach feel as if it was filling up with wall-to-wall butterflies.

Cassidy reminded herself that she'd been so worried about Adam and his fever that she hadn't eaten all day. *That* was to blame for the tight, twisted feeling in the pit of her stomach, nothing else.

Certainly not Will Laredo.

"No," Will contradicted her, "it wouldn't be safe for me."

She scowled at him. "Even when you're being supposedly 'nice,' you manage to make me want to strangle you," she told him.

The smile on Will's face only widened. "Good to know."

Her eyes darkened. "That wasn't meant to be a compliment."

"My mistake," he said. His tone told her that he felt the exact opposite.

Damn it, he wasn't getting to her. He *wasn't*, Cassidy silently insisted. It was just a matter of too little sleep and nothing to eat. And no coffee. Agitated about Adam, she hadn't had her morning coffee. She *always* had her morning coffee, or nothing was in sync for her all day long.

Tomorrow would be better, Cassidy promised herself. Tomorrow she would see this evening for what it was: a fluke, an aberration. A product of a number of minuses, nothing more.

"Well, if you're not going to go to sleep, then I am," she announced.

His smile was nothing if not encouraging. She just *had* to stop letting it get to her.

"That's what I've been telling you to do all along," Will said.

"I'm not doing it because you're telling me to," she informed him. "I'm doing it because it's just a huge waste for both of us to be staying awake like this."

Will spread his hands wide, amused. "My thoughts exactly."

"Stop being so agreeable, Laredo," she snapped. He was putting her on edge, behaving like this. "That's not like you."

That damn sexy smile was back, undulating under her skin, causing more havoc.

"Maybe it is."

She would have let out a scream if it wouldn't have woken up the baby. As it was, it was difficult to conduct an argument in whispers, especially when one of the two people in the argument refused to argue.

She didn't like these new rules. "You're just messing with my mind," Cassidy accused.

Will inclined his head. "If you say so."

She clenched her hands in her lap, curling her fingernails into her palms. She was doing what she could in order to ground herself.

This wasn't getting her anywhere.

Maybe a little reverse psychology might help her out. "Anyway, thanks for trying to spell me."

"Operative word here being *trying*. Thank me once I succeed," he told her, sounding almost annoyingly cheerful.

It told her that he was enjoying this, enjoying getting under her skin, getting in the last word, because that was the way Laredo was built. You couldn't change the spots on a leopard, she insisted. Even a leopard with a very sexy smile.

Especially a leopard with a very sexy smile.

Chapter 15

Will was gone.

When Cassidy opened her eyes again, she looked directly across from where she was sitting to the chair on the other side of the crib and saw that it was empty.

Her eyes swept over the small room with the same results. Will was nowhere to be found.

Adam, mercifully, appeared to be sleeping comfortably. Had he slept quietly through the night? Or had she, for the first time in four weeks, just slept right through his cries?

She noticed the empty formula bottle on the counter and saw that the seal on the pack of disposable diapers the doctor had left had been broken. Sometime during the night, Adam had been changed and fed—and she had slept right through it.

"After all this time, Will Laredo, you've actually

managed to surprise me," she murmured, shaking her head. Who knew?

A noise coming from the front of the clinic caught Cassidy's attention. Thinking that Will was out there, trying to scrounge up some coffee in the minuscule break room, she went out, intending to ask him why he hadn't woken her up to take care of the baby.

But again, she didn't find Will.

Instead, she found Holly, the clinic's other nurse, making coffee in the alcove that was right off the reception area.

Holly swung around the second that she walked into the alcove.

"Oh, Cassidy, you startled me," Holly cried. "I forgot that you were staying here overnight with the baby. How's he doing?" she asked. Putting down the coffee decanter, Holly suddenly appeared concerned. "His fever hasn't gone up again, has it?"

Not waiting for an answer, Holly went quickly to see for herself.

"No, it hasn't gone up," Cassidy called after her. "Adam's sleeping and his head feels cool, thank goodness."

Since she was already there, Holly tiptoed into the room and checked for herself, lightly brushing her fingertips across the baby's forehead.

Adam stirred a little but continued sleeping.

"You're right," Holly whispered as she slipped out of the room. "Cool as a cucumber." She smiled at Cassidy. "I think you've survived your first baby crisis."

Holly led the way back to the break room. "One of the doctors should be here soon. They all usually get in early," she told Cassidy. A smile played on her lips. "You'd think we liked it here, or something."

Cassidy watched as the nurse went back to making coffee. "When you first came in," she began, trying to sound as if she didn't care what the answer was one way or another, "you didn't happen to see anyone else here, did you?"

"Like who?" Holly asked. "Like I said, I'd forgotten about you and Adam staying overnight. Was there supposed to be someone else here, too? Because I didn't see anyone."

That was all she wanted to know. Cassidy shook her head. She definitely didn't want to get into an explanation. "Never mind."

If she said anything about Will being here through the night, Holly might get the wrong idea. That was how rumors started in a town the size of a postage stamp, a town where almost nothing ever happened. The least deviation from the norm and everyone jumped on it, hoping to sink their teeth into something of substance, or at the very least, something diverting.

She could see for herself that Will wasn't here, and if Holly wasn't saying anything, that meant that he had left before the nurse opened the clinic.

Cassidy glanced at her watch. It was barely 7:00 a.m.

How had she not heard Laredo leaving? she asked herself. Or, for that matter, how had she not heard Adam fussing? For the last month, she'd been tuned in to every sound that the baby made, so why was last night any different?

"When did you say that one of the doctors was coming in?" Cassidy asked, then added, "I'm assuming that one of them has to sign Adam out so it'll be okay for me to take him home."

Holly waved away Cassidy's concern. "I'm sure it's

okay to take him home since his fever's gone, but if you want to make it official, Dr. Dan or Dr. Alisha should be here anytime now."

The words were no sooner out of Holly's mouth than they heard the front door being opened.

"There's one of them now," Holly said. "Unless it's Debi," she amended.

But it wasn't Debi. It was Dan, in before eight as had become his habit ever since he'd reopened the clinic several years ago.

"So how's our patient doing?" he asked brightly the moment he saw Cassidy.

"Much better," she answered, relieved. "His fever's gone."

"Told you it would be," he reminded her. He and Alisha had taken turns checking on their littlest patient throughout the day. "Scary stuff the first time it happens, though. And the second, and the third. Gets a little better as time goes on, but never really easier. Worrying is just something you have to come to terms with and get used to."

Cassidy felt that the doctor was talking as if Adam was her baby instead of just a child she found temporarily in her care. She wanted to correct him and remind him that she wasn't really connected to Adam, but decided to let it go.

She played down the "worry" aspect by saying, "I just wanted you to look him over to make sure that I could take him home."

Except that it isn't his home, it's just his temporary shelter, Cassidy reminded herself. She was guilty of making the same mistake that the doctor had just made.

But she had to admit that over the last month, she

had come to regard Adam as her own. She knew she shouldn't, but that didn't change anything.

Dan delivered the same verdict that Holly had a few minutes earlier. The baby's fever was gone. Adam was as healthy as if yesterday had never happened.

"Take the boy home," Dan told her happily.

Although she already knew that the baby was all right, Cassidy still breathed a sigh of relief.

"Thank you!"

And then she put a call in to Connor.

"You're sure you don't mind?" she questioned her brother a little more than an hour later.

Connor had dropped everything and come for them the moment she'd called. They were home now, and her question referred to her leaving Adam in his care while she returned to town to run an errand.

"There're some papers I need to pick up from the office so I can work on them here, but maybe I can do that later—"

Connor nodded. Cassidy might very well be picking up files at the office, the way she said she needed to, but he had a hunch that those files weren't her main focus. He had known Cassidy her entire life—long enough and well enough to see through excuses when she came up with them—like now.

Something else was on her mind. He wasn't about to ask her what, confident that when she wanted him to know, Cassidy would tell him.

"I'm sure. I was planning on working on the books today, anyway, so I'll only be a cry away if Adam wants something. Go, do whatever you have to do," he told her, waving his sister out the front door and on her way.

* * *

Her brother had worded his sentence just vaguely enough—"Go do whatever you have to do"—for her to be able to hide a multitude of deeds within it.

Cassidy made sure she stopped at the law firm first. Something told her that if she left that errand for last, she might never make it to the office. Not that she was a slacker, or flighty, but she'd learned that things had a way of happening when she was around Laredo. Cassidy didn't want to chance not picking up what she wanted her brother to believe was essentially her "main reason" for leaving Adam and the ranch.

Laredo, or rather his ranch, was her next—and last—stop.

Since he had given up his night to stay with her and watch over Adam—in essence being the *only* one who stayed up with Adam after a point—Cassidy felt that she owed Will an update on Adam's condition.

It was, she argued with herself, the decent thing to do.

She was still telling herself that when she pulled up in front of his ranch house, parked her truck and got out. Crossing to the front door, Cassidy's nerve failed her just about the time she raised her hand to knock.

She stood there for a moment, her hand raised but not making contact while she carried on an internal argument with herself.

Will could be out of the house, working on the range. He could be mending fences, training horses or any one of a dozen other things that would've necessitated his leaving the ranch house.

Instead of standing here, debating, Cassidy upbraided herself, she needed to get back to Adam and her responsibilities. She could leave Laredo a message on his phone since she felt she owed him an update.

Engrossed, she didn't hear the footsteps behind her. Not until Will was there, less than a foot away. She was just about to drop her hand to her side.

"Posing for a statue?" Will asked.

This time, she did shriek. Shrieked and swung around, her hand fisted and ready to make contact. Will barely jumped back in time.

"Hey, watch that, Champ," he chided, grabbing her wrist. "You nearly knocked me out."

Cassidy yanked her hand free. She wasn't swinging that hard. "Only if I had some kind of a weapon in my hand when I made contact," she told him sarcastically. "Or have you suddenly developed a glass jaw?"

"Nope, my jaw is hard as ever." His eyes swept over her. "And since you don't have a weapon in your hand, can I assume that you came by for a friendly chat?" he asked, opening his door. "Or did you change your mind about that loan you brought over the other day?"

"The answer's no to both," she informed him. "I just thought, after what you did last night, spending it watching Adam and all, I owed it to you to give you an update on his condition."

"Why don't you come inside?" he urged, pushing the door open even farther when she made no effort to follow him in. "The horses like to gossip. Before you know it, they'll be labeling us a couple, and everyone will be forced to believe it."

"Not if they had any sense," she informed him crisply. But after a moment, she gave in and walked into the house.

"Ah, well, there you have the problem in a nutshell."

When she looked at him, puzzled, he went on to explain, "Having sense doesn't factor into it for most people." Taking off his jacket, Will tossed it onto his sofa. Then, turning back to look at Cassidy, he became serious. "So, how is he doing?"

He switched topics so quickly, she had to pause for a moment so her brain could catch up and make sense of his last question. She realized that the "he" Will was asking her about was Adam.

Of course it's Adam. Who else would it be? You just said you came here to give him an update on the boy.

What was it about Will lately that turned her into a simpleton, unable to rub two thoughts together?

"He's doing great," she told him, enthusiasm entering her voice. "His fever's completely gone and he's hungry." But Will probably already knew the latter since he'd fed Adam while she'd been asleep, she reminded herself. Cassidy pushed on, determined to tell him what she'd come to tell him and then leave. Fast. "It's like seeing a tiny miracle."

"That's what he is, all right," Will agreed, perching on the sofa's arm, "a tiny miracle."

She needed to go, Cassidy told herself. She was suddenly feeling awkward and definitely out of her element. Even so, she needed to know the answer to the main question that kept cropping up in her head.

"Why did you do it?"

Will glared at her. "'It'?" he repeated. "You're going to have to get a little more specific than that."

"Why did you stay with me at the clinic last night? You didn't have to. For that matter, why didn't you wake me up when Adam needed changing and when he had to be fed?" Until last night, she would have bet any amount of money that Will would have left those things up to her, not taken them upon himself to do—and certainly not without immediately taking credit for them.

Will pretended to be confused by her phrasing. "So are you asking me why I did something, or why I didn't do something?"

"Both," she retorted. And then she sighed, reining in her temper. She shouldn't have snapped at him. It was just that being around him like this unsettled her. "Why does everything have to be so difficult with you?"

Will grinned in response. "It's more memorable that way." He saw another hint of impatience crease her brow. It was a look he was intimately familiar with. For once, he didn't want to bait her. In the interest of a truce, he decided he might as well answer her questions without drawing out the process.

He did have things he needed to get to, Will reminded himself. The first of which was to put some distance between Cassidy and himself. The reason for that was a very basic one. He found himself entertaining some very strong thoughts, not to mention urges, regarding the two of them. If he didn't get some space between them—and soon—he was going to act on those urges.

He didn't relish the idea of rejection.

"But to answer your questions, I stayed with you last night because I felt you needed company. The night has a way of magnifying a person's fears, and I didn't want you up all night, worrying about Adam when he was going to be all right."

"And you knew that for a fact," she said sarcastically. The sarcasm was a defense mechanism. She needed a barrier between them, because she was having decidedly unsettling thoughts about him and she needed something to make her stay away. Something to make him *keep* her away.

Will ignored her tone. "Pretty much," he answered. "As for why I didn't wake you when Adam needed changing, well, that was because just before you fell asleep, you looked almost too exhausted to breathe. I thought I'd let you get some rest. Besides, I'm perfectly capable of changing a baby's diaper."

"Because of all your vast experience in changing diapers," she said, falling back on sarcasm again. If she didn't, she was in danger of just melting right in front of him. There was this look on his face that she was having trouble resisting.

"Not vast," he allowed, then added, "but I've had some."

"When?" Cassidy challenged. "When would you have possibly gotten experience changing diapers?"

He debated not saying anything, then decided he had nothing to lose. Besides, it was all in the past. And if it gave her ammunition to rag on him, well, so be it. "During those years I was away."

She was about to discount his statement when it suddenly hit her. Her eyes widened as she stared at Will. "You got married," she said. There was no joy in her voice, no celebratory tone for a friend. If anything, there was a note of crushing disappointment in her voice.

The simplest thing would have been to say yes—but it wasn't true. And he didn't lie.

"No."

Cassidy didn't think that she could feel so relieved over nothing—but she did.

"Then just how would you have gotten that experience with diaper changing?"

He smiled. Cassidy had overlooked a very uncomplicated answer to her question. "I briefly dated a woman with a baby, but I can't say I've had much experience."

He had always attracted women, all the way back to the fifth grade. But she couldn't picture him "dating" so much as just spending time and availing himself of the fruits that were being offered to him. Getting involved with a woman who had a baby was an entirely different scenario, and she was having trouble picturing him in it.

"You?"

"Yes, me." He shrugged, as if the whole thing was of less than no importance to him. "But then I came to my senses. I realized that she reminded me too much of you, so it was never going to work."

"She reminded you of me?" Cassidy questioned, stunned. "Is that why you dated her?"

"No, that's why I stopped," he said simply.

She felt dismissed, diminished. "I came to tell you about Adam because I felt like I owed it to you, but I must have been crazy. To willingly leave myself wide open like this so that you could parade your pathetic wit at my expense—"

"I dated her because she did make me think of you," he admitted to the back of her head.

Cassidy knew she was going to regret this, but she forced herself to turn to face him. "What did you say?"

The woman annoyed the hell out of him—and he wanted her so badly that he ached. What the hell was wrong with him?

"You heard me. She reminded me of you." And then he tried to put it in the proper perspective. "I guess I was kind of homesick after all, and being around someone who looked like you was the closest I could get to home."

But Cassidy wasn't about to let this go. Not yet. "Then why did you break up with her?"

She had no idea how, but she could feel his eyes pulling her in and yet holding her in place at the same time.

Cassidy realized that she had to remind herself to breathe.

"Because she wasn't you."

Chapter 16

Because they were so unexpected—the complete opposite of what she would have thought he'd say—it took a couple of seconds for Will's words to sink in.

And another second before she could actually answer him. Her mouth felt dry as she told him, "I would have thought, from your point of view, that would have been a good thing."

Will slowly nodded, his dark blond hair falling into his eyes.

"It should have been." His eyes held hers as he added, "But it wasn't."

What had happened to all the space that had been between them, she couldn't help wondering. When she'd turned, there'd been at least several strides between where he was standing and where she'd stopped. But somehow, in the last few seconds, they seemed to have just vanished.

She didn't remember walking toward him. When had he walked toward her? And why wasn't she turning and leaving now that he'd answered her question?

She wasn't leaving, she realized, because he *had* answered her question.

That and because she suddenly really, really wanted him to kiss her the way he had that one time, when he'd kissed her so deeply she became seriously in danger of forgetting how to ever walk again.

But as much as she found herself yearning for that kiss, she knew that if he didn't make the first move, she couldn't very well just throw herself at him. If she did, she'd never live it down because Laredo would never *let* her.

This was crazy.

She couldn't just go on standing there like some deer that had been caught in the proverbial headlights. She needed to leave.

Now.

"Well, I'd better be going," she heard herself saying, "since I did what I'd set out to do."

His presence seemed to be almost looming over her, making the rest of the area shrink away. "What's that? Drive me crazy?"

That would require a very short drive, she thought, biting her tongue.

"I came because I was trying to be nice," Cassidy reminded him.

"By driving me crazy," Will repeated, because that was exactly what she was doing, just by standing there—driving him crazy.

Driving him crazy because he wanted to touch her, to kiss her. To make love with her so badly he could scarcely breathe.

"Correct me if I'm wrong, but for once, we're not knee-deep in an argument."

Again, Laredo seemed to have come that much closer to her. He was so close now that if she took a deep breath, her chest was going to bump up against the lower part of his.

"Kind of leaves a void, doesn't it?" he asked her, commenting on her assessment.

"I don't notice a void," she told him defensively. Cassidy turned her face up to his so he could hear her better. Her voice cracked for some reason, as if she couldn't get in enough air to get her voice to carry the short distance between her mouth and his ears.

She struggled to keep from squirming.

"I do," he told her. "The void starts right about here," he went on, touching his chest and moving downward until he reached his lower abdomen. "And ends up here, cutting clear down to the bone."

"Maybe you should see someone about that," she suggested, the words all but falling from her lips in slow motion.

"I just might do that," he responded.

The next moment, there were no more words, no more nebulous speculations that went around in dizzying circles. Because the next moment, Will had finally given in to himself and lowered his mouth to hers, putting an end to the conversation and creating a whole new set of parameters for both of them.

She knew, *really* knew, that she should put a stop to what was happening. Right now. But "right now" seemed to perversely be slipping further and further away from her grasp. Further and further away from what she had, until she'd crossed this line, perceived to be reality.

Her reality.

Suddenly, she wasn't sure about anything, especially about the way she *thought* she felt about Will Laredo. Because if he was the man she loved to hate, why was every part of her lighting up like that huge Christmas tree that Miss Joan had the town decorate every year in the town square?

Light up like it? Hell, she mocked herself, she could easily out-glow it any day of the week and twice on Sundays.

She had dated a lot of cowboys in her time—thought at least three of them were "the one" in their own time. But she had never, ever felt about any of them the way she found herself feeling about Will Laredo. Like she wanted to seal herself to him forever.

Wouldn't Laredo get a laugh out of that if he knew, she thought, trying to work herself up and get angry. Angry enough to pull back and put a stop to this before it was too late.

But it was *already* too late because she didn't want to pull back, didn't want to put a stop to it. What she wanted, Cassidy realized—Lord help her—was to make love with him. Make love with Laredo the way no woman had ever made love with a man before. She was prepared to go down in flames and be reduced to a pile of ashes, as long as those ashes were mingled with *his*.

None of this was making any sense to her.

Maybe she had died plunging into the river after that baby and this was all some wild, afterlife fantasy that had ensnared her.

She didn't know.

Didn't care.

All she cared about was finding a way to scratch

this overwhelming itch she was feeling. An itch Will had created and that only he seemed to have the power to scratch for her.

Had he lost his mind? This was *Cassidy* he was all but wrapped around like some giant piece of cellophane. Cassidy. His best friend's sister, for heaven's sake. The woman who would have sooner argued with him than breathe—and always did.

He was supposed to be doing everything in his power to avoid her, not trying to absorb her into his system as if she was every bit as vital to him for his survival as the very air.

He had to put a *stop* to this.

And yet, every second that he was kissing Cassidy only had him wanting to kiss her that much more. Who would have ever guessed that her lips tasted this good, this tempting, this life-affirming?

Certainly not him.

And yet here he was, kissing her. Wanting her. Wanting more.

The little voice in his head that was so heavily grounded in common sense told him to stop, to make her leave. And if she wouldn't, then he was the one who needed to leave. Right this second.

Hell, he needed to run as if the town's villagers were all coming after him with pitchforks and torches.

But he didn't run, he didn't stop.

He couldn't.

Not when he was on fire this way.

Hell, he could barely remember his own name, much less how to walk away. He certainly couldn't *run*.

Will felt his head spinning so badly, he was certain that he'd fall on the floor if he made a move away from her.

So instead, he made a move *on* her.

With his mouth still sealed to hers, he began to undress Cassidy. To open buttons, tug out shirttails, unnotch the belt on her jeans. He wanted her completely to himself, the way she'd been created.

Completely and utterly nude.

Cassidy's heart was racing so hard, she thought it would burst right out of her chest. Not only was Laredo making the entire world around them shrink to the head of a pin and then just disappear, he was making her body temperature climb to dangerous heights in anticipation of each and every move.

She urgently pulled at Will's clothing, stripping him of his shirt, trying to tug off his jeans until she realized that she'd overlooked one important thing. Or rather, two.

"Your boots, take off your boots," she half begged, half ordered.

And when Will didn't seem to understand what she was saying, or to execute her order fast enough, Cassidy did it herself.

Half nude, she began pulling at his boots, frustrated and eager at the same time.

He thought he'd never seen anything more beautiful in his life.

The moment his boots were off, Will maneuvered out of his jeans.

And then there were no more barriers between them. They were free to do whatever they wanted to.

But rather than take her there and then, the way she'd

anticipated that he would, Will surprised her by continuing to up the ante. He did things to her that primed her body and made her anticipation all the greater.

Will made love to every single part of her before he culminated in making love to the whole of her the way she'd been waiting for him to do.

Before that final moment came, he'd made all of her quiver, all of her feel the small, hard surges of climaxes flowering one after the other until she was quite certain that her entire body was spent and there was nothing more left within her to feel anything else.

But she was wrong.

Because after the caresses, after the long, moist kisses along the length of her body that had her twisting and turning beneath his mouth in absolute sweet, sweeping agony and bliss, Cassidy discovered that there was one last, pulsating reserve she had left to offer up to Will.

With his fingers entwined and locked with hers, he slid his body over Cassidy's and into position. With his eyes watching hers, he entered her and took what had already become his from the moment this dance between them had begun.

His hips against hers, he began to move, urging her to follow until she started to keep up with him.

In sync, they moved faster and faster in anticipation of that one last glorious moment when their union would be finalized in a wondrous shower involving stars, fireworks and blazing sensations. A moment when freefloating was the norm, not the exception.

And when it happened, when it finally captured them both, Will held on to her even more tightly than he had before, as if the thought of letting go meant permanently letting go of her.

Time froze, then slowly moved forward again, bringing back reality as it reluctantly let go of euphoria.

His heart wouldn't stop hammering, as if it was meant to break free of its earthly shell and then meld with the stars overhead. For a few minutes, Will thought that it was going to, leaving him behind in the process— a broken vessel in its wake.

It still took a while for his heart to finally stop pounding. It took longer than that for him to catch his breath.

What the hell had they just done?

Will felt her stiffening beside him, felt the exact second when reality returned to her like a tsunami immediately after an earthquake.

Will caught himself thinking that that was almost appropriate, considering that, at least for him, the earth had definitely moved the way it never had before.

For a fraction of a moment, because it was against his nature to restrain someone who wanted to leave, Will thought of letting her bolt. Of letting Cassidy leave— if that was what she really wanted—without him saying a single word to stop her. He didn't want to prolong whatever she was feeling right at this second that was making her want to flee.

But another part of him, the new, improved part of him that had just been made to see the light, didn't want Cassidy fleeing. He didn't want her acting as if this was all one giant mistake that could somehow be erased with enough denial—especially if it was *mutual* denial.

Most of all, he didn't want to deny what had just happened.

Because to him, what had just happened bordered on a miracle.

And no good ever came of denying a miracle, especially when that miracle had just unaccountably landed right smack in their laps.

The way this one had.

So he closed his arms around Cassidy rather than letting her bolt off the sofa. And when she tried to wiggle free of his grip, he only held on to her that much more tightly.

"Let me go!" she cried, angry at herself for what she'd allowed to happen and angry at him for fueling the flames of a fire that just refused to go out.

He made no move to do anything of the kind. "Not yet. Not until you calm down," he told her.

"Okay. I'm calm," she declared between gritted teeth. "Now let me go!"

"Saying it isn't going to make it so," he told her in a voice she found maddeningly poised and self-contained.

His calm tone just made her angrier. "You can't hold me prisoner like this!"

"Maybe not," he said agreeably. "But I can dream. And for the record, I'm not holding you prisoner, I'm just holding you."

She would have thought that he, of all men, would have wanted to put distance between himself and a woman once the act of lovemaking was over. Will Laredo was the original carefree bachelor.

Just what was he up to?

"Why?" she challenged.

"Because you're soft and, heaven help me, I like holding you. And, in case it escaped your notice, something really nice just happened here. Now, whether you want to admit it or not, it *did* happen, and I suspect that a part of you really enjoyed it despite your protests. I know that more than a part of me did. Actually, I'd say that *all* of me did."

She was not about to admit to anything of the kind. The only thing she would admit was that she was agitated about what had just happened. Agitated because all of her life she'd told herself that she couldn't abide Will Laredo, and now to discover otherwise—to discover the exact opposite—well, it was too much for her to absorb all at once. And definitely too much for her to acknowledge.

Cassidy needed time to come to grips with this. Time and space, and she needed it *now*.

"I've got to go," she insisted. "I left Adam with Connor."

"Wise choice," he told her approvingly, a fact that only got her that much more agitated. "Connor's levelheaded."

She was disoriented and disappointed with herself. Will's words had her instantly jumping to a conclusion. "And I'm not, is that what you're trying to say?"

This was going to take patience, possibly more patience than he had. But he would give it his best shot.

"No, what I'm trying to say is don't run. Because no matter how fast you try to go, that feeling you're trying to outrun is going to catch up to you."

"Maybe," she said, pulling away from him and finally getting up. "But I've still got to try."

Clutching her clothes to her like a makeshift shield, Cassidy backed out of the room and then hurried away to get dressed.

She needed to make good her escape before he broke through her resolve—again.

Chapter 17

Christmas was just a few days away, and Cassidy purposely made herself busier than ever. Christmas had always been her favorite time of year, and it didn't have anything to do with the anticipation of gifts.

For her, it had never really been about gifts—at least not the store-bought kind. The gift of family and love was what was and had always been of major importance for Cassidy. Everything else came second, but she still immersed herself in it. Currently she had her internship at the firm and her online classes to juggle, not to mention that she was taking care of the baby and still finding time to decorate the house for Christmas, something that had always been, without a doubt, her very favorite "chore."

While she kept herself busy with all of this, Cassidy was doing her damnedest not to dwell on what had gone down between Will and her—or even think about it. But her resolve seemed to be made out of vapor, and trying *not* to think about having made love with Laredo just caused her to dwell on it that much more in her unguarded moments. Moments that, for some reason, seemed to be cropping up more and more as the days went by.

The only thing she was grateful for was that neither Connor nor Cole said anything about what had become the elephant in the room.

But finally Connor gave up on trying to stay out of Cassidy's business. So he confronted her in the kitchen late one afternoon.

It must have been obvious that she just wanted to avoid any sort of conversation with him about anything other than Adam or the approaching holiday.

When she tried to get around him, he blocked her exit from the kitchen and bluntly asked, "Okay, what's up with you and Will?"

Cassidy pretended to look at him blankly, as if his changing the subject to Will hadn't caused her to abruptly shut down and try to leave the room.

"Nothing's up with us," she replied crisply. "I find him the same irritating creature I always have."

"No," Connor contradicted her, matching her every move so that she couldn't leave the room, "you're going out of your way to avoid him when he comes by."

Cassidy blew out an annoyed breath. "*Because* I find him the same irritating creature I always have."

"No, that's a lot of bull. Something's changed," Connor insisted. "It has ever since you came home last week after running your 'errands' the day after Adam was in the clinic."

Cassidy scowled. She was not about to have a heart-to-heart with her big brother. Those days had long passed. She was a grown woman and was entitled to live her life without interference. Nowhere did it say she had to open up about what she was feeling.

"You're letting your imagination run away with you," she said dismissively.

There was a knowing look in Connor's eyes as he said, "It wasn't my imagination that noticed the buttons on your blouse were misaligned that day."

Cassidy opened her mouth and then closed it again, momentarily at a loss as to how to respond. Her brother had definitely caught her off guard.

Connor just continued, "I might not have as much schooling as you do, but I'm not just a hayseed cowboy, Cassidy. I do notice things—and you were gone a long time that day. Are you going to tell me that you were running errands all that time?"

That was exactly what she wanted to tell him, but the words seemed to be sticking in her throat. She didn't make it a habit of lying to Connor, but neither did she want to be drawn out on the carpet and treated like a child.

She looked at him defiantly. "Would you believe me if I did?"

"If you swore that it was the truth, I'd have to." He looked into her eyes, wanting to believe that the relationship they'd always had of mutual respect was still alive and well. "Are you?"

She bit the bottom of her lip. She really wanted to swear to him that it was the truth. Because it would put an end to Connor's speculations about her and Laredo, which were definitely coming too close to the truth for comfort.

But she had never once lied to Connor, and she couldn't allow her desire to block that whole day out of her life to cause her to lie to Connor now.

"No," she finally said, defiance in her tone.

He could always read her, although at times it took some effort. "My guess is that you're avoiding Will because it went too well and that scares you."

Cassidy tossed her head. "Nothing scares me," she informed him. "Now I've got a test to study for—" Adam's cries broke through the conversation. "And a baby to change, and I've still got a few gifts to wrap. None of which are going to take care of themselves, so can we table this conversation about a man who makes my blood pressure rise for now?"

"We're going to have to have it sooner or later," he pointed out.

Circumventing Connor, Cassidy crossed into the living room and picked up Adam from the playpen. She began patting his back automatically in soothing concentric circles.

"Later. I vote for later." As she started to leave for her bedroom to change the baby, there was a knock on the front door. She glanced over her shoulder at Connor. The latter was already heading toward the door. "You expecting anyone?" she asked him, a hint of wariness entering her voice.

Cody and Cole were both at work. Besides, neither one of them would knock. Connor shook his head. "Nobody I can think of."

When he opened the door, he found Will standing there.

"You're right," Cassidy commented as she turned away and began to walk up the stairs. "It's nobody."

But Will wasn't about to get drawn into a sarcastic verbal battle. He addressed her back, his voice somewhat strained and formal. "Cassidy, you might want to wait up. This concerns you, too."

But Cassidy just kept on going up the stairs. "There's nothing that you can say that concerns me, Laredo," she retorted.

He didn't bother arguing with her. He just told her the headline. "They found Adam's mother."

Cassidy's arms tightened around Adam as she froze. She put one hand on the banister to steady herself before turning. Her eyes on Will, she came back down. Her mind was going everywhere at once, trying to think, to anticipate what came next.

"Who found her?" she asked him in a stilted voice.

Will came closer to the staircase. "The sheriff and Joe, acting on an anonymous call from someone on the reservation."

Her insides were quivering as Cassidy desperately tried to steel herself. She wasn't succeeding very well.

She didn't remember coming back down the stairs. All she was aware of was that her legs felt rubbery. Her voice sounded hollow to her own ears as she asked, "When will she be coming for the baby?"

"She won't be," Will told her quietly. Before Cassidy could ask him anything else, he added, "They found her in her car. It must have washed up at the edge of the reservation a month ago. There was water in her lungs. She drowned in that flash flood."

"How do they know she was Adam's mother?" Connor asked.

Will's eyes shifted over to his friend. "Joe said they found some baby things in the car, and she had this locket around her neck. There was a picture of the baby pasted inside it."

All three of them were now standing in a small circle. The only one oblivious to the gravity of the conversation was its subject. Adam.

Connor glanced at the boy. "No offense to Adam, but a lot of babies at his age look the same if you shrink their picture down to locket size," he said.

"Which was why Joe stayed on the reservation, following up," Will told them. "Joe figured that since he originally came from there, if he kept at it long enough, someone would talk to him and tell him what happened."

"And?" Cassidy asked, prodding him.

"And he found the girl's aunt who, with enough prodding told Joe the whole story. Seems Adam's mother, Miriam Morning Star, was taking Adam and leaving the reservation the morning the flash flood hit. She was going to go look for Adam's father, a college kid who, along with some other students, had volunteered to work on the reservation a year ago."

Connor, listening, nodded. "I remember. There were ten of them as I recall."

Will nodded. "Miriam and the volunteer had a brief relationship, and then he went back to school. A few letters were exchanged, and then he stopped writing—around the time she told him she was pregnant. Miriam's aunt said that the girl got it into her head that once the baby's father saw Adam—who, by the way, she called Joshua—they'd be a family. Except that she never got too far off the reservation. From the looks of it, the car was engulfed by the floodwater. Miriam lost control."

"And they only found the car now?" Cassidy questioned incredulously.

"The car was partially hidden by debris. Hey, there was a lot of land to cover for three deputies," he reminded Cassidy, "and don't forget, her aunt thought she'd left the reservation. When the truth dawned on her, she wasn't overly eager to talk about a niece who had shamed her ancestors and turned her back on her heritage by giving herself to an 'outsider.'"

"Does the aunt want to take Adam?" Cassidy asked in a wary voice. She was trying to figure out what sort of recourse she had open to her. He might represent a lot of work, but she had gotten very attached to Adam in the last month.

Will shook his head. "She wants him to go to a stable home. She told Joe to do as he sees fit."

"Nobody else in the family?" Connor asked, remembering his own circumstances when he'd taken over as his siblings' guardian. There'd been no other family members.

"Not from anything that Joe heard," Will answered. "And he asked around."

At least that threat was gone, Cassidy thought, suddenly coming to.

"Well, unclaimed or not, Adam still needs his diaper changed. I'll be right back," she said.

"I'll be here," Will called after her.

"That's what I'm afraid of," Cassidy murmured, although loud enough for Will to overhear.

She took her time changing the baby, letting the full import of the information that Will had just finished telling them sink in.

"Well, Adam, it looks like you really are an orphan after all. What do you think we should do about that?" she asked.

The baby made a gurgling noise as if in response, and she laughed softly as she finished changing him.

"Oh, you do, do you?" she said as if the baby had said something intelligible. "Well, I'm going to have to think about that, but I've got a feeling that I might not have all that much time to think. Sometimes things actually do move fast around here." She sighed. "Usually when you don't want them to. Word might get back to social services up in the county." She picked Adam up, thinking how good he felt in her arms. "The truth of it is, I've gotten very used to having you hanging around, even if I don't sleep much anymore.

"Besides, if you're not around, what'll I do with those Christmas presents I bought for you?" Adam made more unintelligible noises, to which she nodded and said, "My thoughts exactly."

When she brought Adam downstairs again, she was all set to announce that she was going to adopt Adam. She clung to the fact that she had been caring for him all this time and that it would act in her favor.

"I get it," Will said the moment she started coming down. Apparently he'd been waiting at the foot of the stairs since she'd gone up.

She had no idea what Laredo was referring to. "Get what?"

"I get it if you don't want to adopt Adam."

"I don't want to adopt Adam?" she echoed, stunned. Just where had he gotten that idea? She'd never said anything of the kind. To be fair, she had never said anything one way or the other about Adam's future.

"Because if you don't want to," Will continued, "then I'll adopt him."

"You?" Cassidy said in disbelief, her tone mocking the very idea.

Connor stepped in and deftly took Adam from her. Her hands free, she fisted them on her hips as she faced Will.

Will felt his back going up. "Yes, what's wrong with that?"

Was he kidding? "Because, in case you forgot that you've always had this love 'em and leave 'em reputation, everyone else around here remembers and that, my friend," she informed him, "is why you wouldn't have a snowball's chance in hell of adopting this baby."

Rather than get annoyed, Will actually smiled at her dismissal. "I've changed—"

To which she responded, "Ha!"

"And I can make further changes," Will continued as if he was already arguing his case before a family court judge. "I can make all the changes necessary in order to be regarded as a good father for the baby."

"Oh?" This was going to be good, Cassidy thought. "And what changes can you possibly make?"

Will dropped the ultimate bombshell. "I can get married."

For a second, Cassidy's jaw dropped, but she came around the next moment. "What woman in her right mind would have you?"

"Well, I guess that rules you out because you've never been in your right mind."

Angry, Cassidy glared at him. How could she have thought that there was something between them? She must have been delirious when she'd made love with this man. Well, she was definitely over him now and thinking straight again.

"I'll have you know that I am very much in my right mind!" she informed him.

"Fine!" he shouted. "Then will you marry me?"

Connor was about to break up the argument when he heard Will's unorthodox proposal and pulled back.

Cassidy was still running on fury. Fury that came to an abrupt halt in the middle of her response. "What the hell are you yelling at me for— Wait, what?" She stared at Will. "Did you just ask me to marry you?" she demanded, stunned close to speechlessness.

She expected Will to laugh at her and tell her that it was all a joke.

But he didn't laugh, didn't say it was a joke.

Instead, what Will did say was "Yes."

She refused to believe he was serious. There was a punch line here somewhere. "You actually want to marry me?" she asked.

The corners of his mouth curved, all but undoing her entirely. "Amazingly enough, yes, I do."

"You want to marry *me*?" she asked again, unable to believe he wasn't somehow setting her up for a fall.

"Pay attention, Adam," Connor said to the baby he was holding. "Your future dad's well-intentioned but kind of slow-witted at times." He turned toward Will. "She's waiting for you to say the words, Will, so say them. Ask her to marry you," he prompted.

Will felt as if he was standing in the middle of someone else's dream—until he realized that it was his dream, that maybe it had *always* been his dream and that only the fear of rejection had put him in denial all these years.

Taking a deep breath, Will plunged in. "Cassidy Mc-Cullough, will you marry me?"

Cassidy still held back. "Are you sure that you're not going to shout 'April Fool's' or something like that if I say yes?"

"It's December 21. That's a long ways away from April Fool's," he told her.

"Take a leap of faith, Cassidy," Connor urged. "And know that I've got your back. If this turns out to be an elaborate hoax, I'll skin him alive for you. Now answer the man," he ordered.

She closed her eyes and took a breath, then opened her eyes again. Will was still there, waiting. She said, "Yes!"

Rather than any proclamations of an elaborate joke being in play, Will echoed "Yes!" as well, then threw his arms around her. Lifting Cassidy off the ground, he kissed her. Long and hard and with all his heart.

Connor waited a moment, then, when it looked like a moment wasn't going to be nearly long enough for his sister and his best friend, he politely turned away from them.

"C'mon, Adam, let's give them some privacy. This looks like it's going to take a while. Grown-ups are funny like that. But the bottom line is that you've got your mom and dad, and that's all that really counts."

Epilogue

It was perfect.

Absolutely perfect.

Cassidy scanned the area and smiled to herself in tired satisfaction.

The tree was up and finally decorated. That had been touch and go for a while. All the gifts that she was in charge of were wrapped and under the tree—finished just by the skin of her teeth, she thought with a grin, if teeth had skin. The spiral ham was in the oven, its aroma competing with the heady scent of pine. Even the table was set.

Everything was ready, including her, for the celebratory dinner that had become a tradition: Christmas Eve dinner.

They had come a long way, Cassidy couldn't help thinking, from that first Christmas she and her brothers had spent the year their father had died. Back then Connor barely had enough money for them to scrape by. Christmas Eve dinner that year was in Miss Joan's house—she had insisted on it.

Cassidy could remember being surprised that Miss Joan actually *had* a house. She had just assumed that the woman lived in the diner. To her thirteen-year-old mind, it had seemed that way.

The jingling noise drew her attention toward the playpen.

Adam was all dressed up and entertaining himself with the silver bells on his shoelaces. Apparently the ringing sound reduced him to giggles.

Cassidy couldn't remember hearing a more heart-warming sound than Adam's laughter.

A delayed chill filled the room, and Cassidy realized that Connor had opened the door. Cody, Devon and their daughter, Layla, had come in.

"What is that wonderful smell?" Devon asked as she shrugged out of her coat while Cody held their daughter in his arms.

"That," Connor informed her, "is a genuine Christmas miracle. Cassidy made dinner and nothing's burned."

"Evening's still young," Cody responded with a laugh.

"Just for that," Cassidy said, looking at her brother as she came forward to greet his family, "you don't get to eat anything."

"I'll have to reserve judgment on whether that's a good thing or a bad thing," Cody told her, then ducked as Cassidy took a swing at his arm.

"Don't listen to him," Devon told her sister-in-law. "When's dinner? We're starved."

"We can start as soon as everyone's here," Connor told her.

"Well, I'm here," Cole declared, overhearing his older brother as he came down the stairs.

Cody looked at Connor. "That's everybody, right?"

"Not quite," Connor told him.

"I thought you said this was strictly a family dinner," Cody reminded his brother, looking toward Cassidy for an answer. "Who else is coming?"

There was a knock on the door just then. "I think that's your answer," Connor told him. He was about to go open the door, but Cassidy managed to get ahead of him. With a smile, Connor dropped back.

Cole and Cody exchanged glances, but neither had an answer for the other. Connor caught the look. "You'll see," he promised his brothers, a rather satisfied smile playing on his lips.

The next moment he saw that both of his brothers appeared completely stunned when Will walked in across the threshold. They grew more so when they saw Will kiss their sister.

Granted it was a quick kiss, but they both expected Cassidy to read their friend the riot act just before she punched him in the gut—but none of that happened.

"What's wrong with Cassidy?" Cole asked. The question was echoed by Cody.

"Not a thing, boys," Connor answered. "Not a thing." He beckoned his family into the living room.

"Why's your camera set up?" Cody asked. The old-fashioned camera—a gift from Miss Joan—had recorded all their milestones over the years. Connor saw to that. But they hadn't seen the camera out and mounted on its tripod since Cody and Devon's wedding.

"I thought it might be nice to get a family picture of all of us together," Connor answered.

Cody slanted a glance toward his sister, expecting some sort of a tirade, or at the very least a dismissal of Connor's suggestion. While he and his brothers all thought of Will as family, Cassidy had made it clear that she thought of Will as the lowest form of lowlife.

"Aren't you going to say anything?" Cody asked his sister, mystified.

"Yes," she replied.

"Finally," Cody whispered to his wife.

"I think that we should take the picture before we have dinner. That way, nobody has to worry about hiding a gravy stain or some other food that's on your clothes—that's not to say that I don't appreciate you eating with gusto, because I do."

"Okay," Cole cried. "What's going on here? I feel like I've just fallen into some alternate universe or whatever they called it in those science-fiction movies Dad used to like to fall asleep to on late-night TV."

"Well," Will began, "I was going to wait until everyone started opening their gifts, but maybe I should do this now."

"Do *what* now?" Cole asked impatiently.

"You know what's going on?" he asked Cody only to have Cody shake his head.

"Do you?" Cole turned toward Connor.

To his surprise, Connor nodded.

Before Cole could quiz his older brother for an explanation, he heard Will say, "This was my grandmother's, and she left it to me, saying that if I ever found that one special woman who I wanted to spend the rest of my life with, I should give it to her." He opened his hand then and held it up to Cassidy.

A small, square-cut diamond ring was in the center of his palm, sparkling as it caught some of the lights coming from the Christmas tree.

"So I'm giving it to you, Cassidy—if you'll have it—and me."

Cassidy could barely suppress the grin that was fighting to take over her entire face. "Well, since you twisted my arm, I guess I can't say no and embarrass you in front of your friends."

"Never stopped you before," Cole quipped, still rather confused.

"Shut up, Cole," Cody chided, finally seeing the light. "You're spoiling the moment."

"You're wrong," Cassidy told him as she held out her hand toward Will and he slipped the ring on the third finger of her left hand. "Nothing can spoil this moment."

Especially, she thought, *since the ring fit.*

Several moments later, her eyes shining, she took her place beside Will who was holding their soon-to-be-adopted son. Her brothers, sister-in-law and niece flanked them on either side.

Connor quickly set the timer on the camera, then darted back into place, instructing them to all say "Happiness!"

It was a good word, Cassidy thought, leaning into Will, because she couldn't remember ever feeling happier than she did right at this moment.

* * * * *

"The Joshua trees and saguaros sure are pretty," Jack
said reflectively. "This sort of looks like the land west
of the Three Rivers Ranch house. Where you showed
me the North Star, remember?"

Remember? Those moments had been burned into
Vanessa's memory. Even if she never saw him again
for the rest of her life, she'd always have those special
moments to relive in her mind.

The thought unexpectedly caused her throat to
tighten, and she wished the waitress would get back
with their drinks. She didn't want Jack to think she was
getting emotional. Especially because she could feel
their time together winding to a close.

"I do. And I just happen to know a place not too far
west of here where there's another special view of the
evening star."

His eyelids lowered ever so slightly as he looked across the table at her. "After we eat, you should show me."

Did he expect her to look at him in the moonlight and not feel the urge to kiss him? Or maybe she'd get lucky, Vanessa thought, and the moon would be in a new phase and the light would be too weak to illuminate his face.

Damn it, Vanessa. Who are you fooling? You could find Jack's lips in the darkest of nights.

Thankfully, a waitress suddenly approached their table, and the distraction pushed the mocking voice from her head…but not the idea of being in Jack's arms again. She was beginning to fear she'd never rid herself of that longing.

Don't miss
The Other Hollister Man *by Stella Bagwell,*
available August 2022 wherever
Harlequin books and ebooks are sold.

Harlequin.com

Love Harlequin romance?

DISCOVER.

Be the first to find out about promotions,
news and exclusive content!

f Facebook.com/HarlequinBooks

🐦 Twitter.com/HarlequinBooks

📷 Instagram.com/HarlequinBooks

📌 Pinterest.com/HarlequinBooks

You Tube YouTube.com/HarlequinBooks

ReaderService.com

EXPLORE.

Sign up for the Harlequin e-newsletter and
download a free book from any series at
TryHarlequin.com

CONNECT.

Join our Harlequin community to
share your thoughts and connect
with other romance readers!
Facebook.com/groups/HarlequinConnection

HSOCIAL2021